THE DIPLOMAT'S WIFE

Surviving the brutality of a Nazi prison camp, Marta Nederman is lucky to have escaped with her life. Recovering from the horror, she meets Paul, an American soldier who gives her hope of a happier future, but their plans to meet in London are dashed when Paul's plane crashes. Devastated and pregnant, Marta marries Simon, a caring British diplomat, and glimpses the joy that home and family can bring, but her happiness is threatened when she learns of a communist spy in British intelligence, and that the one person who can expose the traitor is connected to her past...

THE DIPLOMAT'S WIFE

THE DIPLOMAT'S WIFE

by

Pam Jenoff

Magna Large Print Books
Long Preston, North Yorkshire,
BD23 4ND, England.

British Library Cataloguing in Publication Data.

Jenoff, Pam
    The Diplomat's wife.

    A catalogue record of this book is
    available from the British Library

    ISBN   978-0-7505-3003-3

First published in Great Britain in 2008 by Mira Books

Copyright © Pam Jenoff 2008

Cover illustration © Rod Ashford

The moral right of the author has been asserted

Published in Large Print 2009 by arrangement with
Harlequin Enterprises II B.V./S.à.r.l.

Magna Large Print is an imprint of Library Magna Books Ltd.

Printed and bound in Great Britain by
T.J. (International) Ltd., Cornwall, PL28 8RW

To Phillip, with love

ACKNOWLEDGEMENTS

One of the most remarkable aspects of becoming a published author has been meeting the many talented people who work so hard to bring my books to life. I am forever grateful to everyone at MIRA Books, including my gifted editor Susan Pezzack and the editorial team, Heather Foy and her wonderful colleagues in public relations, Amy Jones and the other brilliant folks in marketing, Maureen Stead who always ensures smooth travels, Jayne Hoogenberk and Adrienne Macintosh for their fabulous work on the eHarlequin.com materials, the terrific sales team, and many others too numerous to count. I would also like to thank the amazing MIRA UK team for their stellar work, including Catherine Burke, Oliver Rhodes, Clare Somerville, Sarah Ritherdon, Alison Byrne, Bethan Hilliard and all of their colleagues. I am also grateful to publicists Margot Weale at Midas PR in London and Gail Brussel in New York for their work on my behalf.

Another wonderful facet of this experience has been the thousands of people who have come into my life from reading my book. To that end, I would like to thank the many booksellers and librarians who have promoted my work, the readers who have reached out to tell me how my writing affected them, and the book clubs who have welcomed me into their homes. I am also grateful to the many authors who have so generously shared the benefit of their experiences with me and to the writers in my writing group for their feedback on my work. I would also like to recognise the Leighton Studios at the Banff Centre for the Arts. The days I spent there during the formative stages of this book were invaluable.

Then there is the continuing joy that comes from those who have been with me from the start. Thanks to my rock star agent, Scott Hoffman, and his team at Folio Literary Management for their flawless judgement, tireless efforts and endless patience in guiding me through the publishing experience. To my friends and colleagues, who have walked this journey with me every step of the way. And, most importantly, to my family: Mom, Dad, Jay and Philip (and Casey and Kitty too) – without you, none of this would be possible or worthwhile.

CHAPTER 1

I do not know how many hours or days I have lain on this cold, hard floor, waiting to die. For some time, it seemed certain that I already was dead, shrouded in the dark stillness of my grave, unable to move or speak.

A sharp pain shoots through my right side. It is not over. Sound comes back next in tiny waves: rats scratching inside the walls, water dripping beyond my reach. My head begins to throb against the icy concrete.

No, not dead. Not yet, but soon. I can take no more. In my mind I see the guard standing above me, an iron bar raised high above his head. My stomach twists. Did I talk? *No*, a voice within me replies. *You said nothing. You did well.* The voice is male. Alek, or Jacob perhaps. Of course, it could be neither. Alek is dead, captured and shot by the Gestapo. Jacob might be gone, too, if he and Emma did not make it across the border.

Emma. I can still see her face as she stood above me on the railway bridge. Her lips were cool on my cheek as she bent to kiss me goodbye. 'God bless you, Marta.' Too weak to reply, I nodded, then watched as she ran to the far end of the bridge, disappearing into the darkness.

After she was gone, I looked down at the bridge. Beneath me a dark red stain seeped into the snow, growing even as I watched. Blood, I

13

realized. My blood. Or maybe his. The Kommandant's body lay motionless just a few meters away. His face looked peaceful, almost innocent, and for a moment I could understand how Emma might have cared for him.

But I had not; I killed him.

My side began to burn white-hot where the bullet from the Kommandant's gun had entered. In the distance, the sirens grew louder. For a moment, I regretted telling Emma to leave, rejecting her offer to help me escape. But I would have only slowed her down and we both would have been caught. This way she had a chance. Alek would have been proud of me. Jacob, too. For a moment I imagined that Jacob was standing over me, his brown hair lifted by the breeze. 'Thank you,' he mouthed. Then he, too, was gone.

The Gestapo came then and I lay with my eyes closed, willing death to come quickly. For a moment, when they realized that I had shot the Kommandant, it seemed certain that they would kill me right there. But then one pointed out that bullets were scarce and not to be wasted, and another that I would be wanted for questioning. So instead I was lifted from the bridge. 'She'll wish we had killed her here,' one said as they threw me roughly into the back of a truck.

Remembering his words now, I shiver. Most days he is right. That was some months ago. Or even years; time here blends together, endless days of loneliness, starvation and pain. The solitude is the hardest part. I have not seen another prisoner the whole time I have been here. Sometimes I lie close to the wall, thinking that I

14

hear voices or breathing in the next cell. 'Hello?' I whisper, pressing my head against the crack where the wall meets the floor. But there is never any response.

When the footsteps in the corridor do come at last, I am always filled with dread. Is it the kitchen boy, who stares at me with dark, hollow eyes as he sets down the tray of moldy bread and brown water? Or is it one of them? The torture sessions come in sudden, unpredictable bursts, none for days or weeks, then several in rapid succession. They ask the same questions over again as they beat me: Who were you working for? Who ordered you to shoot Kommandant Richwalder? Give us the names and we'll stop, they promise. But I have not spoken and they do not stop, not until I have passed out. Once or twice they have revived me and begun again. Most times, like today, I wake up back in my cell, alone.

Yet despite everything, I have said nothing. I have done well. I smile inwardly at this. Then my satisfaction disappears. I thought, almost hoped, that this last beating would mean the end. But I am alive, and so they will surely come again. I begin to tremble. Each time is worse than the last. I cannot take any more. I must be dead before they come.

Another sharp pain shoots through my side. The Nazis operated on me shortly after I arrived at the prison, removing the bullet. At the time, I didn't understand why they would try to save me. Of course, that was before the interrogations began. The pain grows worse and I begin to sweat. Suddenly, the room grows colder and I

15

slip from consciousness once more.

Sometime later, I awaken. The smell of my own waste hangs heavy in the air. In the distance, I hear a low, unfamiliar rumbling sound. Through my eyelids I sense light. How much time has passed? I raise my hands to my face. My right eye is sealed shut by a fresh, round welt. I rub my left eye, brushing away the thick crust that has formed in the outside corner. Blinking, I look around the cell. The room is blurry, as everything has been since they confiscated my glasses upon arrival. I can make out a pale beam of daylight that has found its way in through the tiny, lone window by the ceiling, illuminating a small puddle on the floor. My parched throat aches. If only I could make it to the water. But I am still too weak to move.

The rumbling sound stops. I hear footsteps on the floor above, then on the stairwell. The guards are coming. I close my eye again as the key turns in the lock. The cell door opens and I can hear low male voices talking. I force myself to remain still, to not tremble or give any indication that I am awake. The footsteps grow louder as they cross the room. I brace myself, waiting for the rough grasp and blows that will surely come. But the men pause in the middle of the room, still talking. They seem to be having a disagreement of some sort. They aren't speaking German, I realize suddenly. I strain to listen. '...too sick,' one of the voices says. The language is not Russian or Slavic at all. English! My heart leaps.

'She must go.' I open my eye quickly. Two men in dark green uniforms stand in my cell. Are they

16

British? American? I squint, trying without success to make out the flag on their sleeves. Have we been liberated?

The shorter man has his back to me. Over his shoulder, I can see a second man, pointing toward the door. 'She must go,' he repeats, his voice angry. The shorter man shakes his head.

I have to get their attention. I try to sit up, but the pain is too much. I take a deep breath and cough, then raise my arm slightly. The man who had been pointing looks in my direction. 'See?' he calls over his shoulder as he races toward me. The other man does not reply, but shakes his head and walks out of the cell.

The soldier kneels beside me. 'Hello.'

I open my mouth to respond, but only a low gurgling sound comes out. 'Shh.' He puts a finger to his lips. I nod slightly, feeling my cheeks redden. He reaches out to touch my arm. I jerk away. For so long, human contact has only meant pain. 'It's okay,' he says softly. He points to the flag on his sleeve. 'American. It's okay.' He reaches out again, more slowly this time, and I force myself not to flinch as he lifts my arm, pressing his large, callused fingers against my wrist. I had nearly forgotten that a person could touch so gently. He feels for my pulse, then brings his other hand to my forehead. His brow furrows. He begins to speak quickly in English, his blue eyes darting back and forth. I shake my head slightly. I do not understand. He stops mid-sentence, a faint blush appearing in his pale cheeks. 'Sorry.'

He pulls a metal bottle from his waistband and opens it, pouring some liquid into the cap. Then

17

he takes one hand and places it behind my neck. I allow myself to relax against the warmth of his touch. His sleeve gives off an earthy scent that stirs a childhood memory, pine needles on the forest ground. He lifts my head slightly, cradling it as one might an infant's, bringing the cap to my lips. 'Drink.' I swallow the water he pours into my mouth. It has a salty – slightly metallic taste, but I do not care. I drink all that is in the first cap and a second, too.

As I drink, I study his face. He is no more than a few years older than me, twenty-three or twenty-four at most. His dark hair is very short on the sides but wavy on top. Though his expression is serious now, the crinkles at the corners of his eyes make me think he has smiled a lot. He looks kind. And handsome. I am suddenly aware of my soiled prison dress and matted curls, caked thick with dirt and blood.

I take one last sip. Then, exhausted from the effort, I go limp as he gently lowers my head to the floor. Don't, I want to say, as he slides his hand out from under my neck. His touch is familiar now, comforting. Instead I smile, trying to convey my gratitude. He nods, his eyes wide and sad. I can feel him wondering how I have come to be here, who would do this to me. He starts to stand. Panicking, I struggle to reach up and grab his hand.

'It's okay.' He kneels beside me once more, gesturing toward the door of the cell with his head. 'Doctor.' He means to bring me help. I relax slightly, still clinging to him. 'It's okay,' he repeats slowly, squeezing my hand. 'You will go.' Go. My eyes start to burn. The nightmare is over. It is almost too much to believe. A single tear rolls hot down my cheek. He reaches out to brush it away.

He clears his throat, then touches his chest with his free hand. 'Paul.'

Paul. I stare up at him, repeating his name in my mind. I do not know if I can speak. But I need for him to know my name, too. I swallow, then take a deep breath. 'M-Marta,' I manage to say. Then, overwhelmed by the effort and all that has happened, I collapse into darkness once more.

CHAPTER 2

'Awake now, are we?' A woman's voice, brisk and unfamiliar, cuts through the darkness. Have the Germans returned? I inhale sharply. Something is different. The air is no longer thick with waste, but with smells of rubbing alcohol and fresh paint. Gone are the sounds of the rats and dripping water, too. They have been replaced by gentle rustling, voices talking softly.

Snapping my eyes open, I am stunned to discover that I am no longer in my cell, but in a large room with bright yellow walls. Where am I? A woman stands by the foot of the bed. Though her face is blurry, I can see that she is wearing a white dress and cap. She comes up beside me and touches my forehead. 'How are you feeling?' I swallow uncertainly. There is still pain in my side, but it is duller now, like a toothache. 'My name is

Dava. Do you know where you are?' She is not speaking Polish, but I understand what she is saying. Yiddish, I realize. I have not heard it since leaving the ghetto. But Yiddish is so close to German, and the woman speaks it with some sort of an accent. Perhaps this is just another Nazi trick to get me to talk. The woman, seeming to notice my distress, quickly answers her own question. 'You are in a camp run by the Allies for displaced persons, just outside Salzburg.'

Camp. Salzburg. My mind races. 'Nazis...?' I manage to say. My throat aches as much from saying the word as from the effort of speaking.

'Gone. Hitler killed himself and what was left of the German army surrendered. The war in Europe is over.' She sounds so sure, so unafraid. I relax slightly, letting her words sink in as she reaches above my head to a window and adjusts the curtains to block some of the sunlight that is streaming through. Don't, I want to say. I have lived in darkness for so long. 'There, that's better.' I look up at her. Though her full figure gives her a matronly appearance, I can tell by her face that she is not more than thirty. A lock of brown hair peeks out from beneath her cap.

Dava pours water from a blue pitcher into a glass on the low table beside my bed. I start to sit up, but she presses against my shoulder with her free hand. 'Wait.' She takes a pillow from the empty bed beside mine and, lifting me up slightly, places it atop the one already beneath my head. I notice then that I am wearing a hospital gown made of coarse, light-blue cotton. 'Your body has been through a great deal. You need to move slowly.' I lift my head as Dava brings the glass to my lips. 'Slowly,' she repeats. I take a small sip. 'That's good, Marta.' I look up, wondering how she knows my name. 'It was written on your forehead when they brought you in,' she explains. Then, noticing my surprise, she adds, 'The soldiers who are liberating the camps often write things, names or conditions directly on the patients. They either don't have paper or they're afraid the information would be lost on the way in.'

I take another sip, then lay my head down on the pillow once more. Suddenly I remember the soldier helping me drink on the prison floor. 'How did I get here?'

Dava replaces the glass on the table. 'The Americans found you in the Nazi prison when they liberated Dachau, just outside Munich. We're just two hours south, not far from the German border, so many of the liberated are brought here. You've been unconscious since they brought you in more than a week ago. Your wound was infected and you had a very high fever. We weren't sure if you were going to pull through. But you're awake now, and the fever is gone.' Dava looks over her shoulder across the room, then turns back to me. 'You rest for a few minutes. I'm going to let the doctor know you're awake.'

As she walks away, I lift my head again. Although my vision is blurry, I can make out two rows of narrow, evenly spaced beds running along the walls of the long, rectangular room. Mine is in the farthest corner, pressed against a wall on one side. All of the beds seem to be filled, except the one beside me. Several women dressed in white move briskly between them.

Dava returns a few minutes later carrying a tray, an older man with thick glasses in tow. He picks up my wrist with one hand and touches my forehead. Then he lifts the blanket and reaches for the corner of my gown. Surprised, I recoil.

Dava sets down the tray on the empty bed behind her and steps forward. 'He just needs to examine the wound to make sure it is healing properly.' I relax slightly and let the doctor lift my gown, trying not to feel his cold, unfamiliar hands as they press on my stomach. Then he pulls the gown back farther, revealing the wound. I am surprised to see fresh stitches along the incision line. 'They had to operate again when you first arrived here,' Dava explains. 'There was a piece of bullet still inside you and you had developed an infection.' I nod. In prison I often wondered why my side still ached so long after the Nazis operated on me. Now, not long after the second surgery, it already feels much better.

The doctor replaces my gown and turns to Dava, speaking to her in German too brisk and accented for me to comprehend. Then he hurries away. 'He said you're healing really well. And that you should try to eat something. Are you hungry?' Before I can answer, Dava picks up a bowl from the tray behind her. 'Soup,' she announces brightly. I sit up slowly and this time she does not stop me, but brings the bowl close under my chin. A rich aroma wafts upward. Nausea rises in me and a cold sweats break out on my forehead. Noticing, Dava sets the bowl down on the table and picks up a cup and saucer from the tray. 'Let's just start with some tea.'

I swallow, my stomach calmer now. 'I can hold it.'

Dava hands me the cup and I take a sip. The liquid is lukewarm and soothing to my throat. Cradling the cup in both hands, I look upward. The ceiling is high and decorated with a pattern of some sort. I squint to try to make it out.

'This used to be a formal dining room,' Dava explains. 'The whole camp is housed on the grounds of Schloss Leopoldskron, which was one of the Hapsburg palaces. The Nazis confiscated it from its previous owners, and we took it from them. The palace is very beautiful, as are the grounds. I'll give you a tour when you are well enough.'

'Thank you.' I take another sip of tea.

Dava points upward. 'If you look there, you can see the Baroque influence. The detail is really quite extraordinary.'

'I can't...' I begin, then hesitate. 'That is, I can't see it.'

'What do you mean?' Dava's voice is heavy with concern. 'Did the Nazis do something? A blow to the head, perhaps? Or did you fall?'

I shake my head. 'Nothing like that,' I reply quickly, though of course they had struck me in the head many times. 'It's just that I am very near-sighted. And my glasses were confiscated when I was arrested.'

'Oh, my goodness, why didn't you say something? We have a whole boxful of glasses in the supply room.' What happened to their former owners? I wonder. Dava continues, 'As soon as

23

you've finished eating, I'll bring you a few pairs to try out. Now, let's give the soup another go.' She takes the teacup from me and puts it back on the tray, then picks up the bowl once more. My stomach rumbles with anticipation. I swallow the first mouthful Dava spoons for me, savoring the warm, salty broth as it runs down my throat. Neither of us speak as she feeds me a second spoonful, then a third. 'Let's slow down for a minute and see how that sits,' she says.

I open my mouth to start to protest. It is the first fresh food I have tasted in months and I do not want to stop. But I know that she is right. I lean back and look around the ward. 'I've been wondering, the rest of the room looks so crowded, but there is no one here.' I gesture to the empty bed beside my own.

'You mean, why are you being kept separate from the others?'

'Yes.'

Dava hesitates. 'The others are from the camps.'

'I don't understand. You said I was in Dachau. Wasn't that a camp?'

'Yes, of course. But where you were kept, in the prison, you were not in the general population with the other women.' I study Dava's face. Does she know why I was in that special prison cell? 'The conditions in the general populations of the camps like Dachau were very bad,' she adds.

'Worse than where I was?' I try to imagine what could be more horrible than the beatings, starvation and isolation I endured.

'Not necessarily worse, but different. There were lots of diseases, dysentery, typhus.' Typhus.

My mother died of typhus in the Kraków ghetto. I see her sore-ravaged body, hear her crying out in the delirium brought on by high fever. 'We didn't want to risk you catching something while you were weak from the surgery and infection, so we kept you as separate as we could. That's about to change, though. We're expecting another transport and we'll likely have to use all of the beds then, so you'll be getting a neighbor. But enough about that. Let's have some more soup.'

As Dava spoons the broth for me, I look over her shoulder. Most of the other women lie still in their beds. I am suddenly aware of noises I hadn't heard before, low moans, the whirring and beeping of medical equipment. There is another smell, too: the faint, metallic odor of blood.

I turn back to Dava, studying her face with interest. 'Where are you from?'

'Russia originally, but my family moved to Vienna when I was a child. My parents died in Buchenwald.'

'You're Jewish?' I cannot keep the surprise from my voice. With her ample figure, Dava does not look like she spent time in the camps.

She nods. 'I was in the south of France studying languages when the war broke out. My family wouldn't hear of me coming back. So I signed up as a nurse with the Allies, made my way back to Austria as soon as I was able. But my parents, our house, it was all gone.'

Mine, too, I think, my eyes burning.

'All gone,' Dava repeats a minute later. But her tone is bright and I realize as she sets the bowl back down on the tray that she is talking about

25

the soup now. Gone. Suddenly I am back in my cell without any food, wondering when the next meal will come, whether I will eat again that day. Panic shoots through me. Dava, accustomed to dealing with survivors, seems to read my thoughts. 'Don't worry.' She pats my shoulder. 'The Red Cross supplies our kitchen. There's plenty of soup, and many other kinds of food as well. If you're still hungry and manage to hold down what you've just eaten, I can bring you bread in an hour. But you have to stop eating for now. It's for your own good.'

I lean back, relieved. 'Thank you.'

'My pleasure.' Dava stands up. 'Now I need to go check on some of the other patients. I want you to get some rest. You need to regain your strength.'

My eyelids suddenly seem to grow heavier. 'I am a little sleepy,' I admit.

'It's the food. You rest. Sleep is good for your healing.' Dava picks up the tray and starts to leave.

'Dava,' I call after her, struggling to sit up again. She turns back. 'Yes?'

'I have another question.' I pause, picturing the soldier hovering over me in prison. 'You said that the Americans brought me in. Do you know any of their names?'

Dava's brow furrows. 'I'm afraid not. Why do you ask?'

'There was one soldier I remember helping me before I passed out. I think he was called Paul.' My heart flutters as I say his name aloud.

'What was his surname?'

I hesitate, trying to remember. There had been dark writing on the green lapel of his uniform. I close my eyes, straining without success to read it from memory. 'I don't know.'

'There are thousands of American soldiers in Europe right now, liberating the camps,' she replies gently. My heart sinks. 'I'll ask around when the transports come in from the various camps, but I wouldn't count on too much. Now, you rest. I'll be back when I finish my rounds.'

I sink back in bed, watching Dava as she walks away. Then I look around the ward once more. This is not a dream. I really have been saved. Exhaustion overcomes me and I lean my head back against the crisp white sheets, drifting to sleep.

Sometime later, I open my eyes. How much time has passed? The ward is nearly dark now, illuminated only by a beam of moonlight that stubbornly makes its way through the drawn curtains behind me. The room buzzes with the thick, labored breathing of sick women trying to sleep. In the distance, I hear someone crying softly.

I swallow against the dryness in my throat. Pushing myself up to a sitting position, I reach for the glass on the table beside my bed, which Dava left half full of water. I take a sip, and as I set the glass down I notice several metal objects on the far side of the nightstand that were not there before. Glasses! Curious, I reach over and pick up a pair. I put them on but the room remains blurry. They are too weak. Quickly I try the next pair, which are weaker than the first. Disappointment rises in me as I take them off. What if none work for me? The lenses in the third pair are too strong, making my temples ache when I try to focus. I look at the table once more. Only two pairs left to try. Are there more, if none of these are right? I pick up the next pair, holding my breath as I put them on. The room suddenly comes into focus. They are nearly perfect. I can see again!

I turn toward the window, my side aching from the sudden movement. Pulling back the curtains, I gasp. Majestic, snow-capped mountains line the horizon, their jagged peaks climbing to the star-filled sky. The Alps, I realize. Goose bumps form on my arms. A wide lake sits at the base of the mountains, reflecting their vistas in its glasslike surface.

I stare up at the mountains again, blinking. It is hard to believe that such beauty still exists. What am I doing in this place? How have I been lucky enough to come here, to be alive, when so many others are not? Tears fill my eyes. Should I pray, thank God? I hesitate. I stopped believing long ago, the day I saw my father hanged in the main square of our village for sneaking food to a boy the Nazis had wanted to starve as punishment for stealing bread. I should have died, too, that night on the bridge, or in prison. But I am here, and I cannot escape the sense that some force, something larger than myself, has helped me to survive.

I take one last look at the mountains, then let the curtains fall back into place. I start to lie down once more, then stop suddenly. A young woman is in the bed beside mine. They must have brought her in while I was asleep.

'Hello?' I whisper. She does not respond. Her breathing is shallow, and I wonder if she is un-conscious. I lean in closer and study her face. She

28

looks about my age, though she is so emaciated that it is hard to tell for certain. Her high cheek-bones protrude against her skin as though they might break through at any second and her eyes twitch beneath paper-thin lids. Her hair has been shorn so close that bald patches of scalp shine through.

I scan the room, hoping to see Dava or one of the other nurses to ask about the girl. But the floor is empty. I look down at the girl once more. Her fingers clutch the edge of the pillow, as though someone might try to take it away. The blanket has fallen from her shoulders, revealing a patch of pale collarbone above her hospital gown. I reach over and pull up the blanket to cover her. Out of the corner of my eye, I notice a clipboard on the edge of her bed. Carefully, so as not to disturb her, I pick it up, scanning the top sheet. It is a medical chart of some type, with many long, unfamiliar words written in English. At the top of the page, I can make out a single word: Rose.

'Rose,' I say aloud, setting down the clipboard and looking back at the girl's face. Her eyes flutter beneath their lids. I repeat her name. Slowly, her eyes open and she stares at me, blinking. 'Hello,' I greet her in Polish. When she does not respond, I switch to Yiddish. 'I'm Marta.' The girl does not respond but continues to stare at me with large, almond-shaped violet eyes. I suddenly recall my own confusion at waking up here. She must be terribly afraid. 'You're safe,' I whisper quickly, remembering how Dava comforted me earlier. 'This is a refugee camp run by the Allies.' She still does not answer and for a second, I wonder if she

29

is unfriendly. Just then, Rose reaches out her hand across the space between our beds. I take her thin, burning fingers in my own. 'I'm sure you've been through some really awful experiences. Me, too. But that's all over now.' I squeeze her hand gently. 'We're safe now. We're in a good place and it's only going to get better, I promise. Do you understand?' Rose does not answer but closes her eyes once more.

I study Rose's face, wondering if waking her had been a mistake. Should I call for a nurse? She does not seem to be in any distress. I lay back in my own bed, still holding Rose's hand. I wish that it was morning so I could ask Dava where Rose came from, what had happened to her.

I think then of the bright stars above the mountaintops. Too tired to sit up again, I crane my neck upward to see them. Through the break in the curtains, I catch a glimpse of a star. Do I dare to wish on it as I did when I was little? I hesitate. It seems greedy to ask for anything when I should be grateful just to be alive. Still, I cannot help but wonder what I should wish for, what life has in store for me now that I have survived.

I turn to Rose to tell her about the mountains. But she is breathing evenly now, her expression peaceful. I will not wake her again. There will be time to show her tomorrow. Still holding Rose's hand, I lie back and gaze up at the stars once more.

CHAPTER 3

We sit on the terrace behind the palace, Dava and I on one of the benches, Rose in her wheelchair close beside us. Rose reads aloud in English from *Little Women*, the book she holds in her lap. *'I know I do – teaching those tiresome children nearly all day, when I'm longing to enjoy myself at home...'*

'Those sisters sure can complain,' I interrupt in Yiddish.

'Marta...' Dava shoots me a warning look.

'I mean, really,' I persist. 'They're supposed to be in the middle of a war, but they're safe and warm in their own home. Yet one sister is complaining that she has to teach...'

'Meg,' Rose clarifies.

'And one of the others is upset because she has to sit in a big house and read to her aunt.'

'That's Jo. But, Marta,' Rose says, 'they suffered from the war, too, in their own way. I mean, they didn't have a lot to eat and their father was off fighting...'

'I think that the American Civil War was very different for people who didn't live close to the battlefields,' Dava offers slowly in English, teaching. 'Not like here.' Battlefields indeed. Here our lives were the battlefields. 'War can affect people in many ways,' she adds. She presses her lips together, a faraway expression in her eyes.

31

Rose raises the book. 'Do you want me to keep going?'

'Yes,' Dava replies, patting Rose's hand. 'You're doing great.'

Rose continues reading aloud, but I do not try to follow along. I have been listening for nearly an hour and my head aches from the constant effort of translating each word. Instead, I look up. It is only seven o'clock. Usually, the August sky would still be bright for more than another hour, but the sun has dropped behind thick, gray-centered clouds. I can barely see the hooked peak of the Untersberg through the fog.

I inhale deeply, savoring the sweet honeysuckle smell from the gardens that line the edge of the terrace. It has been more than two months since my arrival at the camp. My health has improved steadily since then, much more quickly, Dava said, than the doctors expected. The incision where my wound had been is nearly healed. It barely aches at all anymore, except when it rains.

'Marta,' Rose says. I turn to find she is holding out the book to me. 'Do you want to try a line or two?'

I hesitate, running my hand along the warm stone bench. Earlier, Dava stopped Rose and let me try one of the easier passages, but as I struggled through the first few words, it was obvious that the text was still too difficult for me. 'No, thanks.' Rose is nearly fluent in English, owing to summers spent with her aunt in London as a child. I, on the other hand, have been taking the English classes offered each morning in the palace library with some of the other camp residents. I've been able to pick up the spoken language fairly easily, but I still struggle to read much beyond children's books. Dava helps me whenever she has the time. Her language skills are remarkable, owing, she told us once, to the fact that her father was a translator. She was schooled in English and French, in addition to her native Russian and Yiddish, and the German she learned growing up in Austria.

As Rose resumes reading, I turn back toward the palace, awed as ever at its size and grandeur. Schloss Leopoldskron is three stories high, with two massive wings jutting out on either side. Large paned windows dot the light-gray stone facade. The ground floor, I discovered when Dava let me get out of bed a few days after my arrival, is taken up by our ward, and a second ward, where the ballroom had once been, houses male patients. The two are separated by a grand foyer with an enormous crystal chandelier hanging from its high ceiling. Two curved marble staircases lead from the foyer to the first floor, where the library and a small chapel are located. The second floor, where the camp administrative offices are located, is off-limits to residents.

Rose pauses reading at the end of a chapter. 'We should stop now,' Dava says. 'I don't want you overdoing things.'

Concerned, I study Rose's face. Her complexion is pale and dark circles seem to have formed suddenly under her eyes. Rose has not had as easy of a recovery as me. The morning after her arrival, she did not awaken again. When I asked Dava, she told me that Rose was nineteen and from

Amsterdam. Though she was only half Jewish, she had been interned in several camps, most recently a camp in Czechoslovakia called Terezin. I remarked that it must have been a really awful camp to make Rose so sick, but Dava replied it actually was not as bad as some. Rather, she explained, Rose had a blood disorder that had been worsened by the poor living conditions in the camp. I didn't know exactly what a blood disorder was, but it sounded very serious. I watched as she struggled in her sleep over the next several days, keeping vigil as much as I could and informing the nurses whenever she awoke for a few minutes so they could give her water and medicine. Dava told me to concentrate on my own recovery, that Rose was not my problem. But Rose had to get better – I had promised her on the night she arrived that things would be all right.

Then one morning I awoke to find her lying on her side, staring at me with bright violet eyes. 'Hello,' she said.

'Hi.' I sat up. 'I'm Marta.'

'I know. I remember.'

Rose stayed awake for most of the day, but her condition improved little. On good days like today, she is able to sit in a wheelchair for short periods of time. But she still tires easily and cannot get around on her own. 'I'm fine,' she insists now. Her cheeks are a bit pinker, as though she willed them to color.

But Dava is not convinced. 'It's going to rain,' she observes, looking up. 'And it's getting cooler, too.' She reaches over to the wheelchair to adjust the sweater around Rose's shoulders, then stands. 'We should go back inside.'

Rose puts her hand on Dava's arm. 'Just a few more minutes,' she pleads softly.

Dava hesitates, her eyes traveling from Rose's hopeful face to the darkening sky, then back again. 'A few minutes,' she repeats, looking over her shoulder toward the palace. 'I do have to go start my rounds, though.'

'Go ahead,' I say quickly. Rose and I will be able to stay outside longer if Dava is occupied elsewhere. 'I'll bring Rose inside soon.'

'Ten minutes,' Dava orders, her expression stern.

'Ten minutes,' I repeat solemnly, winking so only Rose can see. Satisfied, Dava starts walking toward the building. When she is out of earshot, I turn to Rose. 'She's grumpy today.'

'She's just worried about us. And very tired.' Rose sounds so earnest I feel instantly guilty for my remark. The camp is short-staffed, and the nurses seem to work around the clock to make sure all of the patients receive the care they need. And Dava is particularly attentive to Rose and me, the youngest women in the ward by several years. She visits us whenever she has a free moment, often bringing extra food and sweets.

'Dava's really good to us,' I say. Rose nods in agreement. 'She seemed sad when we were talking about the war, though. I wonder if something happened to her.'

'She mentioned a man once,' Rose replies. 'But I don't know if he was her husband and she never said what became of him.'

'Oh.' I wonder, with a stab of jealousy, why Dava

35

shared this information with Rose and not me.

'I'm glad she let us stay out a bit longer, though,' Rose adds, gazing up at the mountains.

I look down at my dress, one of two that I was given when I was well enough to get out of bed. My forearms peek out from the light pink sleeves, tanned from the summer sun. They've grown thicker, too; I've put on weight quickly from the hearty camp meals and no longer see my ribs each time I change clothes. Unlike Rose. I peek at her out of the corner of my eye. Her hair has begun to grow in, forming a tight cap of blond curls, but she is still as thin and pale as the night she arrived. She eats little besides the few bites Dava or I can coax into her at each meal, and often she cannot even hold that down. Though Dava has not said so, I know that Rose's condition is still very serious.

As I watch Rose, a protective feeling rises up in me. We've become so close in the short time we've known each other. Back home, I doubt we would have even been friends. I would have dismissed her as too girlish and timid, too boring. But here, where the other women are older and we are both alone, our friendship seems natural.

It was that way with Emma during the war, too, I realize, her face appearing in my mind. When my mother came back from her job at the ghetto orphanage one day and told me she wanted to introduce me to the new girl who had started working there, I was skeptical. Emma was nearly two years older than me and from the city, not the village like us. What could we possibly have in common? And I had little time for socializing between my official job as a messenger for the ghetto administration and my work for the resistance. But my mother persisted: the new girl seemed lonely. It would be a mitzvah for me to introduce her to some of my friends.

I relented, knowing that it was pointless to fight Mama when she seized upon an idea. The next day, I went to the orphanage after work to meet Emma and invited her to join me for Shabbat dinner with the others at the apartment that served as the headquarters for the resistance. To my surprise, I found that I enjoyed Emma's company – she had a quiet grace that made me instantly comfortable. I liked having someone to confide in; it was as though I had found the best friend I never knew I was missing. We began to spend a great deal of time together, talking over long walks through the ghetto streets after work in the evenings.

Rose and I have developed a similar bond, becoming almost inseparable in our time here. I look past her now toward the sprawling west lawn of the palace. Dozens of large white tents stand in even rows. Residents who do not need medical attention live there, in the main part of the camp. I might have to move there soon, Dava told me the other day. I know that she's kept me in the ward as long as possible for Rose's sake, but she won't be able to justify my occupying a bed that is needed for sicker arrivals much longer.

I turn back toward Rose. Her chin is dipped slightly into her chest, her eyes half closed. 'You look tired,' I offer.

'I suppose. But let's stay just a few more minutes.' I nod. Dava will be furious with me for

37

keeping Rose out so long, but I cannot refuse her simple request. 'Marta?'

'Yes?'

'Where will you go from here? After you leave the camp, I mean.'

I hesitate, caught off guard by her question. I know that the camp is only temporary, that everyone will eventually leave or be relocated elsewhere. Would I return to Poland? I think about it sometimes. A few nights I have dreamed that I went back to our house in the village to find my mother cooking dinner, my father reading by the fire. But I know that things are different now; all of my family and friends are gone. I see the faces of our neighbors who stood by as the Nazis gathered us in the town square and marched us in double lines to the train station. Pani Klopacz, the elderly woman who bought milk from my father each day, peered through the curtains as we passed, her eyes solemn. Others whom we had known for years turned coldly away. No, I cannot live among them again. Nor can I bear the thought of returning to Kraków, which holds nothing but painful memories of Alek and the others who had died for the resistance. But where else can I go? I've heard some of the other women in my English class talking about emigrating to the United States, or even to Palestine. Dava mentioned putting me on the lists for visas to these places, but I know that without a relative to vouch for me, the wait could take years. And even if I could get a visa, how would I survive alone in a strange place? 'I don't know,' I answer at last, feeling foolish.

Rose opens her mouth, but before she can

speak a pained expression flashes across her face.

I lean toward her. 'What is it?'

'N-nothing.' But her voice is strained and her face has gone pale.

I stand up quickly. 'We need to get you inside.'

'In a minute,' Rose implores. Her voice is a bit stronger now, as if whatever was hurting her has eased. 'Don't tell Dava, please.'

'Hey!' A voice yells behind us. Our heads snap in the direction of the palace. As if on cue, Dava is storming across the lawn toward us, hands on her hips.

'Uh-oh,' Rose whispers. I look upward at the early-evening sky, wondering how much time has passed.

'Ten minutes,' Dava says, crossing her arms as she approaches. 'I said ten minutes.'

'I'm sorry,' I begin. 'We lost track of time. I can take her inside.'

Dava shakes her head. 'You'd probably go by way of Vienna and then I wouldn't see either of you for days.' I open my mouth to protest but Dava raises her hand. 'Anyway, I need your help with something, if you're feeling up to it.'

'I'm fine. What is it?'

'We have a small transport of refugees coming in tonight from Hungary and the woman who usually helps with admissions is unwell. Want to do it?'

'Sure,' I reply eagerly. I had noticed other residents working around the camp, in the kitchen and the gardens. Several times I pressed Dava to let me help. But she explained that residents of the medical ward were not allowed to have jobs, that I would have to wait until I moved over to the main camp. They must be really desperate for assistance to break the rules now.

'Great. They should be here any minute. Just go around to the table on the front lawn and Dr. Verrier will explain what to do.'

'No problem.' I look down at Rose. 'Sleep well.'

As Dava wheels Rose toward the door, I start around the side of the palace. Several army trucks have rumbled through the gate from the main road. They sit now on the grass on either side of the long dirt driveway. Soldiers climb from the trucks, open the back doors. One by one, refugees appear, still clad in their tattered, striped prison clothes. Many lean on the soldiers, unable to stand or walk unassisted. All are emaciated, skeleton thin. Did I look like that just a few months ago?

'Excuse me,' a man calls in German. I force myself to turn from the refugees. A man with dark hair and spectacles wearing a white coat stands by a folding table a few meters away. Though he is not one of the doctors who treated me, I recognize him from the ward. 'Are you the help?'

'Yes.' I walk toward the table and sit in the folding chair he indicates.

'Your job is to verify the information for each person on the arrival list – name, nationality, date of birth, if they have it. Then I will tell you whether he or she is going into the medical ward or the main camp. Do you understand?' I nod, studying the line of refugees as they approach the table. They all look as though they will need medical attention. I wonder if there will be room for them in the wards.

I take a deep breath, then look up at the first of the arrivals, a gaunt, bedraggled man. 'Name?' I ask.

The man hesitates, a panicked expression crossing his face. Then he glances down at the row of dark numbers on his forearm. Though I did not receive one, I know that prisoners in the main camps were tattooed by the Nazis. This man is unaccustomed, I realize, to being thought of as anything but a number. I take a deep breath, start again. 'Hello,' I say in Yiddish, smiling gently. 'I'm Marta Nedermann. What's your name?'

The man's expression relaxes. 'Friedrich Masaryk.'

I check him off the list. 'Hungarian. Born November 18, 1901. Is that correct?' The man nods. He is only in his forties. With his white hair and hunched posture, I would have taken him for at least sixty.

Dr. Verrier examines the man. 'Herr Masaryk, you are undernourished, but otherwise well enough to go to the main camp.' I make a note on the chart as one of the soldiers escorts Herr Masaryk away.

The next arrival, a woman, lies on a stretcher, borne between two soldiers. I look up at Dr. Verrier, who shrugs. 'Camp rules, I'm afraid. Even the unconscious have to be registered.'

'Lebonski, Hannah,' one of the soldiers bearing the stretcher reads from the woman's forehead.

I check the list quickly. 'I don't see it.' I scan the list again. 'In fact, I don't see any women's names....'

41

'Is there another list?' Dr. Verrier asks.

'Dammit,' one of the soldiers swears. 'Mattie forgot to give us the list from the women's camp. Jim!' He shouts over his shoulder to another soldier who stands several meters away by one of the trucks. Behind him, I see several of the arrivals cringe. The sound of a soldier yelling, even an American, is still terrifying to them. 'Where's Mattie?'

The other soldier points toward the palace with his head. 'I think I saw him go around the side.'

Dr. Verrier turns to me. 'Would you mind?'

'Not at all.' I stand up and walk quickly around the palace. The back lawn is tranquil, a world away from the chaos of the new arrivals. I scan the terrace, but it is deserted. Perhaps the soldier was mistaken about the one with the list being here. I pause, uncertain what to do. I will ask Dava to help me, I decide, starting for the palace door. Then, out of the corner of my eye, I see something move in the tall grass down by the lake. I take a step forward. A dark-haired soldier is half sitting, half lying by the water's edge. That must be him. I walk quickly down the lawn. He does not look up as I approach. 'Excuse me,' I say. Slowly, as though he had been sleeping, the soldier sits up and starts to turn. As his face comes into view, I gasp.

It is Paul, the soldier who saved me.

CHAPTER 4

I stand motionless, staring down at the soldier. Is it really Paul? His wide blue eyes are instantly recognizable. My breath catches. 'Can I help you?' he asks, cocking his head. Paul's voice, low and melodic, is the one I remember from prison. But his words are formal, his expression unfamiliar. He does not recognize me.

Of course not. He has probably liberated hundreds of people since we met. I hesitate, wanting to tell him who I am, to thank him for saving me. Then I remember the queue of sick and weary arrivals. There is no time for small talk. I clear my throat. 'I–I need...' I stammer, my English faltering. Taking a breath, I try again slowly. 'One of the soldiers said ... Mattie.'

'That's me. Mattie. Paul Mattison, actually.' Paul Mattison, I think. Looking down at him, I feel a strange tug inside me. I have replayed that moment in the prison so many times. It is hard to believe he is here. 'Did they send you for the list?' he asks. I nod. He yawns and stretches slowly, then pulls a piece of paper from his breast pocket and holds it out to me. 'Here.'

As I take a step toward him, my heart flutters. He is even more handsome than I remembered. But closer now, his eyes are bloodshot, as if he has not slept for several days. Fine, dark stubble covers his chin and cheeks and his uniform is

43

coated in dust. As I bend down to take the paper, I recognize his earthy pine scent. There is another smell, too, though, both sickly sweet and sour at the same time. Alcohol, I realize. Paul is drunk, or was. Suddenly I am seized with the urge to flee. 'Thank you.' I snatch the paper, then turn and start toward the palace. Picturing Paul's face, I am disappointed. Is that drunk, sullen soldier really the same man who rescued me?

'Miss,' a voice calls. I turn to find Paul making his way unsteadily up the bank of the lake. 'Wait a minute.' As he approaches, I notice that his hair and face are now wet, as though he dunked his head in the lake. The smell of stale water mingles with the pine and alcohol. 'Don't I know you from somewhere?'

My heart races. He remembers. Then, looking at his unfocused eyes, I realize that it does not matter. 'I–I don't think so,' I manage to say.

He stares at me puzzled. 'But...'

'*Przeprasz...*' I begin. In my nervousness, I have reverted to Polish. 'Excuse me, I have to get back to the arrivals.' I turn and walk around the side of the palace.

Dr. Verrier stands by the table, arms crossed. 'I'm sorry,' I say as I sit down. The soldiers, who had placed the stretcher with the woman on the ground, pick it up again. I unfold the crumpled list, locating the woman. 'Lebonski, Hannah.' Dr. Verrier quickly directs the soldiers to take her to the ward, then moves to the next patient.

As I try to concentrate on my work, my heart pounds. Paul is here. Should I have told him who I am? I lift my head and scan the soldiers who are helping arrivals from the trucks. Paul is not among them. Then I spot him sitting under a tree across the lawn, head in his hands. Drunk and lazy, I think, as I start to process a skeletal older woman. How could I have been so wrong? But through my disgust, I feel something else, low and warm in my stomach. Suddenly he lifts his head and turns in my direction. Our eyes meet for a split second. I look quickly down at my papers once more, my cheeks reddening. The warmth in my stomach grows as I feel his eyes still on me, watching, trying to remember.

Twenty minutes later, when the line has dwindled, I glance over at the tree again. Paul is gone. It is for the best, I tell myself over the small stab of disappointment in my chest. I would rather remember him as I had seen him the day of my liberation, not like this. I finish processing the last refugee, then put the extra forms back into the box and stand up. 'I do know you!' a voice exclaims behind me. Startled, I drop the box, sending forms scattering across the grass. I turn to find Paul standing there, arms crossed.

Suddenly it is as if someone knocked the wind out of me. 'You startled me!' I say, when I am able to speak again. I bend and start to gather the forms.

'Sorry.' He kneels beside me to help pick up the papers. The smell of alcohol is gone, replaced by spearmint gum, and his movements are steadier now, as though he has begun to sober. 'It's just that I remembered where I know you from.' He reaches toward me for one of the papers near my right ankle, bringing our faces close. 'You were

45

the girl in the prison at Dachau. Mary? Martha?'

'Marta,' I say, staring hard at the grass.

'Oh, right, Marta. Sorry.' I feel him studying my face. 'It's just that you look so different. And I didn't think you spoke English,' he adds.

'I didn't.' My cheeks begin to burn again. 'I mean, I don't, very well. I've had the chance to study since coming here.' I am suddenly aware of my accent, of the way I struggle to choose each word.

'Well, you've done great.' He finishes gathering the papers. As he puts them in the box, the back of his hand brushes mine. Reminded of his strong, gentle touch as he tended to me in prison, I am suddenly light-headed. Then he leaps to his feet, extending his hand to me.

'Allow me,' he says. I look up and our eyes meet. A troubled expression flickers across his face, so quickly I wonder if I imagined it. Pity, perhaps, for the girl he rescued in prison?

I hesitate, then put my fingers in his. Warmth, too strong to ignore, rises in me once more. 'Th-thank you,' I stutter as he helps me to my feet. He releases my fingers slowly, eyes still locked on mine. Finally, I turn away, struggling to breathe normally as I place the box on the table and brush the dirt from my dress. Across the lawn the other soldiers are loading supplies onto trucks. 'Are you leaving again fast?' I ask, looking up at him. His brow wrinkles. 'I mean, soon?'

He nods. 'We're trying to make Munich to-night. Then we're shipping out. Haven't told us where, but I'm guessing the Pacific.'

'Oh.' I take a deep breath. 'I never had the

46

chance to thank you. For saving me, I mean.'

He waves his hand. 'It's not necessary. I was just doing my job.'

Before I can reply, another soldier approaches the table. 'Hey, Mattie, change of plans. One of the trucks has a busted axle.' The soldier's words come out in rapid bursts, making it difficult for me to understand. 'It's going to take a few hours to fix. Major Clark ordered us to camp here, then head for Paris at first light.' Paul is not leaving yet, I realize, suddenly excited. The other soldier continues, 'He said we can take the jeep if we want, go into Salzburg to have a look around and get some food.'

'I could use a drin–' Paul begins. Then he stops, turning to me. 'Want to come with us?'

I hesitate, surprised. Paul is asking me to join him in town. My head spins. But camp residents are not allowed to leave the grounds. 'I can't.'

Paul looks from me to the soldier, then back again. 'Give me a minute, Drew, okay?' The other soldier shrugs his shoulders. 'I'd better go with them,' Paul says to me when he has gone.

'Salzburg really is lovely.' I fight to keep my voice even.

Paul reaches out and touches my sleeve. 'It was good seeing you again, Marta. I'm glad to know you're okay.'

'Goodbye,' I reply. Then I turn and walk back across the lawn, still feeling the warmth of his touch. As I round the side of the palace, my eyes begin to sting. What is wrong with me? I should be glad that he is gone. He was drunk and not at all what I expected. I walk down to my favorite

47

spot by the water's edge, beneath the willow tree. Then I drop to the ground and lean over, studying myself in the lake. My wild curls and too-large spectacles stare back. What were you thinking? my reflection demands. Did you really expect him to stay here with you, instead of going into town with the other soldiers? I take off my glasses and brush my eyes with the back of my hand.

Suddenly I hear footsteps coming down the lawn. I replace my glasses and turn, expecting to see Dava, coming to chastise me for being outside so long. But it is Paul, standing behind me, hands in his pockets. He carries a small backpack on his shoulders that I had not noticed before. 'Sorry to sneak up on you again.'

I swallow over the lump that has formed in my throat. 'If you need directions into town...'

He shakes his head. 'Nah, I decided not to go.'

I inhale sharply. 'Oh?'

'I'm kinda tired and the jeep was too crowded. I spend enough time with those knuckleheads, anyway.' He takes a step forward. 'Mind if I join you?' Before I can answer, he drops down close beside me, leaning back and planting one arm on the ground for support. 'It's really beautiful here.' I am too surprised to respond. He did not go with the others after all. We gaze up at the mountains, neither speaking. Out of the corner of my eye, I peek down at his forearm, tanned and muscular. Desire rises in me.

Paul turns toward me. I look away quickly, staring hard at the water and praying he did not notice me watching him. 'I'd love to go for a walk before it gets too dark,' he says, gesturing to a dirt path to the right of where we are sitting that runs along the perimeter of the lake. My heart sinks. He's going to go off and leave me again. But he is still looking at me expectantly. 'Care to join me?'

I hesitate, too surprised to respond. A walk, just the two of us? The idea sounds like a dream. But technically, the path is beyond the camp grounds, off limits to residents. And I barely know Paul; it would hardly be proper to go off alone with him, especially since not an hour ago he was drunk. His eyes are clearer now, though, his face the one I remember from prison. And I cannot bear the thought of him leaving again so soon. I have to find a way to go with him. 'Wait here for a minute.' I stand up and run back into the palace, looking for Dava. The foyer is empty so I walk quickly into the ward. I spot Dava at the far end of the room, checking Rose's temperature.

I race toward them. 'What's wrong?'

'Rose has a slight fever.' Dava's voice is calm but there is concern in her eyes.

'I'm fine,' Rose insists, struggling to sit up. 'How did it go with the new arrivals?'

'Fine.' I force my uneasiness down. 'Dava, I need to ask you a favor.'

She does not look up. 'What is it?'

'I need permission to leave the grounds and go around the lake, just for a little while. I saw someone I know. That is, the American soldier who saved me at Dachau.'

'Paul?' Rose asks eagerly.

I nod. 'Anyway, I want to go for a walk with him.'

'You know the rules, Marta,' Dava replies.

49

'Residents are not permitted off the palace grounds.'

'I know. But I was hoping you could make an exception, just this once. Please.'

Dava hesitates. 'Curfew is in less than an hour.'

'I was hoping you could sign me in at bed check.' Dava frowns and I can tell that I am pressing my luck.

Rose reaches up, touches Dava's arm. 'Let her go, Dava. For me.'

Dava looks slowly from me to Rose, then back again. She reaches into her pocket and pulls out a piece of paper and a pencil. 'Take this pass in case anyone questions your being off grounds,' she says, scribbling something on the paper before handing it to me. 'But I want you back by midnight and not a minute longer.'

'I will be. Thank you.' I lean down and kiss Rose on the cheek. 'And thank you,' I whisper. 'But if you aren't feeling well...'

'I'm fine,' Rose replies softly. 'And I'm really happy for you, Marta.'

I race out of the ward and back through the foyer. When I reach the patio, I stop. The spot where Paul sat minutes earlier is deserted. He's gone, I think. My heart sinks. Perhaps he became tired of waiting for me and went after the other soldiers into town. Hurriedly, I scan the banks. Paul is standing farther to the right along the edge of the lake, head down, back to me, his broad shoulders silhouetted against the last rays of the setting sun. Studying the way his torso tapers to his narrow hips, I feel a tightness in my chest, strong and sudden. I have never felt this

50

way before, not even with Jacob. Easy, I think. It is just a walk, something for him to do while he waits to leave again. I force myself to breathe slowly, struggling to regain my composure.

I start toward him, and as I near, he turns, his face breaking into a wide smile. 'Look,' he says in a low voice, gesturing toward the water with his head. Closer, I can see that his attention has been caught by a mother duck and four fuzzy, yellow ducklings that have drifted close to the bank, heads tucked in sleep. I study his face, boyish with wonder as he watches them.

'Ready?' He looks up from the water, his eyes meeting mine. He blinks, and the serious expression I noticed earlier on the lawn appears on his face once more. Not pity, I decide. Something else.

I swallow over the lump that has suddenly formed in my throat. 'Y-yes.' I follow him toward the low white gate that marks the edge of the palace grounds. He holds the gate open for me and I step through onto the dirt path. A few meters farther along the water's edge, an elderly man sits in the grass, holding a fishing rod, a small dinghy docked at his feet. He eyes us warily as we pass. What a strange pair we must make, I realize. The American soldier and the refugee. But Paul does not seem to notice. He whistles softly under his breath as we walk, looking up at the mountains through the trees.

'It's just beautiful here,' he remarks. 'Reminds me of our ranch in North Carolina. My family farms tobacco, just at the base of the Blue Ridge Mountains. Our mountains aren't as dramatic as

51

these.' He gestures toward the Untersberg. 'But it's still beautiful countryside.' He steps too close to me on the path and our sides brush. 'Sorry.'

I feel a twinge of disappointment as he moves away. 'I'm from the country, too,' I offer, eager to have this in common.

He looks down at me. 'Really?'

'Yes, our village, it's called Bochnia, is close to the Tatra–' I stop mid-sentence, interrupted by the sound of voices. Down the path, there is a group of teenagers coming toward us, laughing loudly. A knot forms in my chest.

Paul notices my reaction. 'What is it?' I do not answer, but gesture with my head toward the youths. 'Do you want to go back?'

'No,' I reply quickly. 'It's just that...' I hesitate, my skin prickling. I have seen so few people, other than the camp staff and residents, since coming here. Staying on the palace grounds, it is easy to forget that we are in Austria, a country that embraced the Nazis so readily. But now, seeing the teenagers, I am terrified.

'I understand. Wait here.' Before I can respond, Paul walks back in the direction from which we had come, leaving me alone in the middle of the path. Despite my anxiety about the teenagers, I cannot help but notice Paul's long legs, his awkward coltlike gait. He approaches the fisherman, gesturing toward the boat. But Paul does not speak German, I realize, watching the fisherman shake his head. I see Paul reach into his pocket and hand the man something.

I walk toward him. 'What are you doing?'

Paul gestures to the boat. 'Your chariot, milady.'

'I don't understand.'

'You wanted to get away from those kids, right?' I nod. 'But you didn't want to go back. So I rented the boat from this man. Indefinitely, if need be.' The fisherman turns back to his rod, disinterested. He would not have loaned his boat to a stranger; Paul must have paid him enough to buy it outright. 'Ready?' He holds out his hand.

I hesitate. I have never been on the lake and it is nearly dark out. But the teenagers are almost upon us now, their voices growing louder with each second. I reach out and Paul's fingers, large and warm, close around mine, sending a shiver through me. I let him lead me to the water's edge. Paul helps me into the boat and I make my way gingerly to the wide wood bench at the far end. The boat wobbles slightly as Paul steps in with one foot, pushing off from the bank with the other. He sits on the middle bench opposite me and picks up the oars. Then he begins to paddle with small strokes, steering us toward the center of the lake. As we pull farther away from the bank, I relax and look around. It is nearly dark now and the gas-lights surrounding the lake are illuminated, their reflections large fireflies in the water. I watch Paul as he looks over his shoulder, aiming for the center of the lake. Warmth rises in me once more.

As the boat continues gently away from the shore, the teenagers' voices fade away and the air grows still. In the distance, a cricket chirps. I swat at a mosquito that buzzes by my ear, then turn back toward the palace. Yellow lights glow behind each of the windows. 'Penny for your thoughts,' Paul says. I shake my head, puzzled. 'It's an expression. I was asking what you were thinking.'

'About my friend, Rose. She wasn't feeling well tonight.'

'I'm sorry to hear that.' He stops rowing and rests the oars in his lap. 'There, that's better.'

He leans forward, resting his chin in his hands and gazing up at the mountains. I study his face out of the corner of my eye once more. He is really here, I marvel. At the same time, disbelief washes over me. Even before the war, in the best of times, I was never the girl whom boys sought out, took for boat rides. I want to ask him why he is here with me. 'So how long have you been in Europe?' I say instead.

'About a year.'

'Do you like it?'

'Depends what you mean by "it." Europe? It's beautiful from what I've seen. The army? I've made some of the best friends of my life, at least those of them that have survived. But this war ... my unit, the Fighting 502nd, they call us, dropped in on D-Day. We've fought in every major battle since. I mean, I would be happy if I never see another goddamn–' He stops suddenly, noticing my expression. 'Pardon my language. I've been around soldiers so long, I don't know how to speak in proper company anymore.'

'I understand.' And I really do. There are some things that only cursing can describe.

Paul reaches into his pocket and pulls out a flask. 'Thirsty?'

I shake my head and cringe as he takes a large swig, remembering his drunkenness earlier. 'Do you do that a lot? Drink, I mean.'

He looks away. 'More than some, not as much as others. More than I used to. That's for dam– I mean darn sure.'

I want to know why, but I'm afraid of appearing rude. 'What did you do before joining the army?'

'College. I was six months short of graduating from Princeton when I was drafted. Not that I was any great brain – I went on a football scholarship.'

'Will you go back? After the war, I mean?'

He shrugs. 'Who knows? I'm not sure of anything anymore. Damn war.' This time he does not bother to catch himself cursing. 'My fiancée, Kim, wrote me a letter a month ago, saying that she was through with me and marrying someone else.' Fiancée. The word cuts through my chest. Paul had been engaged when he liberated me. 'And I'm one of the lucky ones.' There is a hollowness to his voice I have not heard before. 'My cousin Mike was killed at Bastogne. Two guys in my unit died, another lost his legs.'

'I'm sorry,' I say quietly. Paul does not respond but stares out over the water, lips pressed together, jaw clenched. I feel an ache rise within me, my own losses echoed in his. My parents, my friends. I remember lying on the prison floor, realizing that there was no one left who cared, no one who would come looking for me. The idea was as unbearable as any physical pain the Nazis had inflicted. Then Paul had come. Until now, I thought of him and the other soldiers only as liberators, heroes. I never thought of what they sacrificed, how they might resent us for bringing them here. I want to reach out and touch him, to try to offer comfort. 'I'm sorry,' I repeat instead.

'It's not your fault,' he replies, shoulders sagging. 'It's just that sometimes it seems that I've lost everything.'

'No,' I blurt out.

'No, what?'

'No, you did not lose everything. Did you lose your parents?' He shakes his head. 'Your entire family and all of your friends?' Another shake. 'You did not lose your home.' I can hear my voice rising now. 'Or your health.'

He looks down, chastised. 'You lost much more than me, I know.'

'That's not my point. I'm just saying that you didn't lose everything. Neither did I. We're here. Alive.'

He does not respond. Have I angered him? I look out over the water, cursing myself inwardly for saying too much. 'This is so great,' Paul says a minute later. I look back, surprised to find him smiling. Happiness rises inside me. 'The quiet, I mean.' My heart sinks. For a minute, I thought he was talking about being with me. 'You can't imagine the noise, the months of shelling and artillery. Even at night when the fighting stopped, there was no peace because you never knew when it might start again. It's been better since the war ended, but there are still always a hundred guys around, talking and making noise. Don't get me wrong.' He raises his hand. 'I love my unit like brothers. But being in this beautiful place tonight...' He pauses, looking deep into my eyes. 'Seeing you again...'

His words are interrupted by a low, rumbling sound. 'Storm's coming,' Paul observes as I turn.

56

The sky over the mountains has grown pitch-dark. Thunder rumbles again, louder this time, and raindrops begin hitting the water around us. 'We should go back.'

I look from the darkening sky to the shore. We have drifted toward the far edge of the lake, nearly a kilometer from where we started. 'We'll never make it back in time.'

'Then we need to find shelter somewhere,' he replies. 'It's dangerous being on the water in a storm like this.' The rain is falling heavily now, puddling in the bottom of the boat, soaking through my clothes. 'Over there.' Paul points to the bank closest to us.

I wipe the water from my glasses. A few meters back from the water's edge, nestled in the trees, sits a small wooden hut. 'Probably a gardener's shed,' I say.

'Perfect.' There is a large flash of lightning, followed by a loud clap of thunder. Paul begins rowing toward the shore. His arm muscles strain against his uniform as he stabs at the water with short, hard strokes, inching the boat forward into the wind. As we near the bank, he hops out into the shallow water and pulls the boat in, securing it. 'Here.' He holds his hand out to help me to the shore.

We race down the muddy path toward the shed, my hand clasped tightly in his. Paul pushes against the door, which opens with a loud creak. Inside the air is damp, smelling of turpentine and wet wood. I feel a pang of sadness as Paul releases my hand, reaching into his pocket and pulling out a match. He lights the match, illuminating a workman's bench covered with tools. 'A gardener's shed. You were right.' He walks to the bench and rummages around. 'Aha!' He pulls out a small stump of a candle and lights it. The air glows flickering orange around us.

'Th-that's better,' I say, my teeth chattering.

Paul's brow furrows. 'You're soaking wet.' He opens his backpack and pulls out a coarse brown blanket. 'Here.' He wraps the blanket, which smells of smoke and coffee and sweat, around my shoulders. As he brings the edges of the blanket together in front of me, I am drawn nearer to him. We stand, not moving, our faces close. Suddenly, it is as if a giant hand is squeezing my chest, making it difficult to breathe. What is happening here? I wonder.

He reaches down and takes my hand underneath the blanket and for a second I think he means to hold it. But he brings my hand to the edge of the blanket, placing it where his own had been to keep it snugly wrapped around me. Then he steps back, clearing his throat. 'I wish we had some dry wood for a fire,' he remarks.

I drop to the dirt floor, holding the blanket close. 'Probably better if we don't draw attention.'

Paul reaches into his bag and I expect him to bring out another blanket or perhaps a towel. But instead it is the flask again. He opens the cap and takes a large swig.

It is not, I decide, the time for a lecture on drinking. 'Can I have a sip?'

His eyes widen. 'Do you want some? I mean, I'm sorry, I just didn't think that you would...?'

'Drink?' I smile, remembering nights with Jacob

58

and Alek and the other boys from the resistance. We would meet for long hours into the night, planning operations, arguing about strategy. Someone always found a bottle of vodka, and many shots were poured and drunk to the traditional Polish and Hebrew toasts of *nazdrowa* (to your health) and *l'chaim* (to life). 'Not often,' I tell Paul now as he drops to the ground beside me.

As he hands me the flask, our fingers touch. I jerk my hand back, sending the liquid splashing against the inside of the container. Whiskey, I note, as I raise the flask to my lips. The fumes are strong against my face as I take a sip, tilting my head backward like Jacob taught me so I don't taste the alcohol as much. I feel the familiar burning in my throat as I swallow, then my stomach grows warm. 'Thanks.' I pass the flask back to Paul and his hand brushes mine once more. This time I do not pull away. His fingers linger warm atop mine. Suddenly I notice that his sleeve is dripping water. 'You're soaked, too,' I say.

'I guess I am.' Paul looks down, as though noticing his wet clothes for the first time. He shrugs. 'It's not a big deal.' It occurs to me then that he has given his only blanket to me.

'Here.' I pull the blanket open. 'It's big enough to share.'

He hesitates, then moves toward me, taking the edge of the blanket and wrapping it around his shoulders. Trembling, I slide closer along the ground, bringing him farther inside the blanket. 'May I?' He lifts his arm, asking permission to put it around me. Before I can answer, he draws me close. 'Is this okay?'

59

'Fine,' I reply, hoping that he cannot feel how fast my heart is beating.

'I'm sure the rain will stop soon. Then we can head back.'

But I do not want to head back. I look up at him. His face hovers above mine and his eyes dart back and forth, as though searching for something. Then he lowers his head. His lips brush mine, questioning, asking permission. My first kiss. I am too stunned to react. His hand rises to my cheek and his lips press full and warm on mine. I respond, heat rising in me. Suddenly I freeze, putting my hand on his chest. 'Wait...'

He pulls back. 'I'm so sorry. I thought you wanted...'

'I do.' I pause, trying to catch my breath. 'I mean, I thought I did. But you have a fiancée.'

'Had,' he corrects me. 'I think it was over before I left. I mean, we were high school sweethearts. Getting married was what everyone expected us to do, but I'm not sure we were meant to be together, you know?' His words spill out quickly, making it difficult for me to understand what he is saying. 'It's more the idea of having someone back home that I miss.' He pauses. 'Anyway, I'm sorry.' Our eyes remained locked. Kiss me again, I think. But I do not want to be the substitute for another woman, not again.

Finally, I turn away. Listening to the rain pound heavily on the roof, I know there will be no possibility of leaving for some time. I lean my head against Paul's chest, pressing my cheek sideways and feeling the heat that radiates through the damp cloth. He rests his chin on top of my head gently. I take off my glasses, put them on the ground beside me. The shadows dim as the last of the candle burns down. Paul's breathing grows long and even above me. Enveloped in the warmth of the blanket, I feel my eyes grow heavy.

Suddenly I remember another cabin, larger than this one, outside Lublin where Jacob and I used to hide. *Don't*, I think, but it is too late. Jacob's face appears in the shadows on the wall unbidden, reminding me of the long nights we spent together, anxiously waiting for our contact to arrive and deliver information or supplies. We never slept in that cabin, of course, or even dared to light a candle. Instead, we hid in a dark corner, our heads close to hear each other whispering, constantly afraid of being caught. But Jacob made those nights fun, telling me stories or jokes to pass the time.

Then one night, as Jacob was trying to explain some political concept that I did not quite under-stand, he stopped speaking. Outside the cabin came footsteps, too numerous and heavy to belong to our lone contact, followed by a dog's bark. 'Quickly,' he whispered, pulling back the bare carpet and opening a hidden panel in the floor. He pushed me down into the tiny crawl space, then climbed in, closing the door. He lay on top of me – there was no other choice – not moving, for what felt like an eternity as the Gestapo walked the floor above us, searching. His heart beat hard against mine. It was in that moment that I realized I was in love with him.

Then the Gestapo were gone, leaving as quickly as they had come. 'Are you all right?' Jacob whispered, his breath warm.

'Yes.' My voice cracked. 'Fine.'

'Marta...' he began, then hesitated. He lowered his head toward mine. I closed my eyes, expecting to feel my first kiss. But there was nothing. Then I felt him pull back slowly, his weight lessening. I opened my eyes again. 'I'm sorry,' he said.

'I don't understand.'

'We've grown close, you and I. And I like you.' Hope rose within me. 'But Marta, I can't. I'm married.'

Married. It was as if I had been punched in the stomach. 'Who is she?'

'I can't say. Not even to you, whom I'd trust with my life. We have to keep it secret for her safety. That's why I didn't tell you sooner. Marta, I consider you one of my closest friends. I'm fond of you.' He cleared his throat. 'But to be fair, I had to say something before I gave you the wrong impression or things went too far.'

But I want things to go too far, I thought desperately as he opened the crawl space door and climbed out. Of course I did not say this, but followed him out of the shed into the night.

Remembering now, I shiver. A tear runs down my cheek. *Stop it*, I think. This is not that cabin. Paul is not Jacob. Paul. I look up at him. His eyes are still closed, head tilted back against the wall. He holds me tightly as he sleeps, as though afraid I might slip away. It is madness to think he might like me, I know. And even if he does, in a few hours he will be gone. But at least for the moment, he is mine. I turn inward, pressing my cheek against his chest, clutching the front of his shirt in my hand. My eyes grow heavy.

Sometime later, I awake with a start. I blink several times in the darkness. Inhaling the musty air, I remember the boat and the storm. Was it all a dream? Then, feeling Paul's arm wrapped around me under the blanket, I know that it was not. I look up at him. He smiles down at me, eyes wide. 'Sleep well?'

I blush. How long has he been watching me? 'Very well.' It is the truth. Despite sitting upright on a hard floor in soaking clothes, it was some of the most restful sleep I have had since the start of the war. I reach for my glasses. 'How long was I out?'

'A couple of hours.'

'Hours?' I leap up and push open the door of the shed. Outside the rain has stopped and the sky just above the mountains is edged with pink. 'It's starting to get light.'

'Almost dawn,' he agrees, and I detect a note of reluctance in his voice. 'We should get back.' He stands and rolls the blanket up. I try to smooth my hair with my hands. As I start through the door of the shed, Paul follows too closely behind me, brushing against my side. 'Excuse me,' he says, stepping back awkwardly. I turn toward him. He is staring at me, the longing in his eyes unmistakable. My breath catches. I look away quickly, hurrying through the door.

Outside, the night air is cool and still. We walk to the bank and Paul helps me into the boat. Neither of us speaks as he rows quickly across the lake. The air is silent except for some geese calling to one another in the distance. Watching Paul

63

guide the boat toward the opposite bank, I am overwhelmed with sadness. In just a few minutes, he will be gone. We reach the spot on the bank where the fisherman had been the previous night. He hops onto the shore, holds his hand out to me. As I step from the boat, my foot slides on the slippery mud and I stumble. Paul catches me by the shoulders. 'Careful,' he says, still holding me. His breath is warm on my forehead.

'Thank you,' I say.

'Marta, I...' he begins softly, then falters. 'I want, that is to say, I don't want...' I lift my eyes to his face, which is strained with sadness and longing. He does not want to say goodbye, either, I realize. I cannot breathe. In that moment, I know that it is not his ex-fiancée he desires. I reach for him, standing on my tiptoes and placing my hand on the back of his neck. Instinctively, I pull him toward me, pressing my lips against his, taking what I'd been too afraid to accept just a few hours earlier. He hesitates for a second, surprised. Then he responds, his mouth warm and strong. Our lips open, drawing us farther into each other urgently.

A horn blares out suddenly and we break apart. Paul straightens, turning toward the noise. 'They're getting ready to go,' he says breathlessly. 'We'd better hurry.' He helps me up the bank to the path and we walk quickly toward the palace in silence. Sadness rises in me. Don't leave, I want to say. But I know that it is impossible.

In front of the palace, the trucks are assembled in a line, waiting to go. Paul turns to me once more. 'Marta, I don't know what is going to happen. I just wish that there was some way...'

'I know,' I reply quickly, forcing my voice not to crack. Everything is happening too fast. My eyes lock with his and I fight the urge to reach out and touch him again. 'Be safe.'

'Come on, Paul!' a voice behind him calls impatiently. The first trucks are beginning to pull from the driveway.

'Bye,' he whispers, taking several steps backward, his eyes not leaving mine. Then he turns and runs toward the last of the trucks. I watch as one of the other men reaches down and helps him onto the back. The engine rumbles and the truck begins to move. As it pulls from the driveway, Paul turns back toward me. Our eyes meet again and he smiles, raising one hand. Then, as the truck turns the corner, he disappears.

CHAPTER 5

I stand motionless on the lawn as the sound of the engines fades, staring numbly through the clouds of dust kicked up by the truck wheels. I walk to the porch step and sink down, trying to breathe over the lump in my throat. My eyes begin to burn. I raise my sleeve to my face, inhaling Paul's lingering, musky scent. I can still feel his lips pressing down on mine. I desperately want to be back in the gardener's shed, to crawl under the blanket and be close to his warmth again.

Doubt rises in me: Why didn't I ask him for his address in America? Why hadn't he offered it to me? Could I really have felt so much for someone I barely knew? Could he? Perhaps I was just another girl in another town. I dismiss this last thought quickly. I know from the way he looked at me that his feelings were real. But now he's gone. After all I have been through, I suppose I should be grateful for even small moments like last night. Still, I cannot help wanting more.

Enough. I stand up. I should go check on Rose. She will be eager to hear about my night. I head inside and cross the foyer. As I reach the door to the ward, Dava appears in front of me. She blocks my way, arms crossed. 'I'm so sorry I didn't make it back last night,' I begin quickly. 'We were halfway around the lake when the storm started.' I skip mention of the rowboat, knowing it will not help my cause. 'We had to find shelter so we waited in a gardener's hut until it stopped.' I study Dava's face, but there is no sign of anger, only dark circles ringing her bloodshot eyes. I wonder if she was up most of the night caring for Rose, or sitting with her because I was not there. 'And then...'

Dava holds up her hand, then places it on my upper arm. 'I need you to come with me.' Her grip is gentle but firm as she guides me away from the ward.

'Wait, I was going to tell...' I look back over my shoulder through the doorway; but I do not see Rose. Panic rises in me. Had she been taken for some sort of medical treatment? I turn to Dava. 'Where's Rose?' She does not answer, but looks away. 'What is it? What's wrong?'

'Why don't we go outside?' Dava tries again to lead me away from the door, but I pull from her grasp.

'No. Tell me what's going on right now.'

Dava hesitates, then leads me to one of the marble staircases. She drops to the third stair, patting the space beside her. 'Sit down.' I obey, waiting for her to speak. She takes a deep breath. 'Marta, you know that Rose was very sick...'

Was sick. 'I don't understand.'

Dava puts her hand on mine. 'Rose is gone.'

'Gone?' I repeat. 'Did they take her to the hospital?'

Dava shakes her head. 'Not that kind of gone. Marta, I'm sorry. Rose died.'

Died. The word bounces around in my head, not sinking in. 'But that's impossible. She was sitting up last night, talking...'

'You know that Rose had a blood disorder. The medicine that the doctors were giving her made her immune system weaker. She caught an infection and her fever spiked very suddenly. The doctors said no one could have seen it coming.'

Dava continues speaking but I do not hear her. In my mind, I see Rose sitting on the terrace last night, looking up at the mountains. I leap up and race into the ward. 'Marta, wait,' Dava calls after me.

At the far end of the ward, I stop short. Rose's bed has been stripped to the bare mattress, the nightstand beside it cleared. 'No... ' The word rips from my chest.

Dava comes to my side and puts her arm around me. 'She's at peace now.'

I shake my head. 'I should have been here with her.'

'It wouldn't have made a difference. And she was so happy for you last night, knowing that you had found Paul.' Suddenly my night with him seems like a distant memory. 'Now, come with me.' I let Dava lead me outside to the terrace. 'Wait here,' she orders before disappearing again. I drop to the bench where I sat with Rose the night before. My eyes fill with tears. I lost so many people during the war: my parents, my friends from the resistance. People I had known much longer and better than Rose. But the war is over. We are the survivors, the ones who made it. This isn't supposed to be happening now. I put my head in my hands, sobbing.

A moment later, I hear footsteps. I look up and wipe my eyes beneath my glasses. Dava stands in front of me, holding two cups of tea. 'Drink this.' I take one of the cups from her, cradling the warmth in my hands.

Dava sits down beside me. We sip our tea in silence, looking across the lake at the mountains. 'I was with her,' Dava says suddenly. 'At the end, I mean.'

I turn to face her. 'Oh? Did she say anything?'

'She asked me to thank you for trying to help her.' Dava pauses. 'She also asked me to give you this.' She reaches into her pocket and pulls out a small envelope.

Puzzled, I take the envelope and open it. Inside is a folded piece of paper with an unfamiliar seal engraved at the top. Typewritten, it appears to be in English, but I cannot understand what it says.

'What's this?'

'It's Rose's visa to England,' Dava replies.

'Visa? I don't understand...'

'Rose has an aunt in England who sent her a visa to come live with her. She never mentioned it to you?'

I shake my head. 'Only that she had an aunt in London. Nothing about the visa.'

'Rose probably never mentioned it because it was a moot point,' Dava offers. 'She was too sick to travel.' But I know this was not the reason Rose kept the visa from me. Rose knew that I had no one to go to in the West. She did not, I am sure, want to hurt my feelings by talking about her own opportunity. Dava continues, 'She mentioned she was trying to get a companion visa for you to travel with her. She even wrote to her aunt to ask about it. I guess she wanted to see if it was possible first.'

Rose going to England. Me going with her. My head spins as I try to process all of this new information. 'It was a nice idea,' I say finally. 'But she's gone now.'

'Before she died, Rose said she wanted you to have her visa, to go on to London without her.'

I stare at Dava, stunned. 'But this is Rose's visa. How can I...?'

'Technically it isn't transferable, but there are ways. We can get you identification that says you are Rose for the purposes of the trip.'

My mind reels. 'I can't go to London,' I protest. It is too far away, too big.

'You've been studying English,' Dava points out.

'I've read a few children's books. That's hardly

the same as speaking a language, using it every day. And I don't have the money...' I falter, embarrassed. 'For the passage, I mean. And to live.'

'Rose had a little money that she left. It will be enough to get you there.' Traveling to England with Rose would have been daunting enough, but the thought of going alone is terrifying. Dava grasps me by both shoulders. 'Marta, listen to me. I know you are upset about Rose. I am, too. And to consider this trip on top of everything that has happened may seem overwhelming. But this visa is worth its weight in gold. You don't have any special status, no relatives to go to in the United States or anywhere else. The camp won't be here forever, and if you haven't found a place to live when it closes you may not have much say over where you are sent. You need to settle somewhere, make a life for yourself. Do you understand me?' I do not answer. 'Anyway, if you go to London you can take Rose's belongings, tell her aunt personally that Rose is gone. You would want to do that for Rose, wouldn't you?'

'Yes,' I reply. 'But impersonating Rose, I mean, the false identification ... is it safe?'

'Completely. So many people came out of the war without any papers that the border guards seldom scrutinize papers too closely. And making fake identification cards has become big business. I know an excellent source, right here in Salzburg. So does that mean we are agreed?'

I take a deep breath. 'I'll go. Perhaps in a few weeks, after I've improved my English some more.'

Dava shakes her head. 'I'm afraid that is not possible. The visa expires tomorrow.'

'Tomorrow?'

'Yes. Rose planned to have her aunt get the visa extended, if and when she was well enough to travel.' My heart aches, thinking of Rose making plans that would never be. 'But of course that is impossible now. You have to go before this visa expires. If we book you on a train directly to the Channel coast, you can be there by late tomorrow, then take a ferry from Calais to Dover. But you'll have to leave tonight.'

Tonight! My head swims. 'What about Rose? I mean, will there be a funeral?'

Dava hesitates. 'Yes, but I don't think we will be able to have it before you leave. The coroner has to examine her, and there is paperwork. I'll see to it that she has a proper funeral.'

My heart twists at the thought of not being there to say goodbye to Rose. I picture the camp cemetery, a small cluster of headstones on the hill behind the palace. 'She should have a spot by the large oak tree.'

Dava nods. 'I'll have her buried there.' She stands up. 'I need to go into Salzburg to get you a train ticket. I want you to get cleaned up and gather your belongings. Eat and rest. You are leaving tonight.'

After Dava walks away, I sit numbly, staring across the lake. A day ago, Rose was here and Paul was just a faint memory. Now they're both gone and I am leaving, alone.

My entire body sags with exhaustion. I have to try to rest, or I will never have the strength to make the journey. I stand and walk slowly inside, crossing the foyer to the ward. When I reach

71

Rose's bed, I hesitate. I still half expect to see her lying there, waiting to hear about my night with Paul. I run my hand along the bare mattress. Dava is right, I realize. Rose would want me to go.

I take off my glasses and lie on the duvet that covers my bed, still staring at the emptiness beside me. My eyes burn. *I'm sorry, Rosie. Sorry that I couldn't make things right for you.* I roll over and face the wall, pressing my cheek into the pillow and closing my eyes.

I dream that it is a gray March morning in the ghetto, the wind blowing newspapers and other debris across the cracked pavement. I should be on my way to the administration building to report to work, but instead I am walking toward the orphanage. I returned from my mission with Jacob a few hours ago and I am still reeling from Jacob's revelation that he is married. I need to find Emma. Though I never named Jacob, I'd told her about my feelings for him. She will help me make sense of it all. I walk through the door of the orphanage and into the nursery where my mother is diapering an infant. She looks up, relief crossing her face as I approach. Guilt washes over me, knowing the anxiety my resistance work must cause her. 'Hello, *shayna*,' she says, kissing my cheek while not letting go of the infant. *Shayna.* Beautiful. 'How are you?' She does not ask me where I have been, why I did not come home the previous night.

'Fine, Mama. I'm looking for Emma.'

My mother's expression turns serious. 'Disappeared,' she says in a low voice. 'Another girl came to work in her place yesterday.'

Panic rising in me, I turn and run from the orphanage, across Josefinska Street to number thirteen. I fling open the door, taking the steps two at a time to the apartment where we meet for Shabbat dinner and where the resistance is secretly headquartered. I race into the apartment and, too frantic to knock, burst into the back room where the leadership meets. 'Where's Emma?' I demand of Alek, who sits alone at the desk.

Alek looks up from his papers. 'Don't worry, she's fine. We needed to get her out of the ghetto and were able to send her to stay with kin.' I sink into a chair, processing the information. 'I'm sure she would have said goodbye, but we didn't tell her that she was going until it was time,' he adds.

'Oh. I didn't know she had kin outside the ghetto.'

'She doesn't. Her husband does.'

'Husband?' I look at Alek, stunned. 'But Emma isn't married.'

A confused expression crosses his face. 'I thought Jacob told you.'

Why would Jacob tell me about Emma? 'I don't understand...'

'Originally I agreed with Jacob keeping it a secret, even from you.' I can barely hear Alek over the buzzing in my ears. 'But with you two traveling together all of the time, getting so close, it didn't seem fair. We agreed to wait until after Emma was gone. I thought he told you last night.'

'Jacob told me that he is...' The bottom of my stomach drops to the floor. 'You mean that Emma and Jacob...'

'Are married.' *Married.* The word echoes in my

head as the room fades to black.

'Marta,' I hear a voice call. Hands are shaking me gently. I open my eyes, blinking. Am I in the ghetto? No, I realize quickly. Dava is standing above me. I am in Salzburg. I do not know how long I have been asleep. It is still light out, though much later in the day, judging from the way the shadows of the trees fall across the ward. I look over at Rose's empty bed, the grief washing over me anew. 'It's time to get up,' Dava says.

'What time is it?'

'Nearly five.' I blink in disbelief. Dava continues, 'I wanted to let you sleep as long as I could, but the car will be here to take you to the station in half an hour. I'll wait for you out front.'

As Dava walks briskly from the ward, I sit up and swing my legs to the floor. I splash water on my face from the bowl on the nightstand, then put on my glasses and look around the room at the other women sleeping or reading in their beds. On the nightstand sits a small bag that Dava has left for packing. I reach into the drawer and pull out my other dress, the blue one, and some undergarments and stockings. It is everything that I own. I carry the bag from the ward, through the foyer and out the back door of the palace. I gaze up at the mountains, set against a clear blue sky. Thirty minutes, Dava said. A few hours ago I did not even know I was leaving. I see Paul, standing by the water's edge, remember Rose sitting in her wheelchair on the terrace.

Dava comes up behind me. 'All set?'

I hesitate, still looking up at the mountains. 'I think so.'

'Good. Here.' I turn to her and she hands me some papers. 'This top document is your temporary travel card, which you show in lieu of a passport. The second page is your visa. Remember that you are Rose Landyk, if anyone asks, though they shouldn't. And here is your train ticket. It goes directly to Lille–that's in France, not far from the Channel coast. From there you'll take a local train to Calais. And here's a ferry ticket from Calais to Dover, then another train ticket to London. Be sure to make all of your connections. Do you understand?' I nod. 'Good.'

Looking down at the tickets, I am seized with fear. I cannot do this alone. 'Come with me,' I say suddenly. Dava's eyes widen. 'You could find work as a nurse, maybe meet someone and start a family…'

'I can't!' Dava blurts out. Surprised, I stare at her. I have never seen her so emotional. Then she recovers, biting her lip. 'I mean, I can't have … anyway, the discussion is pointless. There is only one visa and no time to argue about it. Besides, I'm needed here. There's much work to be done.' She hands me a small satchel. 'This is for you also.'

'What is it?'

'Rose's belongings, to give to her aunt.' Dava continues, 'Plus some food for your trip.' She reaches into her pocket and pulls out some bills. 'Money. Austrian, French, English, a bit of each. In case you need anything along the way.'

I hesitate. Something tells me that not all of the money was Rose's, that it comes from Dava's own meager wages. 'Dava, I can't take–'

Dava holds up her hand, cutting me off. 'You

are taking the money and I won't hear another word about it.' She smiles. 'Someday, when you are a wealthy Englishwoman, you can repay me.'

'I will,' I reply, overwhelmed by her kindness, by all that she has done for me. 'With interest. Thank you, Dava.'

'Don't worry about it. Just have a safe trip and be well. Write me once you reach London to let me know you've arrived safely.'

I start to thank Dava once more, but she takes my arm and leads me from the terrace. 'Come on.' I steal one last look over my shoulder at the mountains, then follow her reluctantly around the side of the palace. A man whom I recognize as one of the maintenance workers sits in the front seat of a black car, engine running. 'Johan will take you to the station,' Dava says. She grabs me by both shoulders, her familiar clover scent strong as she kisses me firmly on each cheek. 'You are a strong woman, Marta. You have survived when no one thought you would, and you have a wonderful life ahead of you. Don't ever look back.'

'I won't,' I promise, a lump forming in my throat.

'Godspeed.' Dava turns and walks back inside the palace. I turn to thank her once more, but the door closes behind her.

I face the car, pausing nervously. I have only been in a few cars, quick furtive trips while working for the resistance. I climb into the passenger side and close the door behind me. Inside, the brown seats are worn and the air smells of stale cigarette smoke. Without speaking, Johan steps on the gas and the car lurches forward. I'm setting out on the same road Paul took just hours earlier, I realize as we pull from the driveway. I wish that he was with me. Or Rose, or Dava. Anyone. For the first time since prison, I am completely alone. Uneasiness rises inside me and I am seized by the sudden urge to ask Johan to turn the car around. I turn to look at the palace, but it has already disappeared, obscured by the thickness of the trees. Then I hear Dava's voice in my head: *Don't look back.* I can do this, I think. I have to. Steeling myself, I turn forward to face the road ahead once more.

CHAPTER 6

I gaze out the train window, blinking against the bright daylight that shines through a film of dirt and grime. Outside, rolling fields overgrown with late-summer brush and wildflowers stretch endlessly to the horizon. Last night, after we crossed the border into Switzerland, I was lulled to sleep by the gentle rocking of the train as we wound our way through the mountains. I was awakened roughly sometime in the middle of the night by a border guard demanding to inspect my papers at a second crossing. This morning, I opened my eyes to find the sun breaking over the gentle hills of eastern France, the rugged terrain long gone. From the position of the sun, I can tell that we are now heading north toward the coast.

I stretch, looking around the train car. Three

seats, including mine, face another three a meter or so apart. The carriage is dilapidated, the seat cushions torn and stained. There was an older man seated across from me by the door when I boarded, but we did not speak and he is gone now. The air has grown warm and stuffy overnight and smells of sour milk. I reach up to open the window, which refuses to budge.

I peer out the train window once more. How much farther do we have to go? It must be about nine o'clock, judging by the position of the sun – at least another six hours until we reach Lille, according to the itinerary Dava gave me. My stomach rumbles. I didn't eat at all yesterday, with everything that had happened with Paul and Rose and my leaving. I open my satchel, which sits on the seat beside me. Dava packed three sandwiches for me, one meat and two cheese. I unwrap one of the cheese sandwiches and take a bite. The bread is dry, but thick and familiar, a comforting reminder of the camp.

As I eat, I watch the fields roll by. A large, charred piece of metal the size of a horse wagon sits in the grass. It must have been a tank. I saw those in Kraków during the occupation. Little more than a year ago, these peaceful fields were battlegrounds. An image appears in my mind of soldiers, lying motionless on the ground. I think longingly of Paul. It is hard to believe it has been just a day since we said goodbye. The fighting is over in Europe now, but he said he would likely he shipped to the Pacific. I wonder where he is and, selfishly, if he has thought of me.

I eye the two remaining sandwiches. I am still

hungry, but I don't dare eat more now – we are still several hours from the coast, and I have no idea what food will be available at the port or on the boat, or how much it might cost.

Outside, a loud screeching noise jars me from my thoughts. We're slowing down, and the landscape begins to pass more slowly. The braking sound grows louder as the train grinds to a halt. Pressing my head against the glass, I crane my neck, searching for a town or station ahead. But the fields are unbroken as far as I can see. Why are we stopping?

Five minutes pass, then ten. My uneasiness grows. Is something wrong? Have we broken down? Through the door of the carriage, I see the conductor pass by. Taking a deep breath, I stand up and walk to the door and open it. I hesitate. I speak almost no French. *'Entschuldigen sie, bitte,'* I say in German. *Excuse me.*

The conductor turns back, annoyed. *'Ja?'*

I hesitate. 'Why have we stopped?'

'The tracks are broken ahead and we had no word of it when we were sent this way.' I struggle to understand his thickly accented German. 'We'll be backing up to the nearest junction shortly and heading for Paris.'

Panic rips through me. 'But, sir, my ferry leaves from Calais at six tonight. I have to get there.'

'You're not the only one with a boat to catch, miss,' he replies tersely. 'There's nothing to be done about it. You can take a train from Paris to Calais tomorrow. There will be other boats.' He turns and continues down the corridor.

I let the carriage door close and sink into the

nearest seat. My visa expires tonight. I'll never make it in time. A rock forms in the pit of my stomach. What am I going to do? I doubt the money that Dava gave me is enough for a return ticket to Salzburg. If I cannot get to England, I will be stranded with nowhere to go.

Desperately, I reach in my satchel and pull out the visa, scanning the document and trying to understand the foreign words. My eyes go to the seal at the top of the page. There must be a British embassy in Paris. Perhaps if I go there and explain, I can get an extension. I hesitate, considering the idea. Do I really dare walk into the embassy with a visa that isn't even really mine? It is my only hope. Still clutching the papers, I lean back and pray for a miracle as the train begins to roll slowly backward.

I stand by the door, satchel in hand, as the train pulls into Gare l'Est. I open the door and leap to the platform as we slow, not waiting to come to a complete stop. It has been more than seven hours since we stopped in the countryside and began our slow, painstaking detour to Paris. As the train crawled through the seemingly endless countryside, I fought the urge to scream. Instead I hounded the harried conductor for directions to the British embassy, practiced over and over again what I would say when I arrived.

I race down the platform, then pause, staring helplessly at the unintelligible French signs. The massive train station is awash with travelers – commuters mingle with groups of soldiers and families seeming to carry all of their possessions in large bags. To the right, I see a sign with a large *M* on it. The conductor told me the quickest route to the embassy was to take the Métro to the Madeline station.

Weaving my way through the crowds, I run to the entrance of the Métro, then hesitate, staring down the steps into the black hole. The smell of urine wafts upward. Can this possibly be right? Though I have read about subways, I have never actually taken one. But the conductor said it was too far to walk and he did not give me directions by bus. And it is four-twenty, just forty minutes until the embassy will likely close. I take the stairs two at a time, holding the railing so as not to fall. At the bottom, I pause to consult a map and identify a pink line that runs between the Gare l'Est and Madeline stations. Quickly, I buy a ticket from the kiosk, then follow the signs for the pink line to a crowded platform. A few minutes later, a train rumbles noisily into view. I board with the other passengers and find myself pressed uncomfortably into the center of the car between an old man and a group of schoolgirls. There is nowhere to sit, so I reach out and hold on to a nearby pole for balance.

The doors close and the train begins to roll forward. A voice comes over the speaker, announcing the next stop in garbled French that I cannot comprehend. How will I know where to get off? My eyes dart to the route map over the door and I count four stops between Gare l'Est and Madeline. Faster, I think, digging my nails into my palms. What if I don't make it on time? We reach the first stop and the doors open. A few passengers get off, but others board, making the train car more overcrowded than before. Just three more stops, I think, as the train begins to roll forward into the darkness of the tunnel. Suddenly, it halts again. The other passengers groan collectively, mumbling phrases I cannot understand. Why have we stopped? I catch a glimpse of a man's wristwatch. Four-thirty-five. I am not going to make it. A cold sweat breaks out beneath my dress.

The train starts to move again. We reach the second stop, then the third. As we leave the fourth stop, I inch my way through the crowd, trying to get closer to the door. The train creeps into Madeline station. As the doors open, I push through the crowd and race up the steps. At the top, I step onto the pavement and stop, gasping. I am standing at the biggest intersection I have ever seen. Buses, taxis and other cars, at least four deep, race in all directions along two wide boulevards, flanked by enormous buildings. The cities I have seen before, Kraków and Salzburg, in no way prepared me for this. I shiver, overwhelmed by the sheer magnitude of it all.

But there is no time to wonder. A bell chimes once, jarring me from my thoughts. Four-forty-five, the clock on the front of a large stone church across the boulevard reads. The embassy will close in fifteen minutes. I look in both directions, trying to get my bearings. Rue Royale, the street sign at the corner says. I turn left, as the conductor instructed, and run to the next major intersection. In the distance across the boulevard, I see a massive gray building, flags flying atop. That must be the embassy! I step out into the street, then jump as car horns blare out noisily in protest. The traffic light is red, I realize, leaping back onto the curb. When the light turns green, I fly across the intersection and down the street. The distance between myself and the embassy closes, fifty meters, then twenty, At last I reach the front of the large columned building bearing a British flag on the roof.

I rush to the guard booth at the front gate of the embassy. 'Visa section, please,' I pant in English, still breathing heavily from the run.

'The consulate is closed, ma'am.'

My heart sinks. 'But it's not yet five...'

He shakes his head. 'They stop taking applicants at four-thirty,'

'Please,' I plead, pulling my visa from the bag and holding it out to him. 'It's very urgent that I see someone today.'

He does not look down at the papers. 'You'll have to come back tomorrow.'

'But tomorrow will be too late.'

'I'm sorry. There's nothing I can do.'

I step backward, feeling as though a rock has slammed into my chest. I am too late. The embassy is closed. Shoving the papers back into my bag, I stumble away from the gate. The boulevard is crowded now with men in suits on their way home from work, small clusters of young colleagues going for drinks. People living their normal lives. People who belong here. My eyes begin to sting. I brush my hand across them impatiently. Crying isn't going to help. I have to figure out what to do.

Across the street from the embassy, I notice a

small park. I cross the street and make my way down one of the tree-lined paths. Slats of sunlight shine through the leaves. The benches along either side of the path are filled with Parisians enjoying the summer evening. A woman knits silently on one of the benches, a large shepherd at her feet. Farther along, two old men play chess, surrounded by a small group of onlookers. There are people sprawled in the grass as well, smoking cigarettes and reading.

I walk toward the fountain that sits in the middle of the park, finding an empty spot on one of the peeling green benches that surround it. On the other end of the bench a man reads *Le Monde*, the newspaper spread wide in his lap. He does not look up as I sit.

On a bench across from me, I notice two young women with prams in front of them. They are speaking in a Slavic language, and though I do not recognize which, I understand enough to gather that one is describing a night out with a man, perhaps a boyfriend. They rock the carriages with a disinterest that suggests the babies inside are not theirs.

A cool wind blows through the park. Looking up at the dark clouds that have eclipsed the sun, I cross my arms, wishing I had a coat. It will be evening soon. I need to think about where I will stay tonight, and about food. I pull the last of Dava's sandwiches from my bag and unwrap it. I sniff the sandwich, remembering from prison how to judge how far bad it has gone, whether or not it is safe. The meat has a slightly sour smell, still edible but not for much longer. Breathing shallowly, I take a bite. I cannot afford to waste any food now. As I eat, I think longingly of the hot dinners prepared by the Red Cross in the palace kitchen. The Red Cross! Perhaps they help refugees here, too. I hesitate, looking at the au pairs, then stand and make my way across the path. 'Przepraszam,' I say, excusing myself in Polish. Hopefully their language is close enough so that they will understand. The women stop speaking and look up at me, squinting. I touch my chest. 'Refugee.' Then I point at them. 'You, too?'

The women start to stand up, their expressions turning to fear. 'Non,' the younger-looking woman, hair dyed an unnatural red, says quickly in French.

She's lying, I think; their papers must not be in order, either. 'Can you tell me how to find the Red Cross?'

They weigh the question, considering whether to help. 'Americans,' the older woman says in a low voice, pointing in the direction of the embassy.

She must be confusing the British embassy for the United States. 'I've already been to the British embassy and they wouldn't–'

The woman cuts me off. 'American,' she insists. I look again in the direction in which she is pointing. The flag on the British embassy has been taken down for the day. But on another building behind it, an American flag flies. She is trying to tell me, I think, that the American embassy can direct me to the Red Cross. But it is after five now; that embassy will surely be closed, too. I turn back to ask again for directions to the Red Cross, but the girls have looked away, disinterested, and

85

resumed talking in their own language.

I start back toward the bench, but my spot is now occupied by a lady with a poodle. There is nowhere for me to go. Even the bench is taken. Suddenly, tears well up in my eyes once more. This time I let them overflow, run hot and salty down my cheeks, not caring who sees. As if on cue, it begins to rain, thick heavy drops dotting the water in the base of the fountain, splashing against the pavement. Feeling the drops soak through my clothes, I think of the storm that began as Paul and I sat in the rowboat on the lake. Was that really only two nights ago? It feels like another lifetime. But there is no gardener's shed here, a voice reminds me. No Paul to row you to shelter. The voice, long forgotten, is strong and firm, the one that sustained me through prison.

I need to find shelter. I take off my glasses and wipe the water from the lenses. Then, replacing them, I look across the park. At the far end, on the opposite side of the street, sits a massive stone church. I walk closer. Looking up at its turrets climbing toward the sky, I am reminded of the Mariacki Cathedral in Kraków. The first time I saw it, crossing the market square on an errand for the resistance with Jacob, I was staggered by its size. I was even more surprised when Jacob told me that we were to meet our contact inside. As a Jew, churches had always been forbidden; even the tiny one-room church in our village, not much bigger than the synagogue, had seemed ominous. But to the resistance, the churches were safe havens, a place to go under the pretext of prayer, exchanging information with contacts in hushed tones in the back pews.

A safe haven, I think now, staring at the open door of the church. No one will bother me there. I make my way up the stone steps. Inside, the church is cool and dark, empty except for an older woman lighting a candle in an alcove to the right. I slip into one of the back pews, keeping my head low. The wood has an earthy, human smell that makes me think I am not the first to use it as a shelter. I look up. From the rafters, stone statues of saints stare down at me piously. What am I going to do? I ask silently. They look back mutely, their pity useless. Behind me, I hear voices. Two women remove kerchiefs from their heads as they make their way up the aisle, clutching rosaries. I wonder if they are regular parishioners, if they will know that I do not belong. But they do not seem to notice me. When they have passed, I sink back in the pew, suddenly exhausted. My entire body seems to ache.

I will go back to the British embassy tomorrow, beg to have the visa extended, I decide as I watch the women make their way to the front of the church and kneel. And if they refuse? a voice inside me – not the strong one – asks. I push the question down. I must get the visa extended. There is no other option. I wonder if the church is open all night, if I can perhaps stay here until morning. More parishioners enter the church, slipping into pews, spending a few minutes praying alone or in pairs before leaving again. I had always imagined Parisians to be elegant and fashionable. But the people I see are simply dressed, their faces careworn, reminding me that

87

just a short while ago, Paris was occupied, too.

Outside, the church bells ring eight times. As if on cue, a man appears at the front of the church with a broom and begins to sweep. The church will close soon, I realize, as the last parishioners shuffle toward the door. I cannot stay here. I walk outside to the front steps, then hesitate. Where can I go? The rain still falls in heavy sheets, forming a large puddle at the base of the stairs. I look back at the front of the church. Stone columns stand to either side of the entranceway. I make my way toward the one on the right. There, where the column meets the building, is a shallow nook, a meter wide and half as deep. No one can see me here, I think, stepping into the space. I sink to the cold, hard floor, grateful for a place to stay out of the rain. A damp scent rises from the stone.

Wrapping my arms around my knees, I look out into the street at the cold, unfamiliar city. How did I get here? Suddenly I recall once being in the woods outside Lodz. Jacob had left me hidden in a cluster of trees while he went to find our contact. Later I would learn that he had become lost on his way back to me. But in that moment, as I huddled in the pitch darkness, strange, unseen noises coming from the woods around me, I was terrified. What if he never came back for me? Remembering now, a chill runs down my spine. Until that moment, I had not understood what it meant to be completely alone. It was a thought that would later haunt my long, lonely days in prison. I had not thought of it since being liberated, but alone now, I am caught by the memory once more.

My thoughts are interrupted by footsteps. The man who had been sweeping stands in the doorway of the church, still holding his broom, looking at me. We stare at each other for several seconds. Without speaking, he disappears back inside the church. My heart pounds inside my chest. Is he going to make me leave, even call the police? A second later, the man reappears in the doorway and starts toward me, carrying something. A blanket, I see, as he sets it by my feet. *'Merci,'* I say, but he turns and walks back inside the church without speaking, closing the door behind him.

I stare after him for several seconds, caught off guard by his simple act of kindness. Then I reach down and unfold the wool blanket, pulling it up around me. The blanket smells of dirt and cigarettes. I wonder if it is his own, if he has shared it with others who have stayed here. I lean back, the scratchy fabric comforting against my arms. Not so completely alone after all. I look beyond the edge of the cathedral at the rain-soaked street, then up at the dark, cloudy sky, wondering what tomorrow will bring.

CHAPTER 7

I refold the blanket, looking toward the front door of the church. I would like to hand it back to the janitor and thank him, but the door is closed, the man nowhere to be found. Instead, I set the blanket neatly in the corner where I spent the night, then make my way down the steps.

It is morning now and the sun shines brightly, drying the last of the dampness from the pavement. The park is nearly empty, except for one disheveled old man I think I recognize from the previous evening, curled up on one of the benches under a damp coat. Did he spend the night there? I am more grateful than ever for the shelter of the church roof and blanket.

On the other side of the park, I pause, looking up at the Union Jack that flies high above the British embassy. My breath catches as I imagine walking up those steps and through the door, convincing whoever waits on the other side to extend the visa. It has to work. I cross the street and walk to the entrance, where a different guard from the previous evening occupies the booth. I take a deep breath. 'I – I'm here about a visa,' I manage to say in English.

He points to the left. 'Entrance is around the corner.'

'Thank you.' I walk to the end of the block. As I turn the corner, my heart sinks. There is a line of people starting at the corner and running all the way down the street. I walk to the man who stands at the end of the line, then hesitate. The few French words I know seem of little use. 'Visa?' I ask hopefully, pointing at the door. Perhaps all of these people are waiting for something else. He shrugs, turns away. I walk quickly back around the corner to the guard booth. 'Excuse me, I know you said that the entrance for visas is around the corner. But all of those people...?'

'Are waiting for visas, too. Take a number.'

I cock my head, puzzled. I did not see any numbers. 'I already have a visa,' I say, trying again. 'I need an extension.'

'Same line,' the guard replies, pointing once more.

I turn and start back around the corner, my shoulders slumped in disappointment. The line has grown even longer in the minute I was away, two more people joining the queue. I file in behind them quickly. There must be at least a hundred people ahead of me, men and women of every size and age. Some carry babies or hold small children by the hand. If only I had known, I could have waited here all night instead of sleeping by the church.

In the distance a clock chimes nine. Slowly the line begins to shuffle forward. Perhaps this will not be so bad, after all. But then the line comes to a complete stop. Thirty minutes pass, then an hour. I turn and look behind me. At least another twenty people have joined the queue, giving the appearance that it has not shortened at all. We stand motionless for what seems like an eternity, shuffling forward a few meters every half an hour or so. The clock chimes eleven and the sun grows higher in the morning sky, making the air warm and humid.

It is lunchtime, I think a while later, my stomach growling. I have not eaten since finishing the last sandwich the previous evening. The line seems to move more slowly as time passes. People lean against the embassy fence or drop to the pavement and sit in line. I can tell by the weary, accepting expressions on the faces of some of the people around me that they have done this before and are unsurprised by the wait. Anxiety rises in me as the early afternoon passes. What if they do not get to me? I look around, desperately wanting to ask someone if there is a quota, if they take only a certain number of people each day. But I do not know enough French to ask the others in the queue and I cannot leave the line to ask the guard.

Another hour of shuffling and waiting. Finally, I reach the gate and make my way, slowly, painstakingly, up a set of stairs and through a door. Inside, the line snakes through a waiting room. Three glass windows line the far wall, a woman and two men seated behind them. The air here is pungent from too many people in a cramped, warm space. Typewriters clack in the background. I watch as each of the people in front of me in line approaches one of the windows. Some present papers, others simply talk. I cannot hear what they are saying. At the middle window, a woman argues with one of the male clerks for several minutes. When she turns away, I can see that her cheeks are wet.

Finally, it is my turn. 'Next,' the woman in the far right window calls. I step forward, my heart pounding. As I reach the window, I take a deep breath, reminding myself that I am supposed to be Rose.

The woman holds out her hand. 'Yes?'

Catching my reflection in the glass, I hesitate. My dress is wrinkled, my hair wild from sleeping outside. I should have taken time to freshen up. But it is too late now. I push my papers through the slot at the bottom of the window. 'I have a visa to England, but it expired yesterday.' My words, which I practiced on the train, tumble out in a rush, accented and, I fear, nearly unintelligible. 'I was not able to get a train out of Salzburg until yesterday and we were detoured to Paris because of broken tracks. So I am unable to make it to England in time. I tried to come yesterday but the embassy was already closed. I was wondering if it would be possible to get an extension.'

The woman scans the papers. 'You cannot renew this class of visa here.' Her tone is cold, her French accent thick. 'The inviting person must apply for an extension.' She pushes the papers back through the slot at me.

'I have to get to England. Please.'

The woman's expression remains impassive, as if she hears such things every day. 'I'm sorry, but it's beyond my control.'

'But what am I supposed to do?' My voice rises with panic.

The woman shrugs. 'As I said, the only possibility is to get the person who invited you to England to apply for an extension. But you will need to go back to your home country or the country of origin while you wait.

'Dominique,' a male voice calls from behind the window. 'Telephone.' The woman speaks to someone I cannot see in a low voice. Then she turns back to me. 'I'm afraid there's really nothing to be done about it.' Her voice is curt, dismissive. 'Good day.'

'But...' I begin. The woman disappears from the window.

I stand before the window for several seconds, not moving. The visa cannot be extended. For a minute, I consider waiting until she returns, but I know that arguing further will be pointless. I turn and push through the crowd of applicants still waiting to be seen and race back down the stairs. When I reach the street I stop, struggling to breathe. Tears fill my eyes, spill over. I can feel the stares of the applicants still waiting in line as I pass, sobbing openly.

At the corner, I cross the boulevard and make my way into the park. I sink to one of the benches by the fountain, still sobbing. My visa was not renewed. I have failed. What am I going to do?

I study the papers still clutched in my hand. The visa is expired, worthless. I start to throw them in the trash bin beside the bench. Then I stop. These are the only papers I have. But the visa will not get me to England. I wonder for a moment if I could stow away. If I cannot get to England, where will I go? I do not have the money to go back to Austria. Looking at the empty bench across from me, I remember the au pairs I'd spoken with the previous day. Perhaps I could stay in Paris, find work taking care of children or cleaning or in a restaurant. But I have no idea if such things are possible without a French visa, without speaking French.

I tuck the papers back in my bag. The contents of the bag – a second dress, some under-garments, a few coins and the papers – are everything I have in the world. No food. I do not even have a place to stay tonight. I look across the park at the church. Maybe if I go there, they will help me. But I know that the caretaker had little more than the wool blanket to offer, and I cannot sleep on the church steps forever.

The Red Cross, I remember. If I can find the Red Cross, I may be able to get food, a place to stay. Perhaps they can even get word to Dava of my plight. The au pairs had pointed me to the American embassy. I turn around. Behind the British flag, an American flag flies high against the blue sky. It is the same as the one that was sewn to Paul's uniform sleeve, I realize, feeling a small tug at my heart.

I stand up and walk from the park, crossing the street. As I pass the line of applicants still waiting at the British embassy, I keep my head high. But sadness and anger bubble up in me. Would it have cost that clerk anything to bend the rules this one time and extend my visa?

I approach the guard booth at the front of the American embassy. 'Consulate is closed, miss.'

I swallow nervously. 'I – I was wondering if you could tell me if the Red Cross has a shelter in the city.'

The guard pauses, considering. 'I don't know. Sergeant Smith might, but he's gone for the day.' My heart sinks. 'Why don't you try asking at the Servicemen's Hotel. It's just around the corner.'

'Servicemen's Hotel.' I repeat the unfamiliar English words. 'Thank you.' I start to walk in the direction in which the guard pointed. Around the corner is a tall building, set back from the road. U.S. Armed Servicemen's Hotel, the sign out front reads. Several soldiers cluster by the entrance, talking and smoking. Seeing their dark green uniforms and close-cut hair, I cannot help but think of Paul. One of the other soldiers mentioned something about Paris, I remember suddenly. In my panic to get the visa extended, I had nearly forgotten. Could he possibly be here? But he was in Salzburg only two days ago, I recall, picturing the lumbering row of trucks as they pulled from the palace grounds. It seems unlikely that he could be here so soon.

Focus on finding the Red Cross, I tell myself. Taking a deep breath, I walk up to the door of the hotel, feeling the eyes of the soldiers on me as I pass. Inside, I hesitate. The lobby is bright, a thick halo of cigarette smoke hovering in the air. Loud voices and music come from a bar off the back of the lobby. I make my way to the reception desk, which sits to the right. 'Can I help you, miss?'

'Can you tell me whether the Red Cross has any shelters in the city?'

The clerk pauses, scratching his head. 'I think so. Lemme see.' He turns and pulls a thick book from the shelf behind him, then thumbs through the pages. 'Here we are – Red Cross. Nearest shelter is at St. Denis du St. Sacrement – that's a church – in Marais. Go left to the corner and take the number-five bus ... here, let me write this down for you.' He pulls out a piece of paper and scribbles something I cannot read, then hands it to me.

'Thank you.' I start to walk away. Then, looking across the lobby at the bar, crowded with soldiers, Paul's face appears in my mind once more. Easy, I tell myself. Even if Paul was in Paris, there's no reason to think he would be at this particular

96

hotel. There are thousands of soldiers in the city. He could be anywhere. Impulsively, I turn back toward the desk. 'Excuse me again,' I say, then hesitate. 'I'm also looking for a soldier named Paul. Paul Mattison.'

The clerk opens a large register that sits on the counter in front of him and scans one page, then another. 'Mattison ... nope, don't see no Mattison.'

Of course not. I chastise myself inwardly for my folly. Had I really imagined that Paul might be here? 'Thanks again.' I cross the lobby and exit the hotel, feeling foolish.

Outside I start walking toward the bus stop. I pass a café, the tables in its front garden filled with soldiers and civilians, talking merrily over late-afternoon drinks. A delicious aroma of baked goods wafts under my nose. It's not coming from the café, I realize, but from the small patisserie next door. Curious, I walk closer. A delectable display of pastries sits in the front window, a mountain of chocolate tortes in the center. My mouth waters. I reach into my bag, fingering the money Dava gave me. It would be completely irresponsible to spend some of the little money I have on sweets. And I need to get to the shelter right away. But I walk into the shop, unable to resist.

I point through the glass at the plate of chocolate tortes, then raise my index finger. *'S'il vous plait.'* I carefully count out the proper amount of coins as the shopkeeper puts a torte in a paper bag and hands it to me. Outside again, I open the bag, inhaling the rich chocolate aroma. Then I pull out the torte, which is still slightly warm. I know that I should go back to the park or at least find somewhere to sit and eat the pastry, but I cannot wait. I take a large bite, closing my eyes as the chocolate flavor washes across my tongue. Eat slowly, I tell myself. Save some for later. But my mouth seems to have a life of its own, devouring the pastry in several large bites. A moment later it is gone.

I stand motionless on the sidewalk, holding the empty bag, overwhelmed by the rush of sweetness. I look at the people sitting at the café adjacent to the patisserie, casually eating cakes like the one I have just devoured. If all of the food in Paris is this good, perhaps I should forget about London and find a way to stay here.

I look back over my shoulder longingly toward the patisserie, wishing that I could spend money on another torte. Suddenly I hear a loud, familiar laugh. My head snaps in the direction of the tables at the café.

Seated at one of the tables, his arm draped around another woman, is Paul.

CHAPTER 8

Paul! Though I had asked about him at the desk, I never really thought... I blink several times, wondering if he is an illusion, expecting him to disappear. But he remains seated at the café table, smiling broadly, eyes wide. It does not seem possible. What is he doing here? Joy surges through me. I take a step forward. Then, focusing on the pretty young woman seated beside him, I stop. Who is she? Anger rises in me as I watch him smile, then say something to the woman. Was his story about shipping out to the Pacific a lie?

I should give him a good piece of my mind, I decide, starting toward him once more. Then, catching a glimpse of my reflection in the patisserie window, I stop again. My plain pink dress, the same one he saw me wearing two days ago, is wrinkled from the long train ride. Dark circles ring my eyes and there are chocolate smudges on my lips. A disheveled Polish country girl. As I look over at the Frenchwoman, with her perfectly coiffed chignon and low-cut silk blouse, my heart crumbles. How could I ever think that Paul really liked me?

I turn blindly away, crashing into a waiter who is carrying a tray between the patisserie and the café. Cups and plates crash noisily to the pavement. 'Oh!' My face grows hot as I stand helplessly, staring at the scattered dishes. I feel the scornful eyes of the café patrons upon me as the waiter begins to berate me in French. Desperately, I push past the waiter and race down the sidewalk. A moment later I hear the waiter's heavy footsteps behind me. I panic. Is he going to try to make me pay for the broken dishes? Has he called the police? I run faster.

'Marta, wait.' Not the waiter, I realize. Paul. He must have seen me when the dishes fell. I keep running, uncertain what to do. But Paul reaches me easily with his long strides, catches my arm. 'Marta, please.' I stop, too embarrassed to face

99

him. 'Are you okay?' I nod. 'I'm so glad, that is, surprised...' He pauses. It is the first time I have heard him at a loss for words. 'I mean, what on earth are you doing here?'

'I – I...' I falter, my English failing me. Taking a deep breath, I try again. 'I was on my way to London. I had to stop here to try to get my visa extended at the British embassy.'

'What visa?'

I hesitate, looking up. At the sight of him so close, my heart jumps. 'Rose's, actually.'

'I don't understand...'

'She died, right after you left.'

'Oh, Marta, I'm so sorry.' He moves his hand from my arm to my shoulder, but I pull back. I don't want his sympathy now.

'She had a visa to London, so Dava arranged to have it transferred to me.'

'And you're traveling to London all by yourself?' I nod again, unable to bring myself to tell him about my failure to get the visa extension. 'We just got into Paris a few hours ago. I haven't even checked into the hotel yet.' I notice then that he is still wearing the same uniform as in Salzburg, but has added a matching jacket. His hair is freshly combed. In spite of my anger, I grow warm inside. 'We've been given three days' leave before shipping out for the Pacific.'

Paul is leaving again. He really is going to the Pacific, thousands of miles away. And meanwhile I am stuck here with no place to call home. Suddenly, I burst into tears. 'Marta, what is it? What's wrong?'

I can hold back no longer. Quickly, I tell him

about Rose's visa expiring, the embassy's refusal to help. 'I don't know what to do,' I manage to say between sobs.

'So they wouldn't extend the visa for you?'

I shake my head. 'The woman said they couldn't.'

An angry expression crosses Paul's face. As he looks at his watch, I can see his mind working. 'Come on.' He starts down the street toward the Servicemen's Hotel.

I follow, looking back over my shoulder at the café, where the Frenchwoman has risen to her feet. 'What are you doing?'

He does not answer but leads me to the hotel. At the gate, he takes my arm. This time, I do not pull away. His hand is warm through my thin cotton sleeve as he guides me inside, through the lobby to the bar, packed thick with soldiers. 'Where's Mickey?' he asks the bartender, shouting to be heard over the din of music and voices. The bartender points to a blond-haired soldier seated at the far end of the bar. His back is to us and he seems to be telling a story of some sort to a group of men around him. 'Give me your visa,' Paul instructs. I reach into my bag and hand it to him. 'Wait here.'

He disappears into the crowd and I stand alone, self-conscious at being the only woman in the bar. A minute later, Paul appears by the blond-haired soldier, pulling him off his stool and away from the others. I see Paul hand him my papers. Watching as he talks to the soldier, I remember our kiss goodbye, how he held me as I slept in the gardener's shed by the lake. Warmth grows inside me. But then I see the soldier shake his head. Paul returns to my side, his face fallen. 'No dice.'

I tilt my head. 'I don't understand.'

'I thought my pal Mickey could help with the extension. He's helped a few people.' Struggling to hear and understand him over the noise, I lean closer. He bends his head toward me at the same time, causing our cheeks to brush. Closer now, I can smell his familiar pine scent, mixed with soap and spearmint gum. 'He's got a girl over at the British embassy who's sweet on him. Or had, I should say. It seems they're on the outs. I'm sorry, Marta.'

'I appreciate your trying,' I say, trying to contain my disappointment.

As Paul looks down at me, his expression changes, his jaw clenching stubbornly. 'I have another idea.' Without speaking further, he takes my forearm and leads me toward the door of the hotel. I force myself not to shiver at his touch.

'Where are we going?' I ask as he guides me through the hotel garden and out onto the street.

'Back to the embassy.' As we walk back down the street, past the café, I glance at the tables, hoping that neither the Frenchwoman nor the waiter can see us.

I want to tell him that it is hopeless, that the embassy cannot renew the visa from here. 'I didn't think you would be in Paris, at least not so soon,' I offer instead as we pass the American embassy.

'Me, neither,' he replies. 'That axle busted again not long after we left the camp. So rather than crowd us all into the other trucks, they let a

102

few of us hop on a transport flight. We just arrived a few hours ago.'

As we reach the corner of the British embassy, my heart sinks. The visa line is as long as ever. If we wait, it is going to take hours. 'You don't have to...' I begin, but Paul leads me past the line and up the steps. I can feel the stares of the other applicants as we pass, wondering who I am, why I am getting special treatment by this soldier.

'Which one?' he asks as we enter the crowded waiting room.

'The woman,' I say, pointing to the window on the right.

'Hope she isn't Mick's girl,' he mutters under his breath, Leaving me at the back of the waiting room, he walks to the window. When the applicant who is standing there is finished, Paul steps in. The woman behind the glass opens her mouth to protest. Then her eyes dart to the sleeve of Paul's uniform. Before she can speak, Paul pulls my visa from his pocket and slides it under the glass. He begins talking, gesturing to me, but I cannot hear what he is saying. The woman looks over Paul's shoulder at me, but her expression is blank. She does not remember my situation; I am just one of many applicants she has seen that day. Her face remains impassive as she says something in reply. She's going to refuse, I realize, watching the conversation. Not even Paul can help me this time. But she scribbles something on the visa, stamps it and hands it back to him.

'What happened?' I demand as he walks over.

'Your visa, milady,' he says, handing the papers to me. I look down at the papers in disbelief. The original date has been crossed out and a new stamp bearing tomorrow's date added. One stamp. That was all the woman had to do to change a life.

'She would only extend it till tomorrow, so you'll have to leave first thing in the morning. But you're all set for England.'

'Really?' Relief washes over me. Impulsively, I jump up and wrap my arms around him. 'Thank you.'

His arms close around me, warm and strong. For a second, it is as if we are in Salzburg once more. Then I hear someone clapping from the visa line behind us. My mind clears. We are not in Salzburg, I remind myself, stepping back from him. Remembering Paul seated beside the Frenchwoman at the café, I clear my throat. 'We should go.'

A confused expression crosses his face. 'Okay.' I refold the visa and tuck it back into my bag as I follow Paul from the waiting room and down the steps. 'Now we can go to the hotel and get your tickets...' he begins as we reach the street.

'That's not necessary,' I say, cutting him off. 'I mean, I really appreciate all of your help, but I am sure you have other things to do.'

Paul stops, his brow furrowing. 'Other things?'

'Yes.' I pause, swallowing. 'Your friends from the café will be wondering where you have gone.'

'You mean my buddy, John?'

'Actually, I was talking about the French-woman.' I can hear the jealousy in my own voice.

'Oh!' A light dawns in his eyes. 'Marta, I know how it must have looked, but it isn't like that at all. Last year, our unit was in Paris several times.' So he didn't just meet the Frenchwoman, I realize, my heart sinking further. Perhaps she is his girlfriend. Paul continues, 'John has been dating one of the women, Collette, long distance since then. Emilie, the other woman, is Collette's cousin. Collette had to bring Emilie along, or she wouldn't have been able to see John at all today. They invited me along so Emilie wouldn't feel awkward. But I'm not interested in her.'

'Oh?' I study his face, wanting to believe him. 'But don't you need to get back to them?'

'I'm sure old Johnny can handle two French-women just fine on his own. And now that you're here... I never imagined, I mean, I'm so glad...' He hesitates, a faint blush creeping into his cheeks. 'Have dinner with me.'

My breath catches. Is it really possible that Paul wants to spend time with me, not the beautiful Frenchwoman? I open my mouth to accept his invitation, then hesitate. There is nothing I would rather do. But I cannot afford dinner, and I still have nowhere to stay tonight. I need to get to the Red Cross shelter. 'I don't know—'

'Please,' he pleads. 'I'll have the hotel clerk change your train and ferry tickets. Unless you would rather have that done at your hotel.'

'No,' I reply quickly. 'I – I mean, they only seem to understand French at my hotel. I'm afraid they won't get it right.' The lie slips out too easily.

'Then we'll have it done at mine,' he says decisively. 'And grab some chow, I mean, have dinner, while we wait for the tickets.'

Looking into his eyes, I cannot help myself. I

would sooner sleep on the street tonight than leave Paul now. 'That would be nice, thank you.'

'Excellent.' He claps his hands. 'Where are you staying? I mean, do you want to go freshen up before dinner?'

'Th–the Hôtel Dupree,' I fib quickly. I hate lying to Paul, but I cannot bring myself to admit that I was planning to go to the refugee shelter. I glance down at the small satchel that holds everything I own, wondering if it might make him suspicious. But he does not seem to notice. 'It's rather far away, though. Is there a ladies' room at your hotel where I can freshen up?'

'Sure.' We start down the street in the direction of the Servicemen's Hotel. As we walk, I steal glances at him out of the corner of my eye. I am in Paris with Paul. It is almost too much to believe.

A few minutes later we reach the hotel and cross through the garden. Inside the lobby, Paul points to a hallway leading off to the right. 'I passed a ladies' room over there earlier. I don't know what shape it's in. Doesn't seem to get much use these days. And while you're doing that, I'm going to check in and get my key. Why don't you give me your train and ferry tickets? I'll see about having the front desk change your reservations and book you on the train to Calais for tomorrow morning.'

'That would be great.' I reach into my bag. As I hand my tickets to him, our fingers touch. We remain still, neither pulling away. Our eyes meet and I recognize in his eyes the same longing look I saw as we left the gardener's shed that morning. I draw back, my hand trembling.

Inside the ladies' room, I plug the sink and turn the left tap. As the basin fills with warm water, I look into the small, cracked mirror above it, horrified at the disheveled figure that stares back at me. If only I could take a bath, put on my other dress before dinner. I turn off the tap, then splash water on my face and smooth my curls as well as I can.

'Feel better?' Paul asks when I return to the lobby. I nod. 'Good. Let's go.' I follow him out the front door of the hotel to the street.

He raises his hand and a taxi pulls up at the curb. 'I know a great little bistro in St. Germain,' he explains. I nod, as though familiar with the area. 'It's not fancy, but the food is delicious.' He opens the rear door and gestures for me to get in, then climbs in beside me and closes the door, leaning forward to tell the driver the address.

The cab lurches forward. 'My French is awful,' Paul remarks. He sits back, closer to me than is necessary on the wide seat.

'Mine, too.' The warmth of his leg against mine is mesmerizing. I force myself to breathe normally, to look out the window. We turn onto a wide thoroughfare lined with elegant shops and cafés. Since arriving in Paris, I've been so preoccupied – first by my rush to reach the embassy and later with my panic at not receiving the extension – I barely noticed the city. Now I stare wide-eyed at the magnificent architecture, the elegant shops that line the boulevard. 'This is the Champs-Elysées. And that,' Paul says, pointing to the right, 'is the Arc de Triomphe.' I follow his hand, taking in the massive stone arch.

The cab turns left and the arch disappears from view. We start across a bridge and I look back to steal a glimpse of the buildings that line the river. As I turn, my eyes catch Paul's, locking with his. 'It's beautiful,' I say, my heart fluttering.

The taxi reaches the far side of the bridge and begins to climb upward through narrow, winding streets. The architecture is different here, the buildings close-set, rustic. A few minutes later, the taxi pulls up to the curb and Paul pays the driver. He slides across the seat and opens the door, moving away from me. Don't, I want to cry out, instantly missing his warmth. He holds out his arm to me. 'Shall we?'

I hesitate. I could have ridden around the city taking in the beautiful views all night. Reluctantly, I reach out and wrap my hand around his forearm, feeling the warmth of his skin through his shirt. Paul leads me to a bistro with wide-paned windows and a simple wood sign in front that reads Henryk's. Inside, the dimly lit restaurant is overcrowded and warm. A dozen or so tables, covered in red-checked cloths, fill the room to capacity. The aroma of something garlicky hangs in the air, making my stomach growl.

I hang back behind Paul, overwhelmed by the noisy room. A few times during the war, I sat in one of the cafés that ringed the market square in Kraków with Alek and the others during a meeting. But I have never been to a proper restaurant. Staring at the fine plates and wineglasses, my mind flashes back to the café by the Servicemen's Hotel earlier today. I can almost hear the tray of dishes crashing to the ground.

Suddenly, a burly man with a mustache rushes forward to greet us. 'Ah, Monsieur Paul!' he exclaims, taking Paul's hand and pumping it.

Paul steps aside so that I am no longer behind him. 'Henryk, this is my friend, Marta.' Friend. My heart sinks. 'Marta, this is Henryk.'

Henryk steps forward and plants a kiss on each of my cheeks. 'Welcome, beautiful lady!' Caught off guard by his effusive greeting, I forget to be nervous. Henryk leads us to the only empty table, close to the front window, then lights the half-melted candle that sits in the center. 'Monsieur Paul comes to see me whenever he is in Paris.' Henryk's English, though heavily accented, is slow enough to understand. 'But he has never brought a ladyfriend to my restaurant,' he adds as he pulls out my chair. I cannot help but smile at this. 'Usually he come alone, with a book. I tell him this is no good for the digestion. I bring you wine.' He hustles off toward the kitchen.

Paul sits down across from me and unfolds his napkin. I watch him nervously. I have walked with Paul, even spent the night beside him. But sitting face-to-face with him like this feels intimate, intense. I unfold the napkin as he has done, hoping he does not notice my nervousness. 'The restaurant has been in Henryk's family for four generations,' he explains. 'But he closed it during the occupation, rather than serve the Germans.' His leg bumps mine under the table. 'Sorry,' he mumbles, a faint blush creeping up his neck. He's anxious, too, I realize suddenly. It is hard to imagine anyone being nervous around me, but the thought is strangely comforting.

'What books?' I ask, eager to break the tension. He cocks his head, not understanding. 'Henryk said you usually come with a book.'

'Oh, that.' He smiles sheepishly. 'I like to read. Hemingway, Steinbeck.' Now it is my turn to cock my head. 'Those are American authors, although some of Hemingway's books are set in Europe. Classics, too, Dickens and such. Pretty much anything I can get my hands on in English over here.'

'I was reading *Little Women* with Rose,' I offer. 'Before, that is.'

Henryk reappears with a bottle of red wine and a basket of bread. He uncorks the wine and pours three glasses, handing one to each of us. 'To love,' he proposes, raising the third glass. Startled by his toast, I pull back, sending the wine splashing dangerously close to the edge. I do not meet Paul's eyes but look away quickly, feeling my cheeks go warm. 'Dinner will be out shortly,' Henryk announces, before disappearing into the kitchen again.

'He's so subtle,' Paul says wryly. He holds up the bread basket, offering it to me.

I pull out a still-warm roll. 'He said that dinner is coming, but we didn't order anything.'

'I always let Henryk decide for me,' Paul explains. 'His choices are better than anything I could pick.'

I take a bite of the warm roll. My stomach gurgles, reminding me that it is the first thing I have eaten today, other than the chocolate torte I purchased earlier. Feeling Paul's eyes on me, I force myself to chew slowly, to pause before taking a second bite. I look around at the other patrons. Young couples and a few larger groups seem to fill the tables, talking and laughing over heaping plates of food and bottles of wine. 'We're in the Latin Quarter, near the university,' Paul explains. 'Not that many students can afford to eat out. But you get a lot of academics, artists, writers. Fewer soldiers and foreigners than across the river.' He gestures across the restaurant with his head. 'Look.' I follow his gaze to a table in the corner where an elderly couple eat in silence. 'I've seen them almost every time I've been here. But I've never heard them speak.'

'They look like they've been together for many years,' I observe. 'Maybe they've run out of things to say.'

'Maybe,' he agrees with a laugh. 'Or maybe they've been together so long they don't need to talk out loud.' His expression turns serious. 'It would be nice, you know? To spend your whole life with someone, grow old together.' He turns toward the window, a faraway look in his eyes, and I wonder with a pang of jealousy if he is thinking of his ex-fiancée.

Henryk reappears carrying two large bowls. 'First course, vichyssoise,' he announces as he sets the bowls down before us, then disappears into the kitchen once more.

I pick up the same spoon from the table as Paul, then try a mouthful of the soup. 'Potato soup. It's supposed to be cold,' Paul explains, noticing my puzzled expression.

I nod, embarrassed not to have known. 'Delicious.'

Classical music begins to play. I look toward

111

the back of the restaurant. A woman, stout and fiftyish, is seated at a grand piano. 'That's Henryk's wife, Marie,' Paul says. 'Married thirty years and they're still completely in love.'

That word again, *love*. Paul's eyes lock with mine. Suddenly it is as if the other patrons disappear. Neither of us speak for several seconds. Then Paul clears his throat. 'I'm glad to see you again, Marta. I mean, when I left Salzburg, I thought...' His voice trails off and he looks away. 'And you, being here now. It's just unbelievable.'

I nod, unable to speak. Clearing my throat, I force myself to look down at the soup, take another mouthful. A minute later, I glance up again, peeking at Paul out of the corner of my eye as he eats. Taking in his strong jaw, the dimple in his chin, I am reminded of our kiss by the lake. Will he kiss me again? The very thought makes my stomach ache with longing. But we may not have much time together after dinner. How would he manage it? Where? Flustered, I accidentally bang my hand against the table, sending my spoon clattering to the floor.

'Oh!' I cry, starting to go after it, but Paul reaches across the table and touches my forearm, restraining me.

'Don't worry,' he says gently. He pulls away as a waiter, not Henryk, appears and puts a clean spoon beside my plate.

A few minutes later, Henryk returns, looking down at our half-eaten bowls of soup with surprise. 'You do not like?'

'It's delicious,' I reply quickly. 'I'm just saving room.'

Paul winks. 'Good answer,' he mouths as Henryk clears the bowls.

A minute later Henryk brings the main course. 'Poulet à la Henryk,' he declares, uncovering the plates. The dish is a thick stew, served in a brown sauce over rice.

'The city is still under rationing, but Henryk works wonders with what he can get,' Paul remarks after Henryk has gone. 'After the crap – I mean stuff – we ate during the war... Our mess officer, Tommy, tried, God bless him, but there were times last winter...' He stops. 'I'm an idiot. Complaining about food after all that you went through.' A shadow crosses his face and I can tell he is remembering finding me in the prison, starving and near death.

'That's all right,' I say quickly. I do not want him to pity me, not now. 'Tell me about America,' I suggest, trying to change the subject.

'America?' He pauses, considering the question as he takes a bite of chicken. 'That's a tough one. It's such a big place. You've got the south, where I'm from, then places farther south where they talk even funnier.' I cock my head. 'That was supposed to be a joke. Not all Americans talk like me. The states in America are kind of like your countries over here, but instead of languages, we just have different ways of speaking English, faster, slower, pronouncing words differently. Anyway, there's the Midwest and California, which I've never seen. Then there are the big cities, New York, Chicago. There're just so many places to go.' He takes another bite. 'When I get back after the war, I'd like to drive across the

United States. Maybe get a convertible – that's a car where the roof comes off – and just drive, see the whole thing.' His eyes dance, as if he's considering the idea for the first time. I imagine myself, seated beside Paul in a car, with my hair pulled back in a kerchief, wearing large dark sunglasses like the women I've seen in the movies. 'I could go visit the guys from my unit,' he adds.

'The others, they are not from North...' I struggle, trying to remember the name of his home.

'Carolina?' He shakes his head. 'Nah. Well one of the guys, Bill McCauley, is, but he's from clear across the state. The rest are from all over, Texas, New Jersey, Maine. It's funny, we've lived together, sleeping and eating, for so long. It's hard to imagine going back to our own separate lives.'

'You've grown close to them,' I observe, taking a sip of wine.

'Like brothers,' he agrees. Suddenly his expression grows grave. 'I had one, you know. A brother. Jack was five years older than me. He got killed in a car accident when I was twelve.'

'I'm so sorry.' I fight the urge to reach across the table, put my hand on his.

'It was really hard,' he continues, looking away. 'I mean, I love my parents, adore my baby sister, Maude. But Jack was my hero.'

'He would be really proud of you,' I offer.

'You think so?' He looks back, his eyes brightening. I nod. 'I hope you're right. That means a lot. Thanks, Marta.'

We continue eating in silence. I think about Paul losing his brother. I was an only child.

114

Friends like Emma and Rose and Alek are the closest I have come to siblings. Rose. My heart aches as I see her lying in bed the night before she died. I reach down and touch my bag beside my feet, thinking of her possessions inside. *I will get to England for you, Rosie,* I vow silently.

I look up. Paul has stopped eating and is gazing at me, his eyes intense. My breath catches and I look away quickly, feeling heat rise from my collar. Then I catch a glimpse of my reflection in the restaurant window. My hair is still frizzy, my face plain behind my spectacles. What can he possibly see to make him stare so?

When I turn back, Paul is focused on his plate, eating the last of the chicken, scraping the sauce from the plate. But his wineglass is still nearly full. 'Don't you like the wine?'

He shakes his head. 'The wine is wonderful. I could drink the bottle without thinking twice. But you...' He breaks off, looking away. 'There was this girl who made me see I was drinking too much out of self-pity. So I've pretty much decided to stop.'

'Oh.' I think back to our conversation on the lake, struck that my words had such an effect on him. 'I'm sorry if I was preachy.'

'You were right.' He reaches across the table and takes my hand once more. 'You reminded me who I used to be before the war. I want to be that person again.' This time I do not pull away.

Henryk appears at the table then and clears his throat. 'Dessert?'

Remembering the chocolate torte earlier, I am tempted, but I don't want to appear unladylike.

'I couldn't possibly.'

'I think we'd best be going,' Paul adds, handing Henryk several bills.

Henryk puts the money in his apron pocket without counting it. 'Before you go I would like for Mademoiselle Marta to meet my Marie.' Before either Paul or I can respond, Henryk takes me by the arm and leads me through the restaurant. The dark-haired woman at the piano stops playing midsong as we approach. Up close, she is elegant, with sparkling green eyes and large gold hoop earrings. Henryk speaks to her in French, then turns to me. 'This is my wife.'

Marie stands and takes my hand, her bangle bracelets jingling. 'Enchanté.' She turns to her husband, speaking rapidly in French, still holding my hand.

'My wife is quite good at reading palms,' Henryk says. 'She wants to know if she can look at yours.'

I hesitate. Growing up in Poland, I had heard of gypsies from the Roma community who could tell the future from the lines of the palm, but I have never met anyone who claimed she could actually do it. I shrug.

Henryk nods to his wife. She turns my hand over, cradling it in hers. Then she raises it to the light, running her thumb over my palm several times, and speaking to Henryk, who translates. 'You have suffered through hard times.' That is hardly a prediction, I think. Everyone suffered during the war. 'But your life line is strong, and your heart line is very deep. You will have great love...?' As he says this, Henryk looks meaningfully at Paul, who has come up behind me. I

116

shiver. 'And that love,' Henryk prompts, but Marie stops, placing her hand on Henryk's arm to silence him. A troubled look crosses her face. She runs her hand over my palm twice, as if wiping something away. Then she drops my hand as if it is hot and looks up, shaking her head.

'What is it?' I ask.

'Nothing,' Henryk replies quickly, but I can tell from his tone and his wife's expression that there is more. 'I should get back to the other guests.'

'Of course,' Paul replies, shaking Henryk's hand as Marie turns back to the piano. We make our way to the front of the restaurant and onto the street. It is getting dark now and the gaslights have come on, casting a yellow glow on the pavement. 'They're lovely people, but palm reading is a silly game.'

'Perhaps,' I reply slowly, still troubled by Marie's refusal to say all that she had seen.

'Are you tired?' Paul asks. I shake my head quickly, not wanting my night with Paul to end. 'Good. Why don't we walk?' He leads me away from the restaurant along a winding street. The buildings here are narrow, seeming to lean on one another. Voices and laughter spill out from the cafés and bars onto the street. Paul points at the window of an apartment on the third floor of one of the buildings, illuminated in yellow light. A young woman sits on a bed reading to three small children clustered around her. 'Can you imagine growing up here?'

I do not answer. In my mind, I imagine this street during the occupation. What had those children been through? I think then of the children in the ghetto orphanage where my mother and Emma had worked. What had become of them? I wonder, my stomach aching at the memory.

We walk in comfortable silence. Soon the street ends at the river. 'Look.' Paul points to an island where an enormous cathedral sits, its turrets and buttresses bathed in light. 'Notre Dame.' I stop, staring up at the massive structure. The church that seemed so massive when I sought shelter the previous night is dwarfed by comparison. 'You know, they call Paris the City of Lights,' Paul offers.

I continue to gaze at Notre Dame as Paul leads me left along a path that runs parallel to the Seine. Soon we reach a wide stone bridge that crosses the river. 'Careful,' he says, taking me by the arm to guide me onto the pedestrian side-walk, away from the cars that race on and off of the bridge. A jolt of electricity runs through me. Would I ever be able not to shiver at his touch? 'This is the Pont Neuf, the oldest bridge in Paris.' He whistles softly under his breath as we make our way across the bridge. When we reach the midpoint, he stops, pointing at the skyline in the opposite direction from Notre Dame. 'Look.'

In the distance, I can see the Eiffel Tower, climbing toward the sky. I lean against the wall of the bridge, staring. 'This city ... I mean, I couldn't have imagined...'

'It kind of defies words,' Paul agrees, moving so that he is standing close behind me. 'Hard to believe just a few months ago it was still occupied by the Germans.' He puts his arms around me from behind and I can feel his warmth, his heart beating against my back. Other than our brief embrace in the bar, we have not been this close since Salzburg. My desire swells and breaks wide open.

Suddenly, there is shouting on the street behind us, followed by a series of small explosions. We turn toward the commotion. 'What on earth...?' Paul steps forward, putting me behind him protectively. His hand drops to the gun holstered at his waist. There is more shouting, followed by someone singing. On the bridge, traffic has stopped. Car horns begin to blare.

'Sounds like a celebration of some sort,' I suggest.

Paul does not answer but takes my hand and leads me across the bridge to the street, where a small crowd has gathered, shouting and cheering. Some people are drinking directly from bottles, others dancing alone or in pairs. The gathering swells as dozens more revelers come running from all directions. Paul grabs an American soldier by the sleeve as he runs past us. 'What's going on?'

'The Japs have surrendered. The war is over!' The soldier lets out a whoop, then continues running to join the crowd.

Paul turns to me and we stare at each other, too stunned to speak. 'The war is over,' he repeats at last. He bends down and picks me up. 'The war is over!' He spins me around, faster and faster, until the city is just a blur of lights. Then he sets me down, his arms still around me. We look at each other breathlessly for several seconds. Suddenly he brings his lips to mine, and without hesitation I am kissing him back, my mouth

119

open, body pressed tight to his. It is as if we will never stop, as if the street and the people and the world around us no longer exist.

There are more explosions, breaking us apart. 'I'm sorry,' Paul says quickly.

'Don't be. I'm not.' I take a step back, smoothing my skirt. 'Look.' I point across the water. Bright flashes of light, red and blue, fill the night sky.

'Fireworks,' Paul remarks. I nod, staring in wonder at the waves of color that fill the sky like confetti. I have heard of fireworks but never seen them before. 'You would think after all of the bombings, everyone would have had enough of things exploding,' he says a minute later. 'Let's get out of here.' For a second I hope we will return to the bridge and gaze at the skyline once more. But he leads me through the streets back, I can tell, toward the Servicemen's Hotel. The war is over, I think, as we walk in silence. I was thirteen years old when the war began and I spent the past six years running for my life.

'What are you thinking?' Paul asks.

'Lots of things. Mostly about what I lost during the war.'

He smiles. 'Careful, you're starting to sound like me.'

Recalling how I had chastised him for self-pity the night on the lake, I laugh. 'I suppose I am. I really was preachy, wasn't I?'

'Not at all. You were right about being grateful to be alive, earning the chance we've been given. And now, with the war ending, getting to go home. It really is a second chance, isn't it?'

Home. Paul will be leaving, returning to America for good. He stops walking and turns to me suddenly, his expression troubled. 'The only bad thing is leaving you.' My heart pounds against my chest. 'I mean, I realize we haven't known each other very long, but ... I'm going to miss you, Marta.'

So don't go, I want to scream. 'I'll miss you, too.'

We stand staring at each other for several seconds, neither speaking. 'Well, it's getting late,' he says at last. 'We should get back and pick up your papers.' We continue walking and, a few minutes later, approach the Servicemen's Hotel.

Through the closed hotel door, I hear shouting and singing, soldiers celebrating the end of the war. 'Why don't you wait here?' Paul suggests. 'Once I get your papers from Mickey, I can escort you back to your hotel.'

My hotel, I think, panicking. In my excitement at seeing Paul, I had nearly forgotten that I was supposed to get to the Red Cross shelter. 'That won't be necessary...' I begin, but Paul is already through the hotel door.

A minute later, he reappears. 'All set,' he says. There is a new number scrawled across the front of the train ticket. 'Front desk called the station and reserved you a seat on the seven-fifteen train to Calais. It's a bit early, I'm afraid, but the only way you'll make the ferry.'

'Thank you again.' I tuck them into my bag as he leads me down the path to the curb, hailing a taxi.

'Paul, my hotel is clear across town,' I say as the

taxi pulls up. 'There's no need for you to ride all the way there.'

He opens the rear door. 'But the city is crazy right now with all of the celebrating. I'm glad to escort you.'

'I know. But I'd rather you don't. Please.' It begins to rain then, thick drops splattering on the pavement.

'I don't understand...'

'If I don't say goodbye to you now...' I hesitate, looking down the street, then back at Paul again. I take a deep breath. 'If I don't say goodbye to you now, it is going to break my heart.' I reach up and kiss him, quick and hard. Then, before he can respond, I leap into the back of the taxi and close the door. 'Drive, please,' I manage to say in French.

'Where to?'

'Away,' I reply. Paul is still standing outside the cab. Desperately, I come up with the only place in Paris I remember. 'To the Louvre.'

I have no idea what a taxi costs, how far away the Louvre may be. I will stop the taxi and get out, I decide, as soon as I am away from here.

'But the Louvre is closed....'

'Just drive, please!' The cab lurches forward. Don't look back, I think. As we start to move, tears well up, overrunning my eyes. Suddenly there is a banging on the roof of the cab, as though someone has dropped a large rock on it. I jump. *'Mon dieu!'* the driver exclaims, slamming on the breaks. There is another banging noise. It's not coming from the roof, I realize, but the back window. I spin around. Perched on the

122

trunk of the taxi on all fours, is Paul.

He jumps down, then comes around to the side of the taxi. I roll down the window. The rain falls heavily now, plastering Paul's hair to his forehead, but he does not seem to notice. 'What on earth are you doing?' I demand. 'Jumping onto a moving car like that, you could have been killed!'

'I needed to stop you,' he replies simply, opening the taxi door.

'Why? What's wrong? Did you forget to give me some of the papers?'

He does not answer, but falls to the ground. 'Oh!' I reach down. 'Are you hurt?'

Paul does not answer but looks up, still kneeling. He hasn't fallen, but has dropped down on one knee deliberately, as though tying his shoelace. He reaches up and takes my hand. 'Marry me, Marta.'

CHAPTER 9

I stare down at him, stunned. 'Marta, when I had to leave you in Salzburg, I felt so helpless. I mean, I knew I liked you a lot, but we had practically just met. I thought I would never see you again and there wasn't anything I could do about it.' His words come out in a tumble, almost too quick for me to follow. 'And now, well...' He falters. 'I know it's crazy. We haven't spent more than a day together. You barely know me. But there's some reason we seem to keep finding each other. I'm crazy about you. I feel like we've known each other forever. And I'm not going to let you go this time. Not when I can do something about it. Marry me, Marta,' he repeats.

Is this really happening? I close my eyes, then open them again. Paul is still on one knee, gazing up at me expectantly. My mind races. Why is he doing this? For a second I wonder if he is still grieving over the loss of his fiancée, trying to fill a void. But looking down at his face, the intensity burning bright in his eyes, I know that his feelings for me are real. This is crazy. Paul is right, though. There is something special between us, something that makes it seem as though we have known each other forever. Suddenly I remember my first night at the palace, staring out at the mountains and wondering what life had in store for me. Now, at least in part, I know the answer. 'Yes,' I whisper. My eyes start to burn.

'Yes!' Paul shouts. He leaps to his feet, then reaches into the cab and picks me up. We hold each other close, neither speaking. An earthy smell rises from the wet pavement.

'*Pardon*,' a voice says a few seconds later. Paul and I break apart. Behind us stands the taxi driver, arms crossed. 'Louvre, Mademoiselle?'

'The Louvre?' Paul looks from me to the driver, then back again, brow furrowed. Suddenly I want to melt into the pavement and disappear. 'Were you that desperate to get away from me?'

I can lie to him no longer. 'You kept insisting on taking me back to my hotel and I was too embarrassed to admit I didn't have one.'

Paul's expression changes to one of understanding. He walks to the driver and hands him some bills. Then he turns to me. 'Let's get inside out of the rain.' Then he takes his jacket off and holds it over our heads as he leads me into the hotel. The lobby is crowded with soldiers overflowing the celebration at the bar, drinking and singing. As Paul leads me across the lobby through the crowd, a soldier carrying a camera and a dark green bottle blocks our path. I recognize him from Salzburg as the soldier who told Paul that they would be staying for the night. 'War's over!' the soldier exclaims, hugging Paul so hard he is forced to let go of my hand.

'I know. It's fantastic. And more good news – I just got engaged. Drew, meet my girl, Marta.'

My girl. I feel my insides grow warm. Drew turns to me, eyes wide, trying unsuccessfully to place me. 'Congratulations!' He pumps Paul's hand up and down. 'Lemme take your picture.' Paul draws me close to his side as Drew raises the camera. There is a popping noise, followed by a blinding flash. 'This calls for champagne,' he adds, handing Paul the bottle.

Paul takes a swig, then turns to me. 'Do you want some?'

'Sure.' I take the bottle from him, lifting it to my mouth with two hands. Bubbles tickle my nose as I swallow the lukewarm liquid. I pass the bottle back to Paul, who turns to hand it to Drew. But he has already disappeared into the crowd.

'Come on. Let's get out of this mess.' Paul takes my hand again and leads me down a corridor to a stairwell. He drops to one of the stairs, still holding the champagne bottle.

'So what do we do now?' I ask, sitting down beside him.

'Good question. Now that the war is over, they'll be sending us back to the States. But it's still going to be at least a few weeks. I could send you ahead to my family in America and meet you there. Or you can wait here in Paris. Then I can try to get discharged over here and we can travel back together.'

I hesitate. It would be heavenly to spend a few weeks exploring Paris without being worried about the future. I could visit the museums, do all of the things I had only read about in books. But looking down at my bag, I know that I do not have the option. 'I still have to go to London,' I say. 'I have to see Rose's aunt.'

'I could arrange to send her belongings on through the army,' Paul offers.

I shake my head. 'I need to go myself and tell her in person what happened. I owe Rose that much.'

'I understand. But I wish you would reconsider. Traveling across the Channel alone. It's so dangerous.'

Dangerous. Fighting with the resistance, being imprisoned by the Nazis, those things were dangerous. Being alone in Paris without anywhere to go had been scary, too, in a different way. But now that Paul and I are together I feel safe. Really safe. 'I'll be fine.'

'Okay,' he says reluctantly. 'You go on to London tomorrow, while the visa is good. I'll get discharged and meet you there in two weeks and we'll go to America together and get married.' He

126

pauses, thinking. 'Let's say Kings Cross Station, August 30 at seven in the evening. Agreed?'

I nod. 'Paul, there's one other thing....'

He looks down at me. 'What is it?'

'Well, if we're to be married... that is, you know that I'm Jewish?'

'I assumed it when we found you in the camp prison.'

There were non-Jews in the camps, too, I want to say. But that is beside the point at the moment. 'Does that bother you?'

He shakes his head. 'Not at all. I mean, it might give the folks of Ruddy Springs, North Carolina, a start...' He pauses, seeing my expression is serious. 'Is it a problem for you?'

I hesitate. Before the war, marrying a non-Jew would have been unthinkable. 'No. But I wanted to mention it because if we were ever to have children, I would want them to be raised Jewish.' I owe my parents that much.

He smiles down at me. 'We can move to a bigger city, if need be. Somewhere with a synagogue and some other Jewish people. We'll work it out, I promise. It's getting late. Why don't you stay here? Technically we aren't allowed to have guests.' He gestures toward the lobby. 'But my guess is no one is really going to look too closely in this chaos. You're welcome to stay in my room.' He raises his hand. 'I don't mean that improperly. I can stay with one of my buddies so you have the room to yourself.'

'Staying here would be great,' I reply. 'Thank you.'

We stand and make our way up one flight of

stairs, then another. Paul leads me down the hallway. 'Room 303. This should be it.' He unlocks the door and lets me in, then turns on the light. The room is small, barely wide enough for the single bed and washstand. The scent of mothballs hangs heavy in the damp air. 'It's not much, I'm afraid.'

I turn back toward him. 'It's fine. Thanks again.'

'I'm going to bunk with Mickey. He's three doors down on the opposite side of the hall if you need anything. I think we passed a washroom just down the hall to the right. I'll set the alarm and knock so you wake up in plenty of time for your train,' He pauses, looking down at me. Several seconds pass. Then he leans down and kisses me, Heat rises inside me as his lips press against mine, soft and full. A second later, he straightens. 'Good night, Marta.' He walks toward the door.

'Wait,' I call as he turns the doorknob.

He turns back. 'What is it? Do you need something?'

I hesitate. 'No. It's just that, you don't have to leave.'

'I don't understand.'

'Stay,' I blurt out. 'There's no need for you to sleep away, I mean, somewhere else. We already spent the night together once, in Salzburg, remember?'

He smiles. 'I do. I just wanted to give you your privacy. Are you sure?'

I nod. In the morning, I will have to leave and then we'll be separated again for weeks. The last thing I want to do is spend these few hours apart. 'I'll be right back.' I walk past him, out of the

128

room and down the hallway to the washroom. Music and voices drift upward from the bar below. I splash some water on my face, then stare into the mirror above the basin. Paul and I are going to be married. The idea still seems like a dream.

When I return to the room, Paul is kneeling on the tiny floor space, making up a bed of blankets. 'I took a few of the blankets from the bed, but you should still be warm enough,' he says. 'Just let me finish this and I'll step out so you can get changed.'

Inwardly I smile. Paul is still trying to protect me. He does not understand. I could let him continue making the separate bed, I consider. It would be the proper thing to do. But lying apart in the darkness would be torture. I want him beside me. Desire wells up inside me as I kneel down beside him. 'That won't be necessary.' I take the pillow he is holding and put it back up on the bed, then put my hand in his. 'I mean, after all, we are engaged.'

'Practically married,' he replies slowly, turning on his knees to face me. Our bodies press against each other, our faces close. He stands and helps me to my feet. His lips meet mine, probing. Still kissing me, he guides me to the bed, cushioning me with his arms as his weight pushes me gently downward. A second later, he breaks away. 'Are you sure?'

I unfasten the top button of his uniform. 'Positive.' I pull the jacket from his broad shoulders. Needing no further encouragement, he clamps his mouth on mine once more, drawing my

129

breath from me, making me light-headed. Paul's hands run down my sides, cupping my hips, bringing his mouth to my neck. I reach for his white cotton undershirt, pulling it over his head, seeing for the first time the metal chain with three small square plates that hangs from his neck. I run my hands across his torso, his back, while he struggles to unzip his pants. As he caresses me through my skirt, fingers feather-light, a soft moan escapes my lips.

Paul rolls gently on top of me, supporting his weight on his forearms. Suddenly an image flashes through my mind: Jacob above me as we hid in the crawl space of the cabin, his scent close, lips forbidden. I freeze, caught by the memory.

Paul, sensing my hesitation, pulls back slightly. 'I love you, Marta,' he whispers, cradling my face in his hands.

I look into his wide, unblinking eyes. This is real. This is mine. 'You, too,' I whisper, drawing Paul hurriedly to me once more, finding his mouth. He reaches urgently for the hem of my skirt. There is a moment of fleeting pain. So this is it, I think suddenly. I remember watching Jacob furtively, wondering what it would be like with him. I could not have imagined. Above me, Paul tenses and cries out. Desire returns, deeper and more intense within me than before as I move with him. I gasp, then moan softly, not noticing as the vision of Jacob slides from beneath me and fades away.

Paul lies on top of me, not moving, legs inter-twined with mine. His heavy breathing matches my own. 'Wow!' he says finally, lifting his head to

130

kiss my eyelids, my cheeks. Then he shifts his weight off me gently, rolling over onto his back.

I rest my cheek on his bare chest, feeling my body ache dully below. '"Wow" is good?'

He laughs, wrapping his arm around my shoulder. 'Wow is great.' He turns onto his side to face me, his expression serious. His eyelashes, I notice, though long and dark, are blond at the tips. '"Wow" is I never knew it could be like this.' I do not respond. My first time. So different, so much more than what I expected. Paul continues, 'I mean, to feel this way about someone so soon. I'm glad we're engaged. I only wish I had a ring to give you.'

I shake my, head. 'It's not important.'

'I'll get you a nice one when we get to America,' he promises. Then he reaches around his neck and pulls off the chain. 'My dog tags.' He presses them into my hand. 'You can wear these for now.'

I study one of the engraved plates that hang from the chain. It bears his name and a series of numbers I do not recognize. 'But I can't. I mean, this is your identification. You need this.'

'Nah, these are important in combat, to identify me if something happens. But the war is over. I've got two weeks of paperwork until I'm done. Nothing is going to happen. Anyway, I'll go to the quartermaster tomorrow after you've gone, get another set made. Okay?' He places the chain around my neck.

I wrap my hand around the cool metal tags. A piece of Paul to keep close until we are together again. 'Yes.'

'You should try to get some rest,' he says gently,

pulling the blanket up around us. 'You have a long trip ahead of you tomorrow.' I nod, suddenly tired. I roll onto my side, facing away from him, and he presses against my back, cupping his legs beneath mine. His cheek is rough against my shoulder. I listen to the rain as it beats against the window, feeling safe and warm. We are going to be together like this every night. Married. My eyelids grow heavy and I fall into a deep, dreamless sleep.

I open my eyes with a start, trying to remember where I am. In the dim light of morning, I can make out the small hotel room, my bag lying in the corner. Paris, I remember. Paul. Suddenly, the events of the previous evening – the reunion with Paul, his proposal, our lovemaking – come rushing back. I roll over to find him propped up on one elbow, looking down at me. 'Good morning,' he says.

'Don't you ever sleep?'

'I slept a bit. You?'

'Like a baby,' I reply honestly. 'I seem to sleep well around you. But what time is it? I mean, my train–'

'It's okay. It's not yet five. You don't have to leave for an hour or so.' He draws me close once more. A jolt of electricity shoots through me as his hand slides down my side. He pauses at my lower torso, feeling the roughness of my scar. A concerned expression crosses his face.

I pull away, suddenly self-conscious. 'What's wrong?'

'Nothing. But I was wondering how you got that.'

132

I bite my lip. I have not told anyone the story of what happened that night on the bridge, nor the events leading up to it. Not Dava, not even Rose. Now, as I lie in Paul's arms, I am seized with the urge to tell him everything. But will he be horrified, repulsed? It doesn't matter. If we are going to be married, he should know the truth. I take a deep breath. 'In Kraków, during the war, there was a...' I hesitate, trying to find the right words in English. 'A movement of Jews within the ghetto. Fighting back. How do you say?'

'Resistance?' he suggests.

'Yes. Have you heard of it?'

Paul shakes his head. 'I've heard of the one in Warsaw, not Kraków.'

All of the struggling, so many had died. And we were still not even a footnote in history. 'The resistance used to try to do things against the Nazis. One time, we exploded a bomb in a café full of S.S. officers.'

'We?' Paul asks. I nod and he whistles low under his breath. 'I had no idea you were a partisan. No wonder you're so fearless.' Fearless. A warm feeling grows inside me. 'That's why the Nazis had you in the special prison cell, isn't it?'

I nod. 'They wanted me to give up information about the others. I didn't.'

'So were you shot during the café bombing, or did that happen later, when they tried to arrest you?'

'Neither, actually. There was another girl in the resistance, Emma. She was my best friend.' *And the wife of the man I loved*, I think. But I cannot bring myself to speak of Jacob to Paul, not now.

133

'Emma was Jewish too, but she was living under another name as a non-Jew.' I speak slowly, trying to find the right English words to explain. 'She worked for a Nazi, a very big one, and was able to get things for us – security passes, information. She became involved with him. In order to get information,' I add quickly. I do not want Paul thinking ill of Emma, wondering as I sometimes had, why she had really become involved with Kommandant Richwalder. 'She became pregnant.' Paul's eyes widen. 'The Kommandant wanted to take her away from Kraków and marry her, so we had to get her out of the city. I was in charge of helping her to get out and meet up with her husband.'

'She was already married?'

'Yes, to another resistance member. He had been injured in the café bombing and was being hidden outside of town.' Suddenly, I am back in Kraków, waiting for Emma in the bushes outside her aunt's house. I was supposed to pick her up at dawn, but I knew she would never leave Kraków without saying goodbye to her father. Shortly after I arrived, the door to the house opened and Emma slipped out, a shawl over her head. As I followed her silently through the dark, still streets toward the ghetto, anger rose in me. So much was being risked to help her escape and now she was selfishly putting all of us in further danger.

'Marta, are you all right?' Paul is still watching me, a concerned look on his face.

I blink several times, clearing the vision from my mind. 'Fine, sorry. Before we could escape, the Kommandant found Emma and discovered that she was Jewish.' I recount hiding in the shadows, watching the Kommandant confront Emma. 'I had hoped she might be able to somehow talk her way out of it. He seemed to have genuine feelings for her so I thought he might understand. But when he pulled out his gun, I had to do something. I shot him.'

'Oh, Marta.' Paul touches my cheek.

'I killed him. But he managed this first.' I touch my side. 'Then the Gestapo came and arrested me and, well, you know the rest.'

'And Emma?'

'She escaped. When I realized I was shot, I told her to go on without me.'

'She left you?'

I nod. 'I made her go. She didn't want to, but there was no other choice. I told her where Jacob – that's her husband – was hiding. The plan was for them to meet up, cross the border into Slovakia. I don't know if they made it. Anyway, that's how I wound up in prison where you found me.'

He stares at me, his expression one of amazement. 'I had no idea...'

I swallow over the lump that has formed in my throat. 'If you don't want to, I mean, if this changes your mind about me, I understand,' I say, trying to keep my voice from cracking.

'What? Oh God, Marta, that's not it at all.'

'I mean, it's a lot to deal with, I know. I killed a man.'

'You killed a Nazi,' he corrects me. 'To save your best friend.'

'Sometimes it doesn't feel like that.' I burst into tears.

He draws me close and I bury my head in his chest. 'It's okay,' he whispers, stroking my hair.

A few minutes later, I pull back, wiping my eyes. 'I'm sorry,' I say between gulps of air.

'Don't be. I still see the faces of the Germans I killed, too. There was this one soldier, a boy, really. He couldn't have been older than twenty. There were others, of course, but this one... I was only about five feet away.' Though he speaks quickly, I am able to follow his clear, familiar cadence. 'After I hit him he looked so surprised. I think he expected me to take him prisoner instead. Maybe I should have. But his unit had just killed my best friend, David. Grenade in our foxhole. It would have been me, too, if I hadn't gotten up to relieve myself three minutes before. I came back and there was blood everywhere, on our packs, on the cards we'd been playing gin with minutes earlier. I held David while he died.'

'I'm so sorry.' I squeeze my arms tighter around him.

'Me, too. I'm sorry for everything we both had to go through. But it's over now. Just two more weeks.' He smiles. 'I can't wait for you to meet my mom. She's just going to love you. And the ranch! There's a corner of the property, where the stream leads into the woods. I think we should build our house there.'

Our house. 'It sounds perfect.'

'Then we can fill it with, like, twenty kids,' he adds.

I laugh. 'Twenty kids? Let's just start with one.' Suddenly I am concerned. 'Paul, promise me that you'll be careful.'

'I will.' His expression is solemn, but there is a twinkle in his eye. 'I won't eat too many croissants. And I won't dance with a single Parisian girl, I swear.'

'Very funny.' I punch his arm lightly. 'I'm serious. The war is over. Just be careful and hurry back to me.'

'I won't take any chances,' he promises. 'Not now. Not when we have so much to lose.' He looks over my shoulder at the clock. 'But we should leave and get you to your train.'

Reluctantly, I roll away from him and climb out of bed. 'You stay here.'

He sits up. 'I want to take you to the station.'

I shake my head. 'The city is quiet now. I'll be fine. It's better this way. Please.' Saying goodbye was going to be hard and I wanted to get it over with as quickly as possible.

'Are you sure?'

'Positive. The only train station I want to see you at is the one in London, two weeks from now. And, anyway, I want to remember you just like this,' I add, pointing to the bed and trying to sound light.

He leans back for a second, relenting. Then he reaches over to his bag, which lies on the floor beside the bed, and pulls out a small notepad and pencil. 'Write down the address where you'll be in London for me.'

Uneasiness rises in me. 'In case your plans change?'

He shakes his head. 'Nothing will change. I just want to send you a postcard.' I pull my papers from my bag and copy the address from the visa.

137

'Thanks,' he says as I hand the notepad back to him. I dress quickly. A minute later, I sit down beside him on the bed.

'Do you have enough money?' he asks.

'Yes,' I lie, nodding quickly.

He takes my face in his hands. 'Two weeks.'

'Two weeks,' I repeat solemnly. 'Be careful.'

'No chances,' he promises again. 'You, either.' He looks long into my eyes, then kisses me hard. I close my eyes, inhaling his scent, wanting to hold on to the moment forever. But a second later I hear church bells in the distance, chiming the hour.

'I have to go.' Reluctantly, I pull away from him, then stand up and walk to the door. I turn back, fighting back the tears that fill my eyes. 'Goodbye, Paul.'

He smiles. 'See you soon. I love you, Marta. We're going to have a great life together.' I nod, unable to answer without crying. Then I open the door and walk through, pulling it closed behind me.

CHAPTER 10

The bus screeches to a halt at the ferry terminal. The word *Calais* is painted on a large wooden board on the front of the two-story red-brick building. An hour earlier, my train from Paris arrived at a station bearing the same name. The air is different here, though, thick and salty.

138

Behind the terminal I can make out several tall ships, set against a wide swath of sparkling water. My breath catches; I have never seen the ocean before. But there is no time to marvel. The other passengers are standing up, making their way to the front of the bus. I pick up my bag and follow them, stepping out onto the pavement.

The crowd shuffles toward the building. Inside, there are two lines leading to glass ticket windows. I hesitate, unable to comprehend the French signs above each. In the right line stands a woman carrying two large, worn suitcases, four children in tow. Their clothes are clean, but ill-fitting, repaired with crude stitching in several places. To the left, the travelers are better dressed, their bags smaller. A sandy-haired man in a white suit with thin, pale blue stripes stands at the back of that line. Unlike the woman, I do not recognize him from the bus. I join the line of more shabbily dressed travelers to the right.

The line shuffles slowly forward. I look out of the corner of my eye at the other line to see if it is moving more quickly. But the man in the striped suit is still standing parallel to me, shifting his weight from side to side, tapping his foot impatiently. Suddenly, he turns, meeting my gaze. He smiles, revealing small, even teeth, then rolls his pale blue eyes. I look away.

A few minutes later, the woman in front of me reaches the head of the line and sets down her suitcases to give the frowning man behind the window a handful of papers. He stamps them several times, then gives them back to her. 'Lower deck,' I hear him say. 'Next!'

I step forward, handing him my ticket and visa. He scans the papers, then speaks rapidly in French, pointing to the other line as though I've made a mistake. I shake my head, hoping that he will not make me go to the back of that queue and wait again. The ferry will be leaving soon. 'Passport?' he says. I shake my head again, my heart pounding. I do not have a passport. Then I remember the identification card Dava gave me. I reach into my bag, fumbling and feeling the impatient stares of the people in line behind me. My hand closes around the card and I pull it out, then pass it to the man with trembling fingers. I hold my breath as he studies the card and papers. Is he questioning the extension, or whether I am really Rose? Finally, he stamps the ticket and hands everything back to me. I walk hurriedly from the window, clutching the papers, and proceed out the back door of the building as the other travelers did.

Outside, I stop. Twenty meters in front of me sits a row of six ships, each larger than the last. As I catch sight of the green-gray water behind the ships, I gasp. Growing up in southern Poland, hundreds of miles from the coast, I had only played by lakes and streams. I almost saw the ocean once during the war, when I had traveled to Gdansk with Jacob to obtain ammunition from a Danish contact. But it was nighttime, and though we met by the docks, I could not see the ocean, only hear the faint echo of the waves against the shore. Now sunlight sparkles on the water, which flows endlessly to the horizon.

Forcing my eyes from the ocean, I follow the

other travelers down the dock to the third ship. I hesitate. Dava and Jacob had both mentioned taking a ferry across the Channel. But this looks like an ocean liner, its base stretching several hundred meters into the sea. There are three decks, each slightly smaller than the last, stacked like a wedding cake.

A horn sounds loud and low. I walk forward with the others toward the ramp that leads onto the ship. Then, at the base of the ramp, I stop again, losing my nerve. Crowds of passengers push past me, eager to board. I shiver. Why am I doing this? It would be so much easier to turn around, go back to Paris and wait with Paul until he is discharged. Stubbornness rises up in me. I have to go to London. For Rose. Suddenly it is as if she is standing beside me. 'Come on,' I can hear her say, as she slips her delicate hand into mine. I take a deep breath and start up the ramp.

At the top, I give my ticket to the purser, who stamps it and hands it back to me. I take a step forward, pausing to get my bearings. Straight ahead, the deck is crowded, mostly with rough-looking men, laborers. Spotting the family that had been in front of me in line standing by the far railing, I start toward them. 'Ma'am,' the purser calls in English. I turn back, wondering if I have done something wrong. He points left to a staircase that winds upward. 'Your ticket is for first class. Two decks up.'

'But...' I look down at the ticket. Dava could only have afforded a basic fare and she is too practical to have spent Rose's money on anything more. Paul, I think. He must have bought me a more expensive ticket when he changed the reservation. A warm feeling floods through me. 'Th-thank you.'

I climb one staircase, then another, finally reaching the top deck. It is a different world from the crowded galley below. The light wood promenade is open and spacious. A building with large glass windows occupies the center of the deck; inside, I can make out several tables and chairs. Passengers in fine linen dresses and suits sit in the chaise longues or stand in small groups around the perimeter of the deck, sipping cocktails and talking, shielded by parasols from the bright sun. I feel eyes upon me, taking in my coarse dress and thick, secondhand shoes. My face reddens. I don't belong here. I walk quickly away from the other passengers toward the front of the deck.

Underneath my feet, I feel the ship begin to move. My stomach jumps. I am going to England. A few days ago, that would have meant everything to me. And I am still glad to be able to fulfill my promise to Dava and take the sad news to Rose's aunt. But now the trip means leaving Paul, too. It is only for a few weeks, I remind myself. But an uneasy sadness overcomes me as I look back over my shoulder at the shore.

Look forward, I think, remembering Dava's words. I force myself to turn away and keep walking toward the front of the ship. I am relieved to find that the deck is deserted here, perhaps owing to the lack of chairs or the strong breeze that blows off the bow. I stare out at the ocean, captivated. The water has grown choppier now, the green surface broken by hundreds of whitecaps. Seagulls dive to the water, trying to feed, then soar toward the sky once more.

The ship rolls suddenly, then dips to the right. Caught off guard, I stumble. My hands slam against the deck, breaking my fall. 'Easy there,' a male voice above me says in English. A hand grasps my elbow, helping me to my feet. 'Are you all right?'

I straighten, my palms smarting from the blow. Standing in front of me is the light-haired man I noticed in the other ticket line. The orange drink he is holding has splashed across his hand and a single spot stains the fine seersucker fabric of his jacket. But he does not seem to notice. His thin lips are puckered with concern. 'I'm fine,' I reply, brushing off the front of my skirt.

'Didn't want to see you go pitching over the edge,' he adds, his hand on my elbow.

'Thank you.' I pull back slowly, not wanting to appear rude. Up close, I can see that he is not more than about thirty, though his thin, side-combed hair and trim mustache give him an older look. He is nearly as tall as Paul, but slender, with a delicate frame matching his fine, almost feminine features.

'My pleasure.' He extends his hand. 'Simon Gold.'

'Marta Nedermann.' Should I have introduced myself as Rose? I wonder, too late, as I shake his hand.

The small, even teeth appear once more as he smiles. 'Charmed.' He holds my hand for several seconds, his fingers cool and moist. The boat lurches again and I pull back to grab the deck

143

rail. Simon shifts his weight easily with the boat's movement. 'The Channel is a bit rough today. You just need to get your sea legs.'

I tilt my head. 'Sea legs?'

He nods, holding his arms out perpendicular to his sides and leaning from one side to the other. 'You know, balance.'

'Balance,' I repeat slowly. 'I'm sorry, I've only recently learned English.'

'Really?' He cocks his head, appraising me. 'You speak with so little accent, I never would have guessed. But if you would like to keep practicing, why don't we go inside and have tea?' He gestures with his head toward the glass enclosure.

I hesitate. The man is a stranger. And I do not have the money for tea. 'Please join me as my guest,' he persists. 'It will pass the time until we reach Dover. The other guests are woefully boring,' he adds, his smile small and odd. I cannot help but think of Paul, the way his cheeks lift and eyes crinkle with each grin.

'Come along,' Simon says, starting for the enclosure. I did not, it occurs to me as I follow him, actually accept his invitation. I open my mouth to demur. But as Simon opens the door to the enclosure, the aroma of warm pastries fills the air, making my stomach grumble. I step inside as Simon holds the door for me. Then I stop. The café is so grand. Small tables, covered with white linen cloths and set with real china and silver, dot the room. A man in a tuxedo walks over to us and I half expect him to ask me to leave. But instead he escorts us to a table by one of the windows.

A waiter approaches the table with a pot of tea

and plate of scones. As he pours the tea, I study Simon, still wondering if it was proper for me to accept the invitation of a man I do not know, especially now that I am engaged. He is just being friendly, I decide.

'So what brings you to England?' Simon asks after the waiter has left again.

I take a deep breath. 'A friend of mine passed away.' I still cannot see Rose's face in my mind without my eyes burning. 'I'm bringing the news and her belongings to her aunt in London.'

'I'm sorry to hear that.'

I nod. Talking about Rose with this stranger feels awkward. 'And you?' I ask, eager to change the subject.

'I'm British,' he replies, taking a croissant from the plate of pastries that sits between us.

'I guessed that. I meant, what were you doing in Europe?'

'I've been in Europe for several months now for work. I'm a diplomat, you see.' Simon's English is different from any I have heard before, clipped and precise, not difficult to understand. 'I was helping to restore our embassies in the various cities where they were shut down during the war.' He works for the government. I worry again that I should have introduced myself as Rose, in case he sees my papers. 'Now I'm headed back to the Foreign Office. I'll be going back to the department where I was working before this trip, Eastern European affairs.' He gestures to the plate of croissants. 'You should try these, by the way. They're delicious.'

I choose one of the croissants. 'I'm from

145

Poland,' I offer, before taking a bite. The pastry is light and flaky, with delicious bits of chocolate inside. It is not as good, I decide, as the one I had in Paris. I remember the patisserie, my surprise at seeing Paul. Why could it not be him sitting here with me now, instead of this man?

'Really? I thought from your accent that might be the case, but I didn't want to ask. You know, if you're looking for work once we reach London, I could use a secretary, one who speaks Polish...'

'Oh, goodness no,' I blurt out, my mouth still full. I finish chewing, swallow. 'I mean, that's very kind of you, but I'll only be in London for a few weeks.'

'I see.' His brow furrows momentarily. 'And then what?'

I hesitate. 'I'm meeting up with my fiancé and traveling to America to live. He's a soldier and he's coming for me as soon as he's discharged.'

A strange look crosses Simon's face. He looks down at my hand. 'I didn't see a ring.'

'It was very last minute,' I explain. 'The engagement, that is. We didn't really have time to formalize things before I left for England.'

'Of course.' His voice is strained. Were his intentions romantic when he invited me to tea? I study his face, wondering if I had given him the wrong impression. He is not unattractive, with his smooth, even features and blue eyes. But when I think of Paul's rugged good looks, the way he takes my breath away, there is no comparison. 'Congratulations,' he adds, without feeling.

'Thank you.'

He clears his throat. 'It's too bad.' My eyes

146

widen. Could he possibly be that blunt? 'I mean, I could really use your help at the Foreign Office,' he adds quickly.

'My help? I'm sorry, I don't understand.'

'The situation in Poland, throughout Eastern Europe right now, demands urgent attention.'

'What do you mean?' I clutch my napkin in my lap. I heard little news during my time in Salzburg and none in Paris other than that the war had ended. 'What's happening?'

Simon wipes a crumb from his mouth. 'As you probably know, the Soviets liberated much of Eastern Europe.' I nod. I had learned this much from some of the other Polish refugees at the camp. Simon continues, 'The problem is now that the war is over, all indications are that the Soviets won't keep their word on restoring the sovereign leaders of those countries. Take Poland, for example.' His voice rises slightly, his expression growing more intense. 'The Soviets have certain eastern territories like Lwow outright and they've recognized the temporary government in Lublin, which is nothing but a puppet regime. It's the same all over Eastern Europe.'

Anxiety rises in me. The notion of Russian tanks rolling through Kraków is only slightly less terrifying than the Nazi occupation. 'Why doesn't the West do something?'

'We're trying. During the war, no one wanted to upset the Soviets because we needed them to fight Hitler on the eastern front. Now that's all over, but the Soviets have gained a toehold in virtually every country in Eastern Europe, either directly or through satellite communist parties.' I listen carefully, not understanding some of the English words he uses, but comprehending what he is trying to say. 'And because their troops occupy the region, there's little we can do about it. And it's not just in the east – even in places like Germany, the communists have strong political support. You're not a communist supporter, are you?' I shake my head. There had certainly been those among the resistance movement who leaned to the left, believing that socialist ideals were the answer. Jacob had believed in socialist principles but said that he could not support the way in which the Soviets had corrupted them. I had listened to the debate, not forming a view of my own. Simon continues, his voice rising slightly, 'The battle with the communists is coming, Marta. It will be the next great war, maybe even bigger than the last.' There is a sudden intensity to his pale blue eyes.

My head swims. 'I had no idea.'

The ship begins to rock more forcefully. I reach out to steady my teacup. 'We must be getting closer to the coast,' Simon observes, peering out the window.

I follow his gaze to a thin strip of land that has appeared on the horizon. 'I should go freshen up for our arrival.' I push back my chair from the table. 'Thank you very much for the tea.'

'My pleasure,' he replies, standing as I do. 'Would you like a ride to London once we arrive? My driver will be waiting for me. It's really no trouble.'

For a second, I consider his offer. It would be so easy simply to let him take me to the city. But there is something about his attention, about the way he is looking at me that makes me uncomfortable. And I really do not know him well enough to accept. 'No, thank you. I'm being met at the station,' I fib. 'But I appreciate your kind offer.'

A look of disappointment crosses Simon's face. He reaches into his pocket and pulls out a small silver case. 'My card,' he says, handing me a square of paper. 'In case your plans change.'

'They won't,' I reply, hearing the firmness in my own voice.

'Well, then, in case you need anything when you are in London.' His fingers brush mine as I take the card.

I am suddenly seized with the urge to flee. 'Th-thank you again.' I tuck the card in my bag, then turn, feeling his eyes still upon me as I walk quickly away.

The coal-tinged air is cool and damp as I make my way across the tree-lined square toward the row of houses that sit on its far edge. It is dark now, the dim yellow light given off by the street lamps swallowed almost immediately by the thick London fog. The faded street sign at the far edge of the square reads Montpelier Place. The houses rise high behind tall iron gates, thick hedges obscuring their porches from view. Number 33, the address written on my visa, sits on the nearest corner, overlooking the square. I cross the street and stop in front of the massive house. Rose was so quiet and unassuming, I had never imagined her family to be rich. My legs tremble.

Steeling myself, I walk up to the gate and peer through its bars. On the other side, well-tended gardens flank wide marble stairs leading up to a columned porch. I look at the windows, all of which are dark. It is not proper to be calling this late. But when my train pulled in to Victoria Station, I did not know what else to do. Except for my brief meeting with Simon Gold, I know no one in London and I have no money for a hotel. So I found my way here, following the directions a woman on the train had given me, taking the Tube to Sloane Street and then walking the last several blocks. Looking now at the grand house, I feel this was a mistake. Then my hand drops to my bag and an image of Rose's face appears in my mind. I have to do this for her.

I take a deep breath, then press the doorbell. A ringing sound comes faintly from inside the house. There is no response. My heart pounds. Perhaps Rose's aunt is away on holiday somewhere. I press the bell again.

'Yes?' a man's voice says loudly. I jump, then look through the gate, but the door is still closed. 'What is it?' I notice that the voice comes from a small black box with holes in it, just above the doorbell.

I clear my throat. 'I – I'm looking for Delia, I mean, Mrs. LeMay.'

'This is the LeMay residence,' the voice replies stiffly. 'However, Mrs. LeMay is not expecting any visitors tonight.'

'But...' I begin.

The voice interrupts. 'It's late, miss. Come back tomorrow. Or better yet, call first.' There is a clicking sound and the box goes silent.

I start to turn away, feeling my cheeks redden. Then I stop. I have to do this. I ring the bell once more. 'What is it?' the man snaps. 'I just told you...'

This time I speak before he can finish. 'Please. It's extremely important. If you could just come to the door...'

There is no response. I stare at the box. Had he hung up on me again? I look down the street. I will find somewhere to sleep, I decide, then come back tomorrow. As I turn to go, there is a clicking noise on the other side of the gate. I look behind me to see a thin, vertical shaft of light coming from the porch. 'What do you want?' This time, the man's voice comes from the door.

'If you could just open the gate...' The man does not respond but shuffles forward down the steps with great effort. As he emerges from the shadows, I can see that he is bald except for a fine ring of silver hair. He wears a dark pressed suit and ascot that seem formal, given the late hour. I try to recall if Rose ever mentioned an uncle.

The man reaches the gate but does not open it. 'Yes?' I feel myself shrink under his sweeping glance.

I take a deep breath, choosing my English words with care. 'I – I'm here to see Mrs. LeMay.' I raise my hand. 'I know it's late. I should have called first. I'm sorry. But I've traveled a great distance and I must speak with her. It's about her niece, Rose.'

A look of recognition flashes across his face. 'Rose?' he repeats. 'What is it?'

151

I hesitate. Part of me wants to give the news and Rose's belongings to this man and be done with it. 'Are you family?'

'No, I'm the butler, Charles,' he replies. 'But I will pass your message on to Mrs. LeMay.'

I shake my head. 'I'm sorry, but I must speak with Mrs. LeMay directly.'

The man studies my face for several seconds, not speaking. Then he opens the gate. 'Come in, and we'll see if Mrs. LeMay will receive you.'

As I follow him up the porch steps, the thick perfume of honeysuckle rushes up to greet me. Suddenly I see Rose, playing in the garden as a child. Sadness wells up in me. She should be here now, too.

Forcing down my sorrow, I follow the butler through the door. Inside, there is a large foyer, its floor checkered with black-and-white square tiles. Straight ahead, a staircase leads up into darkness. 'Wait here,' Charles instructs firmly before disappearing through the doorway to the left. I stand in the middle of the foyer uneasily. Through a doorway to the right, a clock ticks, breaking the silence.

A moment later, I hear footsteps above me. A light goes on at the top of the stairs and an elderly woman appears. 'Good evening,' she says as she descends the staircase. 'I'm Delia LeMay.' Rose's aunt looks nothing like I expected. Barely reaching my shoulder, she seems nearly as wide as she is tall. Her round face, dominated by full cheeks, is topped with an enormous shock of white hair that has been corralled into a bun that seems ready to burst from its trappings at any second. But her violet eyes are unmistakably Rose's. She eyes me warily. 'Charles tells me you are here about my niece.'

'Yes. My name is Marta Nedermann. I–'

'Marta!' Delia exclaims. Her face breaks into a wide smile, lifting her cheeks until they threaten to eclipse her eyes. 'I had no idea it was you.' She waddles across the foyer more quickly than her girth would seem to permit, then reaches up and kisses me on both cheeks, her flowery perfume tickling my nose. 'Rose wrote me all about you. I sent in the paperwork to extend her visa, and get you one, too.' So Dava was right. Rose had wanted me to come to England with her. 'But I wasn't expecting you girls for a few months yet. What are you doing here?'

I hesitate. 'Do you suppose we could sit down?'

'Of course, how rude of me! You must be exhausted from your trip.' She ushers me through the door on the right into a parlor. The furniture, a couch and two chairs, is covered in matching pink-flowered silk slipcovers. Framed photographs cover the coffee table, windowsill and mantel. 'Charles,' Delia calls loudly. The butler appears once more. 'Two cups of tea, quickly, please.'

'Yes, ma'am.'

After he leaves, Delia gestures to the sofa. I hesitate, not wanting to dirty the fine fabric. 'Come sit,' she urges. 'I'm sorry if Charles was rude. We've had so many people coming to the gate these recent months, beggars mostly. It's a shame what this war has done to people's lives. We try to help when we can, of course, but there have been some unsavory types, too. Hooligans

153

who would just as soon cause trouble. We have to be careful.' As she sits down at one end of the sofa, a large gray cat appears and leaps into her lap. 'This is Ruff,' she says, scratching behind the cat's ears. 'He's nearly fifteen years old. Rosie named him. I tried telling her that the name was better suited to a dog, but she was quite a stubborn child.'

I try to imagine quiet, gentle Rose as stubborn. The war must have changed her so. Then I notice a painting above the mantel of a young girl with a delicate face and strawberry-blond hair. 'Is that Rose?'

Delia smiles. 'Yes. In the summers when Rose didn't come here, we would meet at the family villa on the coast near Trieste. We had a local artist paint her portrait when she was nine. It's always been my favorite.' Watching her eyes dance as she studies the painting, dread rises in me.

Charles reappears with the tea and pours two cups for us before leaving again. Delia hands one of the cups to me. 'No sugar, I'm afraid. We're all out of ration cards until next week and there doesn't seem to be any to be had on the market.' She means the black market, I realize with surprise. It was hard to imagine a woman such as Delia procuring things illicitly, but her tone is matter-of-fact, as if doing so is a routine part of life since the war. 'So how is my dear Rose? And what brings you here?' She stirs her tea. 'I mean, Rose wrote that you were going to be coming with her. Is she not well enough to travel yet?'

I take a sip of tea, forcing myself to swallow over the lump that has formed in my throat. 'Mrs.

LeMay, you know that Rose was terribly ill.'

A grave look crosses her face. 'Yes. She's suffered from her blood affliction for many years. But she wrote me from Salzburg that she was getting much better, stronger every day. Thanks to you and a nurse, Dana or something.'

'Dava. She was very good to both of us.' I pause. 'Rose *was* getting better.'

'Was?' Delia speaks slowly, a look of realization crossing her face. 'You don't mean...?'

'I'm afraid so.'

Her face pales. 'What happened?'

'She developed a terrible fever a few days ago. The doctors and nurses did everything they could for her, but the fever was too much, given her weakened state. I'm so sorry.' Delia stares straight ahead, not speaking. I reach out, take the teacup from her shaking hands and set it down. 'Perhaps I should call Charles?' She does not answer but buries her face in her hands, sending the cat flying from her lap. Her back shakes as she sobs silently.

A few moments later, she looks up again. 'I begged her to come here and live with me before the war. But her father was too sick to travel and she wouldn't leave him. She said Amsterdam was their home, that everything would be fine.' We all thought that, before the war, I want to say. 'I just can't believe that she's gone,' she sniffles. 'She was like my own child.'

'I know.' I reach out and touch her hand. 'She talked about you all the time. She was so excited about coming here and starting a life with you.'

'She was the only family I had left.' Delia wipes

155

her eyes. 'Was ... was she happy? At the end, I mean?'

'Very. She was in a beautiful place, with good care and friends.' I describe for her the palace and the grounds. Then I reach into my bag and pull out Rose's belongings. 'Here.' I show her a picture Rose had drawn of the view from the terrace of the mountains and the lake at sunset.

'It's beautiful.' She reaches into the small pile of Rose's belongings and pulls out a letter. 'This is from me.'

'I know. She kept all of your letters. She loved you very much.'

She does not speak for several minutes. 'And you came all the way here to give me these?'

'Yes. Dava suggested that I come. But I didn't have a visa of my own so I used Rose's. I hope you don't mind.'

'Of course.' Delia wipes her eyes, managing a smile. 'That was very kind of you. But what will you do now? Are you planning to go back to the continent, or will you stay in England?'

I hesitate. It feels strange to speak about my plans for the future so soon after informing her of Rose's death. 'Neither, actually,' I say at last. Quickly, I tell her about Paul.

'An American soldier!' Her eyes brighten slightly. 'That's terribly romantic.'

'He's coming to meet me in London in just under two weeks,' I add. 'Then we'll travel to America together.'

'What will you do until then?'

'I don't know,' I admit. I still have a little of the money that Dava gave me, but it isn't enough to keep me for two weeks, even at the worst of boardinghouses.

'You'll stay with me,' Delia says decisively. I look at her, surprised. 'I have this big empty house all to myself. I can show you London before you go.'

'I wouldn't want to impose...' But even as I say this, I feel myself melting into the comfort of the warm room.

'Not at all,' Delia insists. 'I would love the company. And you can tell me all about your time with Rose. It would be a blessing, really.'

'Thank you. That would be lovely.'

'No, I should be thanking you, for bringing the news of my niece and her belongings home to me. Now, where are your bags? Are they on the porch or did you leave them at the station?'

I shift uncomfortably, then gesture to my small satchel. 'This is everything.'

A look of surprise flashes across Delia's face, then disappears again. 'Of course, how silly of me. Don't worry,' she adds, patting my hand. 'We can get you whatever you need. Charles,' she calls, her voice rising. The butler appears in the doorway again, as if he'd been waiting to be summoned. 'Miss Marta is a good friend of my niece's.' The butler nods and I can tell from his somber expression that he heard our conversation and knows about Rose's death. 'She is going to be staying with us for a few weeks. Please show her to the guest room and see that she has everything she needs.' She turns back to me and pats my hand. 'We'll talk more in the morning.'

'Miss?' Charles gestures toward the doorway. I stand and follow him back through the foyer and up the stairs. At the end of the hallway he opens a door and turns on a light, revealing a spacious bedroom. A wide bed with a wrought-iron headboard is centered against the far wall, covered in a cornflower-blue duvet that matches the curtains. On the opposite wall there is a large oak armoire and a dresser. The room smells pleasantly of dried flowers and spices. It is the nicest room I have ever seen. 'The lavatory is just through there,' Charles adds, pointing to another door. 'Please let me know if you need anything.'

'I shall. Thank you.' When he has gone, I sink down on the bed, trying to process all that has happened. I made it to London, brought the news. And I even have a place to stay. Suddenly I am very tired. I change into my nightgown and climb in between the crisp linens. I picture Paul. Had it really only been this morning that we said goodbye? I desperately wish that I could go back in time. I would gladly trade this grand room for the narrow bed in the Servicemen's Hotel to be with him. But there is no going back, Dava had said. Only forward. And it is less than two weeks until Paul and I will be together again. I reach inside the neckline of my gown and wrap my fingers around Paul's dog tags. My eyes grow heavy and I drift to sleep, clutching the cool metal and seeing his face in my mind.

CHAPTER 11

'Thank you,' I say as I step out of the black taxicab onto the curb. I close the door and, as the taxi pulls away, look up at the hulking Kings Cross train station. Throngs of travelers move briskly through its open double doors. A shiver of excitement runs through me. In less than an hour, Paul will be here.

I join the crowds and make my way inside. A long concourse of shops and kiosks runs down the right side of the station. To the left, perpendicular to the shops, sit a half-dozen train tracks, separated by platforms. Each runs beyond the open arch at the end of the station, then either curves away or disappears into the horizon.

I walk toward the large board that hangs above the tracks announcing train arrivals and departures. It clacks noisily as the numbers turn over, updating the train information. Paul did not say exactly where he would be coming from, or identify a specific train on which he would arrive. Indeed, when I studied a map of London a few days after arriving at Delia's, I was surprised at his choice of station: Kings Cross is to the north of the city, with trains coming in from central England, not the Channel coast as I expected. But Delia explained that there were a number of American military bases located north of London in the Midlands and East Anglia. Paul would

159

likely be flying in with his unit, she explained, and if so he would come to London on the line that ran down from Cambridge, arriving at Kings Cross. The board indicates that a train from Cambridge is scheduled to arrive on track three at seven-fifteen, forty-five minutes from now.

Paul's train. I shiver again. Of course, I don't know for certain that he will be on that one. Seven o'clock was a guess on his part, a pre-arranged time he had set when his travel plans were uncertain. He could have arrived already. I spin around and scan the concourse, half hoping to see him having a coffee or browsing at the magazine racks. But he is not there. It is not seven yet, I remind myself, pushing down my disappointment. I had set out from Delia's house early to allow plenty of time to make my way across the city by Tube. But as I prepared to leave, Delia offered to come with me, or at least have Charles drive me to the station. I politely declined, wanting my reunion with Paul to be private, but she insisted on calling a cab and giving me money for the fare.

Delia's full, smiling face appears in my mind. She's been so hospitable, despite her sadness over losing Rose. 'I'm going to show you the best of London,' she announced at breakfast the morning after my arrival. Over the next two weeks, she led me around the city with an energy that belied her age and size. We had tea at the elegant Food Hall at Harrods, rode a double-decker bus to see Westminster Abbey, Big Ben and Parliament, wandered through the antique stalls and sec-ondhand shops at the Portobello Road market.

One afternoon when it was too rainy for sight-seeing, Delia took me to see *Henry V*, starring Laurence Olivier, at the massive Cinema Odeon in Leicester Square. We talked a great deal, over meals and as we walked, and I told her about Rose and our time together in Salzburg. Delia recounted her travels as a younger woman to Italy and the south of France and even to Morocco. As if by unspoken agreement, we avoided speaking of anything sad. I did not tell Delia of Rose's condition when she had arrived at the camp, or the little I knew about how she had suffered during the war. Nor did I talk about what I had been through in prison. And Delia had her own unspoken stories of hardship, I knew, of long, terrifying nights in the recent war spent huddled in the cellar with Charles as the Nazi bombers roared overhead. It was as if neither of us could bear any more sorrow right now but were content to enjoy each other's company and the memories of happy times.

I found the days with Delia pleasant and I was grateful for her generosity. But each night as I lay in bed, I marked off another day in the calendar in my head: eight days gone, six to go, nine days gone, five to go, and so on, counting the days until I would see Paul. Two days earlier, I received a postcard in the mail from him, bearing a black-and-white photograph of the Eiffel Tower. *Counting the days till our reunion,* he'd scribbled.

Reunion. My heart jumps at the word. I dreamed of this moment so many times over the past few weeks, it hardly seems real. I barely slept at all last night, but lay awake, fretting. What if things are

161

awkward between us, if he doesn't care for me as much as he thought? It is not as if we really know each other very well. Staring at the tracks now, I brush these fears aside. Things with Paul will be as wonderful as ever. But other, more practical, questions persist: What will happen once he arrives? Will he come to the second guest room that Delia graciously offered, or is he planning to stay at another servicemen's hotel? I also wonder how long we will remain in London, what needs to happen before we can leave for America.

Wiping my moist palms on my skirt, I turn back to look down the concourse. It is Friday evening and the station is thronged with travelers – men in suits carrying briefcases on their way home from work, families toting children and luggage for weekend excursions. But signs of the war remain everywhere. A wounded British soldier makes his way painfully across the station on crutches. At the station pub, a group of women, still wearing factory work clothes, talk over pints of beer. An advertisement for the latest autumn fashions sits beside a large sign admonishing that rationing is still in effect.

My gaze stops on the coffee kiosk, where four American soldiers cluster around a small standing table. I scan the group. Perhaps Paul came in at a different gate, arrived with friends. But he is not among them.

Behind me, a train horn sounds. I spin around as a large black locomotive comes into view at the top of track three. The train from Cambridge! As it pulls into the station, I rush forward. I stop, dangerously close to the edge of the platform, wobbling. Suddenly a conductor is at my side, grabbing my elbow to steady me. 'Careful, miss,' he says. 'Step back, please.' Red-faced, I comply. The train glides into the station, wheels screeching loudly as it comes to a halt. I smooth my hair quickly. As the doors open and the passengers begin to pour forth, I study the crowd, watching eagerly for Paul. Suddenly, a flash of olive-green uniform catches my eye. An American soldier is coming down the platform. I start toward him, heart pounding. Then, as I get closer, I stop again. The soldier is too short to be Paul, his hair too light.

The disembarking crowd begins to thin as the passengers make their way toward the main concourse. I turn from the now-empty train, desperately searching the passengers as they disappear behind me. Did I miss him? When the last passenger has made his way from the platform, I walk back toward the concourse, approaching the conductor who had steadied me. 'When's the next train?'

He cocks his head. 'From Cambridge? In about an hour. Same platform.'

'Thank you.' He will surely be on that one. Reluctantly, I walk across the main concourse. Suddenly my stomach grumbles. I was too nervous to eat earlier, despite Delia's attempts to coax me, her admonition that I would faint from hunger. I walk across the concourse to the kiosk where the group of soldiers stood a few minutes earlier and order a coffee and a cheese sandwich.

As I wait for the food, I catch a glimpse of my reflection in the mirror behind the counter. I

163

spent much of the day getting ready, taking a long bath and setting my hair. My dress is navy blue with white trim, one of three that Delia gave me shortly after my arrival. She told me that she had bought them at the secondhand shop months earlier, but I could tell from the crispness of the fabric that they were new and from the size that she had purchased them for Rose in anticipation of her coming to stay. For a second I imagine her beside me, whispering excitedly about Paul's arrival. She should be here, I think guiltily for the hundredth time. Living with Delia, wearing this dress. Pushing this thought aside, I study my reflection once more. My curls, which I worked to smooth, have already returned to their normal frizziness that the London dampness seems to aggravate so much. Paul has seen me looking far worse, I know. But I so want to look beautiful for him, to make him glad about his decision to marry me.

The kiosk tables are full, so after I pay for the coffee and sandwich, I carry them down the concourse, eating as I look in the windows of the station shops. Pigeons peck at some spilled popcorn outside one of the stands until the shop clerk steps out from behind the counter, brandishing a broom and sending them scurrying to the rafters. I pause at the newsstand, scanning the headlines of the *Times*. Delia has the *Guardian* delivered to the house, and almost every night I sit down at the table with the paper and a dictionary, trying to understand as much as possible. But I did not have time today before leaving for the station. I finish my sandwich, then brush off my fingers and pick up the paper. The top article is about the occupation in Germany, I can tell. I do not want to think about the Nazis, not now. My eyes drop to another headline in the middle of the page. *Polish Exiles Warn of Impending Disaster*. I hold the paper closer, trying to make out what the article is saying. I do not understand all of it, but I gather that the Soviets are strengthening their grip on the Polish government. I remember my conversation with Simon Gold on the ship. The fight with the communists would be the next great war, he said. Even bigger than the last. I think sadly of Poland, now occupied by Soviet soldiers instead of Nazis. This is not how we thought it would turn out when we were fighting for our freedom.

'Oy, are you buying that?' the man behind the counter calls. 'This isn't a library.'

I place the newspaper back on the rack. 'Sorry.' I look up at the large clock above the timetable. Eight-ten. I throw my empty coffee cup into a trash bin and make my way back to the platform, where another train is just pulling in. This one is emptier than the last, I realize as I scan the disembarking passengers. At the far end of the platform, I see a soldier get off the last car of the train. Paul! I start down the platform, almost running. But as I draw closer, I stop again. It is not him. For a second, I consider asking the soldier if he knows Paul. But he races past me, down the platform and into the arms of a young blond woman waiting at the edge of the concourse. I look away from their embrace, my stomach aching.

I walk over to the conductor once more. 'Next

165

train from Cambridge?'

He shakes his head. 'That's the last one for the night, I'm afraid.'

Panic rises within me. Has Paul changed his mind? Or maybe he was delayed and did not get discharged from the army when he expected. I walk back to the concourse and sink down onto a bench. There are just two trains left on the timetable, one from Edinburgh and another from Newcastle. Maybe he's not arriving by train at all. But he will be here. My stomach, uncomforted, gnaws.

I look down the nearly deserted concourse, uncertain what to do. Then I reach inside the neck of my dress and lift Paul's dog tags. I have not taken them off since he gave them to me. I trace the letters that spelled out his name. Where are you? My shoulders slump. Half an hour, then an hour, passes. Soon the lights go out at the newsstand. A shopkeeper draws a metal gate closed across the front of the coffee stand.

'Ma'am?' I turn to find the conductor with whom I'd spoken earlier standing above me. 'Do you want me to call you a cab? That is, I'm afraid we don't allow people to stay overnight in the station. Loiterers and all that.' I look at him, puzzled, then turn back to the timetable. It is nearly ten o'clock. The station is empty and all of the trains are gone.

'That won't be necessary,' a male voice says from behind me. *Paul*, I think for a second. But the voice is much older than Paul's, the accent English. I turn to find Charles standing behind me. 'Your car is waiting, miss.'

The conductor looks surprised. 'Good evening, then.' He shuffles off.

'Hello, Charles.' It is difficult to mask my disappointment that he is not Paul. 'What are you doing here?'

'Miss Delia sent me to make sure you are all right.'

'Fine, thank you. Paul's train hasn't come in yet, but I'm sure he's just delayed....'

'Begging your pardon, miss,' Charles says gently, 'but there are no more trains tonight.' He points up at the now empty schedule board. I do not reply. 'I can take you back to the house.'

'I have to wait here.' I can hear the stubbornness in my own voice.

'It's not safe to stay here alone so late,' Charles protests. 'You've given the gentleman our address, haven't you?'

I nod. Charles is right, of course. Paul will be able to find me. I take a long last look around the train station, then follow Charles outside to the sedan parked at the curb. He holds the door for me and I climb numbly into the back. I lean my head against the cool, damp glass, stare blindly out the window as we make our way through the wet streets of north London.

The parlor lights still burn brightly as we pull up in front of Delia's house. Inside, Delia hurries across the foyer to greet us. 'What happened?'

I shake my head. 'The gentleman did not arrive,' Charles replies for me.

'I'm sure he was just delayed,' Delia says quickly. 'You gave him our address here?' I nod. 'Good, he'll come here as soon as he can.'

167

'What if he doesn't?'

'We'll go to the embassy. The deputy chief is a good friend of mine and I'm sure they'll know of various units coming into London. We'll go first thing tomorrow, if he hasn't arrived by then,' Delia promises.

She sounds so positive, I almost feel better. 'Thank you.'

'You're very welcome. Now, why don't you come sit and have some supper? I've kept it warm for you.'

I shake my head. 'Thanks, but I'm not hungry.'

'Then at least some tea,' Delia presses.

'I'd prefer to just go to bed.' I bring my hand to my temple, which has begun to throb.

'Of course. You must be exhausted from all of the waiting.'

'I am.' I start up the stairs, then turn back. 'You'll wake me if...'

'The moment he arrives,' Delia promises.

Upstairs, I undress and climb numbly into bed. I know that the sooner I go to sleep, the more quickly morning will seem to come. But Paul's face stares back at me in the darkness. Where are you? Have you changed your mind about me? His face remains impassive. I close my eyes and force myself to breathe evenly, a trick my mother taught me when I was restless at night as a child. Soon I drift off to sleep, but Paul's face haunts me there, too. I dream that I am standing on the platform in the train station once more. A train pulls in and, as I watch the disembarking crowds, a familiar face appears. Paul! My heart lifts and I start toward him. But he turns away, speaking to

168

the woman behind him. There, holding his hand, is the young woman from the café in Paris. 'No...'

I awake with a start. Bright sunlight streams through the windows. The previous evening comes rushing back to me. Perhaps Paul arrived during the night. I sit up quickly, swinging my feet to the floor. But before I can stand up, a wave of nausea overtakes me. Easy, I tell myself. I reach for the pitcher of water that Charles always leaves fresh on my nightstand and pour a glass. I do not want to get ill just as Paul arrives. A feeling of certainty grows inside me. He will be here today.

I take a few sips of water and my stomach settles. Then I wash and dress quickly, and make my way downstairs. Delia is seated at the kitchen table. As usual, a full English breakfast has been laid out: fried eggs, bacon, stewed tomatoes, beans and toast. My stomach begins to turn again. Delia looks up from the heaping plate in front of her. 'Hello, dear. How did you sleep?'

'I don't suppose there's been any sign of...'

Delia shakes her head. 'No, but I wouldn't worry. Even if he had arrived in London during the night, I'm sure he's too well mannered to go knocking on strange doors at all hours.'

Like I did, I think. But I know her words are not a rebuke. 'I suppose.'

'The embassy opens at nine and we'll be there when they do. Now, come eat.' I start to reply that I am not hungry. My stomach is too knotted to eat. But I do not want to seem ungracious. Reluctantly, I sit down and take a piece of toast, buttering it as Delia pours me a cup of tea.

There are footsteps in the hallway, followed by

a rustling noise. Charles appears, carrying a bag of groceries. 'Good morning, Charles,' Delia says. 'Breakfast is delicious, as always.'

Charles does not respond but stands awkwardly in the doorway, shifting his weight from one foot to the other. 'What is it?' Delia asks.

'Miss Delia, if I might have a word...'

Delia's expression turns puzzled. 'Excuse me,' she says to me before following Charles into the hallway.

I watch as Charles speaks to Delia in a low voice, his head down and close to hers. It is unlike Charles to whisper so rudely in front of me. Then he pulls a newspaper from the bag, shows it to Delia. Uneasiness rises in my chest. I put the toast back on the plate and stand up. 'What is it?' I ask.

Charles stops speaking and they both look up hesitantly as I approach. 'What is it?' I repeat, louder this time. I can hear the harshness in my voice but I do not care. I gesture toward the newspaper. 'What does it say?'

'Marta, dear.' Delia takes a step toward me. I reach around her and before she can stop me, snatch the paper from Charles's hand. The headline is so large it covers nearly half the front page. *American Military Plane Crashes in Channel: All Killed.*

A rock slams into my chest. I scan the article, not breathing. A military plane traveling from Paris to London yesterday experienced mechanical trouble over the Channel. The plane crashed, killing all on board. Dread rises in me. Delia puts her hand on my shoulder. 'Marta, it

170

probably isn't his unit.'

'There are thousands of American troops passing through England right now,' Charles adds.

I do not answer but continue reading. The men were part of the Fighting 502nd, a unit that fought in every major battle since Normandy. I remember Paul calling his unit by that name. Bile rises in my throat. At the bottom of the article, there is a list of soldiers killed in the crash. I scan the names. Paul's is not among them. Maybe he wasn't traveling with his unit. Perhaps he had received permission to leave early, knowing he was coming to meet me. 'He's not on the list,' I whisper, sagging with relief.

Then, at the bottom of the list of names I notice an asterisk, followed by the words 'unidentified soldier.' My hand drops to the dog tags around my neck. Paul promised me he would get another set.

It is a mistake. It has to be a mistake. In the middle of the page, there is a grainy picture of the unit, standing in front of a tank. I scan the faces, which all look remarkably similar with their short hair and helmets. My eyes lock on a familiar face in the third row, far right. Paul's eyes stare out at me unblinkingly. I know then why he had not come for me.

The paper falls from my hands. 'He's gone,' I say aloud. A scream that I do not recognize as my own fills the air. Then the ground slides sideways beneath me and everything goes black.

CHAPTER 12

I stand in front of the timetable at Kings Cross Station, looking out across the platforms. Bright sunlight shines through the slats in the roof, reflecting off the top of the trains. I clutch my purse nervously, waiting. I am early again, of course. But this time I let Charles drive me, gratefully accepting his offer to wait outside with the car until Paul arrives. It had been a mistake, the telegram that arrived this morning had said. Paul had missed his flight, the one that had crashed. He will be arriving today.

A train appears at the top of track three. I start forward, excitement surging through me. Then I stop. Something is wrong. The train does not slow as it enters the station, but barrels forward at full speed toward the end of the platform. It is going to crash. I turn and start running away from the train. A second later, there is a massive explosion behind me, followed by an enormous gust of hot air that slams me forward into the ground. When I lift my head and look over my shoulder, the train has disappeared, engulfed by a ball of fire. 'No!' I cry aloud.

My eyes fly open. Where am I? The familiarity of Delia's house rushes back as I recognize the pale-blue walls. I sit up, trying to catch my breath. At the foot of the bed, early-morning light dances in patterns on the duvet. Voices of

172

children on their way to school ring out as they call to one another from the pavement below. My own unwashed smell mingles with that of fried eggs, left on the nightstand while I was asleep.

Paul is dead. It has been more than a week since I read the news of the plane crash, saw him staring up at me from the photograph. I do not remember dropping the newspaper or fainting, only waking up some time later in bed, not knowing how I had made it there. Delia was seated beside me. 'Hello, darling.' She leaned over and put her arms around me.

'He's gone.' My voice was heavy with disbelief.

'I know. I'm so sorry.'

First Rose, now Paul. The war was over. This wasn't supposed to be happening, not now. Guilt crashed down on me: It was my fault Paul was coming to London. If it had not been for me, he would still be alive. Deep down I knew that wasn't true – Paul's entire unit was on the flight. But the idea suited my grief, its painful jabs welcome through my numbness. Suddenly, I hated Delia, this house, all that was England. 'I just want to be left alone,' I blurted out. A hurt expression crossed her face. 'I mean, I'm very tired.'

'Of course.' Delia stood up quickly. 'Just ring the bell if you need anything.' I turned away, closing my eyes once more.

After that day, I did not speak with anyone, or even get out of bed, except to go to the toilet. Mostly I slept, through the days and nights, trying to escape the pain. But it was no use – I dreamed fitfully of Paul, saw him die a thousand different ways, shot in the Nazi prison as he tried to rescue me, drowned in the lake at Salzburg. Once I dreamed that I was back on the bridge in Kraków, the dead body beside me Paul's instead of the Kommandant's. I dreamed of the others who had died, too, my parents, Rose. Suddenly it seemed that I was to blame for all of their deaths, as well.

Each morning when I woke up, the reality would crash down upon me anew. Paul is dead. The pain was searing, fresh, as though I was hearing the news for the first time. I lay in the semidarkness for hours, seeing Paul's face. I replayed happy memories: Salzburg, Paris, even our first meeting in prison, ran through my head like a movie over and over again, until I drifted to sleep once more. The days passed like this, one after another. Delia, respecting my wishes, did not visit me again, at least not while I was awake. I knew, though, that she was keeping an eye on me through Charles, who brought me food of every variety, hearty stews that went uneaten, fruit that turned brown, ice cream that melted in the bowl. He knocked softly each time, bringing in the tray and setting it on the nightstand, then coming back for it a few hours later, without trying to engage me in conversation.

Charles must have come while I was asleep this time, as the aroma of fresh bacon wafts over me. My stomach grumbles. For the first time in days, I am hungry. I sit up in bed and uncover the tray, then pick up a piece of toast. As I take a bite, I catch a glimpse of my reflection in the mirror over the dresser. My hair is pressed flat against my head. My skin is pasty, with dark circles ringing my eyes. Unwashed and secluded, not eating. It is as if I've put myself back in prison, I think, ashamed. As if everything that has happened since my liberation was for nothing.

I finish the toast, take a few bites of bacon and eggs. Then I stand and walk to the toilet to wash. As I undress, Paul's dog tags fall cool against my chest. I look down at them sadly. Every step forward I take is a step farther from Paul and the time we had together. Suddenly I am overwhelmed by the urge to crawl back into bed. But that is not what he would have wanted, I think, remembering how I had scolded him for self-pity. Quickly, before I can change my mind, I finish washing and make my way back to the bedroom. Inside the armoire, my clothes hang freshly pressed. Delia must have had them cleaned. I have been such an ungracious guest. Quickly, I change into one of the dresses she gave me, green with a light floral pattern.

Downstairs, the kitchen is deserted, the breakfast dishes put away. I scribble a note on the tablet that hangs by the telephone, telling Delia that I've gone out. Then I walk to the front door and step out onto the porch. It is a brisk September morning, the air pleasantly cool. Across the street, the leaves on the trees in the square are still green, but there is a crispness to their rustling that was not there a few weeks earlier. I close the front gate behind me, cutting across the square. As I wind my way through the quiet residential streets, the houses grow even larger and more impressive than Delia's, their porches shielded from view by high hedges.

Soon I reach the wide thoroughfare of Kensington Road, several lanes of cars and buses speeding by in both directions. On the far side of the street sits the wide green swath of grass and trees that signals the edge of Hyde Park. I remember walking the paths with Delia, planning to take Paul for a stroll there after his arrival. My view is suddenly obscured by a red double-decker trolleybus that screeches to a stop in front of me. 'Getting on, miss?' the driver asks. I look up, realizing for the first time that I am standing in front of a bus stop. I hesitate. I have only taken the bus a few times with Delia, never alone. But I suddenly need to keep going, to get as far away from here as possible. 'Yes, thank you.' I board the bus, pulling a three pence coin from my pocket to pay the driver. As the bus lurches forward, I grab the nearest pole to keep from flying toward the rear.

When the bus stops at the next traffic light, I make my way up the stairs, clinging to the rail for support. The top deck is deserted, except for a lone man toward the rear, reading the *Times*. I remember suddenly the newspaper headline announcing Paul's death, his grainy image staring back at me. Forcing the vision from my mind, I drop to a seat by the front of the bus.

I look out the window as the bus reaches the end of Hyde Park and turns left, then quickly right again. The trees disappear and the street grows crowded with tall buildings and signs. Piccadilly, I recognize from my excursions with Delia. We pass Simpsons, the grand department store where she insisted on taking me shopping for new shoes, then the Ritz Hotel. Traffic is slow here, the sidewalks thick with pedestrians making their way between the shops. The bus stops every few minutes. I can hear the voices of the passengers as they board below. But these are commuters, oblivious to the view and they do not come upstairs. Soon we reach Piccadilly Circus. The buildings here are covered with enormous signs advertising products of every kind: Wrigley's Gum, Brylcreem, Gordon's Gin. *Guinness Is Good for You. Gives You Strength*, touts one. The bus grinds to a halt again. Ahead, the traffic does not move at all. All of a sudden I am eager to walk. I make my way down the stairs and step off the bus.

At the corner, I pause, uncertain which way to go. The crowd surges around me and, following, I let myself be carried with the stream. No one here knows or cares what I have been through. For a few minutes, I can pretend that I am just like everyone else. I imagine myself a young British woman on my way to work, perhaps in one of the shops. The sun is higher and the air has returned to its summer-like closeness. My skin grows moist under my dress as I walk.

The crowd loosens suddenly as the narrow street ends at an enormous square. In the center stands a tall obelisk. Trafalgar Square. My eyes travel from the height of the column to the four lion statues at its base, the adjacent fountains. I was here once with Delia on our way to a show in the West End. Then, as now, it seemed large and intimidating, worlds away from the quiet streets of South Kensington. I had not imagined coming this far on my own. A surge of confidence rises in me as I make my way through the swarms of pigeons and pedestrians to the far side of the square.

I turn right onto Whitehall. The wide thoroughfare is lined on both sides with government buildings, large and institutional. I soon reach an intersection, To the left sits the hulking yellow Westminster Palace, Big Ben jutting upward from its foreground. Looking up at the enormous Parliament building, I imagine the politicians inside, making decisions that affect the rest of the world. Suddenly, remembering how the West stood by while the Nazis marched across Europe, I am filled with anger. Why couldn't they have done something sooner?

Big Ben begins to chime. Eleven o'clock. Nearly two hours have passed since I left Delia's house. Ahead sits Westminster Abbey, its spires climbing high above the trees. I cross the wide street toward the grassy park area in front of the church. An ice-cream vendor sits at the corner. I hesitate. I should not spend the money, but I can practically taste the chocolate. I buy a small cone, licking it even as I make my way to the nearest empty bench.

Savoring the rich chocolate, I watch two squirrels playing in the grass. Then I look back across the road toward Whitehall at the pedestrians, men in suits, a few women. They walk with purpose, going to their jobs and other places in their lives. Sitting on the park bench with my ice cream, I suddenly feel very helpless and silly. 'What am I going to do with my life now? It is a question I have never had to answer. Growing up

178

in our village, my future had been presumed: marriage, to someone of a similar, lower-class, Jewish background, perhaps slightly better off if I was lucky. Then children, as many as could be had. That had all changed when the Nazis had come. Even after the war, my plans had not been wholly my own; I agreed to come to London at Dava's insistence, then later accepted Paul's proposal to marry him and move to America.

Now, for the first time, there is no one telling me what to do or offering me a plan. I have been at Delia's house for nearly a month, first waiting for Paul and then mourning him. I cannot impose on her hospitality forever. But where can I go? There is nothing for me in Poland, or in Salzburg anymore. I could apply for a visa to Palestine. Or to America. I imagine meeting Paul's family, paying my respects. But I have no money for the trip, no means of survival once I am there. And Paul's family would hardly welcome a strange immigrant girl, even if she was wearing their dead son's dog tags. We were engaged so quickly I doubt he even had time to let them know about me. To those who loved and will remember him, I never existed. My eyes burn with tears.

Enough. I cannot think about that, not now. Staying in England, where I have a roof over my head, makes the most sense. But I need to get a job, earn some money of my own so I can offer to pay for room and board. It will not be easy. I know from the papers and my conversations with Delia that with the soldiers returning and the economy still struggling to recover, it is hard for women to find work at all right now, much less a girl with a heavy accent and no experience. But Delia knows people, can make inquiries for me. A job in a shop. Boarding with Delia. My head swims. It is not the life I had expected. But it is a life.

Across the park, I spy a group of American soldiers taking pictures of Westminster Abbey. For a second my heart leaps. What if one of them was Paul, if we were magically reunited as we had been in Paris that day? But of course that is impossible. I look down at the ice-cream cone, suddenly disgusted by its gooey sweetness. I walk to the nearest bin to throw it away.

'You know, that's very wasteful,' a male voice says from behind me. I freeze, wondering for a second if my fantasy has come true, if Paul really is there. But the accent is British.

Unexpectedly I am angry. It is my ice-cream cone. How dare some stranger tell me what to do? 'That's none of your...' I turn to confront the stranger. Simon, the diplomat from the ship, stands behind me. 'Oh!'

'Simon Gold,' he says. He steps forward and, before I can react, takes my free hand and kisses it. 'We met on the boat.'

'Of course,' I reply, caught off guard. I remember our conversation over tea, my telling him of my engagement to Paul. It seems like a million years ago.

'My office is just around the corner.' He gestures vaguely toward Whitehall. 'I was just out for my daily constitutional.' I cock my head, unfamiliar with the term. 'It means walk,' he explains.

'Oh.' I feel something cold and sticky running down my hand. The ice cream has begun to melt.

'And I was only trying to say that Mitchell's homemade ice cream is too good to be wasted.' I nod, too surprised to respond. 'But it looks like that cone's had it.' He reaches out and takes the melting cone from my hand. Holding it at arm's length so as not to drip on his light-gray suit, he tosses it in the trash bin. 'Wait here.' I watch as Simon walks quickly over to the vendor where I purchased the ice-cream cone. I am glad to see him, I realize with surprise. A familiar face. A minute later, he returns with two steaming cups. 'Here,' he says, handing me a napkin. I wipe my hands. 'I thought maybe the ice cream had been too cold, so I took the liberty of getting us some tea.'

'Thank you.' I take one of the cups from him.

'Let's sit for a minute.' I follow him to the bench where I had been sitting minutes ago, balancing the tea carefully so as not to spill. 'I must say, I'm surprised to find you still here. I thought you'd be long on your way to America by now with your fiancé.'

I take a deep breath. 'He was killed.' It is the first time I have said this aloud since the morning I learned of the crash.

Simon's mouth opens slightly. 'I'm sorry to hear that. What happened?'

'The plane crash in the Channel.' I dig my fingernails into the bench, willing myself not to cry.

He presses his lips together. 'I read about that in the papers. Dreadful. All those brave soldiers lost. Again, I'm terribly sorry.'

'Thank you.' I look away. We drink our tea in

silence. Across the grass, a group of children kick a football. Their shrieks of laughter ring out.

'So what are you going to do now?' he asks a few minutes later.

I take another sip of tea. 'I'm still trying to figure that out. Stay in London, most likely. I don't have any family back in Poland, or anywhere else. At least here, I have a place to stay with my friend Rose's aunt. But I need to find a job.'

'You know, I'm still looking for an assistant.'

I remember then Simon offering me a job when we were on the ship. 'Oh, my goodness, I certainly wasn't hinting.'

'I know. But I told you on the boat that I would like for you to come work for me. My offer still stands.'

'Really?' He nods. I stare at him, surprised. I thought the offer was just talk, idle conversation. It had not occurred to me that he might have been serious. 'But I haven't any skills or office training.'

'All of that can be learned. You speak Polish, which is a huge asset in my work. And you can make out the other Slavic languages, too, I take it?'

'Yes. Czech and such. And a bit of Russian.'

He waves his hand. 'We have loads of Russian translators. I'm really more interested in your Polish. We have translators for that, too, of course, but it's so time-consuming to rely upon them for day-today matters. Having an assistant who can understand it directly would save a great deal of time.'

'I can understand German, too,' I add.

'And your English has improved a great deal. So what do you say?'

I hesitate. I had almost forgotten Simon's offer on the ship and I wasn't been prepared to consider it now. 'I don't know.'

'Look, Marta...' Simon leans in and lowers his voice. 'The truth is you would be doing me an enormous favor. When we spoke on the ship I told you about the work we are doing to fight communism in Eastern Europe. I really can't say any more until you've been hired and received a security clearance. But I can tell you that the situation has become much more serious in recent weeks.' His eyes burn with the same intensity I saw on the ship. 'We desperately need good people, people like you, to help us. So you wouldn't just be earning a living, you'd be helping Britain and your homeland. How can you pass up an offer like that?'

I bite my lip. 'Can I think about it?'

A surprised look crosses Simon's face, as if he is unaccustomed to people not immediately acquiescing to his requests. 'Certainly.' He starts to hand me a business card.

'I have one already,' I say. 'From the ship, remember?'

He puts the card back in his pocket. 'Of course. I just didn't want to presume that you had kept it. Call me either way and let me know what you decide. And don't wait too long,' he adds. 'I really need to fill this position.'

Then why hadn't he filled it? I wonder, in the weeks since we last spoke. There had to be plenty of Polish immigrants in London looking for work. I stand, brushing off my skirt. 'I really should be going.'

Simon rises and takes my hand. 'It was good to see you again.'

I take a step backward before he can kiss my hand. 'Good day.'

I walk quickly from the park, eager to get away. I am flustered by seeing Simon so unexpectedly and by his job offer. Walking up Whitehall past the imposing gray government buildings, I am flooded with doubt. Me, come to work each day, here? The idea of getting a job in London was frightening enough. I had imagined something simple, working in a store close to Delia's house. A few weeks ago I did not even know if I could get into Britain. The notion of coming into central London and working at the Foreign Office every day seems incomprehensible. My English is not good enough. I do not have any office skills. Simon said that these things don't matter. But in truth, my hesitation is more than that. It just feels too soon. I'm not ready to wake up from my memories of Paul, from my grieving.

Retracing my steps through Trafalgar Square, I make my way back to Piccadilly Circus and board a bus that is going toward South Kensington. I pay the driver, then sink into a seat, not bothering to climb to the upper deck. As the bus lurches forward, I think about Simon's offer once more. A chance to help, he said. I think guiltily of Emma, left behind in Eastern Europe. What was her life like now? Working with Simon, I might be able to make a difference. A shiver runs through me and I remember like a faint dream the feeling I used to have when working for the resistance of fighting for something that mattered. Maybe losing myself in the challenge is just what I need. And it will surely pay more than a job in the shops. I will ask Delia's opinion when I get back to the house, I decide.

I stare out the window at the shops as we make our way down Piccadilly. A few minutes later, as we reach the edge of Hyde Park, exhaustion washes over me. It must be from all of the walking after lying in bed for so many days, I think, my shoulders slumping. The driver slams hard on the breaks, bringing the bus to an abrupt halt. I raise my hand as I am thrown forward to keep from slamming into the seat in front of me. 'Sorry folks,' the driver calls. 'A dog ran across the road.' As I straighten, a sudden wave of nausea sweeps over me. I leap from my seat and race to the front of the bus. 'I need to get off,' I say weakly to the driver.

'But ma'am, we're in the middle of traffic. I'm not allowed to let you off where there's no stop.'

I bring my hand to my mouth. 'Please, I feel very ill.'

The driver shakes his head and I run down the steps and dash hurriedly through the traffic. Horns blare. I cross the sidewalk and reach the bushes on the far side just in time to duck my head behind them. Retching violently, I bring up the ice cream and the tea, then the breakfast I'd eaten that morning. A minute later, when my stomach calms, I look up. The grass and benches nearby are dotted with people eating lunch and talking or reading. None seem to have noticed me being sick. I wipe my mouth with my sleeve, then make my way to a nearby bench. A cool sweat breaks out on my forehead. What is wrong with me? I cannot afford to get sick, not now. Perhaps it's food poisoning. But I was nauseous the morning after Paul did not arrive, too, and that was a week ago. Paul. Suddenly I see his face above me in the Paris hotel room, silhouetted in the moonlight. It has been nearly a month since our night together. An uneasy feeling rises in me.

Impossible, I think. I cannot be pregnant, not from that one night. But the idea nags at me. I remember my last period in Salzburg, count the days. It was due some time ago, I realize now for the first time. In my preoccupation with Paul's death, I had not thought to notice. Dread slices through me. My cycle must be off, I think desperately, from the stress of all that has happened. It will come any day now. But my uneasiness persists as I stand up and make my way back to the road.

Thirty minutes later I walk through the front door of Delia's house. I find Delia in the kitchen, sleeves rolled up, kneading dough. It looks as though a bag of flour exploded – the counter-tops, stove and floor are covered in white. 'Hello, dear,' she says, not looking up. 'I'm just baking some scones.'

I smile. Though Charles does most of the cooking, Delia likes to bake. Or try. More than once, I have seen Charles wait patiently while Delia puts her creations in the oven, then clean up the mess she has made. Later, he will dispose of many of the scones, telling her that they were so delicious he ate them.

The odor of food makes my stomach turn once

more. 'That smells good,' I fib, dropping into a kitchen chair. 'I'm sorry I was gone so long.'

'I saw your note. I was glad to see you up and about. Where did you go?'

'Walking.' I describe my route. 'I would have been back earlier but I ran into someone whom I had met on the ship coming over.' I tell her about Simon and his work for the Foreign Office. Then I pause. 'He offered me a job.'

Delia looks up, puzzled. 'I don't understand.'

'He works on East European affairs for the Foreign Office. He said he needs an assistant who speaks Polish. He made the same offer when we met on the ship.' I swallow. 'Then, of course, I thought I would be leaving for America after a few weeks. But now...'

'Does that mean you are thinking about staying in England permanently?'

I hesitate. 'I am,' I reply slowly. 'I mean, where else would I go? There's no one, nothing back in Poland for me. And nothing in America anymore.' I force down the lump that has formed in my throat. 'Of course, I would find my own place to live. I don't expect you to put me up forever.'

'But I love having you here!' Delia exclaims. 'Can't you see that? It's just me and Charles in this big old house. Having a young person around has given it new life.' I can tell from Delia's voice that she is sincere. I look up at the ceiling, noticing for the first time the places where the plaster had shaken loose from the bombing. They suffered here, too. Maybe not in the same way as we had back home, but no one escaped the war unscathed. Delia continues, 'I understand, a young woman might want her own space. But I really wish you would consider living with us.'

I look around, amazed at how much Delia's house has come to feel like home. 'I would love to stay.'

Delia's face breaks into a wide smile. 'Wonderful!'

'But not for free. As soon as I start working, I'll be able to pay room and board.'

'That's not necessary,' Delia says quickly.

'I know, but I want to. It would make me feel better.'

'We can discuss that later,' Delia relents. 'So what did you tell him? Mr. Gold, I mean. Are you seriously thinking about taking the job?'

'I don't know. It's a big step. Originally, I was thinking of something closer by, like a job in one of the shops. But this would pay well, I think, and be interesting.'

'And this Mr. Gold, is he married?'

'Oh, Delia,' I say, not knowing the answer. I remember the way he looked at me as he kissed my hand. 'I'm not thinking of that. It's too soon.' In truth, I cannot imagine ever wanting to be with someone else. For a second, I consider sharing with Delia my fear that I might be pregnant. But I am too embarrassed. It is probably nothing. 'I think he just needs an assistant.'

'Are you sure you're ready to go to work?'

'I don't know,' I admit. 'But he needs someone to start right away. It may be a good thing, to be busy, to find some purpose again. Sitting around and thinking about what could have been with Paul much longer is going to kill me.'

'It sounds like you've decided,' Delia says, and I know then that I have. She gestures to the phone that hangs on the kitchen wall. 'Why don't you go ahead and call Mr. Gold and tell him you'll take that job?'

CHAPTER 13

'The embassy in Budapest delivered an official communiqué protesting the handling of certain matters with respect to the repatriation of ethnic minorities...' Ian St. James, the white-haired deputy minister, reads from the notes prepared by his aide, papers held close to his spectacles. He has been speaking for more than an hour about the political situation in Hungary and I am still not sure what he is trying to say. His voice is monotone and nasal, its rhythm unchanging regardless of whether he is talking about war or the weather. I imagine him announcing the Allied invasion of Normandy in much the same manner.

I cross and uncross my legs, flexing my feet back and forth to relieve the cramping sensation I always get from sitting in the stiff wooden chairs for too long. I rub my eyes beneath my glasses, then replace them and scan the long conference room table that occupies much of the room. The men seated around it – middle-aged, dark-suited and pale to a one – are the heads of the European Directorate, or in the case of a few of the larger departments, their deputies. Some head up individual countries or groups. ('I'm Benelux,' I heard one man say at a party, which Simon later explained meant that he was in charge of Belgium, the Netherlands and Luxembourg.) Others work in topical areas, economic recovery or political-military. A few, including Simon, specialize in intelligence. They listen to the deputy minister (or the 'D.M.' as he is often called, though never to his face) with varying degrees of interest, some seeming to hang on to his every word, others shuffling through papers in front of them, reading surreptitiously. One man I do not recognize is sleeping, his eyes shut and mouth slightly agape. The perimeter of the room is ringed with other women, secretaries like me in dark pencil skirts and long-sleeved blouses. If they are bored, they give no indication, but sit erect, heads down, scribbling diligently as the D.M. speaks.

I shift my weight, straightening. My eyes travel down the row of men to Simon, who sits close to the head of the table. He wears a scowl, and for a moment I wonder if he noticed me fidgeting and is displeased. His gaze catches mine. A weary smile, echoing my own feelings of boredom and impatience, flickers across his face so quickly I wonder if I might have imagined it. Then he looks up at the D.M., his expression impassive once more.

Simon. My eyes linger on his face. My husband. Though we have been married for more than two years, it is still sometimes hard to believe. Simon first asked me out a few days after I came to work for him at the Foreign Office. His overture was small and tentative: an invitation to drinks after work. 'You should not feel obliged to accept,' he said quickly. 'Just because of our professional relationship.'

At first, I declined. Just weeks after Paul's death, I had no interest in fun. But Simon persisted, asking me to join him for lunch the next day. I remember him standing over my desk, his watery-blue eyes hopeful. 'Fine, thank you,' I relented.

After I accepted his first invitation, he quickly grew more forward, inviting me to dinner or the theater several times per week. Once I accompanied him to a party thrown by a diplomat and his wife who had just returned from a tour in Bombay at their stylish Notting Hill home. I sampled spicy curry dishes that made my nose run, sipped an exotic cocktail called a kir.

'I'm proud of you, Marta,' Delia remarked once. 'For having moved on so bravely with your life after, well, the American boy...'

'Mmm,' I had replied vaguely. Of course, I had not really moved on. Simon's company was pleasant enough. He talked passionately about international politics, told fabulous stories of his travels in Eastern Europe as a student that reminded me of my childhood home. Our dates were a welcome distraction, an escape from the long evenings at Delia's, haunted by my memories of Paul. And I was grateful to Simon, of course, for my job. But sometimes as he squired me to dinners and parties, I felt guilty. Was I misleading him? Simon knew about my engagement to Paul and my recent loss, though, and still seemed eager to court me. I had not thought of it as more, though, and so I was quite stunned when, just four weeks after he first asked me out, Simon proposed marriage.

It was on a day trip to Brighton as we strolled along the promenade by the sea that Simon turned to me and pulled a small velvet box from his pocket. 'I know we've only been seeing each other for a short time. But I'm very fond of you, Marta, and I think we can have a fine life together.'

I did not answer right away but gazed out across the Channel. Considering his tepid proposal, I could not help but think of Paul, dropping to one knee on the rain-soaked Paris street, eyes burning, as he asked me to marry him. I had not considered marrying anyone else. Simon was not Paul. I could never love him in that way. But Paul was gone. I looked back at Simon, who had taken the ring from the box and was holding it out toward me. He was not unattractive, and I knew from the other secretaries that, as one of the only single men in the department, he was considered quite a good prospect, if something of an enigma. He liked me, and he would not be unkind. 'Fine,' I said, realizing too late that mine was not the most gracious of responses. 'I mean, I would love to marry you.'

We were married in a small ceremony in Delia's parlor the following week by a rabbi Simon knew. Neither of us seemed to want a long engagement, or a big wedding. Simon was an only child and his parents had both died, his mother at a young age of cancer and his father of a heart attack shortly after Simon had left for college. I, of course, had no family. So the wedding consisted of Delia and Charles on my side, a few colleagues on his. Simon was unable to get away from work for a honeymoon just then, but he promised me a trip somewhere grand over the winter holiday.

But the honeymoon never took place. A few weeks after we were married, the nausea I felt in the park that day worsened, often making it difficult for me to get to work in the mornings. The doctor Simon insisted I see confirmed my unspoken suspicion: I was pregnant. Seven months later, I gave birth to a baby girl, Rachel.

Voices at the conference room table pull me from my thoughts. The D.M. has indicated that we will conclude for the day, and now the men at the table are standing, shuffling papers as they speak to one another. Inwardly, I groan. I had hoped that the meeting would have finished in one sitting, even if it meant working a bit late. But now the meeting will resume tomorrow morning. I do not relish the prospect of staying awake through a second day of the D.M.'s droning.

As I stand, I try to catch Simon's eyes again. Perhaps I can find an excuse to skip the morning session tomorrow, plead an excess of correspondence to type. But he is engaged in conversation with one of the men across the table and does not meet my gaze. I will ask him tonight, if he does not get home too late. I take my notebook and walk from the conference room toward the elevator, press the down button. Simon and a few of the men enter the corridor behind me, still debating a point about Hungary. The elevator door opens and I step inside, but the men do not

193

follow. As the doors close, I look in Simon's direction one more time. He does not notice, but remains engrossed in conversation.

What happened to that man who courted me so attentively? I muse as the elevator descends to the third floor. At the end of the hall, I push open the door of the office, entering the small reception area where my desk sits. To the left, another closed door leads to Simon's office. He seemed so pleased the day I accepted his proposal. But things changed quickly after we married. I set down my notepad and pick up my bag from behind the desk. Putting on my coat, I make my way to the elevator once more.

I cross the lobby and step out onto the street, joining the stream of government workers headed to the buses at Trafalgar Square. It is nearly dark and the damp air has a biting chill, more winter than autumn now. A few minutes later, I board the bus, still thinking about Simon. It is not that he is unkind. He is unfailingly pleasant, and on the rare occasions when I ask him to do something around the house or go somewhere with Rachel and me, he readily obliges. But the rest of the time, he lives in his own world, spending long hours at the office, holing up in his study at night.

Sometimes, I reflect, as the bus makes its way slowly through the traffic-clogged city streets, I almost wish for the occasional temper or spat, some reaction to my presence. But that would take more energy than he cares to give. Outwardly he appears an attentive husband, holding my arm and listening. Once at a department social function, I overheard him refer to me as his 'dear wife' with a tilt of his head that suggested affection. But the moment we walk through the front door of the house, all signs of interest disappear. It is as if he likes the idea of having a wife, as if I was simply something to be acquired, like a fine car or painting.

Fifty minutes later, I step off the bus at Hampstead High Street, drawing the neck of my coat closed against the wind. Making my way past the closing shops, I turn onto a residential street lined with tall row houses. Ours is second from the end on the right. From a distance it looks like the others, wide windows, a tidy front lawn. Only as one draws closer are the differences apparent: the way the left porch column seems to slump in defeat, the cracks that run up the steps. Simon, who inherited the house from his parents and lived here on his own for more than fifteen years, does not seem to notice the decay. In the early months of our marriage, I tried to improve upon the appearance of the house, tending to the garden and planting flowers, painting the peeling front door a fresh white. But as I grew larger with my pregnancy, I was not able to do as much, and after Rachel was born, I was too busy to care.

Perhaps I would have done more if Simon had seemed to notice. I walk up the porch steps and pick up a toy ball that lies near the front door, carry it inside. A savory aroma fills the air. 'Hello?'

Delia walks into the foyer, wiping her hands on an apron. 'Hello,' she whispers, kissing me on the cheek, then gesturing upward to indicate that Rachel is sleeping. 'I only just put her down.'

'Are you cooking?'

She laughs quietly. 'Me? No, Charles sent over shepherd's pie. I was just heating that up for you.'

'Thank you,' I reply, meaning it. When I announced I was going back to work at the Foreign Office a few months after the baby was born, Delia immediately offered to watch her. I worried that caring for Rachel might be too much, but Delia persisted and we agreed to try the arrangement. It works beautifully – Delia loves being with Rachel and can hardly bring herself to leave at the end of each day. And the baby adores Delia, as well. Sometimes watching the two of them together, I am overwhelmed by sadness that Rachel would never know my parents, who died so many miles away. 'You don't have to warm all of the food, though,' I add, taking off my coat. 'I expect Simon to be late this evening.'

Delia's lips purse and a furrow creases her brow. Though too polite to say anything, she is well aware of Simon's late hours working, how little time he spends at home. 'I'll leave him a plate in the icebox, then. Shall I stay with you while you eat?'

I shake my head. 'That's not necessary.' I enjoy Delia's company, but I know that she is eager to get home to Charles.

When she has gone, I walk into the kitchen. It is spacious, constructed with marble countertops and oak cabinets that had been the finest on offer in their day. But the appliances are old now, the faucets and handles worn. I fix myself a plate, then carry it to the parlor. The house, I think, not for the first time, had once been grand: a large parlor and dining room for entertaining, high ceilings, elegant, detailed molding. But the furniture is faded and worn, the wood floors creak with age.

As I sit down on the sofa, a framed photograph on the mantel over the fireplace catches my eye. It is a picture of Rachel, playing by the pond on the heath last spring. Rachel, I think, my insides warming. Rachel Hannah Gold. Before the baby was born, I hesitated. I wanted to name her after Rose. But the Jewish tradition was to name after someone who had a long, healthy life, and Rose had not. So we named her Rachel and honored the memory of my mother, Hadassah, with Rachel's middle name.

It was Simon who had suggested using the same first letter in English and making her Hebrew name, Rivka, the same as Rose's. Simon is Jewish, too, at least in name. Twice yearly, we dress up and make our way to the synagogue, nodding at the faces we recognize only from the previous year. The grand, formal synagogue could not be more different from our own tiny shul back in the village. I miss the weekly ritual of going to synagogue, the warmth of being surrounded by people whom I had known my whole life. But for Simon, the obligatory semiannual pilgrimage is enough. Once I tried to bring some warmth into the house by preparing Shabbat dinner. Simon watched with an unfamiliar eye as I lit the candles, cut the challah that I had baked from scratch. He politely ate dinner, then excused himself to his study.

I swallow a mouthful of potatoes, still looking at Rachel's photograph. I had hoped that, once Rachel was born, Simon might become more present at home. He makes small outward gestures, placing her picture on his desk and dutifully joining us on a family outing each Sunday to the park or the zoo. But beyond that he is as indifferent to her as he is to me. When he does hold her, it is gingerly and at arm's length, as if childhood is contagious, a disease not to be caught.

Indeed, he did not even seem to notice how quickly Rachel arrived after our marriage. 'Premature!' Delia exclaimed when she came to visit us at the hospital, sounding as though she meant it. I studied Simon's face as he held up the tiny baby for Delia to see. Did he suspect anything? But Simon seemed to accept Rachel's early arrival without question. The respectability that family brought was good for his career.

I finish eating, bring my plate to the kitchen sink. As I wash, I look at the clock. It is not yet eight, which means Simon won't be home for at least an hour. Loneliness rises in me. My days are busy, but it is always this quiet evening hour that is the hardest. I put the kettle on for tea. What did I expect? I ask myself a few minutes later as I carry a cup and saucer back into the parlor, walking slowly so as not to spill. I should be grateful to have a nice home, a husband who comes home each night. I had imagined marriage as something more, though. Intimate looks across a crowded room, shared jokes whispered in the darkness at night. Would marriage to Paul have been any different? I push the thought quickly away. It is not fair, I know, to compare everyday life with Simon to a fantasy frozen in time. And there is no point in thinking about what I cannot have, in making my marriage seem even more pallid by comparison. But it is too late. A dull ache rises in my stomach as I imagine driving across America in a convertible beside Paul, seeing the world and laughing. Marriage to Paul would not have been like this.

Sitting down on the sofa once more, I force my thoughts back to Simon. I know that I should not take his behavior personally. Simon is distant from everyone. He has no family, other than some cousins he's mentioned scattered throughout the north. And he speaks little of his parents. Their wedding photograph, a grainy sepia image that sits on the mantelpiece, is the only reminder of them. There is a trunk, Simon once said, of their belongings in the attic. When I pressed him, he promised to show it to me one day. I want to go through the trunk, to see if there are any family mementos I can pass on to Rachel, since I have none of my own to give her.

I also quickly discovered once we were married that Simon has no friends. The whirlwind of dates and social occasions I experienced during our courtship quickly disappeared after the wedding. Except for the occasional obligatory departmental function, we seldom go out. In the beginning, I considered trying to make friends of my own. But how? Our neighbors, used to Simon's long-standing reclusiveness, keep their distance. The other secretaries, unmarried women without husbands or children, eye me warily, resentful, I suspect, of my audacity in daring to have a husband *and* a job. And Delia lives on the other side of London, too far away for short visits. So I spend my evenings rattling around the creaky old house, until I am unable to read or listen to the radio any longer.

Is it really so much better when Simon is here? The weekend nights, when we have dinner together, are not unpleasant. Simon will update me on some of the meetings I have not attended at work and I will share stories about Rachel. Last weekend, when I told him how she played in the bath, we actually laughed. But those moments are fleeting, pale imitations of what I had thought a marriage to be. And afterward, he retreats quickly to his study. Simon and I are like young children I have seen in the park sitting beside each other in the sandbox but playing alone, not interacting. Two people living separate lives in the same space.

When the clock above the mantelpiece reads nine, I carry my empty teacup back into the kitchen. Upstairs, I tiptoe past Simon's study, pausing in the door of Rachel's room. I fight the urge to go to her and pick her up, settling instead for listening to her quiet, even breathing for several minutes. I walk to our bedroom, then into the toilet to wash and change. I study my reflection in the mirror over the sink. Have I changed so from the woman Simon wanted to court and marry? My jawline has softened a bit and I see a couple of hairs that have turned prematurely gray, a trait I inherited from my mother. I know, too, that my figure is a bit fuller than it once was, owing to a few pounds that lingered after my pregnancy. Perhaps if I lost those ... but even as I think it, I know that it will not make a difference in gaining

Simon's attention.

Do I care? I consider the question as I climb into bed and turn out the light. Things have been this way for so long. And it is not as if I have ever felt passionately about Simon, not in the way I did with Paul. In the early days of our marriage, his lack of interest came almost as a relief, matching my own ambivalence. But his near-constant disinterest bruises my ego, and inside, I ache for affection.

My thoughts are interrupted by noise from below. The front door opening, I realize. Simon is home. I hear him walk into the kitchen, open the icebox door and close it again. Then there are footsteps on the stairs. I sit up. I do not dare to hope for physical attention; our lovemaking is perfunctory and scheduled, thirty minutes on Saturday nights after we've finished dinner and he has had two gin and tonics. But perhaps he will tell me about his day, and then I can ask him about skipping the morning meeting tomorrow. Then I hear him open the study door and close it again behind him. My heart sinks and I lay back down, closing my eyes and willing myself to sleep.

The next morning at eight-twenty-five, I pick up my notepad and make my way back down the hall to the conference room. Most of the secretaries are already seated, the men clustered around the table, talking. The diplomats' conversations, I know, are cordial, professional. But below the surface there is fierce competition and politics. Who has the most relevant information? Whose point of view will hold most sway with the D.M.?

We should all be focused on a common goal, but the disputes are petty, the games personal.

The D.M. enters the room and the men quickly take their seats. 'Let's move on to Bucharest,' he begins, as though we had only taken a short break and not adjourned for the evening. Looking down at my blank notepad, I realize I wrote down nothing of the discussion yesterday regarding Hungary. I scan my memory, trying to remember what was said, but it is useless. I should pay attention, I know. Simon will want me to prepare a memorandum.

Instead, I look out the window across the conference room where the morning sun shines brightly through the bare tree branches. Delia will take Rachel to the park today. Having Delia to watch Rachel made it easier for me to return to work, a decision that had been a source of disagreement between me and Simon. At first, he flatly refused. 'None of the other diplomats' wives work. And now with the baby, it would be unheard of.'

'But my work is important to me. Remember how much you said you needed me, back when we first met?' Simon did not answer, but ultimately he relented, as I knew he would. The truth was, we needed the money. Simon's family had been wealthy, the kind of money, Delia told me once, that had been handed down for generations, rather than earned. But Simon's father lost nearly everything in the stock market crashes, leaving Simon with only the house and a little money for its upkeep or the small fortune to heat it in winter. Simon's government salary had barely been enough to keep the house going when he was a bachelor, I discovered soon after we were married; it would not stretch to support a wife and child. So I continued working at the Foreign Office, though many days like this one, I wished I was home playing with Rachel.

Of course, part of me still wants to work, still believes in what we are trying to do. But that part is getting harder to find anymore. All of my days at the Foreign Office are much like this one, taking notes in endless meetings, then typing up the notes afterward or preparing correspondence that Simon dictates. No one ever seems to actually do anything but talk. Watching the bureaucracy, it is easy to understand how Hitler was able to walk over Europe while the West dithered. Meanwhile, the countries of Eastern Europe keep falling: Romania, Bulgaria, Hungary. Simon keeps a map of Europe over his desk and puts a red pin on each country as it falls. I know he shares my frustration at our inability to stop it.

My thoughts are interrupted by a banging sound. I look up as the door to the conference room swings open. The D.M. stops speaking and all heads in the room snap toward the door. The briefing is classified. Everyone who is allowed to be here is already present and interruptions are nonexistent. A young man I recognize as one of the office messengers pauses in the doorway. 'My apologies,' he mumbles, then walks directly to the head of the table, looking neither right nor left. He hands a piece of paper to the D.M. 'Urgent from the minister's office.'

The D.M. scans the paper, pressing his lips

together tightly. 'Send word back I'll be there within the hour.' The messenger nods and flees the room as quickly as he came. The D.M. turns back to the men gathered at the table. 'I'm afraid I'm going to need to terminate the general meeting. Intelligence principals stay, please.' There is a shuffling of chairs as about half the men at the table stand and leave the room, their secretaries in tow. The remaining half, including Simon, move closer to the head of the table. When the door has closed again, the D.M. addresses the remaining group. 'Bad news, I'm afraid. One of our foreign nationals has been killed.'

A low murmur ripples across the table. 'Where, sir?' one of the men asks.

'St. Petersburg. He was supposed to meet his contact but he never showed. He was found dead in his apartment, supposedly of a heart attack. It's the third one in six months.'

'Fourth, if you count Tersky,' Simon replies. I remember hearing the name before, a contact in Odessa who had survived an attack meant to kill him, but which instead left him in a permanent coma.

'I don't think we can avoid the truth any longer. We have an internal leak. Someone is tipping off the Russians, providing them with names of our contacts and their meetings. We need to find him. Until we do, our intelligence operations are hobbled.'

'What about the list, sir?' one of the men asks. Though I hadn't heard it discussed in the meetings before, Simon mentioned a list that had been intercepted by our station in Vienna last month that was believed to contain the names of those working for the Russians.

The D.M. shakes his head. 'So far no one has been able to break the code. The cryptographers are working on it, but they say it will take time. Time that we don't have.'

'We need to get our hands on the cipher,' Simon remarks. Heads around the table bob in agreement.

'I agree, but how? None of our contacts in Moscow are well placed enough to access it, and even if they were we would have to assume that their identities have been compromised.'

'What about Jan Marcelitis?' a voice at the end of the table asks. All heads turn in the direction of Roger Smith, the youngest of the intelligence officers. Jan Marcelitis. A ripple runs through the room. I cannot help but shiver. Alek and Jacob used to speak of Marcelitis with near-reverence for his work crossing enemy lines to get information to the Allies, and I heard of him again soon after arriving at the Foreign Office. Yet despite all of the talk, no one seems to have ever met or seen Marcelitis. Conversations about him are always mired in legend and myth, the stories as implausible as they are contradictory: He took on a whole unit of the SS single-handedly during the war. He is really American. He is really a communist. Recently I'd heard that Marcelitis had grown distrustful of the West during the war and now worked independently fostering grassroots opposition to the communists. Smith continues, 'I mean, isn't it true that when Dichenko disappeared from Soviet intelligence a few weeks ago, one of the ciphers went with him, headed west? Surely he was taking it to Marcelitis.'

'That's a rumor,' one of the other men replies. 'Dichenko is in all likelihood at the bottom of the Moscow River and the cipher – if he ever took one – is with him.'

The younger man shakes his head. 'I heard that someone saw him in Riga not two weeks ago on his way to see Marcelitis.'

'Saw Marcelitis where?' a voice farther down the table asks. 'We have no idea where to find him.'

'He's like a ghost,' the D.M. agrees. Around the table, heads nod. The communist authorities in various countries have long sought to arrest him, as had the Gestapo before them. As a result, Marcelitis operates from behind the scenes, not keeping a permanent address or residing in one country for very long. I remember Alek saying once that Marcelitis was able to do what he did so well because he had no ties, no wife or family to keep him in one place.

'I've heard that Marcelitis may be on the ground in Prague,' Roger replies. 'It would make sense with everything that is going on there.' Czechoslovakia, I knew from past meetings, had managed to resist Soviet domination, its government a delicate balance of communists and non-communists. But the situation there had grown increasingly unstable, the communist interior minister, backed by the police, trying to force out government ministers with pro-Western leanings. There was talk of a possible coup.

'But even if Marcelitis is there, and has the cipher Dichenko stole, that doesn't mean he'll

206

cooperate,' Simon adds.

'Perhaps,' the D.M. concedes. 'But we have to try. Marcelitis is our best, make that our *only* option, for getting the cipher.' He looks down at his chargé d'affaires, seated immediately to his left. 'Johnson, who are our contacts in Prague, the ones who may be able to access Marcelitis?'

Johnson rustles through his notes. 'There aren't many. Karol Hvany, for one...'

A voice comes from farther down the table. 'I'm sorry, sir, but Hvany was arrested a few weeks ago.'

Johnson continues reading. 'Demaniuk, the fellow from the countryside.'

'We have reason to believe he's been compromised,' Simon replies.

The D.M. takes the paper from Johnson and scans it. 'And Stefan Bak died six months ago.' He throws down the paper. 'Damn! There has to be someone.' A few of the men at the table exchange furtive glances, surprised at the D.M.'s uncharacteristic outburst.

Johnson picks up the paper from the table and scans it once more. 'There is one other possibility. Fellow named Marek Andek.'

Marek Andek. Suddenly it is as if someone kicked me in the stomach, knocking the wind from me. Marek Andek. I repeat the name in my head, wondering if I heard him correctly.

'What do we know about Andek?' the D.M. asks. My heart seems to stop for a second and then beat again very rapidly. Marek was one of the resistance leaders, second in command under Alek.

'Not much,' Johnson replies. 'Except that he is a civil servant and loosely affiliated to the opposition leadership. Andek is known to have gone to Berlin to see Marcelitis a few months ago. Problem is, we don't have anyone who knows him.'

'I do,' I blurt out. All heads snap in my direction.

'Excuse me?' Johnson asks, his voice a mixture of annoyance and disbelief. 'Did you say something?'

I take a deep breath. 'Y-yes, I said that I know Marek Andek.'

CHAPTER 14

The room is completely silent. I look down, desperately wishing that the floor would open and swallow me whole. Out of the corner of my eye, I see Simon's stunned expression. Secretaries do not ever speak in meetings. To do so in here, where the D.M. is present, is unthinkable.

'You know Andek?' the D.M. repeats incredulously.

I hesitate, wondering if I should recant, say that my outburst was a mistake. But it is too late to stop. 'Y-yes,' I reply, my voice trembling. A murmur ripples through the room.

'Marta,' Simon warns in a low voice, then stands up to face the D.M. 'Sir, I am terribly sorry for this interruption. My assistant seems to have forgotten herself.' His assistant, not his wife.

'There is no way she knows this man. I'm sure there's some mistake.' I open my mouth to say that there is no mistake. Then, seeing Simon's furious expression, I close it again.

The D.M. looks from Simon to me, then back. 'Very well.' He turns to the table. 'Keep looking for contacts in Prague who...' I sit motionless, unable to hear him over the ringing in my ears. Marek's fat face and squinty eyes appear in my mind. I never liked Marek. He was boorish, with none of Alek's charm or Jacob's wit. I last saw Marek at a cabin outside Kraków that had served as one of our hideaways, the day after the resistance had bombed the Warszawa Café. He was going over the border to Slovakia, he said, to try to make contact with other resistance groups. Watching him as he stood in the door of the cabin clutching his rucksack, I was flooded with disbelief. He was the only one capable of leading our group now – how could he possibly be leaving? Alek never would have abandoned us if he had lived. But Marek fled, leaving the rest of us to fend for ourselves. Within days, the remainder of the resistance had disintegrated.

It is the same Marek Andek, I am certain. He must have survived the border crossing and the war, then somehow linked up with Marcelitis. Had he seen or heard from Emma and Jacob? Digging my nails into my palms, I force myself to concentrate on the meeting once more. The D.M. is making some concluding remarks, ending much sooner than I had anticipated. Does the abrupt conclusion have to do with the message from the minister's office? Or with my outburst?

When the meeting ends, I slip quickly from the room, not wanting to face Simon. He is usually so calm and even-tempered, I reflect as I make my way down the corridor. But decorum and appearances, his place in the department, mean everything to him. No wonder he was furious. I stop at the ladies' toilet. As I wash my hands at the sink, I berate myself inwardly. I should not have spoken out like that. I have never told Simon about my work with the resistance. I had to tell him the truth about my coming to England on Rose's visa so that he could straighten out the paperwork when applying for my residency and our marriage license. Beyond that all he knows is that I was liberated from the camps. Why hadn't I said anything? In the beginning, I feared that the truth would be too much, that Simon would not want me working for him for fear that my past would come to light and taint him. And later, when we were married and it seemed that I should have told him already, the not telling became a bigger problem than the secret itself. More recently, it had simply become a part of my distant past that I seldom considered, something that no longer mattered. Until today.

When I return to the office, Simon is standing in front of my desk, arms crossed. 'What were you thinking?' he says. Alarmed, I take two steps back, trying to get as far away from him as I can in the tiny, windowless reception area. 'Are you trying to ruin my career?'

Fear rises in me. I have never seen him this angry. 'Simon, I'm so sorry,' I begin. 'I didn't mean...'

'You cannot go forgetting your place, embarrassing me, just because you're my wife.' His nostrils flare. *'Especially* because you're my wife. And what makes you think you know this person? I am sure that there is more than one Marek Andek in all of Eastern Europe!'

'But...' I hesitate. I am sure it is the same man, but I cannot tell Simon this without explaining my entire past.

'Why do you think you know Marek Andek?' he demands.

'That is something I would like to know myself,' a voice from behind Simon says. We spin around to find the D.M. standing in the doorway.

'Sir,' Simon says, surprise replacing anger in his voice. I, too, am taken aback. It is the first time I have ever known the D.M. to come to Simon's office.

The D.M. looks over his shoulder into the hallway, then back into the room. 'Perhaps we should go into your office to talk.'

He is looking at both of us, I realize. I pick up a notepad and follow the two men into Simon's office. It is about three-by-four meters, more than twice the size of the reception area, with a wide window looking down on a grassy area. Simon's desk is dark, institutional wood, and completely bare except for a picture of Rachel in the upper left-hand corner. Aside from a large map of Europe, only his Cambridge diploma and a few certificates of recognition from various government officials hang on the walls.

'Sir, I apologize again for my assistant's outburst,' Simon begins after I have closed the door behind me. His assistant again. 'I was just telling Marta that just because she knew a man called Andek in Poland, there's no reason to think that this is the same one she knew.'

The D.M. turns to me. 'What do you think?'

I swallow, unaccustomed to the question. 'I think he may be.'

'But that's impossible,' Simon interjects. 'For one thing, Andek is Czech, not Polish.'

'Actually, he's not,' the D.M. replies. 'Our intelligence reflects that he fled Poland during the war.'

I nod. 'He told me he was going south over the border the last time I saw him.'

The D.M. crosses the room, drawing close to me. 'Describe him.'

'About this tall.' I raise my hand above my head. 'Brown hair. And he has a scar here.' I move my hand in a semicircle under my right eye, recalling the wound he received when a bomb he was building detonated accidentally. 'Jewish,' I add. 'He was a member of the resistance against the Nazis.'

'And how do you know that?' Simon demands.

I turn, meeting his eyes. 'Because I was a member of the resistance, too.'

There is silence for several seconds. 'The resistance?' Simon repeats slowly, disbelieving. I nod.

The D.M. pulls out one of the two chairs in front of Simon's desk. 'Tell us everything.'

I sit down, then take a deep breath. 'I was living in the Kraków ghetto with my mother when I was recruited by the resistance,' I begin.

The D.M. looks at Simon. 'In Kraków? I

thought the resistance was in Warsaw.'

'There was a resistance movement in Kraków, too,' Simon replies. 'I remember reading about it in a cable. Smaller, not as significant.' His words stab at me.

'Go on,' the D.M. says.

'I worked as a messenger for the resistance, traveling the countryside and gathering information and weapons.' Staring out the window, I tell them about the bombing of the Warszawa Café, how the resistance was decimated in the aftermath. I do not tell them about my friendship with Emma or how I killed Kommandant Richwalder to save her, nor about Jacob. 'And so after the café bombing, most of the resistance leadership was killed or arrested, like me. But Andek was neither, and he told me he was going over the border to Slovakia to connect with partisans there.'

When I finish, I look up. Simon stares at me, stunned. The D.M. turns to him. 'You had no idea?'

He shakes his head. 'We ran a background check for security purposes when she started working here, of course. But it's difficult to get information. All of the papers were destroyed during the war.'

'Why didn't you say anything?' the D.M. asks me.

'I was afraid,' I reply truthfully. 'I came here on someone else's visa. I thought I might be sent back. Plus, I spent a long time in a Nazi camp.' I omit the prison, fearful of raising more questions. 'I was trying to forget that part of my life.'

'You're very brave,' the D.M. observes. 'You should be honored for what you did. And I'm sure our war crimes office would like to talk to you at some point to debrief. But right now we have more pressing matters to contend with. I'm sure I don't have to tell you again how important it is that we get the cipher from Marcelitis.'

'No, sir, I understand.'

'And it seems that the only hope of doing so is getting to Andek.' He pauses. 'Will you help us?'

I hesitate, uncertain how I can be of use. 'I'll do whatever I can.'

'Sir,' Simon interjects. 'What do you have in mind? Do you have an idea of how we can somehow reach Andek from here?'

The D.M. shakes his head. 'I'm afraid that's impossible. We don't know of any secure phone or telegraph line to reach the man. And there's no time to send a courier back and forth. No, I think our only hope is to have Marta speak with him face-to-face.'

Simon stares at the D.M., mouth agape. 'Surely you aren't suggesting...'

I look from Simon to the D.M., then back again. 'I don't understand.'

The D.M. sits down in the chair beside mine. 'I am asking if you will go to Prague to speak with Andek directly.'

I am too surprised to react. For a second I wonder if the D.M. has misspoken. 'Me?' I ask finally. 'You want me to go to Prague?'

'Sir, with all due respect...' Simon splutters. I have never heard him sound so upset, much less in front of his boss. 'You can't possibly be serious.'

214

The D.M. crosses the room toward Simon. 'I'm deadly serious, Gold. Andek is our only link to Marcelitis, and Marta is the only one who can get to Andek.'

'But she isn't a spy, for God's sake! She's not even a diplomat. She's a secretary.'

'She's a former member of an insurgent group.' I have never heard the resistance referred to as this before. 'She has experience with covert operations, firearms. Frankly, she's more qualified than most men.'

Amid my confusion, pride rises in me. I had fought alongside Alek, Jacob and the other men. I am glad not to have to hide it any longer. But Simon is not placated. 'She's my wife. We have a small child and–'

'What is it that you would want me to do?' I interrupt, curious.

The D.M. walks quickly back toward me. 'We need you to go to Prague. We can create some sort of cover for your trip, say that you are there for meetings at the embassy. We have some very good people on the ground there who can help you find Andek.'

'And then what? If I find him, I mean.'

'Ask him to let you speak with Marcelitis. Don't explain too much to Andek alone – we don't have the intel on him to know if he can be trusted. Instead, use your history with him to gain his trust so he introduces you to Marcelitis. I'll give you something written from the foreign minister formally asking for the cipher.'

'Is that all, sir?' I ask.

'What do you mean, is that all?'

'I mean, what are we offering Marcelitis in exchange for giving us the cipher?' I can feel Simon's stunned glare. A secretary questioning the D.M. on policy is unthinkable.

The D.M. pauses, as though the idea had not occurred to him. 'Assurances, I suppose. That Britain is behind them and that we won't allow the Soviets to roll over Czechoslovakia.'

I take a deep breath, emboldened by the role he is asking me to play. 'That won't be enough, sir.'

'What do you mean? Why?'

'Once, before the war, the Czech people believed in the West. We all did. But the West looked on while the Germans took the Sudetenland, then Prague. People have been bitten by empty promises before, and from what I understand, Marcelitis is especially distrustful. If he is to be persuaded to give us the cipher, we will need something concrete.'

The D.M. paces back and forth, stroking his goatee. 'That's a fair point. We would have to put together some sort of package, provide something as a measure of good faith. I'll start working on the needed clearances right away and then–'

'This is madness!' Simon explodes. I turn toward him, stunned by the sharpness of his tone toward the D.M. His cheeks have turned bright red with anger. 'You are proposing to send *my wife* back to Eastern Europe to a country that might fall to the Soviets at any minute? For God's sake, she almost died there just three years ago!'

'We have no reason to think that anything is going to happen imminently with the Czech government. The coalition ministers are resisting resignation and that alone will keep the communists occupied for weeks. Even if they are successful, it will be months until they can form a new government. Nothing will happen before the elections next June.'

'How long?' I ask. 'I mean, if I agree to go, how long would I need to be gone?'

'A few days,' the D.M. replies quickly. 'A week at most. Less if you are able to find Andek and get to Marcelitis quickly.'

'Marta, you can't be seriously considering this,' Simon interjects.

I turn to the D.M. 'Sir, may we have a moment in private?'

'Certainly, though I'm afraid I must ask you to be brief. I need to get over to the minister's office right away, and they're going to want an answer on how we plan to handle the situation.' He walks out of the room and closes the door behind him.

I turn to Simon, who stares at me from the far side of his desk for several seconds. 'The resistance,' he says slowly, his voice a mixture of anger, hurt and disbelief. 'You could have told me, Marta.'

'I wanted to,' I reply, thinking guiltily of all of the other things he still does not know. 'But it was such a painful part of my past. I was afraid.'

Simon crosses the room and drops down in front of my chair on one knee to face me at eye level. 'Marta, this idea of the D.M.'s is madness. Please tell me you aren't seriously considering it.'

I do not answer but study Simon's face. This is the most interest he has shown in me since we have been married, I realize. For a moment I wonder if he is simply jealous that I can contribute something here that he cannot. But the concern in his eyes is genuine. Something tugs inside me. For so long, he has seemed to see right through me. Is it possible that he might actually miss me if I was gone?

I stand up and walk to the window, considering the D.M.'s request. Prague. Eastern Europe. Inwardly, I wince. That part of the world was home to me once. But now that I am safe in London, it seems dark and desolate, the place of a thousand painful memories and broken dreams. How can I possibly go back? Across the park, I can see the edge of the Parliament building. I faulted the British for doing nothing the last time, during the war. How can I now do the same? I turn back. 'Simon, if I am really the only one who can help...'

'What about our daughter?' he demands, gesturing to the picture that sits on the corner of his desk.

I turn to gaze at the image of Rachel taken in the garden last spring. The idea of leaving her, even for a few days, is almost inconceivable. 'I *am* thinking of her. Simon, Rachel is fortunate enough to be growing up in a safe place. For now. But I know firsthand how quickly things can change. You've said yourself that the communist threat is as real and dangerous as the Nazis...'

'Rachel is safe.' Simon walks toward me, placing his arms on my shoulders. His hands seem almost foreign. Simon seldom touches me. Now he is reaching out, attempting to get me to listen to him. I look from his hands to his beseeching expression, then back again. Even now, his touch is not affection, I realize sadly, but a tool of persuasion. 'Rachel will always be safe here.'

'Maybe.' But I am thinking not only of Rachel. In my mind I see Emma and Lukasz, the orphaned rabbi's son she cared for during the war. She had taken him with her when she fled and was surely raising him as her own, along with the child she was expecting when I last saw her. They are likely still somewhere in Eastern Europe while I am living here. What are their lives like? Guilt washes over me. 'I have to try, Simon.' I look into his eyes, pleading for him to understand. 'I can't stand by and do nothing. It's just a quick trip, a few days at most. I'm sorry,' I add.

He pulls back his hands as though burned. The concern disappears and the earlier anger reappears in his eyes. 'So am I,' he replies coldly. Before I can speak further, he turns and walks from the room.

'Simon, wait...' I start after him, then stop again. He is upset, I know, at being defied. But this is not his decision to make.

A second later, the D.M. appears in the doorway. 'I saw your husband leave...'

'He's not happy with my choice.'

'Does that mean you'll go?' I hesitate, then nod. The D.M. crosses the room. 'That's wonderful news.'

'On one condition. I have a young daughter. I cannot afford to be away from her longer than a week.'

'That won't be a problem. All we need you to do is speak to Andek, get him to put you in touch with Marcelitis, get the cipher. That should take a day or two at most.'

'What if he won't give it to me?'

'He'll give it to you. He has to. While you and Simon were talking, I made some calls. A package is being put together for you to take. It contains our key contacts in certain Eastern European countries, information that is valuable to Marcelitis's work We're also going to offer him sizable funds placed in a Swiss bank account that will finance his operations for some time. But he gets none of this unless he gives you the cipher. Once you've obtained it, we'll have someone standing by to extract you.'

'Extract?' I repeat. The word makes it sound as though it will be difficult to leave.

'It's just an expression,' he replies quickly. A strange expression crosses the D.M.'s face, then disappears again so quickly I wonder if I might have imagined it. 'So we are agreed?' he presses.

I swallow, forcing down my uneasiness. 'Yes.'

'Excellent. You should take the rest of the day off and go home to prepare for the trip. I'll finalize all of the arrangements when I return and send further details through Simon later this evening.' Simon. I remember his angry expression before he stormed from the office. 'A car will come for you at six o'clock in the morning,' he adds.

Tomorrow morning. I had not imagined it being so soon. But the sooner I go, the sooner I will be home again. 'I'll be ready.'

'Thank you, Marta,' he says solemnly. 'We owe you more than you know.' Then I watch as he turns and walks out of the office, wondering if I have just made the biggest mistake of my life.

CHAPTER 15

I tiptoe down the creaky wood stairs and across the darkened parlor. The house is still except for the ticking of the clock above the mantelpiece. Five-fifty, it reads, ten minutes until I am scheduled to depart. I walk to the front window and peer out into the deserted predawn street. The smell of roast beef from last night's dinner hangs in the air.

I turn and look up the stairs, fighting the urge to check on Rachel once more. Earlier I stood in the doorway to her bedroom listening to her light, even breathing, punctuated by nonsensical babble as she dreamed. I crept to her crib and looked down, guilt washing over me. How could I leave her? I will be back in a few days, I told myself. She will not even know that I am gone. And someday when she's old enough, I will be able to tell her what I did and why. I reached down and kissed her, inhaling deeply to trap her powdery scent and take it with me.

Forcing my thoughts away from Rachel, I walk to my small suitcase that sits by the door. Uncertain what to bring, I packed two changes of clothing and a few toiletries. I pick up my purse, which sits on top of the suitcase, opening it and checking that the papers I tucked into the lining are still there. Simon gave them to me last night when he returned from work. 'From the D.M.,' he said coldly as he handed the envelope to me in the kitchen.

I took the envelope uncertainly. Was I supposed to open it? 'Simon, please. I know you're upset about my going, but I really need your help.'

I watched his face as he considered my words, his expression softening. 'This contains a list of key contacts for Marcelitis, if he agrees to help us,' he explained. 'Foreign nationals who work for us, in Czechoslovakia, Hungary, Poland and Germany.'

'They really agreed to give him this?'

'You said we had to give him something real to win his trust. This is as real as it gets. Using this list, Marcelitis will be able to forge contacts throughout the region, strengthen his network. I don't have to tell you how valuable this information is, what certain of our enemies would do to get their hands on it.' I nodded, speechless. I had no idea that I would be carrying such important information. 'There's also a wire number to a Swiss bank account containing half a million dollars. We could just take that and run away ourselves,' he added. For a second, I wondered if he was serious. 'Of course, he doesn't get any of this until he gives you the cipher.'

'Of course.' I held up the envelope. 'May I?' He nodded. Inside was a letter addressed to someone named Uncle George, talking about a vacation. 'I don't understand.'

'The list is in code,' Simon explained.

'Will Marcelitis know the code?'

Simon shook his head. 'No, he'll need to go to the embassy and meet with our intelligence officer, George Lindt, who will provide him with the key. That will ensure that he'll cooperate with us.' I wondered if Marcelitis would trust us enough to do that. 'And this is from me.' He pulled from his pocket a small pistol.

I recoiled. 'I – I don't know...' I began.

'Don't tell me that you don't know how to use it.' Simon cut me off, and I could tell from his tone he was thinking of my newly discovered past with the resistance, wondering what else he did not know.

But my hesitation was sincere. The last time I held a gun was the night I shot the Kommandant. 'I – I can't take that.'

'I doubt you'll need it,' Simon replied. 'But it would make me feel better.' I took the gun from him. It was, I supposed, Simon's way of showing concern. 'I still wish you'd reconsider,' he added.

'Simon, we've been through this. You know why I'm going, why I can't back out now.' I took a step toward him, wanting to make him understand. But before I could say more, he turned and walked upstairs.

I look up the darkened stairway now, wishing he would come down and say goodbye. I could tell from his shallow breathing as I dressed that he was only pretending to be asleep. He is really upset, I realize. But is he only worried about my safety? Part of me still wonders if he is jealous that I can help in a way that he cannot.

Taking one last look around the house, I pick up my suitcase, then open the front door and step out onto the porch. I shiver, drawing my coat more tightly around me against the crisp, late-autumn air. Bare tree branches scrape against the front of the house, blown by the wind. The paint is peeling around the door frame, I notice. I had meant to take care of that before the weather turned cold.

Behind me, a floorboard creaks. I turn to find Simon silhouetted in the doorway, a bathrobe over his pajamas. 'Simon...'

'You forgot these.' He holds out a pair of gray wool gloves. 'It's liable to be much colder there.'

'Of course. Thank you.' I take the gloves, touched by his concern. I had nearly forgotten how much more bitter the Eastern Europe winters could be, how swiftly and soon the snows came. Suddenly the magnitude of where I am going threatens to overwhelm me. 'Simon, I...'

'When Delia gets here today, I'll explain that you were called away unexpectedly for a week or so to care for a sick relative of mine,' he offers. I can hear the anxiety in his voice. My departure, even for a few days, is unsettling to him, a shift in the immovable routine of his daily life. In my absence, there is a child for him to consider, arrangements to be made. 'I'm thinking an aunt in Yorkshire would be best.'

I nod. Delia knows I have no family of my own. I hate lying to her, though. Yesterday, when I returned home from the office to find her baking cookies with a jubilantly flour-covered Rachel, I desperately wanted to tell her about my trip. But sharing such classified information was out of the question, even with Delia. 'I'm sure she'll offer to stay and care for Rachel while I'm gone.'

Behind me, I hear the rumble of a car engine,

growing louder. I turn to see a black sedan pulling up in front of the house. 'Time to go,' Simon says.

I face him once more, needing him to understand. 'Simon, I...'

He raises his hand. 'Time to go,' he repeats. He bends down and kisses me stiffly on the lips. 'See you soon. Be careful.'

'Goodbye.' I turn and walk slowly down the porch steps and through the gate. A man in a dark suit whom I do not recognize stands by the open rear door of the car. 'Hello,' I say as I climb into the car. The man does not answer but takes my suitcase and closes the door behind me. I look out the window at the porch, hoping to see Simon. But he has disappeared back inside and the house is dark once more.

The car pulls away from the curb, then turns right from our street onto Hampstead High Street. Suddenly I realize that I have no idea where I am going. I tap on the darkened glass that separates the back of the sedan from the front. The driver opens it. 'Ma'am?' he says, not turning around.

I lean forward; 'Where are we going?'

'Northholt Air Base.' He closes the glass again before I can ask anything further.

An airport. I am flying to Prague. I sit back once more, digesting this information as the streets of north London disappear outside the car windows. I do not know why I am surprised, except that there had not been time to consider how I was going to get there at all. It makes sense; given the urgency of my mission, a slow ferry and train journey would have been out of the question.

We pass by the industrial warehouses on the outskirts of the city. Then the buildings disappear and the roadside grows empty and dark. I have only been north of London once before. Simon took me on a day trip shortly after we were married to show me Cambridge, where he had been a student. We took the train then, and as we rode through the flat grasslands that seemed to stretch endlessly to the horizon, Simon explained to me that those were the fens of East Anglia. I imagine the countryside that way now, though I cannot see beyond the edge of the roadway.

A short while later, the car turns off the roadway at an unmarked gate. We stop and I hear the driver talking to a guard in a low voice before the gate opens and we continue through. An airplane appears out of the darkness, then another, a row of sleeping giants. I have never seen one up close and did not realize they would be so large. Finally the car pulls up close to one of the planes. 'This is it,' the driver says as he opens my car door.

I climb out and hesitate, staring at the enormous plane. An image of Paul pops into my mind. What was he thinking when he boarded the plane for England that last fateful flight? I imagine him laughing, joking with the other men. I am certain he was not worried. He had flown dozens of times, jumped out of a plane into enemy fire. The flight back to England was supposed to be nothing, the first step on the journey home. Perhaps he was daydreaming about our reunion.

'Ma'am?' The driver is beside me now, shouting to be heard over whirring propellers. He hands me my suitcase. 'They're ready to go. You'd better hurry up and board.'

I force Paul's image from my mind and start across the tarmac. As I near the airplane steps, the wind from the propellers grows stronger, whipping my hair against my face. At the top, a woman in a navy-blue skirt suit stands in the open doorway holding a clipboard. Behind her, I see the pilots seated in the cockpit, dials and lights spread before them. My head grows light. 'Miss Nedermann?' the woman asks. I nod, surprised to hear my maiden name. 'I'm Nancy, the stewardess. May I take your bag?' I hand her my suitcase and she stows it in a small closet by the front of the plane, then leads me away from the cockpit into the main cabin. A column of single seats, five deep, lines each side of the aisle. 'Sit here, please.' She points to the only open seat, second from the front on the right. 'And don't forget to fasten your seat belt.' She walks past me down the aisle.

Once seated, I look around at the other passengers. They are mostly young and male; a few wear military uniforms. Who are these people and why are they traveling to central Europe? My thoughts are interrupted by a loud bang as the stewardess shuts the plane door. The urge to stand up and run from the plane engulfs me. But it is too late; the engines roar as the plane begins to roll forward. I fasten the seat belt around my middle, my fingers trembling. Brave like Paul, I tell myself. But I cannot think of him without seeing the fiery crash. I force myself to picture Rachel instead, sleeping peacefully in her crib.

The engines grow louder as the plane picks up speed, pressing me back against the seat. There is a loud bump, then another. My breath catches as I feel the earth disappear beneath us. The plane seems to hover above the ground for several seconds, then begins to climb. Forgetting to be nervous, I look out the window at the sky, which is beginning to grow pink at the horizon.

'Tea?' Nancy stands in the aisle beside my seat, holding a tray.

I hesitate, surprised. I had not known that airplanes had waitresses. 'May I have some water?'

'Certainly.' She pours a small glass, hands it to me. 'Our flight to Munich should take about four hours, not counting the hour's time difference.'

So that is our destination. 'Thank you.' I turn back to look out the window once more. Munich. I shudder. It had not occurred to me that we would be landing in Germany. Dachau was near Munich. Don't, I think, but it is too late. I feel the concrete prison floor beneath my head. Panic rises in me, making it hard to breathe. I dig my nails hard into my palms. I cannot go back there. It is too much. That was a lifetime ago, I think, forcing myself to breathe. The Nazis are gone now. Still, it seems inconceivable that in just a few hours I will be back in Germany again.

I glance around the cabin once more. Some of the other passengers have pulled out small pillows and blankets that are stowed under the seats. I barely slept before the alarm went off. I should try to get some sleep. I lean my head back and close my eyes, lulled by the gentle rumbling of the engines.

Suddenly there is aloud bumping sound. My eyes fly open. Is something wrong with the plane? I sit up. The other passengers do not look afraid but instead are gathering their belongings, buttoning coats. 'Welcome to Munich,' Nancy says from the front of the cabin. 'When you disembark, please proceed inside to Customs and Immigration.' I must have slept through most of the flight and the landing. I look out the window at the snow-coated grass beside the runway.

The plane rolls along the tarmac, then turns and continues for several more minutes. Finally we stop and the door opens. I follow the other passengers down the aisle, collecting my suitcase from Nancy before walking down the stairs. The air is cold and crisp, with a damp smell that suggests more snow is coming. 'This way, please.' Nancy, who has come down the stairs, begins to lead the group toward a drab three-story building.

Suddenly someone bumps into me from the left. Startled, I jump. 'Excuse me,' a woman's voice, barely a whisper, says. As I turn toward the voice, a hand grabs my arm. Instinctively, I pull back. A petite young woman, wearing a dark, boxy man's suit and brimmed hat, stands beside me. I do not recognize her from the plane. 'Marta?' She does not wait for an answer. 'I'm Renata, from the embassy.'

How did she recognize me? I note then that other than Nancy, I was the only woman on the flight. 'Nice to meet you.' I extend my hand, but Renata draws me close, into a cloud of perfume and cigarette smoke, kissing me on the right cheek, then the left.

'Act as if you know me,' she whispers close to my ear in crisp, accented English. 'I need to tell you this now, because once we are in the car you must assume that our conversation is being listened to, possibly recorded. I've been sent to get you. I know why you've come and I'm here to help you.' I am too surprised to respond. Renata pulls me away from the group. 'Come, we have a long drive ahead of us.' I notice for the first time a black sedan like the one that had picked me up at home parked to one side of the plane. She leads me to it and opens the rear door. Inside, she leans forward and says something to the driver, then sits back and removes her hat, revealing a tight cap of dank hair. Her cheeks are pockmarked, scars from past acne, but her features are striking, her eyes a deep chocolate-brown. 'How was your flight?' she asks in a loud voice as the car begins to move. I realize that she is making small talk for the benefit of whoever might be listening.

'Fine,' I reply.

She pulls out a pack of cigarettes and holds it out to me. I shake my head. 'You're lucky that the weather wasn't worse,' she remarks, taking a cigarette from the pack and lighting it with a sleek silver lighter. 'We've had some early snow.' She cracks the window open so the smoke wafts away from me.

Neither of us speak further as the car turns from the airport out onto the main roadway. I peer out the window. In the distance I can just make out the pine-covered Bavarian mountains silhouetted against the pale gray sky. I shiver, drawing my coat closer. How could so much evil have come from such a beautiful place?

'Cold?' Renata asks. I shake my head. 'We'll be at the border in a few minutes. I brought your paperwork from the embassy. Do you have your passport?'

I nod, pulling it from my bag and handing it to her. Simon gave it to me last night with the papers. It was like the others I had seen at the Foreign Office – its cover is black instead of the usual deep red, and the word *diplomatic* is engraved across the front. But when I thumbed through it, I was surprised. Its issuance date was eight months earlier and its pages were worn and stamped. 'We want you to appear as a seasoned cultural attaché,' Simon explained. 'So as not to arouse suspicion.' Amazed, I studied the stamps from dozens of places I had never been, trying to memorize them in case I was asked.

The car climbs one hill for several minutes, then another, without seeming to ever descend again. Soon we reach the border checkpoint. Renata rolls down her window. *'Guten tag,'* she greets the lone border guard in German as she hands him our passports. He does not answer as he thumbs through them, then peers into the car. My breath catches. Will he question me? But he only nods, then stamps the passports and hands them back to Renata. It is like I am someone else, I muse, as the car begins to move once more. Suddenly, I think of Emma. After she escaped from the ghetto to Jacob's aunt, she had to assume a whole new identity as Anna, a non-Jew.

And to make matters worse, she had to go to Nazi headquarters every day to work for the Kommandant. At the time, I had been so disdainful: how could she become close to a man like him? It must have been so difficult for her, wondering if at any moment her secret might be discovered. I wonder if she is well, if she and Jacob were able to escape. Perhaps if I can find Marek, he will have news of them.

As we climb above the tree line, the snow-capped peaks break into full view. I feel a tug, remembering the first time I woke up in Salzburg and saw the mountains. We are north of Austria, I know. Salzburg and the palace are several hundred kilometers away. But I cannot help thinking of Dava. I tried to write to her once after Simon and I were married, enclosing money to repay what she lent me. But the envelope came back undeliverable. I read in the newspaper a few months later that many of the displaced persons camps closed, all of the residents relocated to new countries. I wonder where she is now.

'We still have several hours until we reach Prague,' Renata says sometime later. 'Feel free to nap, if you're tired.'

'I'm fine. I slept on the plane. And I've grown used to getting less sleep since my daughter was born.' I feel my insides grow warm as I think of Rachel.

'How old is she?'

'Eighteen months. Do you have children?'

Renata shakes her head. 'I was pregnant once, but I lost the baby. During the war.'

'I'm so sorry. Maybe you can try again.'

She clears her throat. 'Thank you, but I'm afraid it is impossible.'

Uncertain what to say, I look out the window once more. Soon we reach a small town. The houses remind me of those in my own village, set close to the roadside with long sloping roofs. As we near the center of town, the car slows to let a group of schoolboys cross the road. At the corner sits a house with bright blue curtains. A flash of recognition surges through me: we had curtains that very color in my childhood home in the village. I still remember my mother painstakingly dyeing the material and sewing them, my father shaking his head at the audacity of a color so bright. For a second, I imagine that the house is my parents', and that if I walked up to the door and knocked, I might find my mother inside baking. Then the door opens and a heavyset woman, her gray hair in a thick bun, walks out carrying a broom. Noticing my stare, she eyes the sedan warily for several seconds, then turns her back and begins sweeping the porch. The car begins to move, passing a crudely dressed man atop a horse-drawn wagon, its carriage full of cut brush. Suddenly the village seems foreign and ancient, something out of a long-forgotten dream.

We pick up speed and the houses disappear, the narrow road giving way to a smoothly paved highway. 'The roads are really well kept,' I remark.

Renata nods. 'One of the few benefits of our neighbors.' I know that she is talking about the Soviets. 'Czech industry is critical to their economy, so they keep the roads in top condition. The railways, too. Of course the West is doing the same in Germany. Marshall Plan and all that. If only the two would meet up somehow.'

'I don't understand.'

'The West is building. The Soviets are building. But not together. Take the border, for example. The roads are a mess for that twenty-kilometer stretch on either side of the border because neither side wants to build anything that might help the other. Same with the trains. The Soviets build track at a different gauge width than the rest of the world. If you wanted to take a train east from Prague, you have to change trains at the border.'

'I see.' I wonder if she has forgotten her own admonition not to speak openly, or if what she is saying is such common knowledge she does not care who hears us.

Outside, the landscape begins to change, the forests and fields giving way to industrial warehouses and factories. Smokestacks belch black smoke into the sky. Behind the factories, the hills have been sheared of trees and grass. Strip mining, I realize sadly. Once pristine, the coal-rich land is being pillaged. The pollution from the factories must be awful. I lean my head back, suddenly tired. Then I close my eyes, allowing the motion of the car to lull me into a gentle half sleep.

'Look.' Renata touches my arm, jarring me awake. She points out the front window of the car. In the distance, I see the tops of buildings, interspersed with spires and church steeples. 'We're nearing Prague.' I blink several times. How long was I asleep? The road climbs to the top of a hill. Below, the panorama of the city

234

spreads out like a postcard, an endless sea of red roofs. A wide, curving river divides the city into two halves. 'Hradcany Castle,' Renata says, pointing to a massive, turreted structure that sits atop a hill on the far bank. It reminds me of Wawel Castle in Kraków, only larger. 'And below it sits the Mala Strana, or Little Quarter. That's where the embassy is located.' The car begins to descend the hill, into the narrow, winding streets. The buildings are painted blues and pinks and yellows, their brightness muted by a coating of soot. 'And on this side, we have the Old City. You'll be staying here, at the Excelsior. It is quite close to the Old Town Square.'

'Lovely,' I say, playing along with the charade. 'I will have to be sure to see it.' In truth, I doubt I will have time to visit many of the sights. Speed, Simon told me the night before I left, is critical. I need to persuade Marek to introduce me to Marcelitis and get the cipher before the Soviets have any idea that I am here.

As we stop at a traffic light, I notice an ornate building with Hebrew writing on it. 'A synagogue?'

Renata nods. 'We are just on the edge of Josefov, which is the Jewish quarter. Or was,' she corrects herself. 'Prague used to have an enormous Jewish community before the war. But of the survivors, only those who had nowhere to go came back. The others went to Israel or Western Europe or America.'

Like me. 'You can hardly blame them for leaving.' I can hear the defensiveness in my own voice.

'Of course,' Renata replies quickly. 'I only

235

meant that it's a shame for the city to have lost such a vibrant part of its population.' I study the synagogue. The structure seems to have survived the war intact, but it is in a state of complete disrepair, the stained-glass windows cracked, the front steps crumbling. In my mind I see the tiny synagogue in our village. Is there anyone left to pray in it now? 'The synagogues survived mostly but they're little more than shells,' Renata adds. She drops her voice. 'The communists want to create a Jewish museum, but it's really a Soviet propaganda piece.'

Behind the synagogue I can see a massive Jewish cemetery, crowded with tombstones that seem to be standing on top of one another. Thousands of Jews, I think. Hundreds of years of history. And these are the ones who were lucky enough to die before the war. I study the cracked headstones, tall grass growing between them. Are there no Jews left in Prague to care for the cemetery, or are they too afraid to come here? To Jews, keeping up a cemetery is a moral obligation, a way to pay tribute to the ancestors that came before. I remember my own father walking faithfully to the cemetery each week, even in the worst of weather, to visit his parents' grave and say Kaddish. Even during the war, there were stories of Jews in Kraków sneaking into the cemeteries at night under penalty of death to care for the gravesites that had not been completely destroyed by the Nazis, defiantly leaving a few pebbles on the headstones to show that they were there. My heart aches at the thought of my own parents, denied a proper Jewish burial by the Nazis.

'Here we are,' Renata announces a few minutes later as the car pulls up in front of a hotel. We climb out of the car. 'The porter will take your bag,' she says as I start toward the trunk. I follow her inside to the desk, hanging back as she speaks to the clerk in Czech. The lobby is large and, I can tell, was once grand. But the red carpet is faded and worn through in places, and several lights are broken or missing from the chandelier that hangs overhead. The air smells of over-cooked dill.

A minute later, Renata turns from the counter and hands me a key. 'Well, I'm sure you're tired, so have a good night's sleep.' I look at her, puzzled. Then she pulls me close to kiss my cheek as she had done at the airport. 'Go upstairs and drop off your bag. Wait ten minutes. At the end of the hallway you'll find a second stairwell. Take it and it will lead to the back alley. I'll see you there.' She releases me and strides across the lobby with a jaunty wave.

CHAPTER 16

Upstairs, I unlock the door to the hotel room and flick the light switch. The bare bulb on the ceiling splutters to life. Then there is a popping sound and the room goes dark once more. I feel my way along the wall, finding a table lamp and turning it on to reveal a small, triangular room. A twin bed is wedged into one corner, covered in a garish pink-flowered duvet. To the left of the bed, beneath a window, sits a chair with a worn gold slipcover. A damp odor permeates the room, as if there is some sort of leak.

I drop my bag onto the bed, then walk into the water closet to relieve myself after the long journey. The sink faucet is rusty and the floor tiles cracked, mold growing where the grout should be. There is a claw-footed bathtub, though, inviting and deep. It reminds me of the wood tub in our house in the village, large and sturdy, that my mother would fill fresh with heated water for each of us every week.

I wash and dry my hands, then return to the main room. Renata said to wait ten minutes, but I walk to the door, eager to find Marek. I peer into the hallway, looking in both directions, then make my way to the unmarked door at the end of the hall. At the bottom of the stairs, as Renata described, is a doorway leading to an alley. Outside, the sun is beginning to set, and it's colder, too. I draw my coat closer, blinking and trying to adjust my eyes. The alley is narrow, tall brick buildings close on either side. The air is heavy with the smell of garbage. Something rustles by my feet. A rat. Nausea rises up in me. The rats had been everywhere in prison, scratching inside the walls, running across the floor at night. They were as rampant as flies in the ghetto, too. Once, I awoke in bed screaming as one ran across my neck. Mama chased it down, killed it with a broom. But I was too scared to sleep for days.

Someone grabs my arm. 'Hey!' I exclaim, jumping.

'Shh!' Renata whispers. Still holding my arm, she leads me through the alleyway to a backstreet. 'Be careful,' she adds, gesturing to the slick, wet cobblestones. As we walk, I notice that Renata somehow changed outfits in the few minutes I was upstairs. She is now wearing a short, dark skirt and a pink blouse that dips low to reveal something lacy beneath. Her practical shoes have been replaced with stiletto heels, and she is wearing rouge and bright lipstick. It is as if she is dressed for a night on the town, which, I realize, is exactly the idea, suddenly feeling very frumpy in my wool travel skirt and jacket.

She leads me to a boxy car parked at the corner, so tiny it is almost toylike. The passenger door, its dark paint gouged, groans as Renata opens it for me. I fold myself into the damp car. 'We must hurry,' she says loudly as she turns the ignition. 'Aunt Sophie will be worried if we are late.'

'Aunt Sophie?' I whisper.

'Talk normally now,' she says in a low voice, and I realize that she is speaking for the benefit of anyone who might be listening.

'I – I am really looking forward to seeing Aunt Sophie after so long,' I improvise as she pulls the car away from the curb. These spy games are very confusing to me.

Renata turns on the radio, which blares a mixture of classical music and static. 'Sorry we couldn't take the embassy sedan tonight. Meet Wartburg, pride of German engineering.' She pats the dashboard. 'Careful that your feet don't fall through the holes in the floor.'

I start to laugh, then, looking down, see that

she is serious. 'Are we going far?'

Renata pulls the Wartburg to a halt at a traffic light. 'Just to a bar in the Nové Mesto. It's just a little too far to walk in the cold and...' She stops, peering uneasily in the rearview mirror.

I turn around to look behind us. 'What's...?'

'Don't look,' she whispers, grabbing my arm. I face front quickly, feeling my cheeks burn. As the light turns green, she slams hard on the gas and the car lurches forward. She turns right, then immediately to the left. The wheels skid sideways, sending us careening toward a light post. I grip the seat, bracing myself for the crash I am sure will come. But Renata turns the wheel hard in the other direction, pulling us back into the center of the roadway. A minute later, she slows the car, looking into the rearview mirror once more. 'Sorry. There was a suspicious car and I thought we were being followed, but it's gone.' I cannot help but wonder if perhaps she overreacted. 'I didn't mean to snap at you,' she adds. 'But turning around would only arouse suspicion.'

So would a car accident. 'I'm sorry,' I reply. 'I didn't know.'

'You haven't had any training for this, have you?' I shake my head, uneasiness growing inside me. It had all been so last-minute. Simon had been angry, the D.M. rushed. What else do I need to know that they forgot to tell me?

A few minutes later, Renata pulls the car into a small space along the curb on a residential side street. I look out the window in both directions, but do not see a bar. 'Here?'

'No, but it is best if we park and walk a few

blocks.' I start to open the car door, but she grabs my arm. 'Wait a second. You don't have any crowns, do you?'

I hesitate, then realize she is talking about Czech money. I shake my head. 'I meant to exchange some money at the hotel....'

'Here.' She presses some bills and coins into my hand. 'Don't worry,' she says, cutting me off as I start to protest. 'I'll get repaid by the embassy. Let's go.'

I step out onto the pavement and follow Renata silently through the dark, deserted streets. It begins to drizzle, a light fine mist, and I can feel the curls around my face tightening in response. Renata leads me halfway down the block, stopping in front of an unmarked building. Music and voices rise from below.

'Ready?' Renata asks, I nod, swallowing. The din grows louder as she leads me down a set of stairs and through the door. Inside, the bar is a long brick cellar. Crude wooden benches and tables, seemingly scattered at random angles, are filled mostly with young people, playing cards and talking over large mugs of dark brown beer. Several look up at us across the dim, smoky room, as if they know we do not belong here.

But Renata, not seeming to notice, surveys the room coolly. 'There,' she says in a low voice, gesturing slightly with her head toward the back of the bar.

I follow her gaze to a man seated on the end of one of the benches. 'I see him.' Marek. In truth, I might not have recognized him if Renata had not pointed him out. Once heavyset, he looks as though he has lost at least thirty pounds. His face, usually clean-shaven, now sports a mustache and goatee. He's trying to be Alek, I realize with a start. At the sight of him, my breath catches.

'We need to get his attention,' Renata says.

I nod, too nervous to respond. What will his reaction be to seeing me again? But Marek, engrossed in conversation with a gray-haired man beside him, has not looked up since we entered the bar. 'How?' I ask a minute later. 'I can't just walk up to him.'

'True,' Renata agrees. 'But I can.' She pulls a scrap of paper and pencil out of her bag. She scribbles something I cannot read, then crumples up the paper. 'You wait here.' Before I can respond, she strides across the bar, drawing several appreciative stares in her short skirt and heels. I climb onto a bar stool, watching as she passes Marek, brushing against him, just hard enough so that he notices but the others at his table do not. Then, without stopping, she drops the paper into his lap. Marek looks up in surprise, but Renata has already disappeared into the toilet at the back of the bar. I watch, not breathing, as Marek scans the note. He looks up and our eyes meet. He blinks twice behind his glasses, trying to mask his surprise. Then he leans toward the man beside him and whispers something, before making his way slowly toward the front of the bar.

Before reaching me, he stops, staring as though seeing a ghost. 'Marta...?'

'*Czesc*, Marek,' I say in Polish, struggling to keep my voice even.

'What are you...?' He falters. 'I mean, we

thought that you were...'

'Why don't you sit down?' I suggest quietly.

He opens his mouth to speak, then, appearing to think better of it, closes it again and climbs onto the bar stool beside me. 'Two pilsners, please,' he says to the bartender. Neither of us speak as the bartender pours the beer from the tap. I look over Marek's shoulder, wondering what has become of Renata. She will not come back during my conversation with Marek, I suspect. She did her job by getting him here; the rest is up to me.

I look back at Marek. Images race through my mind: Marek sitting at the head of the table beside Alek at Shabbat dinner each week, laughing and talking. Later they would huddle over papers in the back room of the apartment, plotting in hushed whispers. Then I see Marek again that last night at the cabin when I confronted him as he prepared to flee. He was supposed to lead the resistance after Alek was gone. I know, of course, that there was nothing more we could have done. The movement was in tatters after the café bombing; even a great leader like Alek could not have carried on. But Marek left the rest of us behind at the moment we needed him most. Does he feel guilty, as I do, at having survived when so many others did not?

Enough, I think, forcing my anger down. I wait until the bartender has set the glasses in front of us and walked away once more. 'You thought I was dead. Isn't that what you were about to say?'

He nods. 'The bridge... We heard that Richwalder shot you.'

'He did. I survived that and Nazi prison, too.' There is a note of pride in my voice. Marek had never been a supporter of women helping with the resistance, other than as occasional decoys. He thought us weak, inconsequential. Now, watching his stunned expression, I cannot help but feel smug.

'Did they ask...?'

'About the resistance? They suspected my involvement and spent months trying to beat it out of me. I didn't tell them anything,' I add quickly.

Relief crosses his face, as though the Nazis are still in power and might be able to hurt him if they knew the truth. 'And now? Surely you didn't go back to Poland after all that happened.'

'No. I live in London, actually.'

'England? But how? And what are you doing here?'

'It's a long story.' I pause, looking around the bar for Renata. Has something happened to her? 'I'm afraid we don't have much time.'

Marek's forehead wrinkles. 'I don't understand.'

'Marek, I...' I take a deep breath. 'I've been sent to find you.'

His eyes widen. 'Sent? By whom?'

'The British government.' Marek's jaw drops. 'I work for the Foreign Office. They sent me because I know you. I need you to connect me with a certain leader in the anticommunist underground.'

'I don't know what you're talking about,' he interrupts coldly. 'I'm an employee of the state. I would never associate with such people.'

I lower my voice. 'Marek, there's no time for

games. We know that you are closely involved in the anticommunist movement and we desperately need to make contact with a man named Jan Marcel–'

'Shh!' Marek hisses. 'Don't say his name. Not here.' His head snaps toward the door as though he expects the police to burst in at any moment.

'We need to reach him because he has a cipher that is critical in discovering which of our operatives is really working for the Soviets. In exchange we are offering–'

'Stop.' He raises his hand, cutting me off again. 'You shouldn't have come here, Marta. I can't help you. It's too dangerous, especially now.' He stands up, drains his beer. 'I'm sorry.'

'Marek, please. You don't understand. We want to help you, too. I have valuable information, money. I just need to reach this man–'

'The West? Help?' Marek's cheeks redden. 'Like they did in 1939?'

I hesitate. An image flashes through my mind of looking up at the sky from inside the ghetto. Where were the planes from Britain and America? Why didn't they bomb the camps or at least the train lines running to them, to stop some of the killing machines? I take a deep breath. 'I know. I was there. The Allies didn't come as soon as they could have and by the time they did it was too late for so many. But it's different this time. That's why I'm here, Marek, why I left my family to come see you. We laid down our lives together. You know me and trust me. The help this time is real.' My words tumble out on top of one another, a plea for him to listen. 'I made sure of that.'

245

Watching his face, I realize how implausible my words must sound, the notion that I am in a position to make such assurances.

'Who's the woman you're with?' he asks suspiciously. 'The one who gave me the note.'

'She's my escort from the embassy. She can be trusted.'

Marek looks down, studying his fingernails. 'I'm sorry, Marta. I can't help you. I wish I could. I know you went through hell in prison to protect the rest of us and I'm glad that you survived. But I can't risk it.'

I put my hand on his forearm. 'Marek, please. I want to help.'

He pulls back. 'Go home, Marta. This isn't your fight anymore.' He tosses a few coins on the bar, then turns and walks away.

I sit motionless, watching his back as he retreats. Marek will not talk to me. I stand up. Perhaps if I try to speak with him once more, I can persuade him. But he has returned to his table at the back of the bar, and sits among the other men, not looking up. Approaching him would attract too much attention.

I make my way to the front door and up the steps. Outside, Renata stands by the curb, smoking a cigarette. 'I was wondering where you had gone,' I remark.

'When I went to drop off the note, I thought I saw someone I knew from the university. I didn't want to be recognized, or have to answer questions about why I am here. So I slipped out the back door.' She drops the cigarette, grinds it out with her heel. 'So how did it go?'

'Terribly.'

'He wouldn't talk to you?' I shake my head. 'I'm not surprised. They're a very secretive bunch, especially these days.'

'But if we can't get him to help us...'

'We'll think of something else,' Renata replies. 'Come on, let's get out of here.'

I follow Renata toward the car, my shoulders low with defeat. I didn't even have the chance to ask Marek if he had any news about Emma and Jacob, or the others from the resistance.

As we near the corner, a shadowy figure emerges suddenly from an alley. Before I can react, Renata grabs my arm, pulling me with her as she leaps backward. A man in a dark trench coat and hat stands and faces us, blocking our path. Fear rises in me and I wonder if we are going to be robbed.

'What do you want?' Renata demands.

I notice a lock of gray hair sticking out from beneath the man's hat. 'You're the man from the bar,' I say aloud. 'You were sitting with Marek.' Renata turns to look at me, surprised.

The man nods. 'Marek asked me to deliver a message. Come to Riegrovy Park tomorrow at noon.'

I turn to Renata. 'Do you know where that is?'

'Yes. It's just south of the city. But it's a big park,' she says to the man. 'Where should we meet him?'

'By the fountain. But not you.' He gestures toward me with his head. 'Marek said she is to come alone.'

'But–' Renata begins.

The man cuts her off. 'Come alone,' he says to me. 'Marek will be there, if it's safe.' Before I can respond, he disappears into the alleyway once more.

CHAPTER 17

I pull back the worn window curtain and peer out at the rain-soaked street below. The pavement is crowded with passersby walking quickly, huddled under dark umbrellas on their way to work. I imagine Simon leaving for the office, Rachel looking out of the window after him. Today is her second day without me. Though I know she is well-cared-for by Delia, my heart tugs at the notion of not being there yet another morning when she awakes.

I let the curtain fall again and walk to the mirror, studying my reflection for the hundredth time: dark skirt, cream blouse. Barely able to sleep in the cold, strange room, I awoke early, washed and dressed, painstakingly taming my curls into a low knot. I wanted to look like someone Marek, and hopefully Marcelitis, could take seriously. But the eyes that look back from behind my glasses are hesitant; what am I doing here? I smooth my hair once more, wishing I had thought to bring an umbrella. Then I pick up my coat and bag and walk from the hotel room, locking the door behind me.

'Good morning, madam,' the concierge says to

me in Czech as I descend the stairs into the hotel lobby. I eye him suspiciously. Why is he talking to me? He gestures to the restaurant. 'Will you be joining us for breakfast this morning?'

I hesitate, noticing the smell of coffee and fried eggs for the first time. But my stomach is too knotted for food. 'No, thank you. I really must be going.'

Outside the hotel, I look both ways down the narrow, winding street. The rain has stopped and the cloudy sky is brightening, as though the sun might break through in a few hours. But for now it has not, the breeze reminds me sharply, blowing icy gusts of air upward and sending old newspapers dancing along the pavement. I draw the neck of my coat closed until it meets the edge of my woolen scarf.

In the distance, a clock chimes nine. It is still three hours until my meeting with Marek, too early, I know, to leave for the park. But I've never been to Prague before, and once I deliver the message to Marcelitis, I will be leaving again. If all goes well, I might be headed for home as early as tomorrow. This morning might be my only chance to see the city.

The previous night, when she dropped me off a block from the hotel, Renata offered to drive me to my meeting.

'Marek told me to come alone,' I reminded her.

She waved her hand impatiently. 'I can leave you at the edge of the park. Wait somewhere else, where Andek won't see me.'

'Um, that's very nice of you, but I don't think it will be necessary.'

Renata looked surprised. 'Are you sure?'

I nodded. 'Alone means alone. I don't want to chance him seeing me with someone else.'

'But the park is all the way on the outskirts of the city.'

'I'm from this part of the world, remember? I can still navigate the buses.'

'They may be the one thing the communists do well,' she replied, then shrugged. 'Suit yourself. You can take the C bus from the corner on the far side of the hotel. The park is the second stop from the end.'

'Thanks. Does the same bus run through the Mala Strana?'

'No, that would be the sixteen...' Renata hesitates. 'Why? Where are you planning to go?'

'Nowhere,' I replied quickly. 'I mean, I just want to take a quick walk around the Old Town before my meeting. This might be my only chance to see Prague.'

'I don't like it, Marta. The city is dangerous right now with all of the unrest.'

'I'll be careful.'

'I don't like it,' Renata repeated. 'But I can't stop you. Just stay in the central public areas, Wenceslas Square and such. And don't talk to anyone.'

Remembering now the map I consulted in the hotel room the previous night, I turn left and begin walking in the direction of the Old Town Square. The narrow, winding streets around the hotel are humming with morning activity, deliverymen unloading wagons in front of shops, women walking with bags of groceries. At the

250

corner, there is a man selling snacks from a wooden cart. I fish some of the coins Renata gave me from my bag, buy a coffee and two braided rolls. As I continue walking, I tuck one of the rolls into my bag for later. Then I take a bite of the other, washing it down with a sip of coffee.

At the next corner, I turn right, then stop. Across the street stand three policemen, watching the crowd. My pulse quickens. Easy, I think. They are not interested in you. I force myself to keep walking down the street, trying to look like I belong. As I pass, I sneak a glance at them out of the corner of my eye. Have they noticed me? On the next corner, there are two more policemen. Perhaps Renata was right about this walk not being a good idea. Still looking sideways at the police, I bump into something. 'Excuse me,' I say in Czech, turning to find that I have collided with a woman exiting a bakery with a small child. I bend to pick up her package, which has fallen to the ground. Her eyes do not meet mine as I hand it to her. She looks nervously from me to the police, then back again before dragging the child down the street.

I watch the woman as she disappears around the corner. She is afraid. Just like we were during the war. I recall seeing the Gestapo drag a man from a store as I crossed the market square in Kraków on an errand. Caught stealing fruit, I gleaned from a passerby. People hurried quickly away from the commotion, not stopping or looking as the police pushed the man against the wall of a building. A lone gunshot rang out across the square. Later, when I passed the site on my way

251

home and the police had gone, I crossed back to the site. The man lay motionless on the ground, his blood seeping into the pavement, still clutching the apple he had taken. Crowds continued to walk past his lifeless body, eyes averted, too afraid to acknowledge what had just happened. It is like that here, I realize. The people do not want to draw attention to themselves. They are terrified.

I continue walking, and a few minutes later the street ends at a large, open plaza. Tall, Gothic houses with ornate, sculpted roofs line two sides of the oddly shaped square. On the third side sits a larger stone building, the Old Town Hall. There is a colorful, elaborate clock on the front of the building. I study the design: a gold circle with numbers one to twenty-four run along its inner rim, a smaller circle, ringed with Roman numerals, inside it.

'That's the Astronomical Clock,' a voice from behind me says. He is speaking Czech, close enough to Polish for me to understand. I spin around to face a tall man in a bright yellow jacket. He points up at the clock. 'The outside ring is meant to function as a normal clock, with the inside circle showing the position of the earth in the heavens. It was built in medieval times and functioned for centuries, but it hasn't worked since the Germans hit it during the war.'

'Oh,' I say, surprised at his friendliness, this spontaneous offer of information. He is young, not more than twenty-five, I would guess, with a thin face and brown goatee that remind me of Alek. 'It's beautiful.'

'I'm Hans, by the way.' He extends his hand.

252

I hesitate, remembering Renata's admonition not to talk to anyone. Then I reach out and shake his hand. 'Marta.'

'You aren't from here,' he observes.

I shake my head. 'Is my accent that obvious?'

'Your accent is fine. You just don't see many people staring at the clock. Those of us who live here have grown immune to its charms. And we don't get many tourists these days.'

I curse inwardly at having stood out, hoping that no one else has noticed. 'I'm here on business,' I say slowly, trying my cover story for the first time. 'A cultural project at the British embassy.'

'I see.' I study his face, wondering if he believes me. But he is looking over my shoulder, distracted. I turn, following his gaze to the far end of the square where a group of people have gathered by a statue. 'I'm sorry, but I really must go. It was nice to meet you.' He strides off in the direction of the group.

'Wait...' I begin, but he is already halfway across the square. As he approaches, the group grows larger. People, mostly young men and women, come from all directions until there are several dozen assembled. They begin to walk toward one of the streets that leads from the square. I hesitate. I should head back to the hotel. But, curious, I start across the square, following the group. Ahead, I see Hans toward the front of the crowd, his yellow coat bobbing in a sea of darker colors.

The crowd makes its way down one narrow street, then another. Something is different here,

I realize. The stores are closed, metal grates pulled close across their fronts. The windows in the apartments above are dark, shades tightly drawn. Other than the people who walk with Hans, there are no shoppers or pedestrians on the street. I remember again the passersby who ignored the man shot by the Nazis in Krakow. The people are afraid. They do not want to be a part of whatever is about to happen here. I should walk away, too. But I find myself pressing forward, part of the crowd now, compelled to see what this is all about.

A moment later, the street ends at another square, much larger than the previous one. It is rectangular, narrow at the base where we have entered, with two long sides running upward toward a large, gold-domed building. The National Museum, I recognize from the tour book in my hotel room I thumbed through last night when I could not sleep. This must be Wenceslas Square. As the group surges forward, they are joined by hundreds of others, appearing individually or in small groups. They seem to be mostly students, though I see a smattering of older people, too. Some carry crude homemade signs I cannot read from a distance. A political protest. The group swells and surges forward toward the museum building. At the top of the museum steps, a line of police stand shoulder to shoulder, forming a barricade.

I hang back as the crowd pushes forward around me. I cannot afford to get caught up in this, not now. 'Democracy!' the protesters chant over and over. I inch forward, standing on the tips of my toes to get a better view. These are the very people we are trying to help, I realize, scanning the crowd. Perhaps Marek, or even Marcelitis himself, is here. But I do not see Marek, and I have no idea what Marcelitis looks like. They would be too smart to get caught in something so dangerously public, anyway. Someone a few meters in front of me starts singing the Czech national anthem. The song seems to catch fire throughout the crowd, until it seems that all of the protesters have joined in one enormous voice. Looking at the determined faces around me, I am reminded of our own resistance movement during the war. If only we'd had this kind of support from our people, things might have been different.

As the anthem concludes, the protesters surge closer to the museum building, pressing up the stairs. 'No communism!' they chant in unison. 'Democracy now!' The front of the crowd climbs the steps, reaches the barricade. Some of the protesters exchange heated words with the police. Though I cannot make out what they are saying, they seem to be demanding entry to the building. A policeman pushes a demonstrator roughly, sending the man flying backward down the steps onto the pavement. Shouts erupt in the crowd. Scuffles between the demonstrators and police break out. The rest of the throng, incensed by the conflict, presses forward.

Suddenly a shot rings out in the air, then another. The scuffling ceases and the protesters freeze. The police must have fired into the air to stop the fighting, I think. Then, at the top of the stairs, I spot something bright yellow on the ground. Hans's jacket. He lies motionless, arms flung above his head as though surrendering.

'No!' I gasp. I hold my breath, stifling the urge to scream. The crowd, stunned by the shooting, stands motionless. But the police, having caught the protesters off guard, now take the initiative. They leap forward, brandishing nightsticks. I watch, horrified, as a number of young men are beaten to the ground. Others are dragged away by the police. A cloud of smoke rises from the front of the crowd. Tear gas, I realize, as some of the protesters begin to clutch at their eyes. The crowd begins to flee, police in close pursuit. I have to get out of here, I think, as the protesters stream back past me in the direction from which we came. If I stay here, I am going to be arrested, or worse. I turn around. A police truck has blocked the street from which we entered the square. We are trapped.

I scan the far side of the square, spotting an open alleyway. Quickly, I make my way toward it, expecting a policeman to grab me at any time. When I reach the shelter of the alley, I begin to run, crossing blindly through the backstreets, feeling for the Old Town Square. My lungs burn. At last, I reach the square. Slowing, I look up at the Astronomical Clock as I cross, thinking sadly of Hans.

But there is no time to linger. The chaos of the broken demonstration has begun to spill over here, too. Protesters, their eyes watering from the tear gas, dart across the square alone or in groups of two or three. One man clutches a bloody wound on his temple. In the distance, police sirens wail, as if to remind the protesters that the crackdown is not over. I make my way hurriedly from the square.

A few minutes later, I reach the block where the hotel is located. I catch a glimpse of my reflection in a shop window. My cheeks are flushed from running and my curls have sprung free from the knot. I should go upstairs and freshen up. I look at the clock above the hotel entrance. It is eleven, one hour until my meeting with Marek, and I have no idea how long it will take to reach the park. There is no time. I walk quickly to the bus stop at the corner.

A few minutes later the C bus arrives and I board. It is empty except for a few schoolchildren clustered in the rear. I drop into a seat a few rows behind the driver, then look out the window. As we wind our way through the Old Town, I think about the ruthlessness with which the police tore apart the demonstrators. A shiver runs through me. I had known that the Soviet-dominated communist regimes were oppressive, silencing ideas that were contrary to their own. But I had not imagined that they would actually open fire on their own people. They are no better than the Nazis. I grasp my bag more tightly. Suddenly my mission seems more urgent than ever.

The bus turns away from the Old Town, stopping every few minutes as it follows the river south. At the next stop, the schoolchildren get off the bus and two women board, talking rapidly in Czech about the price of potatoes. One carries a basket only half full with groceries, the other a small pail of coal. The road grows bumpier, the buildings farther-spaced as we make our way from the city center to the sprawling outskirts of Prague. The houses here are smaller, more dilapidated. The bus stops again and the women get off, trudging slowly down a dirt road. An underfed cow stares forlornly out over a fence.

I look around the now-empty bus as it begins to move again. 'Riegrovy Park,' the driver calls a few minutes later, as though speaking to a large group. I walk to the front of the bus as it slows, looking at the driver out of the corner of my eye. Does he wonder what I am doing here? But he does not look up as I step off the bus. The door closes behind me and the bus drives away.

I pause, surveying the park. Flat fields stretch endlessly in all directions, the grass dead and brown. Several hundred meters off to the right sits a thatch of bare trees. I spot a stone fountain beneath them. Drawing my coat more closely around me, I walk toward the fountain. Closer, I can see that it is made up of several statues of small children, their hands reaching upward toward the heavens. Dead leaves lay in drifts in the dry marble basin below. I look around. The park is deserted, except for a cluster of crows, picking at the ground beneath the trees. Where is Marek? He looked so nervous last night. Part of me wonders if he is going to come at all.

It is early, I tell myself, walking toward the trees. The crows watch me with disinterest, not moving. On the far side of the trees, there is a children's playground with swings and a metal slide. Two boys play on the swings. A few meters away from them, on the edge of the playground closest to me, a woman stands by a bench, watching them.

I hesitate, studying the woman's back. I do not want to risk drawing attention to myself, but perhaps she has seen Marek. I walk toward her. 'Excuse me,' I say softly, but she does not seem to hear me over the wind. I move closer. Suddenly, I freeze, a lump forming in my throat. There is something familiar about the honey-blond color of the woman's hair, the way it hangs in a loose knot against her neck. An image flashes through my mind of Emma's hair, bouncing as she ran from the railway bridge. It cannot possibly be. I reach out, touch the woman's shoulder gently. 'Excuse me,' I repeat, louder this time.

The woman jumps, then turns slowly. As I inhale the familiar almond scent, I know there can be no mistake. There, standing before me, is Emma.

CHAPTER 18

'Hello, Marta,' she says calmly, gazing at me in her familiar unblinking way. I stare back, too stunned to move or speak. My mind races. Emma? It does not seem possible. She steps forward to kiss me on each cheek, as though we have simply run into each other on the ghetto street. 'It's so good to see you.'

'Emma?' I reach out and touch her sleeve, checking if she is really here.

'It's me.' She takes my fingers and squeezes them.

'I – I don't understand.' I cannot stop staring at her. 'What are you doing here?'

'Why don't we sit?' Emma walks to the bench. I follow numbly and sit down beside her. 'I know you must be surprised to see me,' she continues. 'I live here now, in Prague. I help, with the political work, I mean. Like you and I did in Kraków.'

So she and Jacob made it out of Poland and over the mountains, after all. If Emma is here, where is Jacob? 'But I was supposed to meet–'

'Marek asked me to come meet you. I was glad to do it, of course,' she adds. 'When Marek told me that you were here, that you were alive, I was overjoyed. It was too risky for Marek to come himself. He thought he was being followed. But he knew that no one would suspect two women with children in a playground. Those are my boys, by the way.' Emma gestures toward the swings. 'You remember Lukasz, of course.' I nod. Lukasz was not technically Emma's – he was the rabbi's son whom Emma and Krysia had hidden after his father was arrested and mother killed by the Nazis. 'And that–' she points to the younger child, who looks to be about six '–is Jake.'

Jake. I stare at the child, remembering. Emma's pregnancy was the reason we had to get her out of Kraków so quickly. The Kommandant found out and wanted to send Emma away to raise his child in Austria. *His child.* That had been the question, though no one had talked about it at the time: had Jacob fathered Emma's baby

260

during their lone reunion before the resistance bombed the café, or had her pregnancy resulted from her affair with the Kommandant? Looking now at the boy, I have no doubt – his steely gray eyes are almost identical to those that stared lifelessly back at me on the bridge the night I killed the Kommandant.

'Jake,' I repeat aloud. At least the child has Jacob's name. Suddenly, my breath catches. Jews name children after those who have died. 'After Jacob...?'

'He didn't make it, Marta,' Emma says, her voice cracking.

Pain rips through my chest. 'No...'

'When I left you on the bridge, I found the Kowalczyk farm and Jacob was waiting there for me, just like you said.' I can barely hear her over the buzzing in my ears. Suddenly I want to reach out and slap her or shake her, anything to stop her words. 'He was still terribly weak, but we knew we had to leave then because the police would be looking for me. The snow in the mountains was so much worse than we expected. Jacob developed a high fever and collapsed, right after we crossed the border into Slovakia.'

I fight the urge to scream. 'Jacob,' I say instead, seeing his face in my mind.

'I stayed with him, Marta.' I can hear the guilt in Emma's voice, her desperate need to explain. 'I stayed with him right until the very end, until he was gone.'

I swallow, struggling to find words. 'And then?'

'I covered his body as well as I could, with rocks and branches. The ground was frozen; it was the best I could do. I didn't want to leave him there, but I had no other choice. I couldn't carry him and we couldn't stay there. We had no food. Lukasz would have died, and the baby inside me, too.' The baby. Resentment fills me. If it was not for the baby, Emma would not have had to flee Kraków and Jacob would still be alive. Emma continues, 'It was like you told me, Marta, the night on the bridge. Those who can go on must.' In my mind I hear myself, insisting that Emma flee and leave me behind wounded for the Nazis. Would things have ended differently if I had gone instead, saving myself? Could I have saved Jacob, too? 'So I finished crossing the mountains and came down into Slovakia. I'd heard rumors that some of those who had survived from the resistance were in Prague. I made my way here and found Marek.'

Emma is here. Jacob is dead. I swallow, trying to process it all. 'Were there others who made it?'

Emma shakes her head. 'No one from Kraków. Everyone was arrested or killed, except for Marek and me. And you, of course, though we had no idea. But there were others who wound up here, from Lodz and Lublin, and from some other countries, too. A lot of people, like Marek and I, who resisted the Nazis, are fighting the communists now.'

'So you're helping Marek with his work?'

'Yes, but...' Emma looks away, staring across the park. 'There's something else you should know. I'm not just working with Marek.' She hesitates, then raises her hand to reveal a small gold band. 'He is also my husband.' I sink back, feeling as though someone kicked me in the stomach. 'Marta, say something,' Emma pleads.

'Your husband?' I repeat, disbelieving.

'It didn't happen right away.' Emma's tone is defensive. 'But when I came to Prague, I was all alone. I had nothing. Marek took us in, provided for me and the children. We grew closer and then he proposed.'

I pause, trying to understand. In the distance, a crow cries out. 'Do you love him?' I ask at last.

'I don't even know what that is anymore,' she replies, her voice hollow.

'But Jacob...'

'Jacob is gone, Marta.' Her expression is hard, unfamiliar. 'I had to be practical, do what is best for my children.'

I follow Emma's gaze to the swings where Lukasz plays. I think of Rachel. I went to work for Simon already suspecting that I was pregnant with her. And in spite of that fact, or maybe because of it, I let him court me. Would I have married Simon if Rachel had not been on the way? It is a question I have avoided asking myself for years.

I remember suddenly a fight Emma and I had when I confronted her on the street the night of the café bombing. How could she be involved with the Kommandant, I demanded, when she claimed to love Jacob? Emma begged me to understand then, too: she was doing what she had to do to help the resistance. At the time, I saw only that it was wrong. If Emma really loved Jacob, she would not be sleeping with the Kommandant. Things were so much simpler then,

263

when the only love I had known was my crush on Jacob. Now I know that it is more complicated than that. I judged Emma once; I will not do it again.

'I understand,' I say at last, reaching out and squeezing Emma's hand. Her fingers close quickly around mine. We are two girls back in the ghetto, confiding in each other.

She looks at me. 'You do?'

Hearing the relief in Emma's voice, I nod. 'Yes. I have a child, too.'

'Oh, Marta, that's wonderful! Boy or girl?'

'Girl. She's one-and-a-half. Her name is Rachel.'

'Then what are you doing here? I mean, Marek told me you live in London now.'

'I'm trying to get back to my daughter as soon as possible. But I had to come here. You see, I work for the British Foreign Office. We both do, my husband and I. We desperately need to reach Jan Marcelitis. When the government found out that the only way to do that was through Marek and that I knew him, they asked me to help.'

'And you agreed?'

'I felt as though I had no choice, as though I had to try to help. Does that make any sense?'

'It does. But you should do what you need to do and get out of here right away. The political situation is very precarious. Any day now...' Emma stops speaking, and her expression grows fearful. 'Anyway, Marek sent me to tell you that he's arranged a meeting with Marcelitis. You are to be at the Charles Bridge tonight at midnight. He said that once again you are to come alone.'

My heart leaps. Marek has arranged the meeting. I will see Marcelitis tonight and then I can go home. I look at Emma. 'What about you?' I ask. 'I mean, will I see you again?'

Emma hesitates. 'I won't be at the meeting tonight, if that's what you're asking. And after that you'll be gone, and God only knows what will be. I certainly never expected to see you again. So I think this is goodbye for now.' A tear rolls down her cheek. 'I want to thank you again for what you did for me in Kraków. You saved my life.'

I put my arm around her shoulder. 'You know, don't you, that you don't have to stay here? I can arrange papers for you and the children to come to London.'

Emma wipes her eyes. 'Thank you, but no. This is our home now. I'm married to Marek and I've taken vows, Marta. Vows that I will not break again.'

Seeing the guilt in her eyes, I know she is speaking of her betrayal of Jacob with the Kommandant. 'It's not your fault that Jacob's gone, Emma.'

'I tell myself that every night,' Emma replies softly. 'But it doesn't change what happened, what I did. I've made my place here now, Marta. This is where I belong.' She stands up. 'Lukasz, Jake,' she calls across the playground to the boys, who trot obediently toward her. Then she turns back to me. 'I must go now.'

I stand up, and Emma reaches over and hugs me gently. 'Goodbye and God bless you.' I open my mouth, but before I can speak, Emma turns and walks away.

An hour later, I walk through the door to my hotel room. Closing and locking the door behind me, I cross the room and sink heavily onto the bed, which creaks in protest. It is not yet two o'clock in the afternoon, more than ten hours until I see Marcelitis. I don't want to risk going out for another walk and running into more trouble with the police. And Renata said before dropping me off last night that she would stop by this afternoon to see how my meeting went; I want to be here when she arrives.

My stomach rumbles and I pull the second roll I purchased that morning from my bag. As I eat, I try to process all that I have learned. Emma is here, married to Marek. Jacob is dead. This last thought hits me heavily again and I feel the pain anew. I picture the last time I saw Jacob, walking into the Nazi café carrying the satchel, a determined look on his face. He insisted on planting the bomb himself, saying that he did not trust any of the underlings to do it properly, that it was more important for Alek and Marek to survive and go on leading the resistance. But the device went off earlier than expected, blowing Jacob through the front window of the café like a rag doll. Alek leapt from the shadows and picked up Jacob's motionless body from the pavement, hauling him from the bomb site before the police arrived. Somehow he survived his injuries. But for what? I wonder now. To die in the mountains a few short months later? At least he was reunited with Emma, was with her in the end.

I pop the last bite of roll in my mouth, then

brush the crumbs from my blouse. I sink back onto the lone, hard pillow. There doesn't seem to be much else to do but nap to pass the time. I close my eyes, imagining that I am home, reading Rachel a bedtime story in her toy-filled room.

A loud bang jars me awake. I sit up as another crash comes from outside the window. Jumping to my feet, I cross the room and peer out through the curtains. At first I can see nothing, but then, pressing my forehead against the glass, I can just make out a small group of people, clustered on the pavement in front of the hotel. More protesters? I wonder. Though I cannot make out what they are saying, their voices are loud and angry. Glass shatters. In the distance, I hear sirens growing louder. Run, I want to shout to the people on the street below. Run before it is too late.

Letting the curtain drop, I force myself to step away from the window. I cannot get involved and risk jeopardizing my mission. I look at the clock on the dresser. Five-fifteen. I had not realized I'd slept for so long. I expected Renata to have been here by now. I look around the room uncertainly. A bath, I decide. I walk to the water closet and turn on the tap.

When the tub is nearly full, I turn off the hot water and undress. I put one foot into the steaming water gingerly, then lower myself in slowly, feeling my skin go red. I lay my head against the back edge of the tub and stare up at the ceiling, thinking of Emma once more. She seems so much older and sadder now. How had I appeared? I had always felt so gawky and adolescent compared to her. Now I want her to see me as mature and poised. She seemed surprised when I told her I was married with a family. In her eyes, I would always be a child. Perhaps I should have told her about Paul.

Paul. His face appears suddenly in my mind. I inhale, caught off guard by the image. I have seldom allowed myself to think of him since marrying Simon. The memories still creep in occasionally, of course, prompted by certain days on the calendar, like the anniversary of his death, a picture of Paris in a magazine, a driving rain on the roof that reminds me of our night together in Salzburg. Most days the memories are fuzzy, an out-of-focus photograph or half-remembered dream. But now Paul's face appears so vividly before me, it seems that if I lifted my hand from the bathwater, I could actually touch him. My insides ache.

Enough. I shake my head, clearing the image. I cannot afford to think of him, not now. What is wrong with me? It is the stress of the mission, of all I have learned. I rub my eyes with wet fists. It is better that I did not tell Emma about Paul, I decide. We are not the friends we were years ago. And some secrets should be kept buried in the past.

A banging sound comes from outside the bathroom. I sit up quickly, sending water splashing over the edge of the tub. Is it the crowd on the street again? No, the sound comes again, louder and more persistent from the hallway. Someone is knocking on the door. Renata. 'One minute,' I call. I stand up and step out of the tub, nearly slipping on the now-wet floor. Steadying myself,

I reach for a towel, drying and dressing hurriedly. The knocking comes again as I cross the room. 'Coming!' I cry, unlocking the door. I reach for the doorknob, then hesitate. 'Who is it?'

'Renata.' The familiar voice comes through the door, low and urgent. 'Open up, dammit.'

I open the door. Renata pushes past me into the room. She looks back out into the hallway, then closes the door and locks it. 'Renata,' I say, 'good news. I'm scheduled to meet–' I stop, noticing that her hair is disheveled and she is breathing hard. 'What is it?' I ask. 'What's wrong?'

'You mean you haven't heard?' I shake my head. Renata looks around the room, as though someone else might be here. Then she pulls a small transistor radio from her bag and turns it on. The announcer speaks very rapidly in Czech, making it difficult to understand him through the static.

'What is he saying?' I ask.

Renata turns the volume lower. 'The police have announced the discovery of a so-called plot by several cabinet ministers to conspire with the West against our great nation,' she says, her voice just above a whisper. 'The ministers have been forced to resign. The communists have seized power.'

Uneasiness rises in me. 'But surely Benes–' I begin.

'Shh!' Renata jerks her head to one side, reminding me the room could be bugged. 'The president is weak. He'll never stand, not without the army or the police behind him.'

I lower my voice. 'But I don't understand. The

deputy minister told me nothing would happen here, not until the spring elections.'

Renata smiles wryly. 'That's Western intelligence for you. Either he didn't know, which is possible, or he lied.'

Because he knew I never would have come if the situation was that dangerous. Simon wouldn't have let me. A rock forms in my stomach. 'But surely people ... I saw the protesters earlier today...'

Renata shakes her head. 'Nothing more than a few thousand students. They're meaningless, unless the general public comes to their aid. Which they won't. People are too afraid.'

'No...' I sink down on the edge of the bed. 'Surely there must be something that can be done.'

'There's nothing anyone can do for us anymore,' Renata says, sitting down beside me. 'And you have to get out.'

'You mean, leave Prague? Give up and go home?'

Renata nods. 'Right away. The borders have been closed.' Closed. Alarm rises in me at the notion of being trapped. She continues, 'There's a group of Westerners, diplomats' families mostly, who have been given permission to fly out in about two hours. I've put your name on the list and I've come now to take you to the embassy.'

I pause, considering what she has said. 'But...' I hesitate, looking at the clock. 'I'm scheduled to meet with Marcelitis at midnight.'

'You need to be thinking of your own safety and the good of your family. It's time to get out while you can.'

Renata's words reverberate inside my head. I should just leave now. For my daughter's sake, I should put my safety first. But I am so close, just hours away, from getting to Marcelitis. I stand and cross the room to the window once more. The crowds below are gone. Two police cars sit parked on opposite corners, lights flashing. I turn back to Renata. 'Has there been any word from London?' I ask, wondering what Simon would want me to do.

'None. Communication is very difficult right now. The government has suspended international calls and telegraphs, so any news would have to go by underground wireless or messenger. I'm not even certain they've received news of the coup.'

So I am going to have to decide this one on my own. Looking out the window again, I remember the demonstrators as they stood in Wenceslas Square that morning, singing the Czech national anthem, Hans lying shot on the ground. I think of Emma and her children, who will have to live with whatever becomes of this country.

This is not your fight, a voice inside my head says. Go to the embassy, leave with the others. The D.M. will be disappointed, but he'll understand. Simon, too – he never wanted me to come in the first place. But stubbornness wells up inside me, blocking thoughts of escape. 'I still have to meet with Marcelitis. This is bigger than just Czechoslovakia. Getting the information to him could help in other countries. I'm sorry, Renata, but I can't leave. Not now.'

271

Renata stares at me. 'You know that you might get stuck here?' I nod. 'And that if the embassy closes, there will be no one to help you?'

'I understand.'

Renata exhales sharply. 'You are nervy, I'll give you that. What about after your meeting with Marcelitis? I mean, will you leave then?'

'Yes. Right away.'

'There is one other possible option, but I didn't want to mention it because I was hoping you would be smart and get on the plane with the others. If we leave right after your meeting, I can try to drive you to the Austrian border, and help you to talk your way across on your diplomatic passport. You can pick up a train to Vienna from there. I can't promise anything. It would be very dangerous, and I'm not certain it would work.'

'We'll have to try. It's our only hope.'

'I really wish you would reconsider and come to the embassy now.'

I shake my head. 'I still have to meet Marcelitis.'

'Alone again, I take it?'

'Yes.'

'You know I could insist that you get on that plane,' Renata says. 'Get the embassy guards, or even the police.'

'I know. But I also know that you won't, because you understand why I am doing this.'

'So,' she says slowly. 'I'll say I came here looking for you, but the room was empty. I'll go to the embassy and tell them that I couldn't find you in time for the flight. But immediately after your meeting with Marcelitis tonight, you are to meet me. Come off the bridge, turn left on Krizov-

272

nicka Street and walk to Platnerska, the first major intersection. You will see an archway beside an antique store. I will be waiting with the car parked there, out of sight. Be there by twelve-thirty,' she adds. 'No later. We need to make sure we can reach the border by dawn, even if we are detoured. Do you understand?'

'So I should pack my things and take them with me?'

'Only your passport and essential papers. You need to leave everything else behind. That way it looks like you are still here if the police come looking for you.'

A chill shoots up my spine. 'I don't understand. Why would they do that?'

Renata walks toward me and takes me by both shoulders. 'The whole world changed tonight, Marta. Now that the communists have secured power here, people are going to start talking. There could be leaks from the embassy, from the anticommunist movement, anywhere. That's why I wanted you to leave with the embassy flight. Things have become extraordinarily dangerous for all of us. There is no guarantee to safe passage if you stay. Do you understand?'

I swallow hard. 'Y-yes.'

'But you haven't changed your mind, have you?' I stare at her unblinkingly. 'I didn't think so. Then get dressed and prepare for your meeting. I'll be waiting for you afterward.' She walks to the door and then turns back again. 'Be careful leaving the hotel. The police are everywhere.'

'I know.' I gesture toward the window with my head.

'And they've imposed a ten o'clock curfew, which you'll be breaking. You need to take the back stairs to avoid attracting attention.' She opens the door and looks both ways out into the hallway. 'Be careful,' she mouths as she backs out of the room. 'And good luck.' Then she turns and races down the hallway.

CHAPTER 19

At eleven-fifteen, I stand in the doorway surveying the hotel room as I have left it. My suitcase is open and my nightgown lies strewn across the bed. The lamp on the dresser burns bright yellow. To anyone who might come in while I am gone, it looks as though I will be back shortly. I clutch my purse, containing the papers for Marcelitis and my passport, as I open the door. Checking to ensure the hallway is deserted, I slip from the room.

I make my way down the back steps into the alley. The hotel door closes behind me with a click. Remembering the rats last night, I move swiftly to the end of the alley and peer out into the street, which appears deserted. Taking a deep breath, I begin walking toward the river, hugging the shadows of the buildings, trying to quiet the soles of my shoes as they scrape against the pavement.

Earlier, as I closed the door behind Renata and leaned against it, my heart pounded. What had I done? The notion of being trapped here, unable to leave, terrified me worse than anything. I fought the urge to run after Renata, to tell her I would fly out immediately with the convoy of other foreigners. Then I steeled myself: this might be the only chance for us to reach Marcelitis. I could not quit so close to succeeding. Resolved, I finished dressing, paced the room until it was time to leave. But now, as I creep through the dark streets of the Old Town, I cannot help but wonder once more if staying had been a mistake.

I make my way down one cobblestone street, then another, until at last I reach the river. High on the far bank sits Prague Castle, its turrets bathed in golden light. The Charles Bridge arches gently across the river, connecting the Old Town with the Mala Strana, or Lesser Quarter. Statues of saints, illuminated by the moonlight, rise from the low walls that flank both sides of the bridge.

I approach the base of the bridge, then pause, shivering as I remember lying on the Kraków railway bridge, the Kommandant's lifeless body beside me. There was another bridge, too, I remind myself, pushing the image from my mind. Paris. I see the Pont Neuf, remember Paul's warmth against my back, his arms around me as we gazed at the Eiffel Tower. From the far bank of the river, cathedral bells begin to chime midnight. Forcing the memories from my mind, I scan the length of the deserted bridge. Emma had not said where the rendezvous was to take place, and if I cross, someone might see me. But I cannot risk missing Marcelitis. I step from the safety of the shadows, begin walking low across the bridge.

The saints look down solemnly on me, their silhouettes cool white against the night sky.

As I near the center of the bridge, a tall figure emerges from the shadows at the far end and starts toward me. Marcelitis. I walk forward, my heart racing. Just before reaching him, I stop. From all of the stories, I expected someone young and vibrant, like Alek and Jacob had been. But Marcelitis is older, his bald head glowing in the moonlight. 'Marta?' I nod. 'I'm Jan Marcelitis.' His English is heavily accented.

I study his pale face and bloodshot gray eyes. 'Did Marek explain to you why I am here?'

'Yes. Give me the information you have for me. The cipher has been left at a dead drop. Assuming the information you offer is acceptable to me, I will give you the location.' I hesitate. The D.M. said only to give the information to Marcelitis in exchange for the cipher. Can he be relied upon to live up to his end of the bargain? 'This is the only way you are going to get the information,' he adds, sensing my uncertainty.

He's right, of course. I have no other choice. I reach in my bag for the papers, trembling. As I start to pull them out, Marcelitis extends his hand expectantly, his pale, bony fingers creeping out from his coat sleeve. Something gold glows on one of his fingers. A wedding ring. But Alek had said that Marcelitis was not married. Uneasiness rises up inside me. Something is not right. Easy, I think. Alek told me about Marcelitis several years ago. Perhaps he is only recently married. But something still seems wrong. I hesitate, uncertain what to do.

'Mr. Marcelitis,' I begin, shifting my weight, stalling for time. 'I understand that we may have a mutual friend...'

'Yes, of course. Marek Andek.'

'Not only him. I understand that you also know another friend of mine, a resistance leader from Kraków during the war?'

'Who are you speaking of?' he asks impatiently. 'The police could be here at any time. I really cannot play guessing games.'

'Alek Landesberg.'

'Yes, of course, Alek,' the man replies quickly.

I take a deep breath. 'Have you had news of him lately?'

'Just last month,' the man replies. 'I saw him in Berlin.'

If this man were really Marcelitis, he would have known that Alek is dead. I look down at the papers in my hand. My heart pounds. 'I – I just realized that these are not the right papers,' I say, putting the papers back in my bag. 'I have to go back to the hotel to get them...'

'Stop playing games,' the man orders sharply. 'Just give me the papers.' He steps toward me and, before I can react, seizes me by both shoulders. I twist, struggling to get away, but the man's grasp is too strong. He reaches down with one hand to grab my bag. He must not get the papers. Adrenaline shoots through me. Quickly, I lift my left foot and bring it down hard on his instep. The man grunts and jerks back, loosening his grip slightly. I pull away hard, breaking free and leaping backward. The man growls and lunges toward me again. He raises his right hand

and I can see that he is clutching something that glints silver in the moonlight. He swings the knife wildly toward me, just missing my shoulder. I step back and he raises the knife, preparing to lunge again. The gun, I remember suddenly, reaching into my bag. But before I can pull it out, he leaps forward. I brace myself and raise my right foot. As he comes at me, I kick him hard in the shin.

'Aah!' the man cries, lifting his leg. But the blow was not serious enough to stop him for long. I have to act now, while he is off balance. I reach out with both hands and push him hard, sending him flying backward onto the ground. Then I turn and begin running toward the end of the bridge.

Behind me, I hear the man scramble to his feet, then start to run after me. Don't look back, I think as his footsteps grow closer. At the end of the bridge, I turn left, running harder. My lungs feel as though they are about to explode. I make a quick right onto another street. Then I duck into an alley, scanning its length. It is bare, completely exposed, except for a door at the end and a large trash bin. Desperately, I run to the door and pull hard on the handle, but it is locked and refuses to budge. I hear footsteps in the street, growing louder. The bald man, whoever he is, will be here any second. I run to the trash bin and climb over the high edge. Trash bags cushion my landing on the other side. The stench of garbage is over-whelming. I hold my breath for as long as I can, then, when I can stand it no longer, take a shallow breath. A gag rises in the back of my throat. Stifling it, I force myself to burrow deeper into the garbage, pulling one of the bags on top of me.

The man's footsteps reach the entrance to the alleyway, stop. I lie motionless, my heart pounding. A minute passes, seeming like an eternity. Then, I hear footsteps again, growing fainter as he disappears down the street.

For several seconds, I remain frozen in the trash bin, too afraid to move. My mind races. The man on the bridge was not Marcelitis, but an imposter who wanted the information I am carrying, enough to kill me. But how had he known that I would be there? I think of Marek, who arranged the meeting. Has he betrayed me?

I have to keep going, I realize. The man might try to come back when he cannot find me on the street. And Renata will be waiting. I climb from the trash bin, brushing myself off as well as I can. I creep to the front of the alleyway, then stop, listening. Hearing nothing, I peer out into the deserted street. My skin prickles. Has the man really gone or is he just hiding somewhere, waiting? I take a breath, then step out into the street, half expecting him to leap out and attack me once more. But the street remains silent. Exhaling, I turn in the direction from which I came and begin retracing my steps.

As I walk, I think again about the bald man. Who is he? And what happened to the real Marcelitis? I was not able to make contact with him or obtain the cipher. For a minute I consider abandoning my rendezvous with Renata and going to the bar again, to try to find Marek and ask for his help once more in reaching Marcelitis. But even as I think it, I know that it is impossible.

I do not even know if the D.M. would want me to continue my mission under such circumstances. I will go meet Renata. She will know what to do.

When I have backtracked to the river, I follow the directions Renata gave me. Soon I reach Krizovnicka Street and follow it until it intersects with Platnerska. I scan the opposite side of the street. There is an archway, as Renata described, but it appears to be empty. Running from the bald man has made me late, I know. Perhaps Renata was not able to wait for me any longer. As I cross the street, the front bumper of Renata's Wartburg comes into view and I can hear the engine running. Relieved, I hurry toward the car.

I wave at Renata through the fogged windshield. Then I open the passenger door and climb inside. 'Something went wrong,' I pant as I shut the door behind me. 'The man who met me wasn't Marcelitis. It was an imposter and he...' I turn toward the driver's seat, then stop. Renata lays slumped forward, her head resting on the steering wheel. 'Renata?'

Dread rises in me as I reach over and lean her back against the seat. Her eyes are closed and her mouth half open, a fine string of spittle running from one corner of her lips to her chin. I shake her, but there is no response. 'Renata?' I lean my head close to her mouth. She is not breathing.

I jump back, staring at Renata's lifeless body, nauseous. Renata is dead. But how? There is no blood or wound that I can see. I look around the inside of the car. Four lines, each made by a separate finger, run down the condensation on the driver's-side window. Renata's fingers, reaching out for help. Otherwise, there is no sign of a struggle or any activity inside the car at all.

I lean over to study Renata once more. Closer now, I can see a small bruise high on her neck, the size of a small coin. At the center of the bruise there is a tiny spot of dried blood. A needle. Someone has killed Renata by injection. I picture the bald man on the bridge, lunging at me with the knife. I am certain Renata's death is connected to him. Could he have killed Renata before coming to meet me, or did he have an accomplice?

The attacker could still be here, I realize with alarm. I spin around, checking the backseat. I have to get out of here. But he could also be outside, waiting for me. I hesitate, uncertain. I am a sitting duck here in the car, I decide. My chances are better on my feet.

I look at Renata's lifeless body once more. I should call someone and report her death. But Renata said the police are controlled by the communists; they could well be connected to the very people who have done this. And I do not know anyone at the embassy, or anyone else for that matter, to call. No, I will have to leave her here, at least for now. 'I'm sorry,' I whisper, reaching over and touching her cool arm.

I open the car door slowly and stare out into the darkness. The night air has grown thick with fog, making it impossible to see more than a meter in front of me. I listen closely for any sign that the attacker might be nearby. Hearing none, I take a deep breath and creep from the car, closing the door softly behind me. I begin to walk swiftly in the direction of the hotel. But the fog makes everything look different, obscuring the street signs and making foreign the route I had taken just a few minutes earlier.

As I make my way through the streets, my mind whirls. Someone murdered Renata. But there were no real signs of a struggle. How had the attacker been able to get close enough to inject her? Perhaps he (I assume for some reason that Renata was not killed by a woman) hid in the backseat before Renata got into her car. Or maybe it was someone she knew, who had been able to get in the car and close to her without causing alarm. Someone she knew. I stop walking. The image of Marek's face pops into my mind. I put one hand up against a building for support. It had been nagging at me ever since I fled the bridge: Marek arranged the meeting on the bridge, and it seemed almost certain that whoever killed Renata was somehow linked to that meeting. Had Marek sent someone to kill Renata, or even done it himself? And if Marek was a double agent, then what did that make Emma?

I look down the street, still shrouded in fog. I have to keep moving. But where can I go? Renata, my guide, is dead. No one else at the embassy knows who I am. I will go to the hotel, I decide. It is a risky choice. Whoever attacked me on the bridge might know where I am staying. But if the man wanted to attack me in my hotel room, he could have done so earlier today instead of waiting for me at the bridge. At least there I can change clothes, try to figure out what to do.

Twenty minutes later, I reach the street where

the hotel is located. I pause. It is long after curfew and I am filthy from the garbage bin and completely disheveled from my struggles. I cannot walk through the lobby like this without attracting attention. I race around the back of the hotel and into the alley, then pull on the service door. It is locked. My heart pounds. I cannot stay here. I need to get into my room. Suddenly I hear footsteps on the other side of the door. I dive behind a tall stack of cardboard boxes as the door opens. A man leans out into the alley and sets down a bag of trash. I wait until he has gone back inside, then reach out and grab the door before it can shut again. I wait several seconds, then hurry through the door and up the back stairway.

At the top, I look down the hallway. It is empty except for a housekeeping cart that one of the maids left at the far end. I walk quickly down the corridor to my room, unlock the door and step inside. As I close the door, I hear a shuffling sound behind me. Someone is here, I sense, my blood running cold. Quickly, I reach into my bag, pulling out the pistol as I turn.

'Marta, no!' a familiar woman's voice cries. My arm freezes in midair, the pistol falling from my hands and bouncing on the carpet.

'Emma!' I stare at her. 'What are you doing here?' She does not answer but stands, pale and wide-eyed, in the middle of the room. I lean against the door, relieved. 'I thought you were...' The events of the past few hours come rushing back. Emma could be the one who betrayed me. 'What's going on?' I demand. I realize that I am speaking loudly and that someone could be listening, but I no longer care. 'I went to the bridge like you told me Marek wanted me to do. A man claiming to be Marcelitis showed but it wasn't him.'

'Good,' Emma says quietly.

I am stunned. 'How can you say that? I was nearly killed.'

'I didn't mean it that way. I mean it's good that Marcelitis didn't show because he would have been arrested or worse. My message must have made it to him in time.'

'I don't understand...'

'Oh, Marta...' Suddenly Emma bursts into tears. 'Marek's been arrested!'

My stomach drops. 'When? What happened?'

'Earlier today, after I saw you. The police came to the house and said he was under arrest for treason. They beat him in front of me and the children, nearly destroyed our home before taking him away.'

I put my hand on Emma's shoulder, my suspicions easing. 'I'm so sorry.

Emma continues through her tears, 'I figured that his arrest was somehow connected to your meeting with Marcelitis tonight. The timing was too close to be a coincidence. And I knew that if they questioned Marek, he would break and tell them the time and location of the meeting. Marek's a good man, Marta. But he's not strong like Alek and Jacob were. Like you. If they found out about the meeting, they would have arrested Marcelitis. So I was able to send word to Marcelitis through certain channels not to come. I wanted to warn you, too, but I couldn't get out of the house. The police stationed a car out front, and they had threatened to hurt the children if I made trouble. I snuck out as soon as I could, but by the time I came here, you were gone.'

'I understand.' My mind races. So Emma did not betray me, after all. The police must have broken Marek and learned about the meeting. But why had they sent the bald man to impersonate Marcelitis and steal the list, instead of just arresting me? And who killed Renata? Something still doesn't make sense. I take off my coat, then walk over to the bed and sink down on the edge. 'How did you get into my room?'

Emma looks away. 'I still remember a few things from the resistance.' I remember then how dangerous Emma's role had been during the war, sneaking around the Kommandant's office and apartment, searching for information. And she risked everything tonight to come here and warn me. She has always been much stronger than she looks. 'What are you going to do now?' she asks.

I hesitate. If Marek really did break and talk, then the police know that I am here and why. 'I have to get out of Prague.'

Emma nods. 'I can show you a shortcut to the British embassy. I know it's late, but perhaps if we explain to the guard–'

'I'm not going to the embassy,' I cut her off firmly. 'I still need to get the information to Marcelitis.'

Emma cocks her head, puzzled. 'But how? Once he received word of Marek's arrest, of the security breach, he surely would have fled. He was going to leave the country, anyway, as soon as he met with you. With the coup, the situation has become too dangerous here. Everyone is pulling up stakes.'

'Out of the country, where?'

'My contact didn't say for certain, but I'm pretty sure he meant back to Berlin. Marcelitis is based there.'

'Do you have his address? Or someone I can contact in Berlin?'

Emma shakes her head. 'I don't. I'm sorry. But Marek did go to Berlin once last winter to see Marcelitis. He told me that Marcelitis lives in central east Berlin above a bookshop. It is right across from a famous synagogue building – Oranienburger Strasse, I think the street was called. I remember because Marek found it strange that a covert operative would live right in the center of town. I pointed out to him that it was just like what the resistance used to do, meeting in the market square cafés in Kraków. The Nazis never thought to look for us right underneath their noses, never imagined that we would be so bold.' I nod, remembering. 'But, Marta, why do you ask? I mean, it's not as if you're going to go to Berlin and find him, are you?'

I do not answer. Berlin. I turn the idea over in my mind. This is not what I was supposed to do. The D.M. sent me to Prague because I knew Marek. My job was to get to Marcelitis through him and leave. Now Marek is out of the picture. I should just take the information about Marcelitis back to the Foreign Office and let someone else pick up the mission from here. I should return to my safe secretarial job in

London, to my daughter. Then I look at Emma, watching me expectantly. She would understand if I just went home. She is a mother, too. But even as I think this, I remember Hans, lying dead on the museum steps, Renata murdered in her car. I cannot quit now. I have no idea how I will get to Berlin, what I will do once I arrive. But I have to try. 'I must find Marcelitis,' I reply at last.

'But to go to Berlin, alone? That's so dangerous.'

'It's no more dangerous than what you and I have had to do in the past.' Emma does not respond, but cringes as memories of the Kommandant come crashing down upon her. 'I can handle it.' I say this as though trying to convince myself, too.

'I would go with you, if I could,' Emma offers.

'I know you would, but you have your boys to think about, and Marek, too. I wish, though, that you would reconsider my offer to come to England to live. It would be safer for all of you there.'

'Thank you,' Emma replies. 'Maybe someday. But I can't leave Marek.'

I start to reply. Then I see the tired sadness in Emma's eyes. This is her life now. 'I understand.'

Emma's eyes widen. 'You do?'

I pause. Time is of the essence. It is not the moment to be sharing confidences. But I do not know if I will ever see Emma again. 'Yes. Before I met Simon, there was someone else.' A strange look crosses Emma's face. 'After the war,' I add quickly, so that she will know I do not mean Jacob. I have always wondered if Emma worried about him and me, if she thought there was something between us. 'An American soldier named Paul. He saved my life, rescued me out of the Nazi prison, and we fell in love.'

'Marta, that's wonderful. What happened?'

'We were supposed to meet up in London and be married. But the airplane he was on crashed before he could get there.'

'Oh, no!' I can tell from the pain in her eyes that she is reliving her own loss through mine.

'With Paul, I finally understood real love. What you had with Jacob. It was worth having that, even for only a short time.'

'And your husband?'

'I actually met Simon before Paul died, on the boat coming to England. But it wasn't until afterward when I started working for him that we became involved.'

'Do you love him?'

That is the same question I asked her before about Marek, I recall, hesitating. 'Simon is a good man. He's kind to me and Rachel, like Marek is to you and the boys. But the kind of love that I had with Paul...'

'It only comes along once in a lifetime,' Emma finishes for me. 'But at least with Simon, he's the father of your child. I mean, he is, isn't he?' I look away, not answering. 'Oh, Marta!'

I cannot lie to Emma. 'Simon thinks she's his daughter. I didn't mean to trick him. It just all happened so quickly. I wasn't sure I was pregnant until after we were married, and then I didn't have the heart to hurt him. I've never told anyone the truth.'

'Until now. Why are you telling me?'

'Because you are my best friend.' Not were, I realize as I say it. Are. 'And to tell you that I understand now how you did the things that you had to do, even though you loved Jacob.'

Emma wipes her eyes. 'Thank you, Marta. That means more to me than you know.'

I nod. 'We don't have a lot of time. You need to get back to your children and I need to get out of here before the police come.'

'How are you going to get to Berlin?' Emma asks.

'I don't know,' I admit.

'You know, when Marek and some of the others went to Berlin, they would take the train to a town near the border. They would get off and walk across the border through the woods, then pick up a train on the other side.' I pause, considering her suggestion. The border is probably guarded more tightly than ever now with the coup. But it is my only chance. 'Is there anything I can do to help?' Emma asks.

'No, I...' I begin, then stop. I need to send word back to Simon about my change of plans. If he thinks I simply disappeared from the streets of Prague, he will be frantic with worry. This way, maybe the Foreign Office can arrange my extraction from Berlin instead. 'Emma, I need you deliver a message to the British embassy for me.' I walk over to the night table and picked up a pencil and a pad of paper. *Change of plans. Meeting Marcelitis in Berlin. Oranienburger Strasse.* I hand the paper to Emma. 'Ask for a man named George Lindt in the consular section,' I add, remembering Simon's mention of his

289

former colleague. 'Only him. Tell him the message is from me, that it is highly classified and urgent, and needs to be sent by secure telegraph to Simon Gold in the Foreign Office at once.'

'Can this man Lindt be trusted with the information?'

'I don't know,' I admit. 'But I don't have any other choice. Wait until morning to deliver the message. That way, even if he tells someone he shouldn't, I'll have a good head start. And you won't attract attention by going to the embassy in the dead of night. Will you be able to get out of your house again with the police watching?'

'I can manage it,' Emma replies. 'If I take the children for a walk during the day, they won't suspect anything.'

'Good. I certainly don't want to put you in more danger. I think we need to get going. You go first and I'll leave a few minutes later so as not to attract attention. Take the back stairway again.'

'Wait, there's one other thing.' Emma walks across the room and disappears into the bathroom. A minute later, she reappears, wearing only her slip. 'Take this.' She hands me her dress. 'Your clothes are too Western. They'll stand out.'

I look from the coarse gray dress she handed me to my own silk blouse. She's right, of course. I take off my clothes, then pull the dress over my head, Emma's familiar almond scent wafting upward as I close the buttons snugly across my midsection. Then I walk to the armoire and take the second outfit I brought with me, a green dress, off the hanger. 'Here.' Wordlessly, she slips it on. 'The hem is a little short for you.'

'It's perfect.' I can tell by the way she fingers the sleeve that she is unaccustomed to such fine fabric. Then she walks over to me and produces a scarf. 'You should tie your hair back, too.' Neither of us speak as she helps me to put the scarf on my head, securing it firmly underneath my hair at the base of my neck.

'Now you'd better get back to your children,' I say.

Emma nods, then steps forward. 'Thank you, Marta. For all that you've ever done.'

I kiss her on the cheek. 'No, thank *you*. I know what you risked coming here tonight. Now go.' Emma turns and leaves the room quickly, closing the door behind her.

Berlin, I think, turning back inside the room. Will I be able to manage it? Should I? But there is no time to deliberate. I walk to the armoire and start to put my clothes into my bag. Then I stop. Renata was right. It is still better to leave my belongings behind so no one knows that I have gone. I can travel more quickly without these things, anyway. I pick up the gun from the carpet and put it in my purse, checking to make sure that my passport and the papers are inside. Then I pick up my coat and, taking one last look around, turn and flee from the room.

CHAPTER 20

I peer out of the doorway of the ladies' room across the deserted train station. Five-fifty, reads the clock on the far wall of the station. I arrived nearly two hours earlier after making my way across the city by foot, hoping to catch a night train. But the departure board was blank and the concourse deserted, except for a Roma family that had set up camp at the base of one of the platforms. The father, a swarthy man with a heavy mustache, informed me that with the curfew, there would be no trains until morning. Not wanting to attract attention by waiting out in the open station, I ducked into the washroom. At first I nearly gagged at the damp, fetid odor that reminded me so much of prison. Then I remembered how to breathe shallowly through my mouth until the smell was barely there at all.

A loud screeching noise comes from the far end of the station. I turn to see a man opening the metal grate on the front of a kiosk, the first sign that the station is coming to life. A few minutes later, I notice an older woman with thick shoes and a kerchief on her head much like the one I now wear, sweeping one of the platforms. The earliest of morning travelers begin to trickle into the station.

I step from the washroom, inhaling deeply to clear my nostrils with the scent of freshly brewing coffee. Then I start toward the departure board to read the listings that have begun to appear. Across the station, I spot two policemen. One holds a German shepherd on a leash. I freeze. Easy, I tell myself. The city is under martial law. There are going to be police. But my heart pounds harder as I force myself to continue walking, looking up at the departure board as though I am any other traveler. There is an express train to Berlin at six-forty-five, though I do not dare take it. A second train, fifteen minutes later, will go to Děčín, a town I recognize from my drive to Prague with Renata as being close to the German border. I will take that one, I decide. I walk to the ticket counter, using most of the money Renata gave me to purchase a ticket, round trip so as not to arouse suspicion. Then I make my way to one of the now-open kiosks, buy a newspaper and a coffee. I sit down at a table and open the newspaper, pretending to read. Peering out over the top of the paper, I see that the policemen have gone.

Relaxing slightly, I look across the station. It has grown crowded now, travelers rushing in all directions toward the trains. My eyes lock on a tall man in a dark trench coat, crossing the station. There is something about his awkward gait, his dark curly hair, that reminds me of Paul. I stand up to get a better look, nearly spilling my coffee. But the man disappears into the crowd. I stare after him. Suddenly I am not in Prague at all but at Kings Cross, waiting for Paul, watching the disembarking crowds in vain. Then, noticing the woman at the next table looking up at me, I sit down again. I pushed thoughts of Paul away for so long. Why am I seeing ghosts now? It must be because I am back on the continent again, I decide. Or because I was just talking about him to Emma.

A minute later, I finish my coffee and stand, carrying the empty cup to a nearby trash bin. The train to Děčín has been listed for platform four. As I start across the station, a phone booth catches my eye. Do I dare call Simon? Renata said communications were down, but at least I can try. Hurriedly I rush to the phone booth and pick up the receiver. 'International operator,' I request in Czech. A second later, an operator answers in English and I give her the number. The phone rings once, then a second time. Answer, Simon, I think; pick up before the ringing wakes Rachel. 'Hallo,' Simon's voice, thick with sleep, comes over the line.

'International call,' the operator says. 'Accept the charges?'

'Yes,' Simon replies, instantly awake. 'Simon, it's me.'

'Where are you? Are you all right?'

'Yes. Still in Prague. But, Simon, about Marcelitis–'

'We know about the coup. We've been trying to get hold of the embassy, but the lines have all been down. There was a convoy of diplomats, we were hoping you would be with them. You have to get out. If you can get to Vienna, I can arrange–'

'Simon, there's more.' Quickly I tell him about the bald man impersonating Marcelitis on the bridge. 'Marcelitis didn't show, but I have an address in Berlin. If I can get there, I still think I can get him to help us.'

'Marta, that's crazy! You don't even know where to find him.'

'I have an address, on Oranienburger Strasse.'

'But you have no support in Berlin. We don't have an extraction plan–'

'I'll be fine, Simon.' Suddenly I notice a policeman walking toward the phone booth, looking at me. 'I have to go now. Tell Rachel I love her and I'll see her soon.' I can still hear Simon talking as I hang up. I look out at the policeman, my heart pounding. A voice comes over the loudspeaker, announcing my train.

I step from the booth. 'Excuse me,' I say, trying to keep my voice calm as I step around the policeman. I force myself to walk past him slowly, looking straight ahead. A few seconds later I reach the gate and join the queue of passengers boarding the train. When I look back, the policeman is in the phone booth, talking.

I board the train and make my way to an empty compartment in one of the second-class carriages. It is similar to the train I took from Salzburg, with three worn orange seats on each side of the compartment, facing one another. I sink into the seat closest to the window, then peer out. The policeman is still on the telephone. He had not been looking for me. Relieved, I lean back against the musty seat cushion.

Soon the train begins to move. As we pull away, the door to the compartment bangs open. I jump, thinking of the police. But it is just an elderly man, carrying a small suitcase. From the doorway, he gestures with his head toward the empty row of seats facing me, asking permission to sit. I nod. The man lifts his suitcase to the overhead rack, then takes the seat across from me nearest the door. He looks at me, and for a second I worry that he will try to start a conversation. Czech is close enough to Polish that I can get by, but my accent would never pass as native. And I cannot afford to stand out, not now. I pull out the newspaper, hoping to discourage him. The man produces his own newspaper and begins to read.

I press my head against the window, too tired to care if it is dirty. My entire body sags with fatigue. Was it really only the day before yesterday that I arrived in Prague? I see the bald man lunging at me, Renata dead in the car. The demonstrators fleeing. The reality of it all crashes down, overwhelming me.

I pick up the newspaper once more, scanning an article about the government. Though the article does not say so, I know that the implications of the coup are much broader than just Czechoslovakia. The country has always been a balancing point between East and West and it is possible that their takeover here might embolden the communists to seek more power elsewhere. I touch my bag, thinking of the papers inside. I have to get to Marcelitis.

Outside, daylight has broken. Hradcany Castle basks in the sunlight, impervious to the plight of the city below. If the state-controlled newspaper is at all correct, the communists will have complete power within days. I look up again at the receding skyline, apologizing silently to the place I have just abandoned.

Soon the city disappears and the landscape grows more rural, the buildings spaced fewer and farther between. I look across the compartment. The old man's eyes are closed and he is snoring lightly. I realize then how dry and heavy my own eyes feel. Between my aborted meeting with Marcelitis and fleeing the city, I did not sleep at all the previous night. I blink hard, trying to stay alert. But I feel myself growing sleepier, lulled by the rocking of the train. Just a little nap should be fine. It is still several hours until we reach the border. I close my eyes, my bag clutched tightly in my arms.

I am startled awake by a loud screeching sound. The brakes, I realize groggily. Struggling to clear my head, I look up at the man seated across from me. 'Děčin?'

He shakes his head. 'This is Karlova. You still have another two stops.'

The station is small, just a single-story building and platform surrounded by trees. Fresh snow has fallen here, covering the ground in white. Pressing my head against the window, I can make out a small group of passengers boarding. At the back of the line, a tall man in a brimmed hat and dark trench coat catches my eye. He looks back before boarding the train, and as I catch a glimpse of his pale eyes, terror shoots through me. It is the bald man, the one who impersonated Marcelitis.

For a minute, I sit frozen, unsure what to do. How did he find me? I have to get off the train. Heart pounding, I stand up and walk to the door of the compartment, looking into the corridor. To the left, I see the bald man entering the compartment behind several other passengers. I can tell from the way he looks in both directions that he has not seen me. I slip out of the car and turn to the right, keeping my head low. 'Excuse me,' I say, pushing by several boarding passengers, squeezing past their luggage. I reach the end of the compartment, cross through into the next, trying to get far enough away so that the bald man won't notice me when I step off onto the platform. I look back over my shoulder. I cannot see him anymore, but I am certain that he is not far behind. I reach the dining car, walking as quickly through it as I can without attracting attention. Now, I think, as I reach the end of the car and approach the door. Get off the train now.

The train lurches as it begins to move. My heart sinks as the station begins to recede. I am trapped. I look back over my shoulder, the cold wind blowing against my face. The bald man has entered the dining car. His eyes meet mine. I take a step forward, looking through the door at the snowy ground that flies by quicker now. As the bald man starts across, the carriage, I know that I have no choice. I take a deep breath and, clutching my bag, leap from the moving train into the whiteness below.

I hit the snow-covered ground with a soft thud, then roll several times down a steep embankment. I am fine, I realize, except for having the wind knocked out of me. As I stand up, I see another figure fly from the receding train. The bald man has jumped, too. I begin to run away from the tracks, across the field toward a thick pine forest. But the ground is soft here, making it difficult to move quickly. Don't look back, I think, but I cannot help it. The bald man runs down the hill, gaining on me with long strides. My lungs burn as I reach for the forest, fifteen meters, then ten. I have to go faster. I run into the darkness of the pine trees, tumbling blindly through the thick branches. Suddenly, my foot sinks into a hole. Pain rips through my ankle as I fall to the ground. I struggle to pull myself up with my arms again, but my leg folds uselessly under me. I cannot go any farther.

I look up in horror as the bald man reaches the edge of the trees. The gun, I remember, reaching inside my bag and pulling it out. With trembling hands, I cock the lever as he descends upon me. I prepare to fire in three, two, one... I squeeze the trigger and a shot cracks through the forest. The bald man stops suddenly less than two meters from me, mouth agape.

A second shot rings out. The bald man falls sideways to the ground. I look at the gun, puzzled. Had I fired again? Behind the spot where he fell, a figure emerges from the trees, holding a pistol larger than mine. It is a man in a long, dark-brown trench coat. A knit hat is pulled low over his forehead so that it almost meets his wide scarf, obscuring his face. The bald man might have had an accomplice, I remember, seeing Renata dead in the car. I sit up, aiming the gun at the second man.

He drops his gun to the ground, raising his hands in a gesture of surrender. An accomplice would not, I realize, have shot the bald man. But that doesn't mean he is a friend. 'Who are you?'

I demand in Czech.

The man shakes his head. He picks up his gun, then walks toward me, taking the pistol from my hand. 'Hey!' I cry, but before I can react, he picks me up and throws me over his shoulder effortlessly, then begins to carry me deeper into the forest. I am too surprised to struggle. My mind races. Who is this man? Is he kidnapping me? Clearly he is not working with the bald man, but he could still be after me or the information that I am carrying.

Several hundred meters deeper into the forest, the man sets me down on the ground. I wince as I try to put weight on my ankle, then limp over to a large stone. We are in a clearing of some sort, beside a large rock formation. The man turns away, bending over and putting his hands on his knees to catch his breath. I turn back in the direction from which we came. Should I try to escape while he is not looking? But the path is obscured by the trees, and I know that I would not make it far on my injured ankle.

'Who are you?' I ask again. 'Or maybe you could just tell me what you want? My husband is highly placed with the British government, so I'm sure whatever you want can be arranged.'

'In English, please,' a familiar voice says. I gasp. 'You know I'm terrible with languages.'

The man turns toward me, and as he does, he pulls the scarf away. 'Oh, my God,' I whisper, and in that moment I am certain that it is I, not the bald man, who has died.

There, standing in front of me, is Paul.

'Hello, Marta,' he says.

'Marta...' a voice calls in the darkness. 'Marta, wake up.' I open my eyes slowly, blinking. I am lying on the ground. Above me kneels Paul, wearing a worried expression. My mind reels with confusion. Am I in the Nazi prison? No, I quickly realize, noticing the bare tree branches forming a canopy splayed against white sky. Paris, perhaps? No, that happened years ago, before Paul died.

But Paul is here, staring down at me. I do not understand. It must be a dream, I decide. Maybe I hit my head. I close my eyes once more, not wanting to wake up and lose the vision of him. 'Marta, no. Open your eyes.' Something warm presses against my cheek. I reach up, closing my fingers around it. A hand. Paul's hand. I know then that I am not dreaming. I must have passed out... I snap my eyes open, tightening my grip, terrified that he will disappear. But he is still looking down at me. 'That's better.' His face breaks into its familiar half smile.

'You're alive,' I whisper, clutching his hand tightly against my cheek. Joy rises in me, mingling with disbelief. 'I don't understand...'

'I'm alive,' he repeats, his eyes not leaving mine. 'And I'll explain everything, I promise. But first things first. Are you all right?'

'F-fine,' I manage to say, still staring at him.

'You went down hard and I was afraid you'd hurt yourself. Can you stand?' I nod. 'Good. There's an army barracks not far from here and someone may have heard the shots. We have to keep moving.' He slides his arm behind my back and helps me to my feet. I wince as I try to put weight on my ankle. 'You can't walk on that,' Paul says. 'Not until we can make sure it's not broken.' Before I can respond, he scoops me up and begins to carry me again. 'There's a shelter close by where we can stop, at least for a bit. Hang on.'

I wrap my arms around his neck as he carries me along the bumpy terrain. His familiar scent overwhelms me. Paul is alive. I wonder again if this is real. My head swims with confusion. How did he survive? And what is he doing here? I stare, dumbfounded, at the back of his neck. His hair is longer now, not military, with dark curls kicking up against the edge of his collar.

A few minutes later, we reach a cave. Inside, it is dark and damp. In the distance, water trickles against rocks. Paul sets me down gently on the dirt floor against the wall. 'I need to see your ankle.' He kneels in front of me and takes off my shoe. I shiver at the touch of his fingers against my bare skin. 'It doesn't seem to be broken. Probably just a bad sprain. I'll tape it for you in a minute.' He takes a canteen from his belt and unscrews the cap. Filling it with water, he offers it to me. 'Here.'

I look from his face to the canteen then back again. He looks different somehow. There is a long scar running from his temple to his chin and his nose juts to one side, as though it has been broken. His hair, once jet-black, is flecked with premature gray. And there is a hardness to his face, the boyishness gone. But his blue eyes are unmistakable. Paul is alive! I throw myself forward, sending the capful of water flying as I wrap my arms around him. A sob rips from my throat.

'You're really here,' I say, burying my head in his neck. I start to cry then, great heaving waves of grief and joy.

He wraps his arm around me, cradling the back of my head tightly. 'Marta,' he whispers.

I inhale deeply, drinking in his scent. Paul is alive. But where has he been all of this time? I pull away from his embrace, sitting straight up. 'Tell me,' I say, wiping my eyes. 'Tell me everything.'

If Paul is surprised by my sudden change in demeanor, he gives no indication. 'I was on my way to meet you in London when our plane went down.' I nod as the horror of the morning after I'd gone to Kings Cross comes rushing back to me. 'It was terrible. One of the engines exploded and we seemed to fall forever. Then everything went black. I awoke in a military hospital in England weeks later. I'd broken twelve bones, had three surgeries for internal injuries. And I was the lucky one. I was the only person who survived, Marta. All of my guys were gone.'

'I know,' I reply. 'I'm sorry.' I reach out and put my hand on top of his. Our eyes lock. Suddenly it is as if we are back in the gardener's shed outside Salzburg, where the rest of the world ceased to exist. But the rest of the world does exist, I remember. Rachel exists. And Simon. I am married now. I have a child. I pull my hand back.

A confused expression crosses Paul's face. He clears his throat. 'Anyway, I spent months recovering in a military hospital north of London.'

He was so close the whole time, I think. If only I had known. 'But why didn't you come...'

He raises his hand to my mouth, silencing me,

then brings a finger to his lips. 'Shh.' He jerks his head toward the entrance of the cave. In the distance, I can hear a rustling noise, voices. He leaps silently to his feet. Then, grabbing me firmly underneath my arms from behind, he slides me farther into the cave, wedging us both into a tiny hiding space between two rocks. 'No matter what happens, don't make a sound.' I nod. The voices grow louder. It sounds as though they are stand-ing directly above the cave now. A dog barks. Surely the dog will smell us in here. I tremble, pressing my head against Paul's shoulder. He puts his arm around me, drawing me close.

Outside the cave, the voices fade. I exhale. They are moving away from us. Soon the air is silent once more. I look up at Paul. So he survived the crash after all. All of that pain and grief for nothing. But why hadn't he come for me? And what on earth is he doing here now?

'They've gone,' Paul says at last, his voice still a whisper. He pulls away slowly, looks down at me. 'That was a close one. We should probably wait here for a while.' He unfolds himself from the hiding place and gestures to the open area of the cave. 'Why don't you let me tape your ankle?'

I slide over to the spot he indicates and he pulls out a roll of gauze from his rucksack. As he reaches for my ankle, I lean over, catching his hand. 'Paul, wait a minute. First I want to know what you are doing here.'

He looks up at me evenly. 'I could ask you the same thing.'

'I asked first.'

He hesitates. 'When I was recuperating from

the crash, a representative from the American intelligence agency came to see me. He told me that I was dead. At least as Paul Mattison, that is.'

'I don't understand.'

'When the plane crashed, I was injured so badly that no one could identify me. And I wasn't wearing any dog tags.' He half smiles. 'Seems I had given them to some girl and hadn't bothered to get new ones before the flight.' I think guiltily of his dog tags, tucked away in my dresser drawer back home. If only he had been wearing them. Paul continues, 'By the time I woke up, everyone had already been told that I was dead. I had no identity, which, according to the man from the agency made me a perfect intelligence operative. So I agreed to stay on and work covertly for our government in Europe and they created a new identity for me.' He extends his hand. 'Michael Stevens. Nice to meet you.'

I do not shake his hand but continue staring at him, trying to process all that he has told me. 'But that still doesn't explain what you're doing here.'

'Look, Marta, the American and British governments have been working closely together to counter the Soviets in Europe, and generally the alliance works pretty well. But we still keep an eye on each other, and recently we've had reason to believe that communist loyalists have infiltrated British intelligence.' He pulls a flask from his pocket and holds it out to me. I shake my head, cringing inwardly as he takes a swig. Why has he started drinking again? But I do not know him well enough to ask that, not anymore.

'So when your mission to Prague popped up on our radar screen, we were curious,' he continues, recapping the flask. 'Our government wanted to trail you, see what you were doing.'

'And they just happened to pick you for the job?'

He looks away. 'When I realized that it was you, I volunteered.'

'Oh.' A lump forms in my throat. 'So have you been following me the entire time?'

'Not exactly. Our intelligence was a little slow, so I was a few days behind you. I got to Prague just as you were leaving, followed you onto the train.' So that had been Paul in the station after all. 'Which brings me to my question, what are *you* doing here?'

Now it is my turn to hesitate. After the events of the past few days, I am not sure that anyone, even Paul, can be trusted. 'You mean, you haven't figured it out yet?' I ask, stalling for time.

He shakes his head. 'I know that it has something to do with Jan Marcelitis and that it's important enough to make someone try to stop you. But that's all I've got.'

I can trust him, I decide, looking into his eyes. 'You were right about Soviet operatives compromising British intelligence. We've been desperately trying to figure out who they are and stop them. We recently came into possession of at least a partial list, but it's coded and no one has been able to break it.'

'So you're trying to persuade Marcelitis to give you the cipher.'

I look at him in amazement. 'You know about

the cipher?'

'Of course. Dichenko's theft of the cipher is hardly a secret, and finding it has recently become the Holy Grail of modern espionage. But no one has been able to find Marcelitis.'

'That's why they sent me,' I reply. 'There was a close associate of Marcelitis called Marek Andek whom I know from my resistance work in Kraków. His wife, Emma, was my best friend.'

Paul lets out a low whistle. 'Isn't Emma the one you told me about when we were in Paris, who spied on the Nazi commander? I thought you said she was married to someone named Jacob.'

I nod, surprised that he remembered the details of what I told him so long ago. 'She was. Jacob died.'

'I'm sorry.'

'Me, too.' I look away, clearing my throat. 'Anyhow, it's a long story, but Emma wound up in Prague with Marek. Our government thought I could convince Marek to put us in contact with Marcelitis, then offer Marcelitis information and money in exchange for the cipher.'

'Makes sense, though I think they are crazy to send you to Prague alone, especially with everything that is happening. They had to have known. But you said Andek 'was' a close associate of Marcelitis. What happened?'

'He was arrested last night. He set up a rendezvous with Marcelitis for me before it happened. But the man who showed up at our meeting claiming to be Marcelitis wasn't really him.'

'Who was he?'

I gesture with my head toward the entrance of

the cave. 'The man we just killed.'

'The bald man? Really?' I nod. 'Marta, that was Boris Sergiev, a well-known Soviet assassin.'

'Assassin?' I repeat with disbelief.

'Yes.' Assassin. A chill shoots through me. Remembering the bald man lunging at me on the railway bridge, raised knife glittering in the moonlight, I am suddenly dizzy. Paul continues, 'The police must have gotten Marek to give up the details of your meeting. Sergiev came to meet you expecting to kill Marcelitis and get the cipher.'

'Except Emma sent word to Marcelitis first and told him not to come,' I interject.

'Right, and when the bald man realized Marcelitis wasn't showing, he must have decided to impersonate Marcelitis to get you to turn over the information. The Soviets weren't messing around when they sent him. You're lucky you weren't killed.'

'I know,' I reply. 'But I still have to get the information to Marcelitis.'

Paul cocks his head. 'How are you going to do that?'

'Emma gave me a location in Berlin where she thinks he might be found.'

'And you're planning to go find him?' I nod. 'Does anyone in the Foreign Office know?'

'I asked Emma to send word through the embassy in Prague. And I called the Foreign Office from the train station before we left.' I cannot bring myself to say Simon's name to Paul.

'And they were okay with what you were doing?'

'I didn't give them a chance to say one way or the other.'

Paul brings his hand to his forehead. 'Marta, this is insane! Prague was dangerous enough, but at least you had the embassy to back you up.' Some backup, I think, remembering Renata dead in the car, my desperate flight through the backstreets of Prague. Paul continues, 'But trying to travel to Berlin alone to find this man... I mean, Berlin is even more of a powder keg than Prague. There it isn't just some puppet regime—it's the Soviets themselves controlling their sector. And they've made noises about block-ading all of Berlin. It could happen anytime now.'

'That's exactly why I have to get there right away.'

'But how? You're in the woods of northern Czechoslovakia, hundreds of miles from Berlin. You have a sprained ankle. And as soon as the Soviets discover that Sergiev is missing or dead, they're going to come after you, harder than before.' I hesitate, trying to think of an answer. 'Please let me just get you out of here. I can sneak you over the border to Austria, get you to the embassy.'

'Paul, I'm sorry. But this is something I have to do.'

He looks across the cave, not speaking for several seconds. 'Okay,' he says at last. 'But we have to figure out a way to get to Berlin unde-tected.'

'We? You aren't still planning to follow me, are you?'

He shakes his head. 'That would be a little difficult, wouldn't it, now that you know I am here? No, I can't follow you anymore. And it doesn't seem that I can stop you from going. So I guess the only thing to do is go with you so I can help you finish this mission and get you safely home.'

I stare at him in disbelief. 'You're going to help me get to Berlin?'

'Yes. It's self-interest, really. Your getting to Marcelitis is good for American interests, as well.' He sounds as though he is trying to convince himself. 'And I can report back fully on your activities,' he adds.

I do not respond. He's trying to protect me, I understand, studying his face. Part of me is glad. Finding Paul again, seeing he is alive, is like standing near a warm fire in winter. I am not ready to go out into the cold again. At the same time, I am hesitant. This is *my* mission. I do not need him rescuing me, not again. But he's right. I need his help. 'Fine,' I relent. 'So what now?'

'First, let me finish taping your ankle.' His hand is warm against my skin as he wraps the bandage several times around my ankle, securing the end and fitting my shoe back over my toes. 'Can you walk?'

I stand up, take a painful step. 'Yes, it feels much better now,' I lie.

'Okay, but you still shouldn't use it too much.' He comes to my side, then takes my arm and puts it around his shoulder. 'There's a village on the edge of the forest,' he says as we make our way slowly from the cave. 'We need to get there and find some transportation.'

Neither of us speak as Paul leads me through the forest. Only the branches beneath our feet break the silence. As we walk, I stare at Paul, fearful that if I look away he will disappear. Soon, the trees begin to thin and I see footprints where others have walked, smell smoke from a nearby chimney. We reach a path that leads us to the outskirts of a village. Paul stops at the end of a tall hedge. 'What are we doing?' I whisper.

'Shh.' He stops at a break in the in the hedge, gesturing toward it with his hand. 'In there.'

'You want me to hide in the bushes?' He nods. I step into the hedge. 'This better be good.'

'Wait here,' he says, disappearing around the corner before I can respond. Anxiety rises in me. I do not want to be separated from him again, even for a few minutes. I stare out from the bushes at the empty street. My mind struggles to reconcile all that has happened. Paul is here. Alive. But this is not two years ago. This is not Salzburg or Paris. You have Rachel, I remind myself. And Simon.

Paul reappears, pushing a two-wheeled vehicle of some sort. As he gets closer, I step from the bushes. I look from him to the bike, then back again. 'Really? A motorcycle?'

'Don't worry, I used to ride all the time back home.'

'But...'

'Look, do you want to get to Berlin or don't you? We can't take the train again and we don't have a car. This is the best way.'

I can't argue with his logic. 'Where did you get it?'

'I borrowed it from a farmhouse down the road. I suspect the farmer will be very pleased to

311

find the money I left, which is about three times what this thing is worth.'

Like the boat in Salzburg, I cannot help but think. I take a step toward the bike, then stop. 'Paul, there's something I have to tell you. I'm married now.'

'I know.'

I stare at him, surprised. 'You do? But how?'

'American intelligence,' he replies stiffly. 'Once we found out about your mission, we made it a point to learn all about you.'

'Oh.' I had hoped he knew because he cared enough to check. 'I just wanted to let you know, in case you were helping me, well, because...'

'I'm helping you because it's good for my country. That's all.' He clears his throat. 'Though I couldn't believe your husband would let you go on such a dangerous mission,' he adds.

'He didn't *let* me go,' I retort. 'I insisted. It was my choice.'

He looks over his shoulder. 'We need to go.'

I touch the seat of the motorcycle. 'Does it run?'

'We're about to find out. I didn't want to start it back in town for fear of attracting attention.' He straddles the bike and steps on the kickstand. The engine splutters then revs noisily to life. 'Come on.' He pats the seat behind him. 'There's no sidecar, like in the movies. You'll just have to hold on tight. Now hurry, before someone hears us.' I hike up my skirt and straddle the bike clumsily. Paul reaches back and hands me a helmet. 'Put this on.' When I have the strap fastened under my chin, he takes my hands and places them around his midsection. I tighten my grip, feeling his torso beneath his coat. As we start to move, I lean forward, resting my cheek on the smooth, cool expanse of his back, trying not to think, grateful for the excuse to be this close to him once more.

CHAPTER 21

I lift my cheek from Paul's back, looking up as he slows the motorcycle, then pulls over to the side of the road. We have been on back roads like this for hours, single lanes winding through rolling, snow-covered hills. Except for the occasional house or car passing in the opposite direction, we have seen no one. 'What's wrong?' I ask now, straightening.

He puts one foot on the ground, then turns to face me. 'Nothing. We're just outside Berlin, but it's only six and I'd like it to be a little darker before we make our way into the city. Hungry?' I nod. I have not eaten anything since the roll in my Prague hotel room the previous day. 'We passed a pub a few miles back, so I thought we'd stop and get something to eat.'

Paul turns the bike around and begins to drive slowly in the direction from which we came. He stopped the bike only once before, pulling off the road before the Czech-German border to bypass the official crossing. My heart pounded as we walked the bike through the woods, branches crackling beneath our feet, expecting that we would be apprehended at any moment. I was so terrified that I barely noticed the throbbing pain in my ankle. But thirty minutes later, we emerged on the German side of the border, pushing the bike up to the road and riding away once more.

For hours as we have ridden, I have clung to Paul, sheltering myself from the wind behind his broad torso. The questions and disbelief keep rising up, threatening to overwhelm me. I have grieved Paul's death for years, the loss immutably woven into the tapestry of my life. How could I have woken and breathed each day, not knowing that he was out there somewhere, alive? How is it possible that he is here again, in this most improbable of times and places? But I push the thoughts down, reveling in the chance to be close to him again, fearful that at any moment the mirage will disappear.

We pull up in front of a small tavern, smoke rising from the chimney. Paul helps me off the bike, his hand lingering longer than is necessary on my shoulder. I shiver, my reaction to his touch even stronger than it was years ago. 'Sorry,' he mumbles, pulling back. I nod and start for the door. He follows closely, a half step behind, as if he is afraid that I will disappear.

Inside, a dozen or so tables fill the small room, empty except for one where a small group of men in hunting garb are gathered. 'I'll be right back,' I say, spotting a sign for the water closet. When I return, Paul is seated at a table in the corner, close to the fireplace but as far from the hunters as possible. Two mugs of dark beer sit before him.

'I ordered us some food, too.'

'But how? You don't speak German.'

He winks. 'I've picked up a thing or two these past few years.' He hands me a mug, then raises the other. 'A toast,' he proposes.

'To what? The success of our mission?'

'No,' he replies quickly. 'That's bad luck. One of the guys in my unit, a replacement for a man we lost at Bastogne, toasted the unit on our last night in Paris. And look what happened.' A shadow crosses his eyes.

'I'm sorry.'

He shakes his head. 'To your happiness,' he says instead.

Happiness. Happiness would have been finding you years ago, I want to say. Instead, I touch my mug to his, then swallow the rich, dark beer. 'Thank you. But what about your happiness?'

He shrugs. 'I don't know what that means anymore really. I mean, I'm fine. I'm not going to wallow in self-pity.' He winks. 'Seems some girl in Salzburg taught me better. It's a miracle I'm alive, and I've got my work. But happiness? I left that behind on a September morning in Paris about two years ago.'

Suddenly it feels as if a hand is squeezing hard around my heart. If I meant so much to you, why didn't you come for me? But before I can speak, a stout woman appears and sets down two large bowls in front of us. The food is simple peasant fare: a hearty beef stew, thick hunks of bread. When the waitress has gone again, I look at Paul, hesitating. Perhaps, I realize, the answer is not one I want to hear.

A loud burst of laughter erupts from the table

315

of hunters, jarring me from my thoughts. A chill runs up my spine. In my desperation to get across the border, I had almost forgotten where I was going. I am in Germany, and not just passing through, as I had with Renata after arriving at the airport in Munich. This time, I am going to Berlin, which had been the very heart of Nazi power. I study the hunters, wondering where they had been during the war. Had they fought for Germany, killed Jews in the camps?

'So what's the plan?' Paul asks. I look back at him, his question a welcome distraction. 'Once we get into Berlin, I mean.'

I hesitate. In my hurry to flee Prague, I hadn't thought much about it. 'I don't know,' I admit. 'Go to Oranienburger Strasse, try to find Marcelitis's apartment, persuade him to talk to us.'

'You know that Oranienburger Strasse is in east Berlin?' I nod. I know from my work at the Foreign Office that the sector is controlled by the Soviets. 'And if he's not there?' Paul asks. 'Or if it's not even his apartment? Or what if he is there but won't talk to you?'

'I don't know,' I repeat. My frustration rises. 'Why are you giving me a hard time?'

'Because I want to ask you one more time to reconsider. You're a diplomat's wife, Marta, not a goddamned spy.' I turn away, too stung to respond. There is a harshness to Paul's voice I have never heard before. 'I know you did some incredibly brave things during the war. But things are different now. You have a daughter.' *So do you*, I think, wishing I could tell Paul the truth about Rachel. But I cannot, not now. 'You need to consider your safety, for her sake. Once we get into Berlin, there's no turning back. We might not even be able to get out if the Russians make good on their threat to blockade the city. Why don't you let me go for you instead?'

'I'm going to find Marcelitis,' I insist.

Paul scrapes the bottom of the bowl, finishing his stew. 'Were you always this stubborn?'

'It's almost dark,' I say, draining the last of my beer. 'We should go.'

Outside, we walk to the bike. 'Here,' Paul says, handing the helmet to me. Our fingers brush, sending a jolt of electricity through me. I look up and our eyes meet. Suddenly his face is above mine, his breath warm on my forehead. 'Marta,' he says softly, staring down at me. He lowers his lips toward mine. Unable to control myself, I raise my face to his. Then a vision of Rachel appears in my mind.

I pull back. 'Paul, stop, I can't.'

He searches my eyes, his expression hurt and confused. 'Do you love him?' he demands.

'What?' I ask, still flustered.

'Your husband – do you love him?'

That question again, I think, remembering Emma. I hesitate. 'I married him.'

'And me?' he presses. 'I know that you still have feelings for me, Marta. I could feel it just now.'

I bite my lip. 'Would it change anything if I did?'

'No, of course not,' he replies quickly, looking away. Neither of us speak for several seconds.

'I'm sorry if you came after me for this,' I say.

He shakes his head. 'I came after you because it was my job.' But the pain underneath his voice

317

tells a different story. I study his face as he stares off into the distance.

'But why...' I pause, biting my lip. 'Why didn't you come after me sooner? After you recovered from the crash?'

'Does it matter?' His eyes are hollow, his face a mask of bitterness I have never seen before.

I reach out and touch his arm. 'Paul, I...'

He turns, pulling away from my touch. 'Let's just concentrate on finding Marcelitis,' he says coldly. 'Then you can go home.'

As I climb on the bike behind him, I can tell that Paul is angry. Jealous. Defensiveness rises in me. It isn't fair of him to blame me for my choices. He was dead, or at least I thought so. It is not as if I chose someone else over him. I am seized once more with the urge to tell him about Rachel. But would the truth just make things worse? Before I can consider the question further, he starts the engine. The motorcycle lurches forward and I grab him quickly so as not to fall backward as we pull onto the road.

An hour later we reach the outskirts of Berlin. It is as if the war ended yesterday, I think as we pass through the residential neighborhoods. The city is a wasteland. The aftermath of the bombings is evident everywhere, street after street of once-elegant houses reduced to rubble. Paul drives more slowly here, weaving between the large craters and debris that litter the roadway. A charred smell lingers in the air. Though it is early evening, the streets are eerily silent. The few houses that still stand are dark and shuttered. Like the Jewish Quarter in Kraków after everyone had been sent away. I remember Jacob and I passing through on our way out of the city, watching his jaw tighten as he took in the once-vibrant neighborhood where Emma had been raised, now an empty shell of its former self. I can still see the curtains blowing through broken windows, feel the shattered glass crunching beneath my feet.

A sense of sick satisfaction rises inside me. So the Germans suffered, too. Good, I think, wrapping my arms more tightly around Paul. We stop at a red light. On the corner sits a house completely destroyed except for the garage. Through the half-open garage door, I see a woman and three small children sitting around an open fire. Nearby stands a man, breaking a wooden chair into pieces for kindling. The smallest child, no older than five, looks out into the street and, noticing us, stands and takes a few steps forward, eyes widening as he takes in the motorcycle, our strange clothes. He is nearly as thin as I had been in prison. For a moment I wonder if he is going to run into the street and beg us for money. But the man hurries forward and pulls him back, scolding him in words I cannot hear. I notice then the rags wrapped around the child's feet where shoes should have been. Children, like those we had seen so long ago through the window in Paris, those on the boat when I came to England. Like Emma's children. These were not the Germans I had imagined. My satisfaction disappears, replaced by a lump in my throat.

It is nearly dark now as we near the city center. Here there is new construction, identical concrete houses set too close together, tall apartment blocks being crudely erected amid the grand architecture of old Berlin. The sidewalks are thick with pedestrians making their way home from work, but the streets are strangely empty except for some buses. 'Not many cars,' I observe.

'Not many people here can afford to own them now,' Paul replies. 'But you make a good point. We should lose the bike so as not to attract attention.' He pulls over to the curb, helps me dismount. 'Wait here,' he says, disappearing around the corner with the bike. I stand on the street, watching the people as they pass, thin, pale and silent. They walk by shells of former buildings matter-of-factly, not looking up. 'Ready?' Paul asks, walking up behind me. He leads me expertly through the streets, turning right, then left.

'Do you know where we're going?' I ask in a low voice.

He nods. 'I've been here a few times in recent months for my work.'

'The devastation...' I gesture upward with my head. 'I had no idea.'

'You should have seen it a year ago,' he replies. 'At least now, with money pumping in from the West, they are starting to rebuild. But it's going to take a long time.' We turn another corner. 'This is it. Oranienburger Strasse.' The right side of the street is dominated by a massive domed building. 'That's the New Synagogue,' he adds as we approach. I look up, not answering. In our village, the synagogue was a single room, no larger than our house, with a lace curtain separating the area in the back where the women sat. Our synagogue in London is larger than that, of course, but even it is dwarfed by the cathedral-size one now before me. The brown-brick facade climbs high into the air, topped by a wide dome. Two narrower towers, identical in design, flank the main structure. But the building is in a horrible state of disrepair. The entire eastern wall of the synagogue is missing. The arched stained-glass windows have been shattered, reduced to jagged shards. Soot blackens the front doorway of the synagogue, as though there had been a fire.

It is Friday night, I realize. Before the war, the synagogue would have been filled with hundreds, even thousands of Jews, chanting the Sabbath prayers. Instead, the synagogue lies silent, a ghost of its former self. Are there any Jews left in Berlin? I wonder. Sadness rises up in me. 'We should keep moving,' Paul says in a low voice, looking furtively over his shoulder. Following his gaze, I see a man walking a dog on the far side of the street watching us curiously. Have we been followed? No, I realize quickly. The man is simply puzzled by the fact that we are interested in the synagogue. Berlin does not have tourists now. We walk farther down the street past the synagogue. 'He's gone,' Paul says.

I turn back. Across the street, as Emma said, is a tiny used bookstore in front of an apartment building. 'There it is.'

We cross the street. As we approach the book-shop, Paul grabs my arm. 'This way,' he mouths, pulling me into a narrow passageway beside the bookshop, separating it from the adjacent build-ing. At the back of the passage, there is a wood door with a high glass window. Paul stands on his toes, peering through. 'Looks like a lobby of some kind. The apartment must be upstairs.'

I notice a button beside the door. 'Here goes nothing,' I say, pressing it. There is no response. 'Maybe it's broken.' I push it again.

Paul presses his ear against the door. 'It definitely works. I can hear it. Well, no one's answering. What do you want to do?'

I hesitate. 'We can't give up. We have to find him.' I turn the doorknob and the door opens. Inside, a single bare bulb casts dim light across the tiny foyer. Paint peels from the walls. 'Hello,' I call, stepping through the doorway. My voice echoes back at us. Paul points toward a narrow metal staircase leading upward. The stairs groan beneath us as we climb them. At the top, there is a short corridor, leading to an open door. 'Hello,' I call again. As we near the doorway, I see that the frame is splintered, one of its hinges ripped away. An uneasy feeling rises in me. Someone has broken in.

Paul grabs me by the shoulder, pulling me behind him. I notice for the first time that he has pulled out his gun, holding it low to his waist. 'Wait here,' he mouths, stepping forward. He enters the apartment, then disappears from view around a corner. 'No...'

'What is it?' Unable to wait any longer, I race through the door. 'Oh, my goodness...' The apartment is in complete disarray. A brown sofa lies toppled backward, its cushions ripped open. In the small kitchen off to the right, shattered glass and dishes litter the floor.

Paul walks to a desk in the corner of the room.

The roller top is open and papers are strewn across the desktop, chair and floor. 'This is Marcelitis's apartment,' he says, picking up a piece of paper and scanning it. 'My guess is that Marcelitis had a visit from the police.'

I walk to the kitchen table, where a cup of coffee lies spilled. 'Still warm,' I say, touching the liquid. 'You think he's been arrested?' Paul nods. An uneasy tingle crawls up my spine. I turn back toward him. 'Do you think it was because of...' I begin, then stop again. Paul has opened the desk drawer and begun rummaging through it. Then he drops to his hands and knees and starts tapping on the hardwood floor by the desk, his ear close to the ground. 'What are you doing?'

'Looking for the cipher,' he replies, sliding away from the desk and tapping on the floor again.

'You really think he would leave it here?'

'I think I want to make...' He stops, then pulls a small pocketknife from his coat and begins to pry at one of the floorboards. I walk toward him as he raises the board, revealing a hollow compartment. 'Aha!' he exclaims, pulling several sheets of folded paper from the ground. Setting the papers aside, he reaches into the hole once more. His face falls.

'No cipher?' He shakes his head. Picking up the papers, he unfolds them and scans the top sheet. He replaces the floorboard, tapping the nails back into place with the handle of the pocketknife. Then he stands, still holding the papers.

'What are you doing with those?'

'Taking them, of course. We can't leave them here. They contain key information about

323

Marcelitis's work. I don't want the police finding these if they decide to come back and search more thoroughly.'

'But I don't understand. Why would they...?' He thinks they may come back after us, I realize. Goose bumps form on my arms.

Paul tucks the papers into his jacket and starts toward me. 'Let's discuss this outside, shall–' A shuffling sound comes from the doorway on the far side of the room. Both of our heads snap toward the sound. Someone is here. The noise comes again, louder this time. I hold my breath as Paul takes a step toward the doorway, raising his gun. An orange cat meanders into view, looking at us with disinterest.

I lean against the table, relieved. 'Just a cat.'

'For now,' Paul replies. He bends over and scoops up the scrawny animal, his face softening. 'She looks hungry.' I cannot help but think of Delia's well-fed cat, Ruff. He walks to the kitchen and opens one cupboard, then another. 'Nothing...' Then he opens the refrigerator and pulls out a bottle of milk. He pulls a bowl from the sink and pours some milk into it, then sets the cat gently down. 'Poor thing,' he says, watching the animal drink greedily. 'Let's go.'

'I didn't know you liked cats,' I remark in a low voice as we make our way back down the stairs.

'Cats, dogs, it doesn't matter. Growing up on the farm we had every animal you could imagine. But during the war...' He shudders. 'You wouldn't believe what I saw. All kinds of animals left on their own to starve or be killed.'

'I know,' I say, remembering the packs of

scrawny dogs that roamed the outskirts of Kraków during the war, searching through piles of garbage. There were stories of people killing them for food. Outside, in the passageway, I stop. 'So what are we going to do?' The darkened street is nearly deserted and the few remaining passersby walk quickly with their coats drawn, heads down. I look sideways through the front window of the bookstore. A thin, balding man stands behind the counter, hunched over a ledger. His eyes flick upward, peering out behind wire glasses. Then, meeting my gaze, he looks downward once more. I gesture toward the bookstore with my head. 'Maybe he saw something.'

Paul shakes his head. 'Even assuming he's not too scared to talk to us, what's he going to say? That he saw the police take a man away? And asking will only draw attention to us.'

'I think we've already drawn attention,' I reply, remembering the ransacked apartment. 'It's worth a try.'

'I'll go check,' Paul relents. 'Wait here.' He looks both ways out of the passageway, then walks into the bookstore. A look of alarm crosses the bookseller's face as Paul enters the store. Then, as Paul speaks to him, the man seems to relax slightly, saying something and pointing out the window to the right. A minute later, Paul walks out of the store. 'Let's get out of here.' He leads me around the corner. As we walk, our steps fall into a natural, easy rhythm, Paul's shortening to match my own. It is as if nothing has changed, as if we had walked the streets of Paris together yesterday, and the years between simply did not exist.

I follow Paul down another block to a café. As we enter, I look up at him, puzzled. 'We need to blend in,' he explains. Inside the atmosphere is surprisingly festive, a respite from the dreary street outside. Tiny Christmas lights and sprigs of fir tree adorn the bar and windows, decorating the otherwise plain room. People crowd the bar, drinking and talking merrily. In the distance, piano music plays. What had this café been like during the war? Had it been frequented by the Nazis, like the one we blew up in Kraków? Perhaps it had been a meeting place for the resistance. Or maybe just a café, like it is now, where ordinary Berliners came to escape their troubles for a while.

Paul ushers me through the crowd to a table in the back of the café. 'Wait here,' he says, disappearing into the crowd once more. I sit down numbly. A minute later, Paul returns with two cups of coffee, handing me one. 'So what did the bookseller say?' I ask, cupping my hands around the warmth as he sits down.

'Pretty much what we expected. Marcelitis was arrested less than an hour before we arrived.' He pulls the flask from his pocket, pouring some of the liquor into his coffee.

This time I cannot help myself. 'You're drinking again,' I observe, struggling to keep my voice even.

'Yes.' He does not offer an explanation but picks up the coffee and takes a large gulp, defiant.

I hesitate, wanting to say more. The accident, everything that happened, seems to have changed him so. But it isn't my place. I am not sure I even know him anymore. I take a sip of my own coffee, hot and bitter. 'Do you really think his arrest has something to do with us?' I ask instead.

'Seems a little coincidental, don't you think? I mean Marcelitis managed to elude the Soviets for years. Sergiev must have told someone that you were headed to Berlin before he came after you.'

'But that doesn't explain how they found out Marcelitis's location and made it to him before we did,' I reply.

'True. You got Marcelitis's address from your friend Emma, right?'

I nod. 'But she would never have given up that information.' As I say this, an uneasy feeling rises up in me. Emma would have broken and talked to save her children. Had the police come after her again?

'Who else?'

'I told Simon over the phone.' At the sound of my husband's name, Paul looks as though he has been slapped. 'But I called from the train station, so I doubt anyone was listening in on the call,' I continue quickly. 'And I had Emma send word through the embassy. I don't know if she gave them the address, though.' My head throbs. 'Anyway, it doesn't matter now. Marcelitis is gone.' Defeat washes over me. 'Dammit. If we hadn't stopped to eat or–'

'Marta, don't. If we had shown up earlier we would be in jail with Marcelitis. You can't second-guess these things.'

I look away. 'I know. It's just that I really thought

if I came to Berlin...' My eyes begin to burn. 'Who the hell did I think I was?' I blink several times, but it is too late. Tears spill onto my cheeks.

'Hey.' Paul leans over and takes my chin in his hand, wiping my cheeks gently. Our eyes lock. He is, I see then, exactly the same man I have always known.

I straighten. 'I'm sorry. I don't mean to be emotional.'

'It's okay. I'm sorry, too.' He pulls his hand back, then hesitates. 'There is one thing. I probably shouldn't even tell you this...'

'What is it?'

'The man in the bookstore said that Marcelitis was taken away in a city police car, not state.' I tilt my head, not understanding. 'That means they're probably keeping him in the local jail overnight before handing him over to Soviet intelligence in the morning.'

'But he's still in prison, so what good does that do...?' I trail off, staring at him. 'Are you saying we can get to Marcelitis in jail?'

Paul hesitates. 'I don't even know why I'm saying this to you, Marta. A few hours ago I was telling you to go home and give up. And I still think that you should.' He taps his jacket pocket. 'But seeing the papers on Marcelitis's operations, well, I understand now why it is so important.'

'So you're saying we can try to help him?'

Paul shakes his head. 'Not we. Me. I can try, but I won't have you a part of this. It's too dangerous.'

'You're not going without me. This is my mission.'

'Marta, be reasonable. You would be risking

your life, even more than you already have. Think of your daughter.' I bite my lip, resisting the urge once more to tell Paul that Rachel is his. 'Anyway,' Paul adds, smiling, 'rescuing people from prison is what I do best, remember?'

I am not amused. 'What's your plan?'

Paul looks upward, thinking. 'I'm sure there's a back way into the police station. The local stations tend to be small, so hopefully there's only one or two policemen on duty. If I can get in and overpower the guard without anyone else hearing, we have a chance.'

A chance. 'You need a decoy,' I reply. Paul cocks his head. 'I can go into the police station, claim I lost my passport. Flirt.' A wrinkle of displeasure forms on his brow. 'That way any other policemen will be distracted while you are in the holding area.' Paul opens his mouth, but before he can speak, I continue. 'Come on. I'm right and you know it. You need my help.'

'I don't know...' Paul begins. 'I mean, what if something goes wrong?'

'Then I'm just another woman in a police station. I can walk right back out the front door. But it could make a huge difference in your being able to get to Marcelitis.'

I watch Paul's face as he searches for another argument. 'Okay,' he concedes. 'But at the first hint of any trouble, I want you to get out of there and go to...' He stops, unable to finish the sentence. I know that he wants to be able to tell me to go to the embassy. Suddenly I am reminded of playing tag with the other children in my village as a child. There was always home base, a safe place that one could run to and not be caught. But we are behind Soviet lines, completely alone. There is no home base here. 'Well, just get out of there, okay?'

'Agreed. When are we going to do this?'

I follow his gaze to the clock over the bar. It is almost nine o'clock. 'Soon, I think. The night shift should come on around ten and hopefully they'll be on a skeleton crew after that.'

An hour later we stand in a doorway around the corner from the police station. It is a drab, one-story concrete structure, no larger than a corner grocery store. 'There's the shift change,' Paul whispers as three policemen exit the station. Their voices fade as they walk away from us down the street. 'You'll go in the front door,' Paul instructs, pointing. 'There should be just one guard at the desk. Talk slowly. I'll go around to the back and find the holding cell. It's probably in the basement.

'What if the back door is locked?'

'I'll get in,' Paul says, his face resolute. 'There's always a way.'

I wonder then about the work he has been doing since surviving the crash, the things he must have seen. 'How long do you need me to stall?'

'Fifteen minutes at least. Twenty would be ideal. Any longer and Marcelitis is either not there or dead.'

A shiver runs up my spine. I hadn't considered the possibility that we might be too late. 'You don't think...'

He shakes his head. 'That they would kill him here? Highly unlikely.' I start to walk out of the doorway but Paul grabs me by the shoulders and pulls me back. 'Marta, wait.' I turn back. His eyes search mine and for a second I wonder if he might try to kiss me again. 'I want to say, I mean, in case something happens...' He falters.

I look up, fighting the urge to touch his cheek. 'Let's just get this done.'

He nods. 'Be careful.'

I cross the street hurriedly. At the door of the police station, I pause and turn back. Paul has disappeared from the alleyway. I take a deep breath, then open the door. Inside, there are two desks, set about a meter apart. A heavyset policeman sits behind the desk to my right, reading a newspaper. '*Ja?*' he says, not looking up.

'*G-guten* a*bend,*' I stammer.

At the sound of my voice, he lifts his head. Taking me in from bottom to top, his expression changes. '*Guten abend, fräulein.* How can I help?'

I summon my most distressed expression. 'I was on my way to visit my aunt when I realized my passport was gone.'

'Lost or stolen?'

I hesitate. 'Stolen, I think. My money is gone, too.'

'You'll need to fill out a report,' the officer says. He reaches into a drawer and pulls out a form.

I approach the desk slowly, stalling for time. 'I'm Lola,' I say softly as I sit down. 'What's your name?'

He gestures to the name on the breast pocket of his uniform. 'Sergeant Schobel.'

'No, I mean your first name,' I press.

Schobel hesitates, and for a moment I wonder

if I have gone too far. 'Joseph,' he replies.

'Joseph, it's nice to meet you. Do you have a pen I can use?' As he hands me the pen, I brush my fingers against his, lingering for just a second. He pulls his hand back and quickly begins shuffling the papers on the desk.

I look down at the form, feeling queasy from the effort of flirting with Schobel. Is this what it felt like for Emma, I wonder, having to be close to the Kommandant? Concentrate, I tell myself. Out of the corner of my eye, I look up. Schobel has picked up his newspaper and begun to read once more, but I can see him taking small furtive peeks at the top of my blouse. On the rear wall, I notice the outline of a wall hanging that has been removed. A swastika, I realize, suddenly nauseous.

Forcing myself to breathe, I turn back to the form. A minute later I look up again. Behind the desks, there is a doorway leading to a corridor. That must be the way to the basement stairs. But I do not see any sign of Paul. I look down at the form again, pretending to write. Suddenly, there are footsteps in the corridor and another officer, older than the first and also heavyset, appears in the doorway. 'What's going on, Schobel?' he asks.

I freeze, pen suspended midair. I was not prepared for a second policeman. 'Young lady was on her way to visit her aunt and had her passport stolen,' Schobel replies.

'You're having her fill out a report?' asks the older man, whose name tag reads Hart. Schobel nods. 'Good. I'm going to check on things downstairs.' He turns and begins walking toward the staircase.

Oh God. If Hart goes downstairs now, he will surely catch Paul. I jump to my feet. 'Excuse me...' I call after him.

He turns back, clearly annoyed. 'Yes?'

I take a step toward him, pretending to read his name tag. 'Officer ... Hart, is it?' He nods impatiently. 'Well, I wanted to ask you and Officer Schobel what I should do now that I have lost my passport and money.' I speak as slowly as I can, stalling for time.

'Officer Schobel will be able to provide any assistance you need. Now, if you'll excuse—'

'But I wanted to ask both of you. I mean...' I stop as something moves behind Hart in the corridor. I recognize the flash of Paul's brown coat before it disappears again. I have to keep Hart talking. 'I mean, that is...' I falter. Noticing my distraction, Hart spins around. But the hallway is empty.

'*Fräulein*, I really must ask you to sit down and let Officer Schobel assist you.'

If I sit down, Hart will go downstairs and discover Paul. 'But surely with your experience...' I press, stalling for time.

Hart draws his eyebrows so closely together they look like a single knot of hair. 'What street does your aunt live on?'

'Excuse me?'

'Your aunt, the one you came to visit in Berlin. What is her street address?'

I hesitate, trying desperately to come up with an answer. 'Number seven, Ringlerstrasse,' I reply, coming up with the name of the only street I remember passing on our way over to the police station, then adding a house number.

Watching Hart's eyes go wide with recognition, I know that I have made some kind of a mistake. 'That's quite impossible, *fräulein*. The houses on Ringlerstrasse have been completely uninhabitable since the last bombing raids during the war.' He grabs me roughly by the wrist. 'Now, what are you doing here?'

Panic shoots through me. 'I – I don't understand,' I stammer. 'I already told you I lost my passport and...'

'A likely story,' Hart says, cutting me off. 'Why are you really here?

Schobel stands up. 'Perhaps she is here because of the visitor.'

'We're not supposed to talk about that,' Hart replies quickly.

'I – I don't know anything about a visitor,' I offer.

'Maybe you did and maybe you didn't, but you do now. We can't let you go.' He turns to Schobel. 'Arrest her.'

'You're arresting me? But I've done nothing wrong!'

Schobel scrambles over to where we stand. 'I told you we needed more staff while Marcelit–'

'Again, we aren't talking about that!' Hart explodes.

'Well, I just thought now that she knows, anyway,' Schobel mumbles defensively, as he starts to put the cuff around my wrist.

'Wait a second...' I begin, stalling for time. Paul said to get out of here at the first sign of trouble. For a minute, I consider trying to run. But there is no way I can break away from both of them.

Suddenly, there is a noise in the corridor. 'What the...?' Hart says, spinning around.

Paul stands behind him, gun drawn. 'Let her go,' he says. Hart's jaw drops and he hesitates, uncertain what to do. Should I try to break away? Then he reaches for his weapon, swinging it wildly toward Paul. 'Don't!' There is a loud bang and Hart's grip on my wrist loosens as he drops to the floor, eyes wide.

Paul turns his gun toward Schobel. 'Let her go,' he repeats. I can feel the younger policeman trembling, uncertain what to do. 'We don't want to hurt you,' Paul adds, stepping forward. Schobel hesitates for a second, then releases me. 'Hands behind your back,' Paul orders, then turns to me. 'It took me longer to get in the back door than I expected. Are you all right?' I nod, feeling his eyes on me, making sure. 'Cuff him.'

I follow his instructions. 'What are we going to do with him?'

'Put him in the cell.'

'Have you been down there yet?'

Paul shakes his head. 'I had to come get you first.'

'Thanks,' I reply, embarrassed. I was supposed to help him by distracting the police and instead I delayed him.

'It's fine,' Paul says, seeming to read my thoughts. 'Let's just go get Marcelitis.'

'So that *is* why you are here,' Schobel exclaims.

'Quiet,' Paul orders. He takes the policeman by the arm and leads him down the hallway to a staircase. 'After you.' Defeated, Schobel starts down the steps, Paul close behind him. 'Wait here,' he says to me.

I nod, watching as they disappear into the darkness. The air below has a damp, fetid smell that reminds me uncomfortably of my own time in prison. 'Hello?' I hear Paul's voice. 'Is there a light up there?' he calls to me. I feel along the wall until my hand touches a switch. I flick it on, illuminating the cellar below in gray light. Unable to wait any longer, I race down the stairs. The cellar is brick, the back half of the room separated by iron bars. Behind the bars in the far corner, a small figure crouches in a ball on the concrete floor.

'Jan Marcelitis?' Paul asks. The figure does not move. My heart sinks. We are too late. Marcelitis is dead.

Paul pulls on the door to the cell, which is locked. He turns back to Schobel. 'Keys?'

Schobel tilts his head downward. 'My back pocket.'

I cross to Schobel and pull the keys from his pocket, then toss them to Paul. He opens the door. He crosses the cell, rolls the crouched figure over. 'Oh, my God...'

'Not quite,' a muffled voice says in English. As the person I have been looking for across two countries sits up and turns to face us, I cannot help but gasp aloud.

Jan Marcelitis is a woman.

CHAPTER 22

'Jan Marcelitis?' Paul repeats.

The woman nods. 'I'm Jan,' she says in accented English. I cannot help but stare. The great Jan Marcelitis is no bigger than me, with a low auburn ponytail and bright green eyes. She looks from Paul to me, then back again. 'Who are you?'

'There's no time to explain now, but I'm American and she's with the British government and we're here to get you out. Are you hurt?'

Jan stands up and brushes herself off. 'No.' She steps out of the cell, shooting Schobel a withering look. 'They hadn't reached that part yet. I think they were waiting until they took me to headquarters.'

'Good.' Paul turns to Schobel and points to the cell. 'You, inside.' Schobel scrambles into the cell.

'You're leaving him alive?' Jan asks, her voice filled with disbelief.

Paul hesitates. I was wondering the same thing. Schobel saw our faces, would be able to identify us. But I know Paul does not have it in him to kill an unarmed man, not if there is another way. 'I don't know...' he says at last.

Jan turns to Schobel, who has turned pale. 'How long until the next shift comes on?'

'N – not until six,' he stammers.

Jan looks at the clock on the wall. A cruel joke to have a clock in jail, I think, following her gaze,

337

remembering my own endless days in prison. 'That's almost eight hours from now, assuming he's telling the truth.' She walks back into the cell and grabs Schobel, who towers over her by at least a head, hard by the lapels. 'You'd better not be lying,' she warns.

'I – I'm not,' Schobel replies. 'We came on at ten and each shift is eight hours.'

Jan stares Schobel in the eyes for a second longer. Then she releases him so roughly that he stumbles backward, almost falling. She walks over to Paul. 'Give me your gun.'

Paul hesitates. 'I don't think we should–'

'Just give it to me.' Jan reaches over impatiently and grabs the gun from Paul's waistband, then strides back into the cell. 'On your knees,' she orders.

'Please...' Schobel begs.

'Wait, I don't think...' Paul begins, but Jan holds up her hand, silencing him. I open my mouth to try to help, then close it again. I was in prison once. I understand Jan's fury.

'On your knees,' Jan repeats, walking behind Schobel. Slowly, Schobel kneels and closes his eyes. I look away, bracing myself for the gunshot. Instead, there is a dull thud, followed by a muffled sound. I turn back toward the cell. Schobel lies slumped on the floor, eyes closed. She really killed him, I think. Then, taking a step closer, I can see that he breathes easily, as though sleeping.

'I clocked him pretty hard,' Jan says, walking out of the cell and locking the door. She shoves the keys into her pocket. 'He won't wake up until the next shift arrives.' She hands the gun back to Paul. 'Now, let's get out of here.'

Wordlessly, Paul and I follow Jan up the stairs and through the police station. Upstairs, Hart lies motionless on the floor, arms splayed above his head, his lifeless eyes staring at the ceiling. He is the second person to die today because of my mission. And he was not out to get us like the bald man; he was just caught in the wrong place.

'We need to hide the body,' Jan says. I look over at Paul. He is staring at Hart and I can tell from the way that his mouth twists that he shares my guilt, that this killing did not come easily to him. 'In the basement cell,' Jan suggests.

I shudder inwardly, imagining Schobel trapped with the body of his dead colleague all night. 'Do we have the time to do that?'

'I suppose you're right,' Jan concedes, then turns to Paul. 'Help me move him behind the desk.' I look away as they drag Hart's body from view.

Outside, the street is deserted. 'Follow me,' Jan says. 'And quietly, we're breaking curfew.' She leads us swiftly through the backstreets, not making a sound. Her auburn ponytail bobs like a beacon in the darkness. Paul follows behind me, so closely I wonder if Jan will think we are a couple. I fight the urge to reach for his hand.

A few minutes later Jan stops in front of a large restaurant. A brightly lit sign above the front door bears the name Meierhof. Paul and I exchange puzzled looks. Surely we aren't going in here. But Jan leads us around the side of the building and opens a cellar door, gesturing with

339

a nod of her head that we should go inside. We climb down the ladder into a dark cellar. Jan follows, closing the door above her.

'Here we are,' she says, lighting a match and taking it to a small stub of a candle that sits on a table. Thousands of bottles, stacked on top of one another, line the brick walls on all sides, climbing to the high ceiling.

'A wine cellar?' Paul asks disbelievingly, looking up.

'Not just any wine cellar,' Jan replies. 'This is the Meierhof wine cellar. Meierhof has been one of Berlin's finest restaurants for more than a century. It has one of the most extensive wine cellars in the world.'

Paul whistles. 'I'll say!'

'And the cellar's construction is incredibly stable. Not a single bottle of wine was broken during all of the bombing raids of the war. The Meierhof family let people take shelter here during the raids.'

German people, I think. They were the enemy then. 'They were just ordinary people,' Jan adds, seeming to read my thoughts. 'Trying to survive the war. The Meierhofs were only saving civilian lives. They would have done the same for either side. And now they are staunch anti-communists, which is why they allow us to use the cellar in emergencies.'

'Won't the waiters be coming down here for wine?' I ask.

Jan shakes her head. 'There is a smaller wine closet up by the kitchen with more than enough for the evening. These are just the reserves.' She points to a small door on the back wall. 'And if a customer has an unusual wine request, Herr Meierhof himself will send a note down in the dumbwaiter and we'll send the bottle up. We won't be disturbed.' She gestures to the table. 'So why don't we sit down and you can tell me who you are and what you're doing here.'

I hesitate, looking at Paul. I have imagined meeting Marcelitis for days and now that we are actually here, I am not sure what to say. 'I'm Michael Stevens,' he begins, using his alias. 'I'm an American intelligence agent. Marta here works for the British government.' I notice that he does not say my last name.

Jan shakes Paul's hand, then mine. 'It's good to meet you. My name is Jan Marcelitis.'

'We know,' I reply. 'You're the reason we're here.'

'We were a little surprised, though,' Paul adds. 'We thought that Jan Marcelitis...'

'Was a man?' Jan finishes for him, then smiles. 'It's a common mistake. The confusion started long ago. You see, Jan is principally a masculine name in many countries, so people who haven't met me often assume that I am a man. I never corrected the assumption because it helps me to keep a low profile in my work. Now why are you here? Who sent you?' Jan's expression turns businesslike once more.

'Sent Marta, actually,' Paul replies. 'I'm just along for the ride.'

'I work on Eastern European affairs for the British Foreign Office,' I say quickly.

Her head snaps in my direction. 'Are you an

341

intelligence agent, too?'

'I'm a secretary, actually.'

'I don't understand...'

'My government sent me to Prague to try to find you because I know your associate, Marek Andek. We used to work together for the resistance in Poland during the war.'

'Andek is a good man,' Jan says. 'Or was. I heard about his arrest.'

'Have you learned anything further?'

'Unfortunately, no. But things aren't looking too good for any of our men who were arrested in Prague before the coup. Andek is either dead or on his way to a Soviet prison.' My stomach twists as I think of Emma. How will she survive on her own with the children? 'What is it your government wants from me?'

I swallow, forcing myself to concentrate. 'Our intelligence work has been compromised of late by a major leak somewhere in the British government. Recently, we came into possession of a list that may identify those individuals who are secretly working for the Soviets. But we can't break the code.'

'So you've come for the cipher?' she says. I nod. 'Even assuming that I have it, what makes you think I will give it to you?'

'We're prepared to pay you half a million dollars. The money is already in a Swiss bank account.'

Jan tosses her ponytail. 'There are a dozen countries willing to pay twice that for the cipher. It's not about the money.'

'The British government, and the Americans,

too, want to offer support to you and your organization in fighting the communists,' Paul says. 'They have promised—'

Jan cuts him off. 'Respectfully, we have very little faith in anything the Western governments promise. Their promises didn't keep the Germans out of the Sudetenland, or out of Prague or even Poland,' she adds.

'I know,' I reply quietly. 'I was there, too. I remember what happened. But this is different.'

She narrows her eyes. 'Really? How?'

'They sent me to give you this.' I pull the papers out of my bag and slide them across the table. Jan takes the papers and holds them close to the candlelight. 'That letter is actually a list of some of our key contacts in this region, contacts who can—'

'I know what it is.' Her eyes widen as she scans the first page. 'How do I get the code?'

'You are supposed to contact a man called Lindt at our embassy in Prague. He'll provide you with the code once I've sent word that you've given us the cipher. Of course, if Prague is too difficult with everything that has happened, I can try to get a contact elsewhere.'

'I can manage Prague,' Jan replies quickly, folding the letter and tucking it into her blouse.

'Does that mean we have a deal?' Paul asks.

I hold my breath as Jan looks from the papers to Paul, then back again. 'Yes, but I have to go get the cipher,' she replies slowly. 'That's going to take a few hours.'

'Do you want us to go with you?' I ask.

Jan shakes her head. 'I can move faster on my

own, attract less attention.' She stands up. 'Wait here.' Before either of us can respond, she walks to the cellar ladder, then climbs up it and disappears.

Paul and I look at each other nervously. 'Do you think we can trust her?' I ask.

'I think we don't have a choice. Anyway, she still needs the information from the embassy to decode the list and she can't get that until we green-light it.'

I nod, remembering the passion in Jan's eyes as she talked about fighting the communists. 'We can trust her.'

Paul nods. 'I agree. I think she's amazing.' Hearing the admiration in his voice, I cannot help but feel a small stab of jealousy. I wish that I was amazing, too, instead of some girl Paul always has to rescue.

There is a noise at the top of the ladder and a second later Jan reappears. 'All set. You can wait here while I go for the cipher. You'll be safe, and I've asked Herr Meierhof to send down some food.'

'Okay,' Paul replies, but his tone is uneasy. 'We need to think about getting out of Berlin, though, before anyone discovers what happened at the police station.'

'We all need to be out of the country by daybreak,' Jan agrees. 'If I can get some new papers for both of you, there's a possibility you can take the early-morning flight to Vienna. Meanwhile, both of you need to stay here, out of sight.' She takes the candle and walks to one of the wine racks and pushes it aside easily, revealing a door.

344

I notice for the first time that the bottles on that rack are empty. Jan opens the door and I follow her through into another, smaller brick room. It is bare, except for a narrow mattress on the floor. 'I'm sorry the accommodations aren't more hospitable,' she says to me in a low voice. 'But at least you can stay together.'

'But we aren't together,' I protest quickly. 'I mean, I'm married.'

'To someone else?' Jan sounds surprised. 'Oh, I'm sorry. It's just that the way the two of you are together, I mean, the way you look at each other ... well, never mind, then. My mistake.'

Paul comes into the room. 'Everything okay?'

'Fine,' I reply, feeling my cheeks redden.

'Then I'm off,' Jan says, handing me the candle. 'I'll be back before dawn to take you to the airport. Help yourself to a bottle of wine if you feel like it. Anything except the 1922 Château Rothschild. It's worth a fortune. Herr Meierhof would kill me. Have a good night, you two.' Her tone makes me wonder if she still thinks there is something between Paul and me.

She walks out of the room, and a few second later I hear the cellar door close. Paul turns to me. 'You did it. Congratulations.'

'*We* did it,' I correct him, setting the candle on the ground beside the mattress.

'Okay,' he agrees. 'But let's hold off on the celebration until we're out of Berlin.'

Before I can answer, there is a banging noise from the front room. I wonder if something is wrong and Jan has returned. 'Wait here,' Paul says. A minute later he reappears, carrying two steaming plates heaped with meat and noodles. 'These came down in the dumbwaiter. Hungry?'

'No, but you go ahead.' Paul shrugs, then sets the plates down on the floor and drops to the mattress. I sit down beside him, watching him eat.

'You should try this,' he says between bites. 'It's really good. World-famous cuisine from the Meierhof. When are you going to have the chance to try this again?'

'Fine,' I relent. He stabs a piece of meat and covers it in sauce. Then he brings the fork to my mouth, cupping his other hand beneath it to catch any drips of sauce. As I take the meat from the fork, our eyes lock. Then I pull away, swallowing. 'Delicious,' I say, my voice cracking.

'Do you want more?' I shake my head. He finishes eating, then carries the two plates, his empty and mine untouched, to the table in the front room. 'It's hard, isn't it?' Paul asks abruptly as he reenters the room.

My heart skips a beat. 'What is?'

He sits down on the mattress beside me once more. 'Being back in Germany, after all that you went through here. It must be difficult.'

'Lots of things are,' I reply evenly. Paul looks away. Neither of us speak for several seconds.

'Do you want to play?' Paul asks finally, drawing a deck of cards from his bag. 'We might as well kill some time.'

I hesitate. 'I don't know too many games. Gin is my best. I used to play it with my grandmother, Feige, when I was a child.' I see her stout fingers shuffling the deck of cards, her brown eyes glinting with anticipation as she arranged her hand.

'That's funny, so did I.' Paul shuffles the cards. 'Play gin with my grandmother, I mean. She would always let me win.'

'Not mine. She was really good and she always played for real. But every time she beat me, she would say, "Someone will love you very much."'

'Really?' Paul begins to deal the cards. 'What did she mean?'

'There's some old saying, "lucky in cards, unlucky in love." Or maybe I have it backward. But the point is that if you are a bad card player, you are supposed to be lucky in love.' Lucky in love. Someone will love you very much. Bubbe Feige's words echo in my head as I arrange my hand of cards. Had she been right? Simon loves me in his own way, I know. But 'lucky' would have been finding Paul years ago, before it was too late.

I look up from my cards to see Paul staring at me. 'Your turn,' he says. I pick up the top card from the stack, a queen of clubs, and put it in between the two other queens I am holding, then discard the ten of diamonds.

'So tell me about your life,' I say. 'Not the classified parts, I mean. But where do you live when you're not working?'

'Nowhere, really.' Paul takes a card from the top of the deck and discards it right away, revealing a five of diamonds. 'There's an apartment in Zurich and another in Brussels where myself and a few of the other guys can catch some sleep, get cleaned up, change clothes. But those aren't home to me any more than this room. Mostly I keep moving, take as much work as they can give me. It's not hard, there's lots to be done right now.'

I pick up the five of diamonds, rearranging my hand to start a run of the suit. 'Do you ever get back to England?'

He shakes his head. 'Not since I got out of the hospital. I haven't been back to Paris, either.' Or Salzburg, I guess silently as he takes his turn. And if there had been an assignment at the prison in Munich he probably would have turned that one down, too. He is avoiding the places that remind him of me, I realize. Trying to outrun his memories. 'The work's not just in Europe, though,' he adds. 'I've been to Africa twice and I'm supposed to make my first trip to Asia next. When we're done here, I mean.'

When we're done here. The reality slams into my chest like a rock: this is going to end. As soon as we get out of Germany, I am going to get on a plane back to England and Paul will be off on his next mission. We will never see each other again. I stare at my cards, not seeing them. 'You're up,' he says gently. I did not realize he had taken his turn. My hand trembles as I blindly pick up a card, then throw it down again. It was the seven of diamonds, I realize too late; a card I needed. Paul picks it up and shuffles his cards. 'Gin!' he declares, laying down all of his cards in neat succession.

I set down my cards. 'Congratulations.'

'You know what they say, lucky in cards...' His voice trails off.

'Unlucky in love,' I finish for him. 'Do you really believe that?'

He shrugs. 'Look at me. I was on the way to meet the one girl I ever loved when–'

I cut him off. 'I'm sure there must have been others since. I mean, Brussels? Zurich? You probably have a girl in every port, as they say.' I try to sound light, chiding. But the mention of Paul with other women makes my stomach hurt. Suddenly I understand how he must feel, knowing about me and Simon.

Paul shakes his head. 'Not at all. I wish I could say otherwise. The truth is, there's been no one. A few dates here and there over the years. Once I had what we had...' He looks away. 'I mean, what's the point?'

'Paul...'

He turns back to me. 'I still love you, Marta.' My breath catches at the words. 'I've always known it, and, well, seeing you again ... I know that's wrong to say, but it's the truth.'

I take a deep breath. I can hold back the question no longer. 'Then why?'

'Why what?'

'Why didn't you come for me?' My words, pent up since our reunion, tumble out on top of one another. 'When you recovered, I mean. If I meant so much to you, why didn't you come find me?'

He pauses. 'I did.' Suddenly I cannot breathe. 'Marta, the truth is that as soon as I could get out of bed, I left the hospital. The doctors said it was too soon, that I was going to relapse. But I knew that I had to find you.'

'But you never came...'

'I did,' he repeats, his voice rising insistently. 'For God's sake, Marta, of course I came for you. How could I not? I went to that address in Kensington you gave me back when we were in Paris, your friend's aunt.'

'Delia's house?'

He nods. 'She wasn't there. But her butler told me you had gotten married.' He pauses, swallowing as if the words hurt his throat. 'He said that you moved out, gave me your married name. I looked you up. Even then I knew I had to see you. I went to find you, Marta.'

'You came to our house?'

'Yes. I saw you. You were working in the garden.' His eyes grow hollow and faraway in the candlelight, as though reliving the moment once more. 'I wanted you to know that I was all right, even if we couldn't be together. But then you stood up and I could see that you were pregnant.' His voice cracks. 'You looked so beautiful. You were already married and expecting a child. There was no way I could interfere with that. So I turned around and left without saying anything.'

I do not answer. In my mind, I see the day he is talking about, an early-spring morning. I can almost feel the cool, moist dirt on the backs of my hands as I planted bulbs. I remember thinking that someone was there, behind me in the garden. It was a thought I often had in the months after Paul died, on the street and in the shops, too. I turned around but as always no one was there. Or so I thought. Oh, God. If only I had known. If only he had known. I see the moment again in my mind, only this time when I stand and turn, Paul is there. I drop the gardening basket in surprise and, heedless of the neighbors or anyone else, run across the yard and throw myself into his arms.

'Marta?' My vision clears and I am in the wine cellar once more. Paul searches my face, concerned. 'Are you okay?' He really had come for me. Suddenly I can stand it no longer. I reach across the mattress and grab Paul by the shoulders, drawing him close and bringing his full lips to mine. For a second he is too stunned to respond. Then he begins kissing me back hungrily. We cling to each other desperately, as if to go back to that moment in the garden and rewrite history. 'Are you sure?' he whispers between kisses, as he had that night in Paris. I do not answer, but rip his jacket open, hear the buttons as they break and scatter across the floor. He presses me back too hard, banging my shoulder against the wall. Playing cards crush beneath me. Clutching fistfuls of his hair, I bury my head in his neck to muffle my groans. Then he touches me and it is as if we are in Paris again, two young people in a time and place where shoulds and shouldn'ts do not exist. It is our first time, our reunion and our honeymoon, all of the nights that fate took from us.

When it is over we lie breathless beside each other on the mattress. 'Are you okay?' he asks, his fingers still entwined in my hair.

'Yes,' I reply. 'I'm glad it happened.' My body aches as it did after we made love years ago.

'Really?' he asks. I nod. 'Well, that's a relief. I

wouldn't have wanted to add this to our list of considerable regrets.'

I smile. 'Me, neither.'

He touches my cheek. 'I meant what I said before. I still love you.' His face is relaxed now, boyish, all of the hardness and pain gone.

'I love you, too.' The words feel warm and natural on my tongue. 'I never knew you came looking for me. I mean, when I first saw you again, I wondered why you hadn't.'

'I did. I was surprised you had met someone else so quickly,' he added.

I hesitate. Tell him the truth about Rachel, right now, a voice inside me says. But I am uncertain how he will react, and I do not want to ruin the moment. 'You were gone,' I reply uneasily. 'Forever, I thought.'

'I understand. I was glad that you were happy.' The sincerity of his voice shatters my heart. Happiness would have been being with him. He rolls onto his side, facing me. 'So what now?'

'Now we try to get out of Berlin alive.'

'You know what I mean, Marta. What about us?'

I take a deep breath, swallow. 'I'm married, Paul.'

'Do you love him?'

I look away, unable to lie. 'I took vows...' I hear the echo of Emma's words in mine.

Paul rolls away, slamming his hand against the stone wall so hard I am afraid he might have broken a bone. 'Dammit, Marta. Why did things have to turn out this way?'

'I don't know.'

'You could leave your husband, you know. Get a divorce. Women do it sometimes.' Divorce. My mind whirls. I have heard about divorce, read about it in books, but I never thought of it as something people actually did. Paul continues. 'I would care for your daughter. Love her as if she were my own.'

She *is* yours. My eyes fill with tears and in that moment, I know I have to tell him. 'Paul, there's something that I–' My words are cut off by a banging sound coming from the front room.

Paul leaps up, pulling on his pants. 'Someone's here.' Our eyes meet uneasily. Jan is not supposed to be back so soon. Has someone else found us? Paul reaches for his gun. I pull the top of my dress closed as the door flies open and Jan rushes into the room. I cringe, knowing how ridiculous we must look, half dressed, playing cards scattered across the floor.

'Jan, we were just...' Paul begins.

But if Jan notices anything strange, she gives no indication. 'Get dressed quickly,' she instructs, crossing the room toward us. 'We have to leave.'

'I thought the flight wasn't until morning,' I say.

Jan shakes her head. 'It is nearly morning.' Paul and I exchange surprised glances. How much time has passed? 'Anyway, the flight is out of the question now.' She holds up a newspaper. Printed across the front page under the headline are unmistakable sketches of Jan, myself and Paul.

CHAPTER 23

'I told you we should have killed that police officer,' Jan says to Paul, her voice recriminating. I take the paper from her and scan the article.

'What does it say?' Paul asks, looking over my shoulder.

Jan answers before I can. 'That two foreigners liberated the notorious criminal Jan Marcelitis,' she reads, her voice wry. 'And murdered an unarmed police officer in cold blood.'

'Unarmed, that's bullsh–' Seeing my warning expression, he does not finish the sentence.

'How could this have possibly made it to the paper so soon?' I ask.

Jan shrugs. 'Someone must have come in shortly after we left and rescued that officer. I doubt he could have escaped on his own. The police brought the description to the paper right away, demanded they print it. Does it matter? Going through the airport, with Immigration and Customs, is out of the question now.'

'Maybe we hole up here for a while?' Paul asks. He sounds almost hopeful, I note with surprise. But I understand. Even with everything that is happening, the urgent need to escape, part of me wants to stay in the cellar and be with Paul.

Jan shakes her head. 'Impossible. The wine cellar is a good hiding place, but it's not un-detectable. I won't put Herr Meierhof in danger

354

by keeping you here any longer.'

I refold the newspaper, my heart sinking. 'So what are we going to do?'

'I've come up with one other possibility. There's a freighter ship, the SS *Bremen*, leaving for Britain later today from a port city north of here. If we can get you into the hull, you can stow away.'

'How long will the trip take?'

'Considerably longer than if you had been on that flight. A day, maybe two. But I think it's our only option. I've arranged for a truck to take you to the port. Come on.'

Jan starts for the door. As Paul buttons his jacket, I race after her. 'Jan, wait. I want to explain. Earlier, I told you that Pa – I mean, Michael and I weren't together, that I am married to someone–'

Jan raises her hand. 'You don't owe me any explanations.'

'But I *want* to explain.' I hesitate. Jan has trusted us with so much; I cannot bear for her to think I have been less than honest. But I am not sure how to explain what I do not quite understand myself. 'You see, Michael and I were together years ago. We were engaged, but then something happened and I thought that he was dead. I married someone else, but then a few days ago I found out that Michael is alive. So we...' I falter, realizing how improbable my explanation must sound. 'Anyway, it's complicated. But I didn't want you to think I had lied to you.'

'Life is complicated,' Jan replies. 'It is also unpredictable and short. You two obviously care for each other. But remember, there's always a price to be paid for our choices.'

She stops speaking as Paul approaches. 'What are you talking about?'

'Nothing,' I reply quickly.

'Nothing,' Jan echoes. 'Let's go.' We follow her back into the main wine cellar, but instead of walking toward the ladder, she goes to another bookshelf. Paul and I exchange puzzled expressions as she walks to one of the wine racks and begins pushing against it with her shoulder. 'This one is heavier. I need you to help me,' she says to Paul. He goes to where she stands and pushes in the same direction. Slowly, the rack begins to move to the left, revealing a small wooden door. Jan opens it. 'This way, quickly.'

Jan goes through first, crouching to fit inside the low doorway. I follow, wondering if the space is large enough to hold all of us. On the other side, I gasp. We are in a tunnel of some sort. Here the ceiling is high, the walls well carved out of stone.

'These are the Nussen tunnels,' Jan says, not looking back. 'The first ones were created in medieval times, and they were expanded by independence fighters during the Prussian war, who used them to avoid foreign troops. They connect to points all over the city. Come.'

'Were they used during the war?' I ask. 'The recent one, I mean.'

'They were used by what little resistance managed to survive in Berlin. Fortunately the tunnels are a well-guarded secret and the Nazis either never discovered them or didn't understand their true value. Berlin would have been a much harder city to take if the Allies had to fight the war down here.'

Jan does not speak further but leads us through the tunnel. My ankle begins to throb as I struggle to keep up with her swift strides. 'Are you okay?' Paul, noticing my limp, asks in a low voice behind me. I nod. Ahead, another tunnel intersects with ours. Jan turns right into it without warning. The new passageway slopes upward, causing us to climb as we walk. Ahead I can sense cool dawn air. A few minutes later we reach the end of the tunnel. Above us is a hole, revealing the star-filled sky.

'Wait a second,' Jan says, reaching into her pocket. She hands me a small metal object. 'I believe that's what you came here for.'

I hold up the cipher. It is a cylinder, no bigger than my thumb. 'Thank you.' I tuck the cylinder into my pocket.

'And these are yours,' Paul says, pulling the papers he took from Jan's apartment out of his pocket and handing them to her. 'We took them for safekeeping in case the police came back to your apartment.' I had nearly forgotten about the papers. I realize now that Paul held them back deliberately as insurance until Jan gave us the cipher.

'Thanks.' Jan tucks the papers into her pocket. 'I guess I'll have to work with you now that you've seen my operational notes.' Before either of us can answer, she locks her hands and lowers them to her knees as if to give me a boost out of the tunnel. 'Here.'

Paul steps forward. 'Let me.' Before I can react,

he puts his strong, warm hands around my waist and lifts me over his head. My head swims as I remember his earlier touch. I raise my head through the hole, then use my arms to pull myself up and outside to the ground. Standing up and brushing the dirt from my dress, I discover that we have reached a park.

Jan climbs out of the hole. 'All clear?'

I nod, then point to a truck that is parked several hundred meters away. 'Except for that.'

'That's ours,' Jan replies as Paul appears beside us. 'Let's go.' We hurry across the grassy field to the truck. Jan waves to the driver, then leads us around to the back carriage, which is covered by a tarp. 'In there. Stay away from the edge, out of sight.'

'You're not going with us?' Paul asks.

Jan shakes her head. 'The driver, Milo, is a good man and can be trusted. He'll get you past security into the harbor and as close as he can to the ship. After that it's up to you.'

'What about you? Where will you go?' Paul asks.

'South.' She touches her pocket. 'To make use of the information you've given me.'

'You're going to Prague?' I ask. Jan nods. 'Is that safe now?'

'It will be fine,' Jan replies. 'They'll never expect me to come back so soon.'

'Jan, there's one thing. Marek Andek's wife, Emma, is a good friend of mine. She's still in Prague with the children.'

'I'll look in on her,' Jan promises. 'Andek gave up everything for us. I'll make sure his wife is safe, that she has whatever she needs.'

'Thank you.'

'No, thank you. I know what it has taken for you to bring me this information, what both of you have risked. I won't let it go to waste.' She shakes Paul's hand firmly, then reaches over and kisses me on the cheek. As she pulls back, she lingers for a second, her lips close to my ear. 'Don't let him go again,' she whispers before straightening. I am too stunned to reply. 'Now, get out of here.'

Paul turns to me. 'You ready?' I nod, and he helps me onto the back of the truck and climbs in himself, pulling the tarp closed. I drop to the wooden floor. As Paul follows me, the truck begins to move, sending him flying toward me. He reaches out to break his fall.

I look out the back of the truck, hoping to catch one last glimpse of the famous Jan Marcelitis. But she has already disappeared into the darkness. 'She's pretty remarkable, isn't she?'

'You're pretty remarkable yourself,' Paul replies.

'Me? I'm just a diplomat's wife.' I look away, remembering his earlier words.

'Marta, I'm sorry about that. I didn't mean...'

'I know.' I turn back inside the carriage. It is mostly empty except for some wooden crates piled against the wall that separates us from the driver. Curious, I crawl toward the crates. Closer to the front of the carriage, I notice that some floorboards have been peeled back, revealing the road beneath us as we drive. 'Paul, check this out.'

He crosses the carriage to me on his hands and knees. 'Careful,' he says, putting his arm around my waist and pulling me back from the edge of the hole. 'I don't need you falling through.'

I look up at him. Our eyes lock. Neither of us speak for several seconds. 'Marta, about what happened—'

I cut him off. 'We shouldn't talk about it.'

'I understand. I just wanted to say I'm sorry. I never should have kissed you.'

'You didn't. I kissed you, remember?' Paul does not answer. 'Anyway, like I said earlier, I'm glad it happened.'

'Me, too,' he admits, leaning back against the crates. 'But it's kinda difficult, you know? Remembering how good it was between us...'

'And knowing it can't happen again?' I finish for him. He nods. 'I know.'

I lean back beside him and he puts his arm around me. 'This is okay, though, isn't it?' He gestures with his head toward his arm. 'I mean, it's like that night in Salzburg. Innocent.'

Innocent. I look from his face to his arm around my shoulder, then back again. There's nothing innocent about our feelings. But soon we'll be home and Paul's arm around me will be a distant memory again. 'It's fine,' I say at last, reaching up and squeezing his hand.

We bounce along in silence, not speaking. 'How long do you reckon until we reach the harbor?' he asks.

'A few hours. I wish we hadn't left the deck of cards back in the wine cellar. I'd like a chance to redeem myself at gin.'

'True,' Paul agrees. 'Why don't you take a nap?'

'I am a bit tired,' I admit. 'But it's probably not a good idea.'

'You go ahead. I'll stay awake. Honestly, I'm not at all tired.'

I lean my head against Paul's chest and close my eyes. His arm tightens around me, drawing me close. Like Salzburg, I think. I can almost smell the turpentine, hear the rain on the roof of the gardener's shed.

Suddenly, the truck screeches to a halt, jarring me awake. I sit up groggily. 'What is it?'

Paul turns around and pulls back the tarp slightly, peering out. 'We've reached the harbor,' he whispers. 'But the trucks are stopped ahead. It looks like there is some sort of checkpoint at the gate.'

Panic rises within me. 'What are we doing to do?'

'Maybe they won't look back here.' But as he continues to look outside, his face falls. 'No, they're inspecting each vehicle very closely. We need to get out of here. The floor,' he says suddenly. 'We need to get out through the hole in the floor.'

'But Jan said to stay on the truck, that it would drive us right to the ship.'

Paul shakes his head. 'That isn't going to work anymore.' He crawls over to the hole in the floor. 'You go first. When you hit the ground, I want you to move away from the truck quickly so you don't get hit if it starts to move. Stay low to the ground, out of sight.'

'What about you?'

'I'll be right behind you,' Paul replies quickly. An uneasy expression crosses his face. 'Now hurry.'

I crawl to the hole, then pause, looking up at him. 'Paul–'

He cuts me off. 'If anything happens... I mean, the ship is the SS *Bremen*. Find your way there and get on it.'

I freeze. It had not occurred to me that we might be separated again. I open my mouth to protest. But he touches my cheek, silencing me again. 'No matter what happens, you keep going. Get home to your daughter.'

'I won't go without you.'

'You won't have to,' he promises, looking deep into my eyes. 'I stood you up once in London and look what happened. I'm not about to do it again.' Outside the truck, the footsteps and voices grow louder. He reaches down and kisses me hard and quick. 'Now go.'

I slip through the hole, cringing at the soft sound of my feet hitting the ground. Then, remembering Paul's instructions, I crouch low and crawl from beneath the truck, away from the voices, finding cover beneath some bushes beside the road. I made it, though my heart is pounding. Suddenly, I hear an engine sound. I spin around, looking through the brush at the underside of the truck, searching for Paul in the dim light. But he isn't there. The truck begins to roll forward, moving closer to the checkpoint. Paul's still inside!

I hesitate, uncertain what to do. Keep moving, Paul said. Get inside the ship. I duck into the bushes and make my way toward the metal fence that surrounds the harbor. But it is nearly three meters high; I cannot possibly climb over it. I look sideways toward the gate. Where is the truck? Is Paul still on it? The bushes obstruct my view. Keep moving. I crawl along the fence farther into the brush. I spy a small tear in the fence, low to the ground. I drop to my knees, pulling against the bottom of the fence to lift it farther from the ground. Lying on my stomach, I try to force myself through the opening. It is working, I realize, as the jagged edges tear at my clothes and skin.

I stand up. I am inside, I think with relief. Suddenly, I hear shouting and loud noises coming from the direction of the gate. Paul! Crouching low to the fence, I make my way back toward the commotion. The truck is stopped at the gate, a guard standing by the rear. I can see a flashlight shining beneath the tarp, illuminating the inside of the carriage. My heart drops as two guards climb from the back of the truck, dragging Paul behind them.

Paul has been caught. I start toward the truck. I have to do something. Then Paul's eyes flick toward me. He shakes his head, almost imperceptibly, then looks away. Keep going, I can hear him say. No matter what happens.

I hesitate for several seconds, my heart pounding. I cannot leave Paul. But if I stay here, I will surely be caught, too. Rachel's face flashes through my mind. I have to get home to her. I cannot turn back now. *I'm sorry*, I think, looking back at Paul one last time. Then I begin to run desperately into the harbor, my ankle throbbing.

Away from the bushes, the harbor is open, exposed. I slow to a walk, not wanting to attract attention. Ahead, the pier juts out into the sea like a long finger, massive vessels lining either side. Stevedores carry large crates from trucks, loading them into the hulls of the ships.

As I near the dockside, I duck behind a tall stack of crates, then begin to scan the side of the boats. SS *Bremen*, I read, on the side of one vessel that sits at the far end of the pier to the right. I start toward it, crouching behind stacks of cargo, moving as quickly as I can. I hear a gunshot in the distance, followed by another. I stop and turn. *Paul!* I scream inside, my heart breaking. But there is nothing I can do for him now. I have to keep going. Desperately, I turn and race down the pier, past the stevedores, who have been distracted by the gunshots.

When I reach the base of the *Bremen*, I stop, staring up the massive ramp that leads upward toward the main deck of the ship, lined with trucks. I start up the ramp, keeping low beside the passenger sides of the trucks as I move. At the top, I duck behind a large pallet of boxes, then crawl away from the ramp toward the stern of the ship. I made it. I look back out at the pier. In my mind, I see Paul being dragged from the truck by the police. I fight the urge to run off the ship after him. If I can get back to Britain, I can send word to the Americans about what happened to him. Get him help. Then I remember the gunshots. It is too late for help, I realize numbly. I have lost him all over again. *Goodbye, my darling Paul.*

Thank you for saving me once more. My eyes fill with tears.

A minute later, the trucks begin rolling off the ramp. Then a loud horn sounds and the ramp begins to retract from the deck. We are leaving. I must have made it just in time. I look behind me for a hatch, a way to get below deck out of sight. Suddenly I see something moving on the pier, a figure coming closer. I duck down below the railing. Has someone spotted me? Then I look up again at the figure running toward the ship. Recognizing the awkward gait, my heart leaps. Paul! He is alive and he is trying to make it.

Hurry, I pray, fighting the urge to call out to him. But the ramp has been lowered and the ship is beginning to pull away from the dock. He cannot possibly get on board. He keeps running toward the ship, looking straight ahead toward a small dingy attached low to the outside of the ship. Paul, coatless now, runs to the end of the dock and without hesitating jumps into the water. It must be nearly freezing! Surely he will not be able to survive long. My heart pounds as he swims toward the lifeboat with sure, swift strokes. Hurry. His hand catches the edge of the lifeboat, but slips off. Then he grabs it, firmer this time, and climbs in. He made it! But choppy waves, stirred up by the wake of the ship, crash over the sides of the tiny craft, battering him. He won't be able to last long down there. He reaches up, grabbing the thick rope that holds the lifeboat to the side of the ship. I watch in amazement as he begins to climb, slowly, painstakingly, up the rope. I race to the side of the boat where the rope is secured. As he nears the top, I hold out my hand. Taking it, he hoists himself over the edge.

'Paul!' I cry. He is soaking wet and the front of his shirt is covered in blood.

'I told you I wouldn't stand you up again,' he manages to say, then collapses to the deck.

CHAPTER 24

'Paul!' I kneel beside him, touching his blood-soaked shirt. His eyes are half open, his breathing weak. *Oh, God.* I have to get him out of the cold and out of sight. About twenty meters down the length of the boat there is a doorway. I do not know what is inside, but it has to be better than staying exposed on the open deck, waiting for someone to find us. 'Paul, can you hear me?' He grunts. 'I need your help. We can't stay here and I can't carry you. Can you move?'

He does not answer. I take his right arm and wrap it around my neck, then put my left arm around his waist. Taking a deep breath, I try to raise him to a standing position. But he remains limp, too heavy to lift. I shake him hard. 'Paul, listen, I know you're hurt. But I need you to help me, just for a few minutes. On the count of three. One, two...' Using all of my strength, I struggle to stand up again with him. This time, I feel a slight movement in his legs, his whole body trembling with the effort as he helps me to raise him. How badly is he hurt? I wonder. Panic rises within me as I drag him to the doorway.

Leaning Paul against the side of the ship for support, I open the door and roll him around the edge of the door frame. We are inside a stairwell, with one set of stairs leading up, one down. Above us I hear voices speaking in German. 'Paul, downstairs, quickly,' I whisper. I do not know if there are more sailors below, but I have to chance it. He blinks, seeming to revive slightly. I help him down one flight of stairs, then another. We reach the bottom of the ship, and I blink to adjust my eyes. The cavernous hull seems to run endlessly into the darkness, filled with crates and boxes piled high to the ceiling. I inhale the damp air, which smells of wet wood and burlap. Hopefully no one will come down here until we reach England and they are ready to unload.

Beside me Paul wobbles. He cannot last much longer on his feet. I help him farther into the hull, finding a narrow path through the piles of crates. Soon we reach a small clearing where three stacks of boxes seem to form an alcove against the wall of the ship. 'Let's rest here,' I suggest. Paul does not respond but lets me help him to the ground. I gather some empty burlap sacks that lie nearby, propping them against the wall to form a makeshift pillow behind him. 'Now, let me see your wound.'

'I'm okay,' he says, breathing heavily.

Lifting his shirt, I gasp. His lower torso is bathed in thick, fresh blood. I have to stop the bleeding. I look around desperately for something to use as a bandage. Then I remember the gauze Paul used to tape my foot. 'Do you have more gauze?' I ask him. He does not answer. I move up to study his face. His eyes are half open and his face is pale. It must be the blood loss. 'Paul,' I say. He does not respond.

I reach over and open his pocket. Inside, I push aside his pocketknife and some soggy crumpled papers. At the bottom, I see a small photograph. Curious, I pull it out. It is a picture of me and Paul, the one taken in Paris the night he proposed. I stare at the picture, stunned. How could he possibly still have this, after everything he had been through?

I put the photo down beside him, then check his other pocket for gauze but find none. Desperately, I unwind the piece that Paul had used to wrap my ankle, now black with dirt. I cannot put this near his wound without risking infection. I reach around to his back pocket and pull out the flask, but it is empty. I look up at the crates that fill the hull. There has to be something here that can help. Standing up, I scramble through the boxes, trying to read the labels in the near darkness. A familiar word catches my eye: *Zyborowa.* Polish vodka! Quickly, I try to open the crate but it is sealed shut. I race back to where Paul lies, pulling the pocketknife from his jacket and carrying it back to the crate. I work at the seal with the knife, then use it as a lever to open the box. Inside there are dozens of bottles of vodka, cushioned in straw. I take one, opening the top as I carry it back to Paul.

I kneel beside him once more. Dousing the gauze in vodka, I use it to wipe the blood from

Paul's wound. I touch his skin lightly, studying the site. The bullet pierced his midsection, slightly to the left. It is almost the exact spot where my own gunshot wound was. He groans as I lift him slightly to study his lower back. 'Sorry,' I say. There is a neat hole where the bullet exited. But as I set him down again, the blood pours fresh from the front of his torso. I have to dress the wound, try to stop the bleeding. I pick up the bottle of vodka and rinse the now-red gauze once more. Then I lean over and put my head next to his ear. 'This is going to hurt,' I whisper, 'but it's for your own good.' I put my hand over his mouth so that he does not attract attention if he screams. Taking a deep breath, I pour the vodka directly onto his wound to clean it. He cries out weakly. I wrap the gauze around his midsection as tightly as I can, tucking in the end.

I study the dressing. Blood is already beginning to seep through the gauze, but it will have to do. I pull his shirt down over the wound, then touch his forehead, which is burning hot and covered with a fine layer of perspiration. My panic grows. There has to be something else I can do. Suddenly, I remember the canteen he had been carrying. Praying that it is still there, I reach around to the far side of his waist, careful not to touch the wound. Relief washes over me as my hand closes around the canteen. There is only a tiny bit of water left, I note as I shake it. Paul would tell me to save the water, that we will need it later in the journey. But if I don't bring his fever down, there might not be a later.

'Paul,' I say. There is no response. I shake him

and repeat his name, louder this time. He grunts, as though being awoken from a deep sleep. Carefully, I fill the cap of the canteen with water. Cupping his head and lifting it, I bring the water to his lips. The same way he did with me in the prison, I think. But there is no time for nostalgia. I pour a few drops of the water into his mouth. 'Swallow,' I implore. He does not respond, and a second later, the water trickles out of the corner of his mouth. Desperately, I tilt his head back slightly, pouring the rest of the capful of water through his barely parted lips. 'Drink.' This time, his Adam's apple moves slightly and the water does not reappear. Picking up the canteen again, I pour a few of the remaining drops of water on my hand, then rub Paul's forehead to cool it.

I replace the cap on the canteen, studying his face again. There is nothing more to be done. He shivers. I crawl across the ground, grabbing some more of the burlap sacks and dragging them back over to Paul. I lie down beside him and pull the sacks over us for warmth. Then I place my head on his chest and close my eyes, willing the ship to sail more quickly toward Britain. A few hours ago, I dreaded reaching our destination, knowing that upon arrival we would be forced to say goodbye. But now, reaching land and getting medical attention, if it is not too late, is Paul's only hope. I'm not going to lose you again, I think, wrapping my arm around him protectively.

My eyes grow heavy with the gentle rocking of the ship. I should stay awake, I think. But it does not matter anymore. If someone discovers us, it will not matter if we are asleep. We have done

370

everything we can. Everything we set out to do. Now it is only a question of whether or not we make it back alive to deliver the cipher. Clinging tightly to Paul, I drift off to sleep.

Sometime later, feeling Paul move, I awaken. I sit up quickly, studying his face. His eyes are open slightly. 'Can you hear me?' I ask. He nods. 'How are you feeling?'

'It hurts,' he replies matter-of-factly. 'It hurts a lot.'

'I know.' I touch his forehead, which feels hotter than before. Then I reach for the canteen.

He raises his hand slightly. 'Save it.'

'Paul, you're burning up. I'll find more water later.'

He does not answer but lets me bring the canteen cap to his lips, grimacing as he swallows. I remember then how in prison, I tried to forget pain by pretending I was somewhere else, was back in my family home in the village, or at Shabbat dinner with my friends in the ghetto. 'Let's pretend we're not here,' I suggest. 'Remember the night in Salzburg, how we stayed up in the gardener's shed talking, listening to the rain?'

He manages a faint smile. 'That was wonderful. So quiet after all the months of fighting, I thought I had died and gone to heaven.' Then his expression grows serious again. 'The whole war, I managed not to get shot. And now...' He lifts his hand slightly in the direction of his wound.

'This is all because of me,' I say. 'You never would have been here otherwise. I'm so sorry.'

'It was worth it,' he replies quickly. 'I love you, Marta.'

'I love you, too. But when I saw the port guards pull you from the truck and heard the shots, I thought...'

'That you lost me again?' Paul finishes for me. I nod, suddenly overcome with all that has happened. My eyes well. 'Nah, you won't get rid of me that easily. They were about to cuff me and then I would have been sunk,' he adds. 'But I was able to slip out of my coat and grab the gun of the one who was holding me. I shot him, wounded the other two.' His voice cracks, as much from the memory of shooting the men as the effort of speaking. I see in his eyes the same remorse as I had in the Berlin police station, looking down at Hart's body. Killing did not come easily to Paul, even when it was to save his life.

Or mine.

'I love you,' I repeat, lowering my lips to his, wanting to take away his pain.

'Me, too. I do wish you hadn't moved on quite so quickly, though.' He tries to sound light, but there is a seriousness to his expression that belies his pain.

I know then that I have to tell him. I take a deep breath. 'I didn't.'

Paul looks up at me. 'I don't understand. Didn't what?'

I hesitate. Telling Paul will change everything. But he needs to know the truth in case... I shudder. The thought is almost too unbearable to finish. But if something happens to him, I want him to know. 'I didn't move on,' I say at last.

Paul's expression is puzzled. 'But you married

372

your husband so quickly...'

'I didn't marry Simon because of my feelings for him, or because I had forgotten you. I married Simon because I was pregnant.'

'But you wouldn't have slept with him if...' Paul's voice trails off and a light of recognition appears in his eyes. 'You didn't, did you?'

'Sleep with him? No. Not until we were married.'

'So the baby...?'

I nod. 'Rachel is your daughter. I'm sorry that I didn't tell you sooner,' I add.

I watch his face as he processes the information. Is he angry? 'Daughter,' he mumbles softly, closing his eyes again. I lean over quickly to check his shallow, even breaths, wondering if the shock was too much. He is just delirious from the fever, I decide, touching his forehead. He will not even remember what I told him. But at least he knows. I lie back down beside him, holding him tight. Whatever happens now, he knows. I drift off to sleep once more.

Sometime later, I blink my eyes open, feeling the gentle rocking of the boat and smelling the damp wood. Paul has fallen away from me and lies motionless on his side. Dammit, I swear, crawling over to him. I never should have let myself sleep. 'Paul,' I whisper, touching his cheek, then his forehead. He seems cooler now, but his eyes remain closed. I roll him back toward me, lifting his head into my lap. 'Paul, wake up, please.'

His eyes flutter open. 'Oh, hello,' he says, half smiling.

'You're awake. How are you feeling?'

He raises his hand to his side. 'Still hurts.'

I pull back his shirt to examine the wound. Blood seeped through the gauze at some point, but he does not seem to be bleeding further now. I should redress the wound, I know, but there is nothing else to bandage it with. I let the shirt fall once more. 'The bleeding seems to have stopped,' I report. 'At least as far as I can see.'

He nods. 'There's something still going on inside, though. I can feel it.'

'You're less feverish.' I try to keep the worry from my voice. 'You should drink a bit more.' I reach behind me and pick up the canteen.

'I can do it,' he says, taking the bottle from me. 'Not much left. Did I drink all of that?'

'Some. And I used some to bring your fever down.'

'Did you drink any?'

'Yes,' I lie, looking away.

'Marta...' He reaches up and touches my lips. I had not realized until then that they are dry and cracked with dehydration. 'You need to drink, too.'

'I'm fine,' I insist. 'I'll go find some more water for us soon.' I look around the hull, which remains in perpetual semidarkness. 'I wonder what time it is.'

'Dunno. Speaking of drinking, why do I smell like a distillery?'

I laugh softly. 'That's my fault. I needed something to clean out your wound. The only thing I could find was some vodka.'

'That must explain why I feel so good,' he says

wryly, handing the canteen back to me. 'Seriously, thank you.'

'You're welcome. You've saved my life twice. It seemed the least I could do.'

He does not answer but closes his eyes. I study his face, wondering if he remembers our conversation about Rachel. I consider mentioning it again, then decide against it. Instead, I reach down and pick up the photograph. 'I wanted to ask you about this. I found it in your pocket when I was looking for more gauze.'

Paul half opens his eyes. 'Oh, that's a girl I had a fling with in Paris.'

'Very funny. I remember having this taken. But how do you still have it? I mean, with the crash and all...'

'Would you believe they found that on me when I was rescued? I was unconscious, practically naked, no identification whatsoever. Seems that was the only thing that made it.'

'But how...?'

'Medic told me I was holding it. Clenching it so hard they could barely pry it from my hand.' He looks away. 'I guess I must have been looking at it when the plane went down.'

A lump forms in my throat. 'And all this time...'

'I've carried it with me. Figured it was my lucky charm, the reason I survived.' His voice is strong and clear. 'I know I'm crazy. It's two years later and I'm still carrying a torch for a girl who's with someone else.' I wonder again whether he remembers our conversation from the previous night, if he understands that I married Simon because of Rachel. He continues, 'I mean, I'm shot and lying in the bottom of a ship with no doctors, no pain-killers...'

'We'll be in England soon.'

'I know, but that's the crazy part. I don't care that we're in this boat or even much mind the pain. I don't want to get to England. Being here with you is enough. It's all I want. I mean, last night when I was delirious, I thought maybe finding you again was a dream. But finding out it's real ... this is the best morning of my life.'

My heart pounds. 'I feel the same way.'

'You do?'

'Yes, except for the part about not caring whether you get to a hospital.'

His expression turns serious. 'But when we get to England...'

I lower my hand to my lips. 'Shh. Don't say it. I just want to be with you right now.' He pulls me down and kisses me with such strength I almost forget he is wounded. A few seconds later, I break away. 'You need to rest.'

He nods. 'I know. I wish I wasn't so injured so that I could, I mean we could...'

'Make love again?' I ask.

'Yes.'

I do not answer. Lying next to Paul, I desperately wish the same thing. It would be wrong, I know. Betraying my marriage once had been bad enough, but somehow I could justify it as unexpected, the heat of the moment. Letting it happen a second time, intending it, seems worse somehow. But in a few hours we will reach England, be torn apart by real life. My mind races. I cannot wait to hold Rachel. England means married life, though, going back to Simon. And then Paul will be gone again.

Above us, the horn sounds and the rocking grows heavier. 'We're almost there,' Paul mumbles.

'Yes.' We should sneak off the boat as soon as it docks. But looking at Paul's pale face, I know that will be impossible. He cannot make it up the stairs. For a minute, I consider going for help, but I am too afraid to leave him alone. We will have to wait here until the ship is unloaded and we are discovered. 'Just rest,' I whisper to him. 'Hang in there. It's almost over.' He does not respond.

A few minutes later, the boat bumps against something hard. Above come voices and footsteps, growing louder. I hear the door at the top of the stairs open with a creak, someone descending the stairs. A flashlight shines down inside the hull. Taking a deep breath, I stand up. 'Hello?' I call, raising my hands.

The flashlight swings around, illuminating me. 'What the...?' a man's voice exclaims in English.

I shield my eyes, unaccustomed to the bright light. 'Can you help us, please?' I can make out two men in uniforms making their way toward us through the boxes. English Customs officers, I realize with relief.

'Stowaways!' the second man exclaims.

'Please,' I say. 'My name is Marta Gold and I'm from the Foreign Office. And this man is Michael Stevens with the American government. Call his embassy. But first call an ambulance. He's been shot and he needs medical attention at once.'

The men look skeptically from me to Paul, then back again. 'Don't move,' one of the men says, then turns to the other. 'Radio in to headquarters to check out their story. And send for an ambulance.'

'Please hurry,' I add. The second man turns and scrambles back through the boxes and up the stairs. I drop to my knees beside Paul once more. 'It's all right, darling.' I squeeze his hand. 'We've made it and we're going to get you some help.'

Paul shivers, eyes still closed. I bring my other hand to his forehead. He is very cold now – a fact that scares me more than the fever had. He mumbles something. I lean my head close to his. 'What is it?'

'A-about what you said before...' His voice trails off.

I shake him lightly. 'Paul, wake up.'

'Mmm,' he mumbles.

'You were asking me about something I said,' I remind him gently. 'What was it?'

'I – I can't remember,' he replies.

'Just rest. You need your strength.'

The second man reappears at the top of the steps. 'It's all true,' he says, breathing hard. 'Someone anonymously wired a message saying that there would be two stowaways aboard, a man and woman, British and American. They didn't say anything about an injury.' Jan, I think. She tried to help by sending a message, but of course she hadn't known about Paul being shot at the port. He turns to me. 'The ambulances are coming now.'

Ambulances, plural. 'I don't need medical attention,' I say.

A minute later, I hear sirens in the distance, followed by more footsteps and voices overhead. Several medics race down the stairwell past the guards and come to Paul's side. 'Ma'am, if you would step aside so we can treat him,' one says. Reluctantly, I stand up and take a few steps back. 'What happened?' the medic asks as he kneels.

'He was shot,' I reply.

'Any idea what kind of weapon?'

I shake my head. 'East German. Soviet, maybe. Beyond that I don't know.'

He looks up at me. 'How long ago?'

I realize that I have completely lost track of time. 'Yesterday, I think.' The medic's eyes widen. Turning back to Paul, he lifts Paul's shirt and examines the wound, not speaking for several seconds. Finally, I can stand it no longer. 'How is he?' I demand.

The medic looks up at me, his expression grave. 'Are you family?'

'Yes,' I reply quickly. 'I mean no. He doesn't have any family. I – I'm a close friend.'

'He's seriously wounded and he's going to need surgery immediately.' He turns to the other medics. 'Let's get him out of here.' As they lift Paul, he cries out in pain. I follow them as they carry him up the stairs.

Outside on the dock, I blink, adjusting my eyes to the daylight. The sky is a blanket of thick, gray clouds, and light, misting rain is falling. The brackish salt air fills my lungs, replacing the dank, dusty air from the hull of the ship. I walk quickly to Paul's side as the medics place him on a stretcher. 'Paul,' I whisper. He does not respond.

'We have to keep moving,' one of the medic says. I clutch Paul's hand tightly, walking beside the stretcher as they wheel him from the deck, past several other ships, to one of the two ambulances waiting at the base of the dock.

The medic opens the back doors of the ambulance, then turns to me. 'We have a second ambulance for you.'

'I'm fine. I don't need medical attention.'

'Yes, you do, but there's no time to quarrel about it. You have to let him go.' I open my mouth to reply, then close it again. Arguing will only delay Paul's care. I release his hand and the medics lift the stretcher into the ambulance, closing the doors quickly behind them. Then, as the ambulance drives away, I fall to the ground, sobbing.

CHAPTER 25

'Marta,' a voice calls in the darkness. Paul. Are we still in Germany? 'Marta,' the voice says again. My heart sinks. The accent is British. It is not Paul.

A hand touches my arm, shakes me. Reluctantly, I open my eyes. Simon stands above me, brow furrowed.

'Simon,' I whisper. Simon, not Paul. I wonder if I am lying in our bed at home, if finding Paul alive and being reunited with him was just a dream. Tears fill my eyes.

'Darling.' Simon touches my cheek, mistaking my tears for happiness. 'You're home now. Safe.'

But I am not home, I realize, looking around the sterile, unfamiliar room. Suddenly I remember huddling with Paul in the bottom of the ship. 'Where am I?'

'You're in the hospital. We received a message at the Foreign Office the day before you arrived that you were coming back by ship, and then Customs reported finding two stowaways aboard the *Bremen*.' I picture the medics wheeling Paul away, the ambulance door closing. Where is he now? Is he all right? Simon continues, 'You managed to tell them who you were and ask them to contact the Foreign Office. But then you became hysterical and refused to let the medics treat you, so they had to give you a sedative. How are you feeling?'

'Fine,' I reply, sitting up. 'How long was I asleep?'

'Just overnight. You were suffering from severe exhaustion and dehydration, but the doctor says you're fine otherwise.'

I swallow. 'We ran out of water and...' I take a deep breath, wondering how much Simon knows about Paul. 'The man they found in the boat with me. How is he?'

'I don't know,' Simon replies. 'He was in pretty bad shape when they found you two. Shot, I believe, losing a great deal of blood.'

I try to keep my voice calm. 'Did they say who he was?'

'Apparently an American intelligence operative. Michael something-or-other.'

He called Paul by his assumed cover identity, I note with relief. He does not know that the man on the ship is the same man I was engaged to before we were married. 'Can I see him? To thank him, I mean.'

'Impossible, I'm afraid. They transferred him to a military hospital for surgery.' My stomach twists. 'Would you like me to find out how he's doing?'

'Please.' I struggle to keep my voice even. Then I notice a vase of fresh-cut flowers on the nightstand. 'Did you bring those?'

'I wish I could take credit, but those are from the D.M. He sends his tremendous gratitude and congratulations on a job well done.'

I look back at him. 'The mission was a success?'

Simon nods. 'The medics found the cipher on you when they brought you in and turned it over to me. It's being used to decode the list as we speak. Marcelitis has already been in touch with the embassy and is helping us to identify key contacts throughout Eastern Europe. And the Americans are very excited to work with us on this, too.' He pauses, cocking his head. 'How did you and that Michael fellow meet up anyway?'

In a prison in Salzburg, I think. 'It's a long story,' I say aloud. 'Would you mind if we talked about it later?'

'Of course, you must still be exhausted. There will be plenty of time for debriefing once you've been home and had a chance to rest.'

Home. 'Where's Rachel? How is she?'

'She's with Delia and doing just fine.'

'Delia,' I repeat slowly. 'Does she know?'

Simon shakes his head. 'Only that you are in the hospital. She thinks you took ill while tending to my aunt.' I wince inwardly at the lie, further compounded. 'Anyway, Rachel is fine,' he continues. 'She'll be very excited to see you, I'm sure. She's invited to a birthday party this weekend.'

I gaze out the window, across the road at the rolling fields, blanketed in thick fog. Children's birthday parties. Two days ago I was running from the police in Berlin. With Paul. It seems like another lifetime. In my mind's eye, his face grows fainter, like a dream. Then I look back up at Simon. 'When can I go home?'

I settle against the sofa cushion and adjust the blanket that is draped over my legs. Then I pick up the still-warm cup of tea Delia brought me and look out the window. Outside Delia and Rachel play with a ball on the front lawn. As if she knows she is being watched, Rachel looks back over her shoulder and smiles widely at me. Even from this distance, I can see the flash of white where a new baby tooth has started to come in. I missed that while I was away. Swallowing my guilt, I wave and blow her a kiss.

I lean back once more, looking across the room to the fire that burns brightly in the fireplace. It has been nearly three weeks since I woke up in the hospital. Simon was right – there was nothing wrong with me other than a little dehydration, and I was discharged the following day. I could have gone back to work almost immediately, but Simon insisted that I take a few weeks off to rest and recover. At first I resisted, thinking of Jan and the others, the promises we made to help them. 'You've done your part,' Simon said. 'Let others pick up the baton.' So reluctantly, I agreed to a brief sabbatical. Delia still came every day, again at Simon's insistence, to keep me company and help care for Rachel. But I spend almost all of my time playing with Rachel or watching her. She seems completely unaffected by my absence, which bothers me a bit in a selfish way. She does not understand how close I came to not making it home. I will go back to work in time, but I know that I will never leave her like that again.

A few minutes later, I watch as Delia scoops up Rachel and carries her into the house. Rachel pouts, her tiny upper lip quivering. 'What's wrong, darling?' I ask as Delia brings her over to me.

'She didn't want to come in.' Delia answers for Rachel who, still bundled, points out the window. 'She was hoping that Sammie would come out and play with her after he returns from nursery.' Sammie, the little boy across the street, is almost three. I look at Rachel in amazement. Can she really have a crush at her age? Delia continues, 'But the sun is going down and it's getting colder. She needs a bath before bed.'

I smile. Delia keeps Rachel's schedule with the efficiency of a general. 'You can play outside again tomorrow,' I say to Rachel. 'Maybe Mama will even join you. Now, give me a kiss.'

Delia lowers Rachel and I kiss her cold cheek,

inhaling the smell of fresh earth in her dark, curly hair. In the kitchen, the telephone rings. Delia looks over her shoulder. 'I should get that.' I know she worries about Charles, home alone all day with only Ruff for company.

'Here,' I say, taking Rachel from Delia. 'I'll hold her.' Rachel settles against my chest, babbling.

'Hello?' I hear Delia say in the other room as I unbutton Rachel's coat. 'Hello?' There is silence followed by a click. A moment later, she re-appears in the doorway.

'No one there?' I ask. She nods. 'Strange.'

'It happened once yesterday, as well,' she says as she crosses the room to me. 'I meant to tell you.'

I shrug. 'Probably just a wrong number. If it happens again, I'll call the phone company.'

'Bath for you, young miss,' Delia says to Rachel, taking her from me and carrying her to the stairs. 'There's a roast in the oven,' she calls over her shoulder. 'I'll fix you a plate after I put her down.'

I start to reply that it is not necessary, but Delia disappears up the stairs, talking to Rachel. I look back at the fire, still seeing my daughter's face. She reminds me more of Paul than ever since I came home. Suddenly I see him as the medics carried him away from me on the dock, face pale, eyes closed. A few days ago, Simon told me in an offhand way that he had news of the American. 'He made it through the surgery and is recovering at one of the military hospitals.' I was barely able to contain my relief. 'He's to be shipped back to the States as soon as he's well enough to travel,' Simon added. I wondered if this last part was true. Paul told me that he never goes back to America; he will surely head out on his next mission as soon as he is well enough. My heart ached at the thought of him leaving England. 'If you'd like to send a note to offer your good wishes, I have the address of the hospital,' Simon offered.

'I'm sure the Foreign Office has thanked him sufficiently,' I replied. What would I say? That since coming back from Germany, I have thought of him every waking moment? That when I do sleep, I see him endlessly in my dreams? The truth is unspeakable. And to say less would feel like a lie. No, I decided, a note from me would just hurt him more by reminding him of everything that could never be.

The phone rings in the kitchen, jarring me from my thoughts. 'I'll get it,' I call to Delia, standing. There is a second ring as I cross the parlor to the kitchen. I pick up the receiver. 'Hello?' I say. There is no response. I think then of the two earlier calls Delia had mentioned. 'Hello?' A wrong number perhaps, or a bad connection? But I can hear breathing on the other end of the phone. There is something familiar about the sound, the way the caller inhales, breath seeming to catch and hold for a second. My heart skips a beat. 'Paul?' I whisper.

'I'm an idiot,' he says remorsefully. 'Calling like I'm a twelve-year-old boy with a crush.'

At the sound of his voice, strong and deep, warmth rises in me. I swallow, forcing myself to breathe. 'How are you?'

'I'm fine,' he replies quickly. 'I called earlier but someone else answered so I hung up.'

'That was Delia.'

'I figured. And just now, well, I guess when you answered, I almost lost my nerve. I know I shouldn't be calling. But I couldn't help it.' He pauses. 'I needed to hear your voice.'

I bring my hand to the mouthpiece. 'Me, too,' I whisper, my voice cracking. I clear my throat. 'I thought you were still in the hospital.'

'That's the official story. We've said that because...' He stops, catching himself. Is he afraid of speaking openly on the phone, or of telling me too much? In Germany, we were a team. But now, back in our separate worlds, there are things that cannot be said.

'I'm glad to know you're well,' I say.

'I'm not,' he replies. 'That is, physically I'm on the mend. But I can't stop thinking about us, about...' His voice trails off.

'Me, neither.' I pause as a vision of the cellar in Berlin, Paul's torso beneath me, flashes through my mind. Then I remember Delia and Rachel, just one floor above me. Simon could be home any minute. 'But we can't do this, Paul.'

'I know. I'm sorry,' he says, his voice choked. 'Goodbye, Marta.'

'Paul, wait...' There is a click and the line goes dead. I stare at the receiver for several seconds. Paul called me. He has not forgotten. Tears fill my eyes. Impulsively, I pick up the receiver once more, ring the operator. 'I'd like to get the last number that called this line,' I say. There is a pause. I jot down the numbers that she recites on a pad of paper. I start to dial, then stop again. What would I say to him? Calling Paul will only make things worse for both of us. But he sounded so upset when he hung up, and the notion of him being sad or angry with me is unbearable. I start to dial the number.

Suddenly, there is a noise behind me. I drop the receiver, which clatters to the counter, and turn. Delia is standing at the entrance to the kitchen. 'Y-you startled me,' I say, picking up the receiver and replacing it on the hook.

'Another empty call?' she asks, crossing to the stove.

'Yes,' I reply, feeling guilty at my lie. 'I was just going to try to get the number from the operator.'

Delia does not respond but turns on the stove burner beneath the tea kettle. Then she opens the oven door and begins pouring some of the juices that have formed in the bottom of the pan over the roast. 'Rachel went right down,' she says a moment later, closing the oven door. 'Nearly fell asleep in the bath.'

'She was more tired than she knew.' I sink to one of the chairs at the table.

'More tea?' I shake my head, still reeling from my conversation with Paul. Suddenly, unable to hold back any longer, I burst into tears. 'What is it, dear?' Delia asks, startled. She rushes to the table and sits down beside me. 'What's wrong?'

'I'm sorry,' I say through my sobs.

'There, there,' Delia says, stroking my hand. 'You've been through a lot. It's all catching up with you.'

I look up at her, puzzled. How much does she

388

know? I consider telling her that it is the stress of caring for Simon's aunt and getting sick. Then suddenly I can lie to her no longer. 'Delia, I need to tell you something. When I was gone, I wasn't actually caring for–'

Delia raises her hand. 'I know.'

'You do?'

She nods. 'Simon isn't a terribly good liar.'

'I'm sorry for not telling you the truth. It was government business.'

'My dear, there is no need.'

'Anyway, while I was gone, I saw...' I hesitate, studying her face. I should stop there, I know. But I have to tell someone about what happened in Germany, to make it real and make sense of it all. And Delia was with me when I lost Paul the first time. 'Do you remember Paul, the American soldier whom I was supposed to marry?'

'Of course.'

'He's alive!' I blurt out.

Delia's jaw drops. 'I don't understand.' Quickly, I tell her how Paul had survived the crash, followed me to Prague and rescued me from the bald man. Watching her eyes widen, I realize how unbelievable my story must seem.

'Oh, my goodness!' She brings her hand to her mouth. 'That is really quite remarkable. Where is he now?'

'At one of the U.S. military bases. And the calls,' I say, gesturing to the phone on the wall. 'They weren't wrong numbers.'

'I see.' She studies my face. 'He still has feelings for you?' I nod. 'And you?'

I hesitate. 'I'm married.'

'Yes, and you have a daughter...' Delia stops, remembering. 'Rachel was premature. That is, she really wasn't, was she?'

'No,' I admit. 'I'm sorry I didn't tell you at the time.'

'I understand,' Delia replies quickly. 'But you don't have to be ashamed. You were young and in love.' I bite my lip. I cannot bring myself to tell Delia that I was with Paul again in Germany, that I betrayed my marriage. 'Does Paul know that Rachel is his?'

'I don't know. I tried to tell him on the ship, but he was half conscious at the time.'

Delia looks away, staring out the window. 'You've never asked me why I didn't marry or have children.' She raises her hand before I can reply. 'Oh, don't worry. I know you were just being polite. I was in love once many years ago. We wanted to get married, but my father wouldn't hear of it. He said he would disinherit me if I shamed the family by marrying a man who worked as our butler.'

'Charles?' I interrupt, surprised. I had known for some time that their relationship was more than a working one, but I had no idea the history went back so many years.

Delia nods. 'My father fired him over the affair. Charles begged me to leave with him, but I was too afraid. So he left, married, had children. And I remained alone. Years later, after his wife died, he came back to me. My father was long since gone by that time. We never married; it would have been too painful for his children and it wasn't something either of us needed. We just

390

wanted to be together, and we're quite happy now. But when I think of all the years we missed, the family we might have had together... I don't know, Marta. I can't tell you what to do. You have stability here, a good life. But second chances don't come often. And when they do, well, you kind of have to wonder.'

We sit, neither of us speaking, for several minutes. The clock in the parlor begins to chime. 'It's seven,' Delia remarks, sounding surprised. 'I had no idea it was so late.'

'You should go,' I reply. 'Charles will be worried.'

Delia does not respond but walks toward the door and begins putting on her coat. For a minute, I worry that she is angry with me, judging my feelings for Paul. But then I see that she is lost in the memories of her own past. 'Delia?' She turns back to me. 'Thank you. For telling me, I mean. And for understanding.'

She smiles. 'Good night. I'll see you tomorrow.'

After the door closes behind her, I sit for several minutes, thinking. Delia's words echo in my mind: second chances, what might have been. It all happened so fast. I think of Paul and me in the Meierhof cellar, clinging to each other desperately, and I ache with longing. But not with guilt, I realize suddenly. Except for my hesitation at telling Delia, I have not felt at all badly about what happened between us. What kind of woman am I, to betray my husband and feel nothing?

It was a moment, I tell myself now. Old lovers caught up in memories. But even as I think this, I know that it is not true. Our feelings are still as real as they were two years ago. And now he is gone again, just as quickly. I hear his voice in my mind, desire slicing through me anew. How can I bear to be separated from him again? I stare at the phone, fighting the urge to try to call him. What could I possibly say that would change things, not make them worse?

A noise at the door jars me from my thoughts. 'Hallo?'

Simon. I wipe my eyes with the back of my sleeve, straighten my hair. 'In here,' I call.

'Hello, dear,' Simon says as he enters the kitchen. 'Good day?' he asks. A faint clover smell tickles my nose as he bends to kiss me on the cheek.

'Fine. And you?' Our evening colloquy is always the same. But something is different, I think, as he steps away from me. His suit, usually well-pressed even at day's end, looks rumpled beneath his overcoat, and his thin hair is tousled as though there was a strong breeze. The bus must have been more crowded than usual, I decide. I imagine the riders packed tightly together, Simon standing in the aisle, wedged uncomfortably between an old lady with shopping bags and a woman holding a crying baby.

'Busy.' He raises his briefcase. 'Loads of reading to do tonight. I'd best get started.'

'The roast is in the oven. It will be ready in a few minutes if you're hungry,' I offer, but he shakes his head.

'Too much to do, I'm afraid. And there was a late lunch meeting. If you would just leave me a plate in the icebox, that would be lovely.' Before

I can answer, he is gone again, his footsteps echoing against the stairs. I slump against the counter, relieved. There were times before my trip when I wished Simon would have eaten dinner with me, when I would have welcomed some company. Now, lost in my thoughts, I am grateful not to have to manage a conversation.

My mind spins back to Paul once more and I replay our dialogue over and over in my mind. 'I can't stop thinking about you,' he'd said. He wanted to hear my voice. I grow warm. Suddenly I am seized with regret. Why had I pushed him away? Because you are married with a child, a voice inside me says. Because it was the right thing to do.

I walk to the sink and reach into the cupboard above me for a glass, then turn on the cold water tap, letting it run for several seconds. As I fill the glass, I spot an unfamiliar item on the counter-top: a pair of spectacles. I turn off the tap and pick them up. Delia's glasses. She must have set them down while making dinner. I raise my hand to my own face. I know how disconcerting it is when I cannot find my glasses, even for a few minutes. She will surely be missing them.

I look up at the clock. Delia left about twenty minutes ago and won't be home yet, but I can leave a message with Charles, telling her the glasses are here. I walk to the phone and pick up the receiver, remembering Paul's voice on the other end of the line. I bring the receiver to my ear. But instead of a dial tone, I hear voices talking. I freeze, surprised. Simon must be on the extension in the study. Unusual, I think. Simon

393

seldom uses the phone. I wait for him to say something, to chastise me for interrupting his call. But he does not seem to have heard me pick up the line. Who is he speaking with? Probably one of the men from the office.

I hesitate. I should hang up. But instead, I place my hand over the mouthpiece and listen. 'The arrangements are made?' I hear Simon ask.

'Luton Airport...' a voice replies. A woman's voice. The hair on the back of my neck stands on end. 'Tomorrow. Seven o'clock.' She has a clipped, foreign accent that is somehow familiar.

'Seven o'clock,' Simon repeats. 'I will be there with the package.' There is a click and the line goes dead.

CHAPTER 26

I stand motionless, still holding the receiver. Who was Simon speaking with? I replay the conversation in my mind, hearing the young woman's voice. It surely did not belong to Biddie Newman, the secretary who had been assigned to help Simon during my office leave and who had been with the department for nearly forty years. Perhaps one of the other assistants in our department, calling to convey a message. I run through each of them in my head, but all except me are British-born. None of them have an accent like the woman on the phone. Who is she and why is Simon calling her?

I replace the receiver and walk to the oven, considering the question. I could just ask Simon, I rationalize as I take the roast from the oven, making up two plates of meat, potatoes and vegetables. I put one in the icebox, carry the other to the parlor. We have no secrets at work, at least none that I know of – even during my sabbatical, he's kept me updated about events at the office. But to ask, I would have to admit that I heard him on the phone. Though it was inadvertent, I feel somehow guilty about eavesdropping.

It has to be someone from the office, I decide, cutting a piece of roast. Simon does not have any other friends or associates that I know of... My hand stops midair, brown gravy dripping onto the plate. That I know of. Is he having an affair?

I turn the thought over in my mind, considering it for the first time. Don't be silly, I tell myself, setting down the fork. Simon is so cold and distant, so focused on his work. It is hard to imagine him summoning the passion for any woman.

But it is not impossible, I admit reluctantly. Suddenly I am not hungry. I carry my plate back into the kitchen, scrape my uneaten dinner into the garbage bin. Perhaps he is so disinterested in me because he has feelings for another. He has been working later at the office since my return, many nights not returning until after I am asleep. And then there was that business trip to Brussels several months ago... Suspicion bubbles in my mind.

I then remember Simon's strange appearance

when he walked into the kitchen earlier, the unfamiliar scent as he kissed me hello. I walk quickly down the hallway to the coatrack that stands by the front door and lift Simon's overcoat from the hook, bringing it to my nose. An unmistakable clover smell lingers by the collar. The perfume of another woman.

It could be nothing, I tell myself, replacing the coat. A female passenger pressed too close on the bus, her scent lingering. But that does not explain the phone call. I walk back to the kitchen. An affair. I wash the dishes, still considering the idea. An hour ago the notion was inconceivable. What if it is true? I hardly have the right to be angry, after all that happened with Paul. It would almost be ironic. But I nevertheless feel a stab of jealousy. Who is this woman who Simon prefers to me?

You cheated, too, I remind myself. But Paul and I were different, two old lovers finding each other for a single moment in time. Our coupling was unplanned, instinctive. I imagine Simon's affair to be calculated and sustained. Furtive plans made for secret meetings. Lies told to cover his tracks. Anger rises in me. Has Simon been playing me for a fool? An hour ago, I turned away Paul on the phone. And for what? Is my marriage to Simon a charade?

Easy, I remind myself as I dry the last of the plates. You don't know for sure that Simon is having an affair. A few words on the phone, some perfume. That is not proof. But doubt nags at me harder now. I need to find out.

I turn out the kitchen light and make my way

upstairs. Tiptoeing into Rachel's room, I reach into her crib and place my hand on her back lightly so as not to wake her, feeling her gentle, even breathing. Farther down the hall, the door to Simon's study is closed. I hesitate, looking at the thin shaft of light beneath the doorway. Suddenly I am seized with the urge to burst in and confront him with my suspicions. I take a step toward the study, then stop again. Simon would never admit to having an affair. I can almost imagine his calm denial, so matter-of-fact as to make me feel foolish. No, if I am to find proof, I will have to manage another way.

I continue down the hall to our bedroom, my mind turning as I wash and climb into bed. I pick up the book that sits on my nightstand, but I am too agitated to read. I look around our bedroom at Simon's nightstand, his armoire. If there is evidence of Simon's infidelity, where would it be hidden? I do not dare look now, of course, but perhaps tomorrow when he is at work. I force myself to turn to the book until at last my eyes grow heavy and I drift to sleep.

I do not hear Simon come to bed. When I awake in the morning, the duvet on his side is freshly made, as though he had not bothered to climb underneath. The events of the previous night, my suspicions about Simon, come rushing back to me. Perhaps it is all in my head, I think, staring up at the ceiling. And even if it is not, do I really want to know? 'Borrowing trouble,' my mother would have called it. My life is safe here, stable. I could leave well enough alone. Simon would never ask for a divorce – the scandal would be too much for his career. A sensible woman would not dig for answers. But I need to find out.

I go to Rachel, who is sitting in her crib, babbling to herself. Carrying her downstairs, I find Simon's breakfast dishes washed and stacked. There is a hastily scribbled note on the table: *Early meeting.* I look at the clock above the stove. Six-fifty. Uneasiness rises in me. Simon always leaves at exactly seven-twenty. I wonder if he knows that I heard him on the phone last night, senses my suspicions and is avoiding me.

I carry Rachel over to her high chair and put some dried cereal on the tray in front of her. At seven-thirty, there is a noise at the front door. 'Good morning,' Delia singsongs from the foyer. I look over to the counter where her glasses still sit. In my confusion over hearing Simon on the phone, I forgot to call her and tell her they were here.

Delia comes into the kitchen wearing a pair of spectacles I do not recognize. I hold the ones she left behind out to her. 'I was wondering where those were!' Delia exclaims.

'I meant to call you and tell you they were here.'

'No worries. Fortunately I had my old pair.' Her sleeve is damp as she takes the glasses from me, replacing the older ones and tucking them into her bag. I look out the window over the sink, noticing for the first time the rain that falls in heavy sheets. My heart sinks. I had hoped that Delia would take Rachel to the park, giving me a chance to look through Simon's belongings. Perhaps the weather will change.

But the sky remains solid gray throughout the morning. Delia takes Rachel back up to her bedroom to play and I join them for a while, trying to focus on the building blocks Rachel loves so much. Later, I leave them, still playing, and retreat to the parlor with my book. But I stare out the window at the rain-soaked street, unable to concentrate. Is Simon really at work, I wonder, or off somewhere with that woman? For a minute I consider calling him at the office to see. But a call from me would be unusual and would surely make him suspicious.

A short while later, Delia carries Rachel back downstairs and deposits her on my lap. 'I'll make lunch,' she says, disappearing into the kitchen. I wrap my arms around Rachel, burying my nose in her dark curls.

I think then of Paul. If Simon really is having an affair and I confronted him, perhaps he would leave me, after all. Maybe then Paul and I could be together. A shiver runs through me. The idea is almost inconceivable. Would Paul even still want me under such circumstances? He might not even realize that Rachel is his, I remind myself. A romantic affair while on the run in Germany is one thing. A relationship with a divorced woman who has a young child is quite another.

Delia reappears with two trays bearing sandwiches and soup. She turns on the radio to the BBC and a newscaster's voice fills the parlor. We eat in silence, listening to the broadcast. I feed Rachel small bites of sandwich from my plate. After we finish, Delia clears the lunch trays and returns with cups of tea. The news ends and another program, 'Woman's Hour,' begins. We sit, listening to the radio while Rachel plays on the floor. Neither Delia nor I mention our conversation from the previous day about Paul. I consider briefly sharing my suspicions about Simon with her, then decide against it.

The afternoon passes slowly, the rain beating incessantly on the roof. I look at the clock above the fireplace. It is just after three o'clock. Delia usually doesn't leave until at least six and I will not dare look through Simon's belongings at such a late hour for fear he will come home.

'How's Charles?' I ask when Delia switches off the radio.

'He's a bit under the weather,' she replies, 'but it's just a cold.'

'You should go home and be with him,' I say quickly, seizing the opportunity.

'Are you certain?' she asks.

I nod. 'Rachel and I will be fine.'

Delia hesitates, then stands. 'Thank you. I'm sure Charles will appreciate it. I'll fix her bottle before I go.' She goes into the kitchen and returns a few minutes later with the warm bottle, which she hands to me. She walks to Rachel where she plays, bends and kisses her on the head. 'See you tomorrow.'

When Delia has gone, closing the door behind her, I stand and scoop up Rachel, who squawks in protest. 'Nap time, darling,' I say, pushing down my guilt at not playing with her for longer. I carry Rachel upstairs, depositing her into her crib, then walk back out into the hallway. Simon's study, I think. He would surely keep anything private there. I hurry into the study. It is immaculate as always, the desktop bare except for a notepad in the upper-right-hand corner and a cup of perfectly sharpened pencils beside it. The sweet smell of pipe smoke hangs faintly in the air. I walk behind the desk. There are three drawers on the right-hand side and a shallower one running across the middle. I pull on the handle of top-right drawer, but it refuses to open. The other drawers are also locked.

I pause. I have been in Simon's desk dozens of times, looking for paper clips or pens. It has never been locked before. What is he hiding? The gnawing in the pit of my stomach grows sharper. Where is the key? I scan the top of the desk, the bookshelves behind it. He must have taken it with him.

Suddenly there is a noise at the front door. I jump, moving hurriedly away from the desk. Delia must have forgotten something. 'Hallo?' Simon calls from the foyer. I freeze, panicking. What is he doing home so early? I race from the study, pulling the door quietly closed behind me. A second later, he appears on the staircase.

'I – I just put Rachel down,' I stammer, gesturing toward the nursery, hoping he has not noticed the direction from which I have come. 'You're home early.' I start down the stairs past him, trying not to shake. Did he hear me in the study?

But if he is suspicious, he gives no indication. 'I have a dinner tonight at seven,' he replies, following me into the parlor. 'Have to get changed.

401

Here.' He hands me a long box. 'For you.'

'What's this?' I tear off the paper. Inside, I recognize the dark green cardboard of Harrods department store.

'I know how much you like the mint chocolates,' he says as I lift the lid. 'You haven't had any since you've been back.'

'Thank you.' I try to make my tone sound appreciative. But my mind reels. Simon never brings me gifts for no reason. And Harrods is in Knightsbridge, clear across town from the Foreign Office. What was he doing in that neighborhood? Perhaps he was meeting the woman on the phone for a romantic tryst.

'I had a lunch meeting in Kensington,' he adds, as though sensing my suspicion. I do not respond but replace the lid and set the box on the coffee table. 'Aren't you going to have one?'

'I had a big lunch with Delia so I'm not hungry. I'll enjoy them later. What's the occasion for the dinner tonight?'

'To honor the outgoing chargé d'affaires from Copenhagen. I mentioned it a few days ago.'

'Of course,' I say. I have no recollection of him mentioning the dinner, but I have been so distracted since coming home. 'Not a problem for you to go alone, I take it?'

He shakes his head. 'It's a stag dinner, in fact. I'm going to look over some papers and get changed for the evening. I'll see you before I leave.'

I watch nervously as he crosses the room and climbs the stairs. Had I disturbed anything in the study that would give any indication that I had been inside? And why were the drawers locked? I think back to the phone conversation I overheard. Seven o'clock tonight, the woman said. And now Simon is going to this dinner... I stand up and walk to the kitchen. On the wall by the icebox hangs the calendar on which Simon writes all of his appointments. I look at the small white square for December 20, today's date. It is blank. The dinner, which Simon claimed to have told me about days ago, is nowhere to be found.

My uneasiness grows. It is probably nothing, I tell myself. He just forgot to write down the dinner. Simon is too meticulous for that, though. I make my way back to the parlor, my mind racing. For a minute, I consider confronting him once more. But what would I say? Whom did I hear you speaking with on the phone while eavesdropping? That I could not snoop because your desk drawers were locked?

A short while later, Simon appears on the stairs, wearing his dinner jacket, hair slicked back.

'Y-you look nice,' I say.

'Thank you.' He gestures toward the box on the coffee table. 'How are the chocolates?'

'I don't know. I still haven't tried them.'

'Well, let's have one before I leave, shall we?' I do not answer as he opens the box and holds it out to me. I pick a piece of candy, unwrap the foil and take a bite. The melted chocolate, thick and rich, seemed to stick in my throat. 'Delicious,' I say, forcing myself to swallow. But I cannot manage the rest of the piece. I close my fist around the rest of the chocolate, then tuck it in a napkin when Simon is not looking.

'I'll have mine after I eat supper,' he says, putting it in his pocket. He leans down and kisses my cheek. 'I won't be terribly late.'

'Have a good time,' I say, struggling to keep my voice even. I want to stop him, to demand that he tell me the truth. My heart races as he closes the door behind him, fighting the urge to leap up and run to his study. He will be gone for hours, I tell myself. I need to wait at least thirty minutes or so, to make sure he is really gone, that he doesn't return because he has forgotten something. I lean back, closing my eyes, eager for him to leave once more.

Suddenly, I sit up with a start. I must have fallen asleep, but for how long? My head is strangely heavy, my mouth dry as though I have been asleep for hours. 'Hello?' I call, rubbing my eyes. There is no response. I stand and make my way unsteadily to the kitchen, splashing water on my face. Then I walk back across the parlor to the front window. Simon's car is gone.

Shaking my head to clear it, I hurry back up the stairs to Simon's study, more determined than ever to find out what is going on. My eyes lock on a letter opener standing in the pencil cup, the lamplight reflected in its sharp, silvery end. I pick up the opener and turn it over in my hand, considering. If I break the lock, Simon will know I was here. Suddenly I do not care – I need to know the truth about what he is doing, about the woman on the other end of the phone. I wedge the letter opener into the small space between the top-right drawer and the underside of the desk and turn it sharply. The lock opens with a pop.

Inside the drawer sits a thick stack of papers. I lift the top few and rifle through them. What am I looking for? I wonder. Love notes, receipts from presents or hotels? But everything here appears to be work-related. This is ridiculous, I think. Why am I doing this? But I continue skimming through the papers. The first few pages are department cables. For a second, I hesitate. Perhaps there are classified documents that I am not cleared to see. Nonsense. I risked my life. I have the right. Simon would not have classified documents stuck in a desk drawer, anyway. Or at least I do not think so. I look down at the cables. They are nothing I have not seen in the office, but I am surprised to find them shoved inside the desk in no particular order. Simon always files papers alphabetically in folders and then by date order within, in the metal cabinet that sits behind his desk.

Farther down the stack, my thumb brushes against something thicker than the rest of the papers. I pull out a manila folder. Inside is a sheet of paper, listing dates, times, destinations. A travel itinerary with today's date. The name at the top of the itinerary is Dmitri Borskin. Probably just the travel plans of a visiting dignitary, I think, scanning the page. Someone who was attending the dinner. Simon must have been confirming his travel plans. I close the folder. The phone call about the flight from Luton makes sense now, I think, suddenly feeling very silly. I look down at the broken lock. I will have to think of something to tell Simon.

I replace the file and start to close the drawer. Then, still curious, I pick up the papers once more and thumb farther down in the stack. More cables. Suddenly, a piece of paper, yellow, and smaller than the others, catches my eye. I pull it from the stack. It appears to be a telegram of some sort. The document is written in Russian.

I stare at the piece of paper, my heart pounding. Simon does not read Russian. What could he possibly be doing with this? I scan the paper, trying to recall the Cyrillic alphabet I learned from my grandmother as a child. I make out a name: Marek Andek. The telegram is dated November 26, 1947. That was the date I arrived in Prague and first met with Marek. The day before he was arrested. My hand trembling now, I lift up the next document in the stack, another telegram in Russian. This one is dated a day later. It contains the name Jan Marcelitis, gives her address in Berlin.

I set the stack of papers down and sink into the chair, my legs weak. Someone was sending telegrams, revealing information in Russian about Marek and Jan. But who? And why does Simon have them? Perhaps it is part of the investigation into the leak. But why hadn't Simon mentioned them to me? I pick up the stack of documents, scanning more quickly now, looking for an explanation.

My hand touches the manila folder and I pull it out once more, rereading the itinerary. Dmitri Borskin. A flight from Luton Airport to Moscow tonight at eight. That must have been what the call was about. Did Borskin have something to do with the telegrams? The words on the page begin to blur. I set down the folder and rub my eyes beneath my glasses, trying to focus. As I pick up the folder once more, my hand brushes against something hard on the bottom. I turn it over. Taped to the back of the folder is a brown envelope. Curious, I pry the envelope away from the folder. Leave it alone, a voice inside me says. But I've gone too far to turn back now. I open the envelope, trying to undo the seal gently so I can close it again. A piece of paper falls out and flutters to the floor. It is a photograph, I realize as I bend and pick it up, with something hand-written on the back in Russian. I scan the Cyrillic letters, sounding it out. Dmitri Borskin, the name reads. Then, turning over the photograph, I freeze.

The face that looks up at me is Simon's.

I stare at the photograph, my mind whirling. There must be some mistake. The man in the photograph is younger, his hair and mustache thick, but the eyes are unmistakable. Heat rises in my neck. Are Simon and Dmitri Borskin the same person? Why does he have a Russian alias? My mind turns back to the telegrams I have just found, referencing my meeting with Marek, Marcelitis's address in Berlin. Simon was the leak, I surmise, dread and disbelief rising in me.

I pick up the itinerary again. Borskin is scheduled to fly to Moscow tonight. Simon must be fleeing the country. Still clutching the paper in my hand, I race from the study to our bedroom, the ground seeming to wobble beneath me. I throw open Simon's armoire, half expecting his clothes to be gone. But his suits hang neatly, all present except for the dinner jacket he was wearing when he left. I lean against the armoire, relieved. Simon's things are still here. There must be some sort of mistake. I scan the itinerary once more. It clearly indicates that Borksin is leaving for Russia tonight. A box at the bottom of the page catches my eye. Number of travelers: three.

Simon is leaving, and he is not traveling alone. Rachel, I think. My blood runs cold. Dropping the piece of paper, I start toward the baby's room. 'Rachel?' I call into the darkness as I run into the nursery. There is no response. Even before I reach into the crib, my hands closing around the emptiness, I know that my daughter is gone.

CHAPTER 27

For several seconds I stand in the middle of the nursery, too stunned to move. 'Rachel?' I call out, hoping in vain that perhaps she managed to crawl from her crib and is hiding somewhere. There is no response. Simon has taken Rachel; I am sure of it. But how? He left the house alone. But he could have come back after I fell asleep. Surely I would have heard him, though, if he came in and took Rachel. I'm usually such a light sleeper, hearing Rachel every time she makes a

sound and hopping up to check on her. I fell asleep so quickly on the couch, though, and I was so groggy when I woke up.

The chocolates. I remember then Simon giving me the box, his insistence that I try one. He must have drugged me so he could get Rachel out of the house. What did he put in them? Instinctively, I lean forward and put my fingers down my throat, vomiting a gooey brown mass onto the hardwood floor. Then I stand up unsteadily, the room spinning. How much of the drug has entered my system already? I race to the toilet and turn on the cold tap. Cupping my hands, I gulp several mouthfuls of water to flush the rest of the drug from my system. Suddenly, I heave again, this time just making it to the toilet.

A few seconds later, I straighten, wiping my mouth. My vision is a bit clearer now. Racing back down the hallway, I grab the itinerary from the floor. The flight leaves at eight, just an hour from now. I have to find them.

Clinging to the railing for support, I make my way down the stairs. I race into the kitchen and grab the phone. I have to call someone, but who? If Simon is a traitor, then there is no telling who at the Foreign Office can be trusted. And the police will not interfere with diplomatic matters, even if they believe me. For a second, I consider calling Delia and Charles. But they live in the wrong direction, and it would take them at least half an hour to get here, longer still to reach the airport.

Something white on the countertop catches my eye. I look down. It is a tablet of paper, the phone

number I had taken down earlier scrawled across the top sheet. The number the operator had given me. Paul's number.

Hurriedly, I pick up the receiver and dial the number. 'Lakenheath Air Base,' a man's voice – not Paul's – answers.

The room starts to slide from beneath me once more. 'Paul Mattison,' I say. Clutching the edge of the counter, I force myself to focus on the window above the sink.

There is a pause. 'There's no one here by that name.'

I swear inwardly, trying to remember Paul's alias. 'I mean Michael. Michael Stevens.'

'I'm sorry but he's gone for the day.'

My panic rises. 'I have to find him. It's urgent.'

'Who's calling?'

'Tell him this is Marta. It's an emergency and I need him to meet me at Luton Airport right away.'

'But...' the man begins.

'An emergency,' I repeat, then throw down the phone. I do not know if he will get the message, but I cannot wait any longer. My eyes dart to the clock above the stove. Ten past seven. I race into the foyer and grab my coat and purse. Then I dash through the front door, slamming it closed behind me.

Outside I pause. The cool night air revives me, clearing my head. I have to get to the airport, but how? Simon has taken the car and there is no possibility of getting there by bus or train. I look at the row houses on either side of ours, wishing I knew our neighbors well enough to ask for help.

But the doors of the other houses are closed, shutters drawn tight. A taxi, I think. I sprint down the steps and through the front gate toward Hampstead High Street. But the taxi stand at the corner is deserted. My heart sinks. I look desperately up and down the street. Should I try to hail down a stranger, beg for a ride?

At the far end of the street, I spot a lone taxi, making its way slowly up the road. I wave my hand desperately, willing it to pull over. Finally, it reaches me, veering to the curb. 'Luton Airport,' I say as I climb into the back.

The driver looks over his shoulder, surprised. 'Luton's almost an hour away. I don't know...'

He stops mid-sentence as I throw a wad of bills over the seat. 'Here. Luton Airport, as fast as you can, please. It's an emergency.'

The taxi swerves away from the curb, throwing me back against the seat. Faster, I pray, steadying myself with my hand as we race through the streets of North London. How much time has passed? My heart pounds. Simon is working for the Russians. I cannot believe it. I had gone into his office looking for evidence that he was an adulterer. Instead I discovered that he is a traitor. Perhaps there is another explanation, I think again. A secret assignment, with a cover so deep he cannot tell anyone, even me. Or perhaps they threatened him, I think suddenly as we reach the motorway. Said they would hurt me or Rachel if he did not cooperate. But even as these ideas run through my head, I know that they cannot possibly be true. No, Simon's betrayal is real. Still, I am flooded with disbelief. He has always

been so passionate about his work. What could the Russians possibly have offered him to make him to turn against his own country, to take Rachel away?

'Rachel,' I whisper aloud, seeing her face. The road seems to stretch endlessly ahead of us. Staring out at pitch darkness on either side of the car, I fight the urge to scream. I look desperately at the clock on the dashboard. Twenty past seven. If the plane takes off, Simon will be beyond the authorities' reach and Rachel will be gone forever. Bile rises up in my throat and I lean my head against the seat in front of me, praying we will make it in time.

Twenty-five minutes later, we pull up in front of Luton Airport and I leap from the taxi. Through the glass, I can see that the building is dark inside. The parking lot is deserted, except for a lone man lifting a bag from a garbage can. I run to him. 'Excuse me. I'm looking for a flight to Moscow this evening.'

The man cocks his head. 'Moscow? We don't fly there. Airport is closed for the night, anyway.' My heart sinks. They are not here. Had Simon left the itinerary as a red herring to throw me off his trail? 'Unless it's a flight from the private hangar,' the man adds.

My breath catches. 'Where's that?'

He points behind the building to the right. 'But you can't...'

Not listening further, I start to run in the direction he indicated. Behind the airport building is an open field. Commercial planes stand idly in a row. To the right, far in the distance, I see

another building, hear a low whirring noise. I begin to run toward the building, my lungs burning. As I draw closer, I can make out a single plane on the tarmac, smaller than the commercial ones. A man walks around the side of the plane and starts up the open stairs. At the top, he turns to look back. I recognize Simon's silhouette in the doorway. I run faster. They have not left yet. But the propellers are starting to spin now, ready to go. He starts inside the plane.

'Simon!' I yell over the noise of the engine as I near. He does not hear me. 'Simon!' He turns back. At the sight of me, his jaw drops. I can see him thinking that I should have eaten the chocolates, that I should be unconscious on the floor. 'Where's Rachel?' I demand, racing up the stairs.

'I don't know what you're talking about,' he says patiently, as though talking to a child. 'Rachel was at home with you.' His voice is so sincere that for a second I almost believe him. Then his eyes dart toward the entrance of the plane.

'Rachel?' I call, starting up the steps.

As I try, to push past him, he grabs my arm roughly. 'You shouldn't have come here,' he growls, his expression turning to rage.

Who is this man with the harsh face, the foreign, angry eyes? His fingers dig into my arm like a vise. For a moment, I consider playing dumb, stalling for time. But I cannot contain myself. 'I know, Dmitri. I know everything.' His eyes widen. Anger flares inside me. He had been so arrogant, so certain I would never find out. He had not even bothered to destroy the evidence. 'I know that you are working for the Soviets.'

He opens his mouth to start to deny my accusations. Then, looking over my shoulder at the deserted tarmac, he shrugs. 'I'm a communist, Marta.' There is a hint of pride in his voice.

I stare at him, disbelieving. I had assumed that the communists had somehow persuaded Simon to spy. It had not occurred to me that he might be one of them. 'For how long?'

'Years before I met you. Since college, in fact.'

Before he met me. Before we were married. I am flooded with disbelief. 'But why? You were so insistent that I come to work for you, that I help you with your work...' My mind reels back to the day I heard Marek's name in the meeting. 'You needed me to find Marcelitis,' I say slowly, realizing aloud. He does not respond. I remember Simon's anger at my going to Prague, his concern. It had all been an act. 'You needed me to get the cipher. But you gave the cipher to the department...' Even as I say this, I know that it was a lie, too. I lunge toward him, reaching for his jacket. 'Where's the cipher, Simon?'

He holds me off easily with one hand, his grip stronger than I've ever known it to be. 'The cipher is going back to Moscow where it belongs,' he informs me coldly. 'And it is just a matter of time before Marcelitis is taken from the picture altogether.' He pushes me away hard.

I stumble, grabbing the railing to avoid falling down the stairs. You have to catch Jan first, I want to say. I am glad that I had not told him Jan was a woman. 'But how did you know that I knew Marek, that I would volunteer to go?' I ask

414

instead. 'You knew, didn't you? About my work with the resistance, my contacts?' Simon does not answer. 'But how?'

There is a noise behind Simon. 'Hello, Marta,' a familiar voice says. My heart stops. A woman appears in the door of the plane, and at the sight of her brown hair and full figure, I gasp.

There, in the door of the plane, stands Dava.

I stare at her, not breathing. I remember the clover scent on Simon's coat last night, the woman's voice on the phone. It does not seem possible. Dava who nursed me back to health in Salzburg. Dava who told me to go to England. 'Dava?' I manage to say at last. She does not reply but looks back at me unblinkingly.

'When Dava found you at Salzburg, we knew you were perfect,' Simon says. The Soviets must have planted operatives in the displaced persons camps to look for refugees to work for their cause. Simon continues, 'She knew that you had been a political prisoner so we did some checking. Your experience, your connections, made you a natural.' I suddenly remember the conversations about the war Dava and I had sitting on the terrace at the palace. It had never occurred to me that she was assessing my political views for the communists. 'But we knew you would never work for us willingly,' he adds.

'So you found a way to bring me to England and meet me,' I say slowly, thinking aloud. 'But I didn't plan on coming to England. I didn't even have a visa until Rose...' I stop, the awful truth dawning on me slowly. I turn to Dava. 'You killed Rose.'

She looks down. 'It was the only way.'

'Dava,' Simon says, his voice cautioning. 'That's enough.'

I remember meeting Simon on the ship, his job offer. 'But I was engaged to Paul, so I could not have possibly...' A rock seems to hit me in the stomach, knocking me backward. 'The crash wasn't an accident, was it?' Dava turns away. Neither of them answers. I lean against the stairway railing for support. The newspaper headline, announcing the plane crash, appears suddenly in my mind. 'All of those men, gone.' Murdered. 'You knew that once Paul was gone I would have no choice but to come to work for you,' I say.

He nods. 'The fact that you were pregnant and I could marry you to keep a closer eye on things was a bonus.'

I stare at him in disbelief. 'You knew about Rachel?'

'That she wasn't mine, you mean? Yes. I can add. I didn't care, though. Having a wife and daughter added to my cover, gave me an air of respectability at the Foreign Office I would not otherwise have had as that odd bachelor chap everyone suspected might be homosexual. And Rachel will continue to give me that same credibility in Moscow.'

'No!' I cry. Breaking free of his grip, I run up the steps of the plane and push past Dava.

Inside, the plane is a smaller version of the one I took to Munich, a single column of seats, three deep, along each side. Rachel sits on the floor of the aisle. I run to her, touching her head, making sure she is all right. Seeing me, she smiles. 'Ma...'

'Yes, darling, it's Mama.' Hurriedly, I pick her up. I turn toward the doorway, but Simon and Dava are blocking my way. 'Sit down, Marta,' Simon orders.

'But...'

'You're coming with us. I hadn't planned it this way. But you've interfered, complicated things like you always do. You know too much. And I can't leave a body behind on the tarmac.' The chocolates, I remember. He wasn't just trying to drug me but to kill me. Thank goodness I had only taken a bite.

'But, Dmitri,' Dava interjects. 'You don't mean...?' I can hear the surprise and conflict in her voice. After all that she has done, can she really be concerned about killing me?

'He already tried to kill me once,' I inform her. I turn to Simon, whose eyes have gone wide. 'I know the chocolates were poisoned.'

'You never said anything about killing Marta,' Dava says.

He turns to her angrily. 'It's none of your business.'

'But I didn't think...'

The plane is going to take off soon, I think, while the two of them continue to argue. For a second I consider racing into the cockpit, pleading with the pilot for help. But he is surely working with the communists, too. I have to get out. There is a small gap between Simon's back and the door frame. Clutching Rachel, I charge at it. 'Oh, no you don't,' Simon says, grabbing me and pulling us back.

Suddenly there is a noise at the door of the

plane and Simon jerks backward. Standing behind Simon, grasping him in a chokehold, is Paul.

Paul! Relief floods through me. So he received my message after all. But then I see Simon reach for his waistband. 'Watch out!' I yell as he yanks a knife from his belt. Rachel, hearing my distress, begins to cry. Paul pulls Simon backward out the door of the plane, away from the baby and me. Struggling violently for control of the knife, they tumble down the stairs of the airplane, landing in a heap at the bottom, Simon on top of Paul. Paul tries to get up, but Simon punches him, knocking him back to the ground. Paul is still weak from surgery. He cannot possibly overpower Simon now. Holding Rachel close to me, I start down the stairs.

Behind me there is a clicking sound. 'Not so fast,' Dava says. I turn to see her pointing a gun at me. 'Sit down.'

'Dava,' I say slowly. But her face is a stony mask now, her loyalties clear. As I stare at the gun, panic rises in me. I have to get Rachel out of the line of fire. 'Don't do this, Dava,' I say slowly, raising my hand. 'We're friends. You saved my life.'

'I know,' Dava replies. 'And I don't want to kill you. But he told me that in Moscow we can be together as a family, and you're getting in the way of that.'

Suddenly I understand. 'You love Simon, don't you?' I ask, trying to make my voice gentle. Rachel, her sobs subsiding, watches Dava and me with interest. Out of the corner of my eye, I look through the door of the plane. Simon and Paul are still fighting on the ground, but I know that Paul cannot last much longer. I have to get out of here before Simon comes back. But Dava's gun is still trained on Rachel and me. 'How long have you felt this way?'

'Forever,' she replies sadly. 'Years. Well before I met you. I knew Dmitri in Moscow before the war. I was going to have his baby once, too. But he made me get rid of it, said it would interfere with our work.' Her face hardens. 'And I can't have any more children now because of that.' I remember speculating with Rose about Dava's past, how she had seemed so sad and resolute when I talked about starting a new life. 'Now sit.'

I drop to the first seat on the right, still holding Rachel, who has grabbed a fistful of my hair. Dava comes toward me, picks up the seat belt to tie me up. As she leans over me, her head turns slightly away for a second. Taking a deep breath, I knee her in the stomach. She flies backward to the floor of the plane with a grunt, still clutching the gun. Quickly, I stand up. Then, looking at Rachel, I hesitate. I do not want to let go of her, even for a second, but I have no choice. Reluctantly, I pull my hair from her fingers and set her down in the seat. I lunge toward Dava as she tries to sit up, landing on top of her, trying to pry her fingers from the gun. But she clings tightly to it, struggling to raise it above her head. Keep it close, I think, wrapping my hand tightly around hers, forcing her arm down. If the gun is between us, she cannot shoot Rachel. Suddenly a shot rings out. We both freeze. Then Dava rolls back away from me, her arm limp. Blood appears on her chest. 'Dava...' I pull back, staring at her. Even though she betrayed me, I cannot help but feel her pain. But there is no time to linger. I race back to Rachel and pick her up. If she was upset by the gunshot, she gives no indication. I carry her to the door of the plane. Paul lies motionless on the ground below. Dread rises in me. Simon turns from Paul and starts back up the stairs of the plane.

'Is she dead?' he asks, his voice devoid of emotion.

'She loved you,' I say.

'I know.' His voice is cold, matter-of-fact. 'Which made it easier to get her to do what I needed. Because she really never wanted to do this to you, Marta. But she wanted a family more.' He looks over my shoulder into the plane. 'I guess that's all over now. So you'll get to take care of Rachel for a little while longer, after all. At least until we get to Moscow.'

'Simon, please listen. No one has to know what happened. We can go home.'

'Moscow is my home,' he replies, his voice sincere. It occurs to me again that I have spent two years married to a stranger. 'Now, get back in the plane,' he orders. He raises the knife again and now I notice that it is wet with blood. Paul's blood. 'You killed Paul...'

'Paul?' A stunned look crosses Simon's face. 'I thought that was–'

'Michael?' I finish for him, taking pleasure in for once knowing something that he does not. 'Michael and Paul are the same person, Simon.

The soldier you thought you killed in the plane crash two years ago. He survived and he found me while I was looking for Marcelitis. Paul is Rachel's real father,' I add.

A stunned expression crosses Simon's face. He turns to look at Paul's motionless body on the ground behind him. As he does, I reach out and kick him hard. He tumbles backward down the stairs, landing close to where Paul lies. I run down the stairs, desperately wanting to stop and check on Paul. But I know that it is only a matter of seconds before Simon gets up again. Carrying Rachel, I start to run away from the plane in the direction of the airport. Taking this to be a game, she laughs giddily. I look ahead desperately for somewhere to hide, but the airfield is open, exposed. Behind me, I hear Simon getting up. Desperately, I start to run toward the airport in the distance. Let the maintenance man still be there, I pray. Let someone be there. But carrying Rachel slows my gait. Simon's footsteps grow louder and I know that it is only a matter of seconds until he catches us.

Suddenly I hear a shot, then another. I drop to the ground, falling on top of Rachel to protect her. I will give up, I decide, stop running and let Simon take us to Moscow rather than risk her being shot. I stare at the ground, waiting for Simon to pounce upon us. But there is silence. At last I look up. Simon has fallen to the ground and lies motionless. Behind him, holding the gun, stands Dava.

Looking from Dava's outstretched arm to Simon lying prone on the ground, I am overcome with a strange sense of déjà vu. Have I been here before? No, that was me shooting the Kommandant to save Emma's life, long ago. This time it is I who has been saved.

'Dava!' Setting down Rachel, I race to Dava's side. Blood seeps from the front of her dress and she is breathing hard. But she is still alive.

She leans on me for support and I help her to the ground. 'I thought he loved me, too,' she says weakly. She must have overheard our conversation on the stairs of the plane. 'I'm so sorry.'

I hesitate, staring down at her. Hatred rises in me. She killed Rose. I fight the urge to take the gun and finish her off myself. But she might have information that is valuable to the government. I help her to a sitting position on the ground. Suddenly the maintenance man appears at the door of the airport. 'Call an ambulance!' I yell as loudly as I can. I stand up and walk to where Simon lies, eyes staring blankly at the sky. I reach in his jacket pocket and pull out the cipher. Tucking it in my own pocket, I pick up Rachel, then start running back across the airfield toward the plane. Paul still lies on the ground, not moving. 'Paul!' I cry, dropping to the ground beside him. He does not respond. I lower my face to his. Is he dead? Rachel reaches over, pats his cheek with her tiny palm.

'Mmm,' he mumbles.

'Paul, wake up,' I plead.

He opens his eyes. 'Marta? Are you and the baby okay?' he asks weakly.

My body sags with relief. 'We're fine. But you've been stabbed.' I set Rachel down. There is a gash between his chest and shoulder that is bleeding heavily.

'I don't think he hit anything major.' He grimaces. 'I may have broken my shoulder, though.'

'When you didn't move, I was afraid that...'

'I think I just bumped my head when we fell.'

'Thank goodness you received my message and made it in time. Simon was a traitor, Paul. It was him all along.' Suddenly I feel very foolish.

'You couldn't possibly have known,' he says, reading my mind. 'Where is he now?'

'Dead. Dava shot him.'

'Dava, the nurse from Salzburg?' he asks. I nod. 'I was wondering who the woman with him was. She was in on it, too?'

'It's a long story. Apparently it was all a deliberate plan set up by the Russians to have me use my contacts to find Marcelitis. And there's something else.' I take a deep breath. 'The plane crash, it wasn't an accident. Simon arranged it deliberately, to keep us apart.'

I watch his face as he processes the information, trying to grasp the full extent of the damage and pain Simon had caused. Then he shakes his head and the shadow lifts from his eyes. 'He's gone now and he can't hurt us anymore.' He reaches out to Rachel, who is trying to crawl away. 'Now, isn't it about time that you introduced me to my daughter?'

EPILOGUE

I stand on the deck of the ocean liner, looking out at a flock of gulls that dive low to the water, searching the wake for fish. Behind me, the coast of England grows smaller. A chilly breeze blows across the deck and I draw my coat more closely around me.

'Mama!' a voice calls. Behind me I turn to see Rachel toddling unsteadily toward me, bulky in her winter coat. Paul follows, his arm still wrapped in a sling.

'Hello, darling.' I stoop to pick up Rachel, who seems to grow heavier by the day. She babbles animatedly, pointing at the gulls. I study her face for the hundredth time, wondering if she has any memory of what happened. But her eyes are bright and clear.

Rachel turns in my arms and strains toward an enclosed glass area about ten meters away where a bunch of children sit at tables, drawing and painting. 'You want to go play?' She nods.

'I'll take her,' Paul offers, taking Rachel from me with his good arm. I watch as he carries Rachel over to the play area and speaks with the governess in charge. A moment later, he returns to me. 'She'll be fine playing with the other children.'

I smile. 'I know.' In the weeks since we were reunited, Paul has been as nervous as a new father, scarcely letting Rachel out of his sight. I, too, have been watching her more closely since that night at the airfield, waking in the middle of the night and tiptoeing to her in the darkness, touching her to make sure that she is still there.

I turn back to face the water, and Paul wraps his arm around me, resting his chin on the top of my head. More than a month has passed since the confrontation at the airport with Simon. We buried him in a private graveside ceremony in his family plot at a Jewish cemetery west of London on a rainy Sunday morning, just the rabbi, Rachel and myself, Paul, Delia and Charles standing a respectful distance behind. At first, I had not wanted to go. Simon was a murderer. Every single thing he had said or done since I met him had been a lie. In the end, it was Paul who convinced me to go. I looked at him in amazement. His entire unit had died because of Simon. 'For closure,' he explained. 'I mean, I hate him, too. But we should go for Rachel. Simon is the only father she has known until now and someday she will want to know things.'

So in the end we went. As his casket was lowered into the ground my rage burned white hot. How could he have done this? He killed so many innocent men. He played with our lives, made us nothing more than pawns in his game. The rabbi passed me a small handful of dirt, and as I threw it into the grave, my anger began to wane. You lost, Simon, I thought, feeling strangely triumphant. Then, staring down into the dark hole, my curiosity burned. There were so many things I wanted to know about what had happened and why he had done it, questions to which I would never get answers. Suddenly I realized that it did not matter. 'Y'isgadal, v'yis'kadash,' the rabbi began. As I joined him in the Mourner's Kaddish, I did not pray for Simon. I prayed for my parents and Rose, for Jacob and Alek and all those I carried with me. The years I spent with Simon would forever be part of the tapestry of my life, but I would not let it destroy the good. My voice grew stronger as I thanked God for sustaining me and bringing me to this place. When the prayer ended, Paul stepped forward and took my hand, and he, Rachel and I walked slowly away together.

Dava survived her gunshot wound and agreed to cooperate with the government in exchange for amnesty, a reduced sentence. 'It's actually better this way,' Paul told me a few days earlier as we packed up the house. 'There won't be a public trial.' In fact, somehow the whole incident had been kept out of the media, though I knew that the scandal of Simon's death and my departure would be whispered about in diplomatic circles for years. 'And hopefully we'll learn the full extent to which the communists had infiltrated the British government,' he added.

Hopefully, I think now, shivering. We learned a great deal more about Simon in the investigation following his death, how he had been targeted by the communists for recruitment while a student at Cambridge, invited to Moscow by a college classmate for spring vacation. It was not hard to imagine Simon, alone and in need of money after his father's death, being drawn in, warmed by the prospect of being important and needed. There he had taken on the identity Dmitri Borskin, met Dava. Later another diplomat, also secretly working for the Soviets, had helped him secure his place at the Foreign Office.

Hearing this, I pictured the faces of the other men in the department – Ebertson, Fitzwilliam, even the D.M. – how many of them were really communist spies? I worried that someone might come after me and Paul, seek revenge for what we had done. But the investigators assured me that they would all be arrested. Paul said, too, that the Soviets would no longer be interested in me. But I was still glad to be putting an ocean between us.

Dava's face appears in my mind once more. Her betrayal is the hardest to believe. I remember her as she had been in Salzburg, caring and kind. It had all been a lie. I hate her for what she did to Rose, and I want her to go to prison, to suffer. I will never forgive her, but in a strange way, I can almost understand. She was blinded by her love for Simon. And she did not let him kill me in the end. If it was not for Dava, I wouldn't be standing here today.

I look up at Paul, wanting to pinch myself to make certain that it is real. We have been so lucky. Though the cut Simon gave him had not touched any major organs, the struggle had caused internal bleeding at the site of his gunshot wound. I clung to his hand as they loaded him into the ambulance that night, fearful that if I let go, he would disappear again. 'Come back to the States with me,' he suggested before they closed the ambulance doors and took him away. He repeated the invitation as his first words when he woke up in the hospital following surgery the next day.

I hesitated. Going to America with Paul was a long-forgotten dream, something that had died years ago. But what did I have left here? I could hardly go back to the Foreign Office after all that happened. And our house, Simon's house, held nothing but painful memories. Delia was here, of course. But even she was talking about moving on, getting married at long last to Charles and retiring to the south of France.

'Life's too short,' she explained. Too short indeed. That night I told Paul I would come with him to America. We stayed in London just long enough to finalize affairs: I arranged for the sale of the house through an agency Delia recommended and Paul secured visas to America for Rachel and me. A few weeks later, we were ready to go.

Before we left, I sent Emma a letter, too, telling her what had happened and giving her Paul's address in America. I wrote that if she wanted to come to America, I would try to arrange papers for her and the children. I wonder if I will get a response.

'Happy?' Paul asks now, jarring me from my thoughts. Still staring out at the sea, I hesitate. I am still getting used to all that has happened, trying to convince myself that it will not fall apart. I am too scared to be happy. But I nod, anyway. 'I have something for you,' Paul says.

I turn around to face him, the wind whipping

my hair across my face. 'What is it?' Paul reaches into his pocket and pulls out a box, then starts to lower himself to one knee. My breath catches. 'You're asking me to marry you?'

He nods. 'Again.' Then he opens the box to reveal a white-gold band with a solitaire diamond on top.

'It's beautiful.' I lift the dog tags that hang around my neck. 'But I kind of like these.'

He smiles. 'You should have had a ring then, too. I was such a dumb kid.'

'We were both kids.'

'So is that a yes?'

I laugh. 'I feel like we're already married.'

'Me too. But I think we should make it official as soon as we get settled. I want everyone to know that I'm your husband and Rachel's father.'

I do not answer. That is how the whole mess started in the first place. If I had not been worried about appearances, I wouldn't have married Simon just because I was pregnant with Rachel. Enough, I think. That is all in the past now. Everything that happened, for better or worse; contributed to where we are right now. Happy. Together.

I look down at Paul, who is staring up at me, the ring box still held in his palm. 'I'd love to,' I say. 'Yes.'

He takes the ring from the box and slips it on my finger. Then he stands up, drawing me into an embrace. Suddenly, I laugh aloud. 'What is it?' he demands. 'Don't you like the ring?'

'The ring is perfect,' I reply quickly. 'It's just that this all seems so ordinary. So wonderfully, perfectly ordinary.'

Paul shakes his head. 'That,' he replies, brushing my hair back and kissing my forehead, 'is the one thing I doubt we'll ever be.'

'True,' I say, suddenly exhausted. 'I think I'll go upstairs to the cabin for a nap.'

He looks down at me, his expression worried. 'Are you all right?'

'Fine, just a bit tired. Want to come with me?'

'I don't think you'll get much rest if I do.'

'Agreed. Want to come with me?' He hesitates, looking over at the nursery. 'Rachel is fine with the other children,' I add.

'Let's go.' As he takes my arm and leads me across the deck, it finally seems as though our journey together has just begun.

This Large Print Book for the partially sighted, who cannot read normal print, is published under the auspices of

THE ULVERSCROFT FOUNDATION